RACHANEE LUMAYNO

I0639276

HEIR OF
SECRETS
AND
SPECTRES

KINGDOM LEGACY BOOK FIVE

Thank you for reading, I hope you enjoy Heir of Secrets and Spectres!
If you have the time, please leave an honest review on Goodreads or wherever you purchased this book! Thanks!

Also By Rachanee Lumayno

Kingdom Legacy

Heir of Amber and Fire

Heir of Memory and Shadow

Heir of Magic and Mischance

Heir of Crowns and Curses

Heir of Secrets and Spectres

Heir of Illusions and Others

Heir of Immortals and Empires

CONTENTS

Join the Newsletter

PROLOGUE

NIGHT DESCENDED ON SHONN, quiet and peaceful. The silent stars watched over the kingdom, as they always did.

But tonight the stars weren't the only thing keeping an eye on the kingdom.

Since the death of King Finvarra and Queen Oona of Faerie at Samhain, the kingdom of Shonn had been on edge. For Shonn, the easternmost kingdom in the Gifted Lands, was the one with the strongest ties to the otherworldly realm. The Veil, that magical border that separated Faerie and the Gifted Lands, was just outside Shonn's capital city, and many of the Fae mingled, married, and did business with the humans there.

But with the sudden and violent death of the Faerie royals, relations between the two areas had been strained, at best. Just little things—a broken contract between Fae and human merchants, an engagement between a human groom and his Fae bride being called off. Outright violence was unlikely, as Valdonne's Treaty would keep the Fae from retaliating in physical or magical harm against the citizens of Shonn for the murder of their leaders—even though no one in Shonn was responsible for it. To be a human in Shonn at this point meant being watchful and wary.

And sad, over losing dear friends due to politics beyond anyone's control.

It was now Midwinter, a day of thankful celebration that the winter would soon be over. In the evening, when the festivities were done, the citizens of Shonn settled into their homes. Only when all the occupants of a home were asleep would a household Fae make their appearance, as was their nightly custom. Most households had a brownie who took pride in keeping their chosen home clean, and a pixie who loved keeping their home's garden well-tended.

Once the moon had risen and all was quiet, Keela the brownie popped up from her favorite hiding spot and sniffed the air. All were asleep. Time to get to work. Whistling a jaunty tune to herself, she bustled to the side window and waved at her friend outside. The pixie smiled and waved back, then turned and put a hand on the cold, hard ground, mouthing something Keela couldn't hear. It was still too early for their humans to plant any seeds, but singing to the earth helped prepare it for that time.

Keela grabbed a broom and started sweeping. Out of the corner of her eye, she noticed something passing by the front window. She stared, but nothing seemed to be there. She shrugged and kept working. The night wasn't getting any younger.

Wait. There it was again. What was it? It shouldn't be any of her humans; they were all asleep, worn out from the day's festivities. Maybe it was her humans' dog. That animal was sweet—a little silly, sometimes, but still quite sweet—but she didn't want it inside, getting underfoot. And worse, tracking dirt all over her nice, newly cleaned floors.

But then again, she didn't want the poor creature to freeze out there....

Sighing, she went over to the door and opened it. "Here—" What was the dog's name, again? She could never remember. She only ever heard her humans refer to it as "boy." What an odd name for a dog. "Here, boy! Come here, boy!"

A chill swept over her, but it wasn't from the night air. Even though she called for the dog once more, it didn't appear. Well, she couldn't stand here all night. She had work to do. She closed the door, shivering, but not knowing why.

She turned. A short, wordless scream escaped her lips as she felt her mind and body go numb. A presence settled within her, taking control of her. Stiffly, she walked over to the shelf and started pulling books and knickknacks down, tearing out pages and breaking as many decorations as she could. She overturned tables and chairs, raking her sharp nails down the wooden surfaces. The fire in the hearth had gone out. She swept ashes from the hearth into the room, streaking the curtains and walls with soot.

Then Keela walked into the kitchen, opening up the pantry and pulling bread and cheese from the shelves, shredding the food as she did so. She grabbed some eggs that lay in a bowl on the table and threw them, watching the yolk streak yellow down the walls. It was still cold enough that her humans could store milk just outside; she opened the door and grabbed the full pitcher, dashing it against the floor. A huge white puddle soon formed at her feet. That would certainly stink in the morning.

Keela kept up her destructive whirlwind. Her brownie magic ensured that no matter how much noise she made cleaning, her humans wouldn't hear. So they wouldn't be alerted to this—unless she wanted them to be.

The pixie in the garden peeked into the house, wondering at the noise from inside. Red eyes met her blue ones. She gasped, and suddenly knew no more.

Within moments, the garden lay in ruins, the earth turned up and scattered, and bits of shattered pots everywhere.

The pixie lay near one of the pot shards, unmoving.

Inside the house, her brownie counterpart sprawled, face down, in the milk puddle. She did not stir either.

Its purpose fulfilled, the grey apparition floated away in search of its next victim.

In the morning, Keela's humans awoke to find two strange creatures dead in their home, one in the garden and one near the hearth. They'd never seen their household Fae before, although they were aware of their presence, so it took a few moments before they realized who the poor things were.

Sad, truly. But strange as well—for all around Shonn, other households were waking up to find that their household Fae had also perished in the night. And even stranger, just like in Keela's home, it looked like the household Fae had destroyed the homes they had once lovingly kept, before dying inexplicably.

What had happened? Who had done this? Would it come for the humans next?

And with the death of more Fae in the kingdom of Shonn, would more blame fall on the people of the Gifted Lands?

1

—·—

CHAPTER ONE

"So, when's the big day?"

I paused, pointing my bow with its nocked arrow down at the ground. My hand relaxed slightly as I pondered Queen Jennica's question.

Truthfully, I hadn't given much thought to planning my wedding. I assumed, like so many other things about my relationship with my betrothed, that things would just fall in place somehow and I wouldn't have to worry about it too much.

I shrugged, shaking my head so the wisps of my lavender hair would fall away from my face. My hair was pulled back in its usual braid, but it had an annoying habit of coming loose and getting in the way. "I'm not sure. I mean, Rhyss and I have only been engaged for a few months."

Jennica laughed as she raised her own bow, surveying the target ahead. "It may only have been a few months, but it took you two over a decade to finally get together."

I chuckled as well. She had a point. My friend—now fiancé—Rhyss and I had practically grown up together in the predominantly Seeker kingdom of Orchwell. Our love was built on a solid foundation of friendship and exasperation, and I wouldn't have had it any other way. "You're right. We should probably get going on getting married. Otherwise, it will be another ten years before we actually walk down the aisle."

I raised my bow again and let the arrow fly. It landed with a satisfying thud in the wooden target several yards away. My arrow landed a few inches shy of the center. I nodded, satisfied.

Jennica took a deep breath and released her own arrow, which hit the target in the top right hand corner. She smiled ruefully and wiped her brow. Some tendrils of her dark hair clung to her cheek, and she pushed them away. "It might be a while before I get to your level of proficiency, Farrah. Maybe I should just stick with magic."

"No, no, Your Majesty. You're actually doing quite well. And besides, you only just started your archery three weeks ago. I've been doing this for years."

Jennica smirked. "Okay, now I know I'm bad at this. You only call me 'Your Majesty' when you're teasing me."

I laughed. "You can always use your magic to make the arrow shoot perfectly."

The queen gave a mock gasp of horror. "That would be cheating. I am determined to learn this archery thing correctly." She giggled. "But I'll keep it in mind as a last resort."

I put my bow down on the nearby small wooden table and poured a glass of lemon-and-honey water from the glass pitcher that sat on it. A servant had just delivered the pitcher and two glasses, and I wanted a drink while it was still fresh.

"Ready to take a break?" I said, holding the full glass out to Jennica.

"Yes." She spoke so readily I had to laugh again. The archery lessons were apparently harder than the queen wanted to admit.

I poured the second glass for myself, then took a sip and looked around. King Beyan of Calia, Jennica's husband and my friend and former employer, had had a small corner of the castle grounds set up as a private archery range when his wife had expressed an interest in learning. In theory, she could have practiced with the Calian soldiers at their training grounds, and any of the guards would have been happy to instruct their queen. In theory.

Calia didn't have a standing army, which also meant they didn't have a place for soldiers to train. Wherever the Calian army—such as it was—sparred, it was somewhere outside of the kingdom's capital where it wouldn't have been wise or safe for the queen to go.

Not that Jennica usually had to worry about her safety. As a master level magician, she could hold her own against all but the strongest mages. And with her ability to shapeshift into a fire-breathing dragon, she could easily wipe out an army—and had, on the occasions when her country was threatened.

So she didn't really need to learn how to use any weapons. But when I had asked her why, she had said, "Because even magic fails sometimes, and if something should happen and I couldn't transform into a dragon ... well, it's a good idea to have a backup plan."

But now I was beginning to think she wanted to learn archery as a not-so-subtle way to question me.

"Have you begun any sort of planning?" Jennica asked, after taking a long sip of her lemon-and-honey water.

I shrugged. "Not yet. I think until we know where we're having the wedding, we can't really hammer out any other details."

"Where *will* you have the wedding?"

I sighed. "That's really the question, isn't it? Rhyss and I both live in Orchwell, but our dearest friends—you and Beyan—live here in Calia."

Orchwell, the kingdom directly south of Calia, wasn't so far away that Jennica and Beyan wouldn't be willing to travel to it, but—knowing they couldn't leave their royal duties for too long—Rhyss and I didn't want them to be inconvenienced.

"Rhyss doesn't have any other family left in Bomora?" Jennica asked, naming Rhyss's home kingdom.

"No, his only family—his cousin Enlar—is here in Calia now. And after our last trip there, I don't think Rhyss is too keen to return."

Recently, Rhyss and I had traveled west to Bomora to rescue Queen Jennica and King Beyan's newborn baby boy, who had been kidnapped by a power-hungry secret society. While the adventure had helped put some painful parts of Rhyss's past to rest, it had also stirred up those sad memories to begin with, and I knew Rhyss would be happy if he never had to return there.

"What about Shonn?" Jennica raised her eyebrows. "Or are there bad memories back there, too?"

I took a long sip of my sweetened water, trying to figure out what to say. Shonn, a kingdom in the far eastern part of the Gifted Lands, was where I had been from originally. Although I had been about six or seven when I left, so honestly, I considered Orchwell more my home than Shonn ever was.

Still, Shonn had left its mark on me. In the form of my half Fae blood, and the innate magic that came to those of Faerie.

"Well, I just sent word to my mother back in Shonn about the engagement," I said. "I'm sure she'll have some opinions on our wedding plans."

Jennica snorted, still sounding surprisingly queenly despite the rude sound. "Fortunately, my mother was too busy with her own wedding and honeymoon to fuss too much over mine. And I think, after the Prince Anders debacle, she was just as happy to stay away from anything wedding-related."

I chuckled. A few years ago, Jennica had been betrothed—against her will—to Anders, and the match had ended in a rather spectacular fashion.

"I understand he lives in Shonn now with his wife." I grinned wickedly. "If we decide to hold the wedding in Shonn, I could invite him."

Jennica groaned good-naturedly. "I'll make sure to come to the wedding in dragon form, then. And stay in it."

The idea of Jennica attending my wedding as a big golden dragon caused me to double over in laughter for several minutes. "Oh, dear. I don't know if we'll be able to find a church big enough."

Jennica grinned. "Shonn shares a magical border with Faerie, doesn't it? Maybe you should ask the Fae, perhaps their court would be willing to let you marry on their side of the border. With their magic, they'd definitely be able to accommodate a dragon."

Now it was my turn to groan as I picked up my bow. "No, thank you. I want my wedding to be as drama-free as possible."

"Tell you what." Jennica waved her bow in the air. "We'll shoot for it."

I smirked. "If you insist."

At Jennica's wave, I nocked my arrow and sighted. Taking a deep breath, I drew my bow and released the arrow. It flew straight and true, hitting the wood with a loud thump, a mere finger's length from center.

I gave Jennica a self-satisfied smile and dipped into a curtsey. "Your turn, Your Majesty."

She chuckled, shaking her head at my antics. "You be careful. Pride goes before a fall, and all that."

I crossed my arms, smirking. Jennica took aim, then loosed her arrow.

My eyes widened and my jaw dropped as the smirk fell from my face.

Queen Jennica's arrow, for once, had flown just as true as mine. And it had embedded itself in the exact center of the target.

The queen turned to me, eyebrows raised and a smile quirking her lips.

"Beginner's luck," she said modestly.

"Very well done," I commended her.

Jennica laughed. "You don't have to talk to the Fae, you know. It was just a joke."

"Oh, I know." I eyed Jennica's perfect bullseye again. Even though we had made the wager in jest, I couldn't shake the feeling that I had lost more than just a bet.

2

CHAPTER TWO

QUEEN JENNICA LED ME back inside the castle, which was thankfully cool after the heat of the noon sun.

"Are you sure you don't want to stay and eat?" she asked.

"It's tempting—and it's obscenely hot out—but we do need to get back to Orchwell," I said.

Jennica addressed a page who was waiting just inside the castle entryway. "Do you know where the King and Lord Rhyss are?"

The page said, "I believe they're in the nursery, Your Majesty."

Jennica blinked, surprised. I raised my eyebrows, equally surprised. I had thought the two men would be walking the grounds, or out for a ride, or similar.

Not sitting around drinking tea, minding a child.

Jennica smiled. "Please have the kitchens wrap up some of the midday meal, and bring it to the front of the castle."

The page nodded and started off, even as I said, "Oh, thank you, but it's not necessary—"

Jennica waved away my protests. "Nonsense. I know you need to get home, but I also know Rhyss's appetite."

We headed down a stone hallway. Paintings of various sizes lined the walls on both sides, a history of the Calian royal family immortalized in art.

Just past the king and queen's suite of rooms, Jennica opened the door that led to Crown Prince Coran's nursery. The room, decorated in cheery shades of yellow and purple, also boasted two overstuffed chairs, perfect places for the queen to nurse her baby in comfort.

I giggled as I got a good look inside the nursery. I had been wrong about the tea, but the scene before Jennica and me was just as good.

Toys and some items of baby-sized clothing were strewn around the room. A sleeping King Beyan sprawled in one of the chairs, head lolling to the side. My intended, Rhyss, sat in the other chair, bouncing baby Coran on his lap and murmuring nonsense words at him. Coran gurgled and smiled, but the moment he caught sight of his mother, he instantly held his little chubby arms out to her.

After exchanging quick greetings with Rhyss, Queen Jennica scooped up her son. Coran turned his big brown eyes on me. When I wiggled my fingers at him, he grabbed one and stuffed it in his mouth.

"My, he's getting big," I said. "Imagine what kind of dragon you'll be one day!" This to the baby, who was quickly turning my finger into a sticky, wrinkly mess.

Jennica tried to gently pry Coran from my finger, but to no avail. "I do wonder what he'd look like as a dragon. If he can even transform into one. Maybe he'll get Beyan's abilities."

"Or both. That would be interesting." I managed to extract my finger and wiped it on my skirt. "I wonder when he will start showing his powers?"

"If it's Seeker ability, then probably around five or six," Jennica said. "As far as shapeshifting—most likely the same age, maybe younger. I apparently showed signs when I was little, but without someone to teach me properly, I couldn't transform until I was an adult. But that shouldn't be the case with Coran."

Rhyss stood up and stretched. Jennica turned to him. "Thank you for watching over Coran. It looks like he was quite a handful today." She indicated the mess around the room.

Rhyss gave me a quick kiss on the forehead, then put his arm around me. "It was no trouble. I wanted to spend some time with my godson before I had to leave today."

I smiled. I never would have thought I'd see the day that Rhyss got all sentimental over a baby. My betrothed was a live-in-the-moment, act first, ask questions later kind of man. While he'd always been kind and happy-go-lucky, I'd never seen this softer side of him until a few months ago, when King Beyan and Queen Jennica asked him to become Crown Prince Coran's godfather and regent of Calia. Surprisingly, Rhyss took to his new role and responsibility quite well, and he actually enjoyed his new duty.

Thinking about that, I sighed inwardly. Along with our upcoming wedding, it was one more thing we'd have to figure out—where to live, eventually. Thanks to his new status as Coran's godparent, Rhyss received a sizable allowance from the Calian crown. He didn't have to continue his job as a mercenary-for-hire to the Seekers of Orchwell, and he had told me he had plenty of money to cover my expenses as well, but we both enjoyed the work. And while Rhyss didn't have to live in Calia, it would be wise to stay nearby in case—gods forbid—anything happened to Beyan and Jennica, and Rhyss had to step in as regent.

Gods forbid. Ha. After all these years, it's being engaged to the man that has me sounding like him.

Well, there'd be plenty of time to think about that future stuff later.

"Shall we get going?" I asked Rhyss. He nodded, then turned to the still-sleeping Beyan.

"Beyan." Rhyss nudged the King, who groaned in his sleep but didn't wake up. Rhyss reached over and shook our friend's shoulder. "Beyan!"

Beyan came awake all at once, jerking violently and swatting at the air. "What? What's happened?"

"Rhyss and Farrah are going back to Orchwell," Jennica said as she bounced the baby on her hip.

Beyan slumped back against the chair, sighing. "Oh my goodness. I thought we were under attack or something."

"We'd better not be," Jennica said. "I just want a few quiet months, with no magical or mundane plots to take over Calia. It doesn't seem like too much to ask."

Beyan got up, and as our group walked toward the front of the castle, I said, "Perhaps we *should* have the wedding in Shonn. Then you two could get out of Calia, have a vacation of sorts."

Jennica laughed. "You never get a vacation from running a country. Still, though, the idea has merit."

"Wait, what's this?" Rhyss asked me. "We're getting married in Shonn?"

Now it was my turn to laugh. "Not unless you want to. It was just something Jennica and I were discussing during archery."

We said our goodbyes, with promises from Rhyss and me to return to Calia soon. Rhyss and I rode off, settling in for the journey back to Orchwell.

Once we reached Orchwell, at the gate that led into the capital city, Rhyss and I also said our farewells.

"I'll see you in a few hours," I laughed as Rhyss kissed me again. "You're coming over for dinner, after all."

"I know," he said. "But still ..."

I gave him one last quick kiss. "If you don't get your errands done now, then you'll be late for dinner. And if *I* don't get *my* errands done, there won't be any dinner to speak of. So get going!"

Rhyss chuckled and, with a small wave, headed into the city's center.

I smiled as I watched him go, then turned and headed the opposite way, toward the capital's residential area. We had stayed in Calia for five days visiting Beyan and Jennica, and I definitely had things to attend to at home. Even though traveling to Calia took less than a day on horseback, we often just stayed there for several days when visiting our friends. And ever since Rhyss's appointment as Coran's godfather, as well as our engagement, it felt like we spent more time in Calia these days than we did in Orchwell.

I reached the street of brick row houses that included my modest home. I quickened my pace, eager to get home, unload my bag, and relax a little before I had to leave again to shop in the marketplace before it closed for the day. I suppose I could have joined Rhyss on his trip to the market—that's where he had been headed when we parted ways—but part of me craved some time to myself.

My steps slowed as I neared my home. A little grey sphere leaned against my door, small enough that it would escape most people's notice. And even if it hadn't, most people would have taken it to be a rock, probably left there to serve as a convenient door stop.

But I had a feeling I knew what it was.

And as I scooped up the little ball and rolled it around in my fingers, I was sure: someone had sent me a magical message.

3

CHAPTER THREE

"So, what's for dinner?"

I pointed at the center of the table as Rhyss sat down, sniffing the air expectantly. He looked at the table, then up at me. Some dishes and silverware sat to one side, along with a bottle of mead and two glasses. But in the middle of the table, between Rhyss and me, was the grey spell ball. "That's odd. I could have sworn I smelled roast chicken, but perhaps I was mistaken."

I smirked. "Well, I could have saved it for after dinner, but I knew once I mentioned it, you'd want to open it right away. So we might as well get it over with so we can eat."

"Or lose our appetite entirely," Rhyss said, but he poked at the magical message ball curiously. A small spark shot out.

"Hey!" He pulled his finger back and shook it, then examined his finger. He stuck his finger in his mouth. "Darn thing zapped me. I thought you said it was a magical object."

"It is," I said, picking up the grey sphere. "And don't talk with your mouth full."

He removed his finger from his mouth, sticking his tongue out at me in the process. "Magic isn't supposed to affect me, since I can't use it. Or so I thought. Okay, now I'm cranky *and* hungry. Let's listen to your message so I can eat, already."

I laughed, shaking my head at him. Then I quieted down, closing my eyes and concentrating, focusing on the cool ball in my hands.

You could send messages any number of ways in the Gifted Lands, from the mundane—letters, carrier pigeons, word of mouth—to the magical. Queen Jennica and I often communicated by a magic calling spell, and we had even worked out a way to infuse an object with the spell so non-magicians could use the calling spell as well.

But all of those ways were susceptible to being intercepted. Letters could be tampered with, word of mouth could be misconstrued. You could be overheard when using the calling spell.

So if you wanted to be sure that your message would get to its intended recipient intact and remain private, then you sent it via a magic message ball. Or you paid a magician to create one for you. They were expensive little things, but worth it. Only the person the message was meant for could open the sphere, and anyone else who tried would be roundly denied.

As poor Rhyss had just found out.

I opened my eyes. The sphere cracked open, and both grey halves fell away.

I expected to find a note tucked in one of the halves, but instead, a cool white light filled the space in front of me. A voice, deep and liquid and warmly familiar, filled the room.

"Darling, I was overjoyed to learn about your engagement. Rhyss is a wonderful young man, although it took him long enough to propose—" I smirked at my betrothed, who rolled his eyes at me "—and we're looking forward to welcoming him into the family. And speaking of family ..."

My breath hitched as my mother's voice trailed off momentarily. In the message, Mother also took a deep breath, steeling herself for whatever she would say next.

"My darling, there is an important matter in regards to our family—and your future—that we must discuss, and soon. It would be best if you could come to Shonn where we can talk with each other in person, instead of relying on unreliable messages, whether they be through magic or mundane means. Please return home soon. I eagerly await your reply, or even better, your visit. All my love."

The light dimmed, then winked out completely. Rhyss and I sat across from each other in my dining room, stunned into silence.

The sound of Rhyss's growling stomach broke the quiet.

"Sorry," Rhyss said sheepishly.

I laughed, standing. "I get the hint."

I walked into the kitchen and grabbed the roast chicken where it was beginning to cool on the counter. In my short absence, Rhyss had set the table and poured us two glasses of mead. I nodded my thanks as I placed our dinner on the table.

Rhyss carved up the chicken. After we both had been served, he sat back and took a bite. "Mmm. Delicious."

"And you thought I couldn't cook," I smirked.

"I know you can cook. It's just that I cook better," he said around a mouthful of meat.

"Don't you worry. You'll get your chance to show off your cooking skills again soon."

Rhyss looked at me quizzically. "What are you talking about? We don't have any Seeker jobs lined up, at least that I know of."

When any of the Seekers in Orchwell hired Rhyss and me for help on the road, it was usually for my healing skills and Rhyss's sword. And often Rhyss served as camp cook as well. Over the many years we had worked together, he had proven to be surprisingly adept at making delicious dishes from whatever we could find while traveling. A fact he enjoyed lording over me whenever he could.

I grimaced. "I wish we did. I think battling bandits would be preferable, honestly. No, you heard my mother's message. We need to go to Shonn."

"We do?" He sighed. "I was kind of hoping to stay close to Orchwell for a while."

I understood Rhyss's reluctance to leave Orchwell again, so soon after returning. The last few months had been filled with constant travel—first to Calia for Crown Prince Coran's christening, then to Bomora and back to save the baby prince. Even after things had settled, we had gone back and forth several times from Orchwell to Calia to visit King Beyan and Queen Jennica.

And that didn't even count for the days or weeks we'd have to spend on the road eventually, actually working.

I smirked. "I never thought I'd see the day that you'd want to be settled and stay in one place."

Rhyss blushed but shrugged, trying for nonchalance. "Guess that's how you know we're getting older."

"Well, before I buy you a cane and a rocking chair, we'll have to go to Shonn. We don't have to get married there, but we definitely have to travel there before we get married." I eyed the two halves of the broken message ball. "Something about what she said ... I hope I'm wrong, but something seemed off."

"Don't worry," Rhyss reassured me. "We'll head to Shonn as soon as we can. It will be nice to see your family again. It's been a while."

I nodded, relieved. I had hoped Rhyss would agree to accompany me without an argument. Because, honestly? I had also been looking forward to spending some time in Orchwell. But my mother's vague message left me feeling uneasy. I would relax—maybe—once I knew what it was about.

Sighing, I smiled at Rhyss. "I wish we could just elope."

"I'd be fine with that."

I toyed with the food on my plate. "It could be any number of things, but if she wants to see me in person … I'm worried it might have something to do with my father."

I fell silent, lost in thought about my estranged father. The man who had loved my mother and then broken her heart by disappearing one day, without a hint of a reason why or where he had gone. I had barely known him, but he had given me my lavender hair and Fae heritage and the innate Fae magic that flowed through my veins.

Rhyss stuck a piece of chicken in his mouth and chewed thoughtfully. "I haven't encountered the Fae much, except for you. Any of our commissions with Beyan that took us to Shonn kept us in the wilderness, going after elemental dragons, not wandering into Faerie. Is dealing with the Fae really that bad?"

"You can't even imagine," I said wryly.

Rhyss shrugged, a teasing gleam in his eyes. "Well, they do say relations with your in-laws can be tough."

I didn't respond. Instead, I downed my mead in one swallow and poured myself another glass. It was paltry fortification, but I was going to need all the courage I could get.

4

CHAPTER FOUR

RHYSS AND I STAYED in Orchwell for two more days, just long enough to get our affairs in order and stock up on provisions before we had to travel again. Shonn wasn't far—less than a week's travel going roughly straight east—but it was mostly unclaimed wilderness between the two kingdoms. So, no roadside inns with hearty meals and soft beds for us. Instead we could look forward to days of foraging and camping at night.

Among other, more worrying things.

I sought out the person who had delivered my mother's message ball. A dark-haired, dark-eyed man just a little older than Rhyss and me, it was easy enough to find him—word had spread of a handful of travelers newly arrived from out east.

When I asked him if he was in Orchwell to hire a Seeker, he nodded. "I would have sent a message, but I knew it would take longer than usual to get a reply. Very few who leave Shonn right now are willing to return immediately. Not unless you can travel with a companion, or better yet, several. The roads have gotten treacherous. The gangs of roaming bandits have gotten bolder, attacking travelers more frequently. The kingdom has its hands full trying to keep them in check. So that's allowed the wild animals to get worse, too."

"Not to mention the Fae," said a blue-haired lady who had traveled with the messenger. "Ever since their king and queen died, they've been acting against humans more often. You have to be careful when traveling through the forests. And be especially careful if you have to bathe, or clean your clothes, or refill your waterskins in one of the lakes or rivers."

I nodded soberly and thanked them both, then left to finish my other errands around Orchwell. I visited shops and made my purchases a bit distractedly, mulling over what the man and woman from Shonn had told me.

My half Fae heritage gave me a little bit of immunity from the tricks my full Fae counterparts liked to play on unwary travelers. At the very least, it allowed me to see through their glamours and be more aware of Fae magic. But my human side still attracted them to me, to see if they could catch me off guard. And Rhyss, fully human, would definitely be a target.

I also mulled over the news the blue-haired lady had shared—that the Fae were not afraid to harm humans in the wake of the deaths of their king and queen. The Faerie royals had died a few months ago, at the hands of a Bomorran human. I had assumed that the Seelie Court had already appointed new monarchs, especially since time flowed differently in that magical realm. Our "few months" could be several years to the Fae, or vice versa.

But if the Fae living in human lands were actively harming humans—something that was forbidden, thanks to Valdonne's Treaty, enacted after the Great War had nearly decimated all of the humans and Fae of the Gifted Lands—then that meant the Fae were leaderless. For only the Faerie king and queen could keep that lot of tricksters in check.

Or worse, what if the land of Faerie *did* have a new king and queen—and the new rulers sanctioned the blatant breaking of Valdonne's Treaty?

I shook my head, as if that could clear it of its troubling thoughts, and hurried home. No sense in worrying about it right now, I reasoned. I'd find out the state of affairs in Faerie—and in Shonn—soon enough.

But that night, my thoughts returned to my conversation with the travelers in the marketplace. As I drifted off to sleep, I couldn't decide which was worse: dealing with bandits, dealing with the Fae, or dealing with my upcoming wedding.

5

—·—

CHAPTER FIVE

OUR HORSES' HOOVES CLOP-CLOPPED steadily on the hard-packed dirt road as Rhyss and I rode out of Orchwell. Soon the Gifted Lands would welcome spring in earnest, but in certain places, winter still held on stubbornly with its chilly grip.

Camping in cold weather had never bothered me—we had gotten used to traveling under all sorts of conditions with Beyan and other Seekers—but, in light of the travelers' news from last night, I did worry about things like making fires at night. I said as much to Rhyss, after relaying what I had learned.

"It'll make travel much slower, that's for sure," he said. "But there's no way around it. It's still cold enough that we need a fire at night, or we could possibly freeze to death."

"We'll have to take turns keeping watch," I said. "Too bad no one else was going out this way. It would have been nice to have an extra pair or two of eyes to help out."

Rhyss shrugged. "We've dealt with worse. I'm not worried."

Well, I was glad that at least *he* wasn't worried.

I sighed, looking up at the sky as two large shadows temporarily blotted out the sun. A pair of ice dragons winged overhead, their cool blue scales appearing nearly translucent in the light. I smiled at the sight. Pretty soon all the ice dragons would either migrate to the far north, beyond the Gifted Lands, or retreat to their caves and hibernate through the end of spring into late fall, avoiding the hottest parts of the year.

In our initial hours on the road, we saw many travelers headed in the opposite direction from us, going to Orchwell. It wasn't odd to see people traveling on the east-west road between Shonn and Orchwell, but it was unusual to see such a large amount of people only heading one way.

Some of the travelers gave us funny looks, as if wondering why we were going east. I looked down the road behind us. Rhyss and I were the only ones heading toward Shonn, it seemed.

"Do you get the sense everyone knows something we don't?" Rhyss said to me in a low voice as a large group of travelers, the third in so many hours, appeared on the road in front of us.

"There *is* something strange about it," I mused, trying not to stare too openly at the group on the opposite side of the road. "These travelers don't look like the regular sort. They're carrying way too much. They look a bit like—"

"Refugees?"

The group was nearly upon us. I nodded, not wanting them to overhear our conversation.

As we approached this new group, I finally got a better look at them. I doubted they were adventurers—while there were several adults in the party, they lacked any kind of armor or weapons, and they traveled with three small children who walked alongside their wagon. Their tired, sad faces and haunted eyes hinted at some recent and severe troubles.

"Ho, travelers!" One of the men called out to us, holding up his hand in greeting. "Are you heading to Shonn, by any chance?'

Rhyss and I halted our horses. Rhyss greeted the man in return. "Greetings to you as well, good man. We are, indeed, traveling to Shonn." His eyes swept over the group. "Is there any reason we shouldn't go there?"

One of the children darted forward, his small hand outstretched to pet Rhyss's horse. A woman—presumably his mother—reached out and grabbed the child before he could potentially startle the horse. "Please pardon my son," she said. "He loves animals."

"It's all right," Rhyss reassured the little boy. He gestured to his horse. "Thistle is quite tame." He slackened the reins, allowing the little boy to reach the horse's head as his mom cautiously let her son move toward Thistle again.

"We had to sell or set free most of our animals before we left Shonn," the mother said, watching her son happily stroke Thistle's nuzzle. She spoke matter-of-factly, but I could hear the tinge of sadness in her words.

"You're not going back?" Rhyss must have also picked up on the woman's sadness, because his tone was gentle.

The man who had hailed us spoke up. "Not for a long while. Perhaps not ever. There's nothing left there for any of us."

"What do you mean?" I asked.

"There's been strange doings lately," the man said. "More Unseelie sightings, and they're quite bold in their tricks against us. As far as the Seelie go—they've been carefully neutral since the death of their rulers, but now there's hardly any left. They've been bowing out of any dealings with humans, some going so far as to leave Shonn entirely. And a few weeks ago we woke up the day after the Midwinter celebration to find that all our household Fae were dead."

"Dead?" I found that impossible to believe. The Fae tended to be long-lived, and any of the household Fae in Shonn would have served several generations of a certain family.

And the news that the Unseelie were acting up was unsettling. The realm of Faerie was divided into two Courts: the Seelie, of which the late King Finvarra and Queen Oona oversaw, and the Unseelie. While both groups favored trickery in their dealing with humans, the Seelie tended to have better relations with us, even intermingling with us sometimes. The Unseelie Fae were wild, lawless, and malevolent, but kept in check by the Seelie's favoritism toward us. If the Seelie were leaving Shonn ...

The man nodded. "Yes. And even stranger, it looked like they had all destroyed the homes they kept before dying."

I frowned, but before I could ask another question, the man sighed and eyed the position of the sun in the sky. "We must get going. We still have a long way to go. Most of the others who left planned to settle in Orchwell, since it's so close. We're going to travel on to Annlyn, where hopefully it will be less crowded. Best of luck to you, travelers. If you're headed to Shonn, you'll need it."

He nodded his head at us, then called to the woman and the boy, who was still petting Thistle. The boy seemed disinclined to leave, and when his mother finally was able to pry him away from the horse, there were tears shining in the child's eyes.

The group of refugees continued on their way to Orchwell. Rhyss and I exchanged a loaded look, but stayed silent as we clicked at our horses to start moving again.

As the day wore on, the large groups of travelers began to thin out. We came across a few stragglers here and there, but by the afternoon Rhyss and I were the only ones on the road.

Soon the sun hung low in the sky, and, without even needing to say it aloud, we both started looking for a place to camp. As we set it up, I reflected on how well Rhyss and I knew each other. After years of traveling together and fighting side-by-side, I suppose it would be surprising if we didn't.

I glanced at Rhyss surreptitiously. What if there ever came a time when we weren't so in harmony with each other?

"What?" Rhyss's voice startled me out of my thoughts.

"What, what?" I asked.

"You're staring at me."

Suddenly embarrassed, I didn't voice my actual thoughts. Instead, I said, "First the pair of travelers in Orchwell, then the families we saw on the road today. I've never seen so many people eager to leave my home kingdom. What do you think we'll find when we reach Shonn?"

Rhyss shrugged, his arms full of firewood. "Who knows? It doesn't seem like there's anybody left."

I frowned, looking toward the road. "I wonder how long it's been happening. We've been on the road so much ourselves recently, you'd think we'd have noticed."

"Not necessarily." Rhyss dropped the bundle of wood he was carrying on the ground, near our packs. "We spent most of our time in the west. People aren't keen to move to Bomora or Rothschan."

He had a good point. Of all the kingdoms in the Gifted Lands, Rothschan, the strict military kingdom to the southwest, and Bomora, the seaside kingdom in the far west that was home to pirates, thieves, and other unsavory sorts, were places that most casual visitors avoided.

"And," Rhyss continued as he started to build a fire, "if we weren't out west, then we were in Calia. We barely spent any time in Orchwell. So we probably missed seeing the groups of refugees coming into the kingdom. And it sounds like some of them have continued on to Annlyn in the south. So we definitely would have missed them, in that case."

"Perhaps." I turned my frown on Rhyss. "Should we be making a fire?"

Rhyss didn't pause in his work. "We've talked about this already. There's no way around this, not unless we want to freeze overnight." He looked up at me. "Can you set a ward?"

"I can, but it won't protect us from physical, mundane attacks." I yawned, already feeling so weary, even though night hadn't fallen yet.

Rhyss looked at me sympathetically. "I'll make dinner, then you go to sleep. I can take first watch."

I yawned again. "You sure?"

He laughed. "You're about to fall asleep on your feet. Yes, I'm sure."

The rest of the night passed uneventfully. Rhyss made a wonderful dinner—which he was quick to point out, eliciting an eye roll from me—and I fell asleep right after. Nothing happened during my watch, either, and I was happy to tell Rhyss in the morning that no trouble had found us that night.

Most of our travel also remained trouble-free. Occasionally we'd catch a flash of something in the trees, or hear high-pitched giggling nearby. Neither Rhyss nor I felt any inclination to investigate, as we both knew the stories of the Fae luring unwary travelers. During the night we would hear phantom riders and see strange bobbing lights, but nothing tested the magical wards I set, and nothing approached us.

One sobering thing, however, was seeing the husks of abandoned farms dotting the landscape as we got closer to Shonn. While some had fallen into rot and ruin due to time or weather, others had been deliberately burned or destroyed. I stared, horrified, at the sight.

Shonn, a small kingdom, didn't have any towns other than its capital city. The area farmers were often the first ones to welcome visitors and put travelers up for the night. Very few people tried to take advantage of a Shonn farmer's hospitality. Despite Valdonne's Treaty—or perhaps because of it—the citizens of Shonn and those of Fae held a deep respect for one another, and even a little protectiveness. The two worlds often intermingled here. I was proof of that.

So to act against a citizen of Shonn was nearly akin to acting against a citizen of Faerie. And the Fae did not take kindly to one of their own being hurt or swindled, unless it was done fairly.

Passing by these sad, decrepit buildings, I wondered, who had destroyed them and driven the farmers away?

And why had the area Fae not stepped in to protect them?

6

--.--

CHAPTER SIX

TWO DAYS BEFORE REACHING Shonn, we saw a lone hooded figure sitting in the middle of the road in the distance. Rhyss and I exchanged wary glances as we slowly rode forward. The person was squarely in our path; if we wanted to avoid them, we'd have to leave the road and go through the forest. But if we did that, it would be too easy to get lost, especially if the rumors of the Unseelie Fae now roaming through the woods to help travelers go astray were true.

As we drew level with the mysterious figure, a lilting feminine voice called out. "My lady! Sir! I need your help!"

"What seems to be the problem, my good woman?" Rhyss asked.

She lifted her head slightly. A tumble of auburn curls spilled out of her hood, and big green eyes looked out at us from a lovely, heart-shaped face. "I'm traveling to Shonn. My horse spooked and threw me, then ran off. I'm lucky I didn't break my neck in the fall. As it is, I twisted my ankle and cannot walk all that way."

A single tear slid down her beautiful face. "I saw you riding my way and used the last of my failing strength to step into the road to get your attention. If you could take me to Shonn, I would be ever so grateful."

Her eyes held the perfect amount of hope and humility. In fact, everything about her seemed too perfect—from her face and figure, to the story she had just finished sharing about her plight. She reached out a slender hand toward Thistle, who shied away from her touch.

Rhyss wavered. "It isn't far to Shonn—we should be there on the morrow. If my companion is fine with it, I would—"

"No!" I shouted, reaching over to try to clap my hand over Rhyss's mouth. No easy feat when you're both on horseback, but I couldn't let him finish that sentence.

The woman's eyes flashed, and her eyes changed from their gorgeous green shade to an evil red. It happened so fast, you could have easily thought your eyes were playing tricks on you, if you didn't know what to look for.

But I did.

And no Fae trickster was going to harm my beloved.

I slapped Thistle's flank, trying to get the horse to run. At the same time, I urged my own mount forward. Frightened out of their minds, neither horse followed my direction, although I'm sure we all wanted to put as much distance between us and the Otherworldly woman as we could.

Or I should say, creature. Not woman. Not human.

A terrified Thistle snorted, rolling her eyes and backing away. But she kept backing into my mount, who was equally frightened. The beautiful woman reached out once more, trying to get on Rhyss's horse. But instead of a lovely, slender hand peeking out from the cloak, a yellowed skeletal hand clawed at the horse. The hooded creature turned the red eyes I had spied earlier on us, and an inhuman cackle pierced the air.

"Rhyss!" I yelled, trying to break the spell that the hooded Fae creature had spun with her words to entrap my intended. "Go, go!"

Dazed, Rhyss shook his head, and I could sense that the tether between him and the Faerie woman had broken. Getting Thistle under control, he spurred her forward. The skeletal creature's grasping hands just missed grabbing onto Rhyss's horse. It turned to me, but my horse, seeing Thistle flee, had already broken into a run.

The Unseelie Fae's eerie laughter followed us as we rode away.

When we had gone far enough to be sure of our safety, we slowed our horses.

"What was that?" Rhyss asked, looking back the way we had come.

"A boggart," I said. "They're shapeshifters. And tricksters." I glanced behind me too, as if the evil creature was still pursuing us. Thankfully, it wasn't. When it didn't accomplish its goal, it would have stayed in its domain to wait for the next unwary traveler.

"What would have happened if we had given it that ride it asked for?"

"Death, probably. Injury, definitely. To both you and Thistle."

Rhyss shuddered. He looked at me. "Thank you for saving me."

I smiled. "You would have done the same for me."

"If I had known how to see through that thing. Which I didn't." He sounded ... embarrassed? Ashamed?

"Hey," I said, trying to lighten the mood. "You're not the first man to be taken in by a pretty face. You're just lucky you have me around to look out for you."

He smiled back. "What would I do without you?"

I laughed. "Let's hope you never have to find out."

The rest of the day passed uneventfully. That night, I set the magical wards and we settled in for our usual nighttime watch routine. I hoped the encounter with the boggart was the worst of any encounters with the Fae we would have.

How wrong I was.

7

——·——

CHAPTER SEVEN

As I SAT THERE during my watch in the dark solitude of night, I thought about what awaited us in Shonn.

Next to me, Rhyss let out a soft snore. We had fallen into a routine on our journey. He would make dinner for us and then take the first watch. I would set up a ward and sleep until Rhyss woke me for my turn at keeping watch.

I reached out mentally and tested the ward I had set up earlier. Still strong and intact. Good. I breathed a silent sigh of relief. One more night, and then I would be reunited with my family once more.

It would be wonderful to see my mother again. It had been far too long. And when I saw my sister Halianna—truly, my half-sister, although I rarely thought of her that way—I would give her the biggest hug—

Something rustled in the darkness.

I sat up straighter, all senses on alert. Barely breathing, I strained my ears to listen. But there was nothing else, beyond the sound of the wind sighing through the trees.

I relaxed a little bit. Perhaps I was just a little too excitable right now, thinking about the journey's end.

I glanced up at the sky. I estimated another hour or so until sunrise. The sky was beginning to lighten, turning the bluish-purple of twilight.

Another rustle sounded. Then another.

I grabbed for my weapons and my pack even as I hissed in Rhyss's direction. "Rhyss! Wake up!"

He came awake instantly. Seeing what I was doing, he started to grab his things as well. "What's going on?" he asked in a low tone.

"There's something out there." So far, nothing had actually approached our campsite, but I knew we were easy targets, silhouetted by the dying embers of our fire.

"Is it magical? Or human?"

I narrowed my eyes as I reached out with my magic, testing. My brow furrowed. How strange … it couldn't be …

My eyes flew open. "Rhyss … it's both."

He frowned as he quickly belted his sword around his waist and checked to make sure his dagger was in place. "Let's get back on the road, if we can. If whatever's out there is both, it might be better if we outrun it instead of fight it."

I nodded, and we hurried to mount our horses, who were sleeping peacefully nearby. Right on the edge of my magical ward.

The rustling noise started up again, this time coming from multiple directions. Rhyss nodded at me. "Ready?"

I nodded back. In one quick movement, I pointed at the fire and doused it with a quick spell, plunging our camp into semi-darkness.

In the very next breath I snapped my fingers, and felt my magical ward dissolve around us.

A tall, gaunt figure jumped out of the darkness at me, snarling and grabbing at my arm, my leg, anything it could grab on to.

I screamed. And kicked. My horse whinnied in fear, and it took all I had to keep my seat while trying to get rid of the monster that was trying to drag me away.

Except, in the hazy purple air, I saw it wasn't a monster. It was a man, although so thin and feral I wouldn't have first thought they were human. But this man who was attacking me wasn't one of the bandits I had been warned about—this person was attacking me with hands and teeth, not swords or bows.

Nearby, I heard Rhyss swear, followed by the sound of his sword being pulled from its scabbard. "I'm coming, Farrah! Just as soon as I get rid of this one!"

I could hear more snarling and rustling around us, and I realized we would soon be surrounded. And if the others were just as relentless as the man currently clinging doggedly to my leg, then we would soon be overcome if we stayed here.

My attacker grabbed my hand.

I shouted, and heat shot down my arm and into my hand, bursting into flame when the spell connected with the tall, thin man. Eerily, he didn't even flinch or yell as the magical flame consumed him. He just turned into ash at my horse's feet.

I pointed toward the center of camp and shouted again. The fire I had doused just a few moments earlier shot up in a column of fire, illuminating the area around us.

Which was filled with more of the feral humans, making their determined way toward Rhyss and me.

I turned, catching a glimpse of Rhyss just as he neatly lopped off his foe's head with his sword. "That oughta do it!" he said proudly.

"Uh, Rhyss?" I began.

Rhyss glanced over his shoulder. His eyes widened as he took in what I had just seen. "Let's go!"

We both spurred our horses forward, headed for the road.

The crowd of feral people began running after us.

We reached the road and started toward Shonn, urging our mounts to run faster. The air around us had lightened more, and in the slowly growing light I could see the indistinct shapes of the people coming toward us. I couldn't count properly, but I estimated at least a dozen. Possibly more.

And even though we urged our mounts to run faster, as fast as they possibly could, the wild people behind us also ran faster.

Faster than I thought humans could possibly run.

I ducked low over my horse's head, trying to create as little wind resistance as possible so she could run faster. Next to me, Rhyss did the same. Our poor horses were already at their limit, their mouths foaming from the effort. They could sense our fear, and the strangeness of the beings behind them. Adrenaline kept them going, but I knew soon their energy would flag. And we still hadn't reached Shonn.

And then finally, in the distance, I could see the gates of Shonn ahead of us. The slowly rising sun's light glinted off the heavy iron wall, tightly closed against invaders—be they human or monster.

Atop the wall, I spied two guards watching our rapid approach.

Rhyss and I began to yell as loud as we could. "Open the gates! Open the gates!"

The two guards seemed to hesitate. They couldn't be so heartless as to keep the gates closed and abandon us to our fates.

Could they?

And then, ever so slowly, the gates began to open.

8

—·—

CHAPTER EIGHT

AT THE RATE RHYSS and I were traveling, we'd be there within moments. And although the horde of human-like monsters was still behind us, we had a good enough lead that we would be able to slip through the gates and close them again before a single pursuer had a chance to approach.

I hoped.

Just a little bit more ... we were nearly at the gates. They loomed ahead, getting larger and larger with each passing moment.

And then my horse, traveling at breakneck speed, tripped over an invisible rock in the road.

Jostled by the sudden stop, I lost my seat and tumbled off her back, hitting the dirt road hard. I landed on my side, feeling the jolt of pain from the fall travel up the length of my body. My mind cried out, *Move! Move now! Run!* But my body was too stunned and bruised to obey.

Rhyss brought his horse to a halt—no easy feat at the crazy speed he had been going. "Farrah! Are you okay?"

I tried to get up but collapsed back onto the ground, groaning. As I stared down the road, I could see the snarling crowd of monster-humans were quickly closing the distance between us. I waved frantically at Rhyss. "Go on! Get into the city!"

He dismounted from Thistle and ran over to me. "Are you kidding? Come on!" He tried to help me up, but I yelped in pain.

"Just go, Rhyss! I'll be fine!"

"You've never lied to me before, Farrah. Don't start now." Rhyss stepped in front of me and drew his sword, and then there was no more time for talking.

The first of the attackers sprang at Rhyss, falling away in a bloody mess as it impaled itself upon his outstretched sword. More quickly took their fallen friend's place, crowding around Rhyss, me, and our terrified horses.

From my position behind Rhyss, I flung a hand out and shouted in the direction of the feral human closest to me. A spark of purple light shot out from my fingers, momentarily stunning the creature and causing it to stumble back a few paces. I sent more jolts into the crowd, but they did little damage beyond creating a brief annoyance for whoever was on the receiving end.

I ceased my spells, stunned. Usually that magical spark was enough to knock a person out, if not outright kill them.

"This isn't working!" I yelled, even as I began ineffectively zapping our attackers again.

"Too late now!" Rhyss yelled back. While he was still holding his own fairly well, I could tell his energy was flagging.

Overhead, the sun continued its ascent. Long rays of sunlight crept over the ground all around us.

I pulled my dagger from my belt and tried to hold the weapon, but my right arm, sore from falling on it, wouldn't cooperate. I switched the knife to my left hand. I wasn't as good at fighting with my left side—something that Rhyss had hounded me about correcting, for years—but if I could at least get one good throw in, that might do ... something.

I raised the knife and took aim.

An arrow whizzed over my head, just missing Rhyss, before embedding itself firmly in the throat of one of the feral humans. It went down instantly.

Additional arrows found their marks in various parts of our attackers, and then several swordsmen wearing the colors of Shonn—silver and purple—suddenly were at our side, helping Rhyss fend off the horde of monster-humans.

"Should we run?" Rhyss called to the closest Shonn swordsman.

"Hold your ground, if you can," the man advised, neatly dodging a swipe from one of the feral humans before slicing its arm off. "In just a few moments—"

And now sunrise was fully upon us. As daylight touched our faces, our attackers suddenly stopped their assault. Instead, they stood there, motionless and uncomprehending, for a brief moment. Then, one by one, with a sick, small popping sound, each feral human exploded into a shower of gold sparkles, settling into a little mound of dust at our feet.

Rhyss poked at one of the dust mounds with his sword. "Are they truly gone?"

The guard who had spoken earlier eyed the dust with distaste. "Yes, thankfully so. Otherwise they'd be a bigger nuisance than they already are."

"What were those things? They looked human, but acted like monsters." Rhyss looked around at the piles of dust surrounding us. "Were they undead? They're the only creatures I can think of that can't abide daylight."

"They weren't undead, unless you count the Fae-touched among that lot," the guard said.

I gasped. "The Fae-touched? But ... I thought that didn't happen much anymore?"

Every child in Shonn had grown up hearing the horror stories of the Fae-touched. Even I had, although I had only spent part of my childhood in Shonn before moving to Orchwell.

The Fae-touched were humans who ended up living in Faerie, whether by choice or by trickery. The longer one stayed in that otherworldly realm, the more likely it was their mind would be seduced by its glamour and illusion. Faerie was a land of confusion and guile, and few humans could stand against it for long. Eating or drinking Faerie food was another surefire way down that path of becoming Fae-touched. And, as time ran differently between the land of Faerie and the Gifted Lands, a person could find that they had spent decades in Faerie, when only a few days or a week had passed back in the human world.

Valdonne's Treaty supposedly had put a stop to many Fae machinations, including the creation of the Fae-touched. But even if the Fae couldn't harm humans outright, due to the terms of the treaty, they could still find ways to get to humankind indirectly. And humans were no better, willing to sell off or give away their own to gain money or power. As Rhyss and I well knew.

The guard shrugged. "As you can see, it still does happen. And if recent goings-on are any indication, it happens quite a bit." He eyed the mounds of dust, now blowing away in the morning breeze, and bowed his head. "Poor fellows."

I bowed my head along with him in a brief moment of respect. One other thing about the Fae-touched—and possibly the saddest fact of all—was that any Fae-touched human outside the land of Faerie would die by sunrise. This was due to the difference in the flow of time between the two worlds. Many of the Fae-touched would have walked the Gifted Lands generations ago, and would have been way past their mortal life span if they were still regular humans.

As I recalled that fact, I eyed the guard suspiciously. "You heard us calling for help, and you saw we were in trouble. Why didn't you and the others come help us sooner?"

"Let's get you two inside the city." The guard neatly sidestepped my question as he waved the other swordsmen over. One tended to my injured horse, while two others reached down to lift me gently to my feet. I followed Rhyss and the other guards into the capital city of the kingdom of Shonn.

9

—·—

CHAPTER NINE

THE GATES SWUNG SHUT behind us.

The resounding clang reverberated off the stone walls with a finality that made me shudder. Were the citizens of Shonn keeping trouble out?

Or keeping us in?

Although it had been several years since I'd returned, I was shocked at how different the city looked from my childhood and the various times I'd visited my family.

Shonn, due to its proximity to the land of Faerie, had always enjoyed a touch of magic that made the kingdom come alive. It wasn't a large or fancy kingdom by any means, but it gave visitors a cozy, welcoming feeling. Bright and always clean streets, neat and tidy-looking houses. The air usually carried a sweet-smelling freshness that delighted your nose, ever so slightly, and it seemed to sparkle just a bit no matter the light or the season.

But now?

Now, I mourned the beautiful capital city from my childhood memories.

The once-sparkling streets were grimy, coated with a layer of dirt and sludge that squelched under our boots as we walked. I grimaced to myself, not looking forward to having to clean the muck off later.

Next to me, Rhyss wrinkled his nose at the stink in the air, which suggested rotted food, and sewage in the streets.

Even the buildings looked tired and rundown. Several were boarded up, with planks of wood nailed hastily over windows. The water in the city's fountain looked dull and flat, instead of its usual sparkling cool blue.

The lead guard turned to Rhyss and me. "Why did you two come to Shonn?"

I bristled at his rude question. I nearly said, *Our business is our own*, but I stopped myself before the words slipped out. He and his men had saved Rhyss and me from the Fae-touched.

Even if they had waited until the last possible moment to help.

"We're here to visit my family," I said.

The man looked me over, really taking me in this time. I fidgeted under his stare, knowing my lavender-colored hair would be an obvious giveaway. "The magic you used on the Fae-touched earlier ... are you Fae as well?"

"Half Fae, not full."

He nodded, as if I had confirmed his suspicions. He indicated my hair, pulled back in its usual braid. "Probably best to keep that knowledge to yourself, although with that hair it'd be hard to hide your heritage. Unless you dyed it or wore a hat. Right now, the people of Shonn—those that are left, anyway—aren't too keen on anyone with a touch of Fae blood. I suppose it's only fair though; those of Faerie feel the same way about us humans."

"That's what we've been hearing. But why?"

The guard stiffened and looked around warily. Was he afraid we were being watched? I scoffed inwardly at the ridiculous idea. The Fae who lived in Shonn—at least, those who were still here—were the harmless, human-loving sort.

Or had been. I thought of what the refugee had told us.

As before, the guard sidestepped my question. "One of my men will see to your horses, and make sure your injured mount is taken care of properly." Out of the corner of my eye I saw one of the silver-and-purple clad men lead our horses into the city's stable.

The man continued, "And if you would be so kind as to instruct us where to go, we'll escort you to your family's home."

The unspoken other part of that sentence hung in the air: *To make sure you don't attract unwanted attention and cause any more trouble.*

I told the men where my family lived, and we made our steady, silent way down the street. We didn't have far to go—my mother and half-sister lived in a small apartment above a storefront in the Merchants' District, just past the city's fountain.

My eyes widened as we approached. Usually my mother's talents as a seamstress were displayed in the shop windows as ready-made garments. But no one would be able to see her handiwork anymore, as the windows were boarded up. In addition, the two lamps that often shone cheerfully on either side of the door, beckoning and welcoming people passing by, were cold and unlit.

I made a choked squeaking sound and quickened my pace.

The lead guard noted my reaction. "Is this the place?"

I nodded, too dismayed at the sight of my mother's business to speak.

Rhyss knocked on the door, politely at first, then more insistent when no one answered. He looked at me, puzzled. "Does your family still live here?"

I frowned, stepping back slightly to look above the boarded shop windows. "I thought they did. If they had moved, Mother would have said so."

Rhyss turned to the three Shonn swordsmen who had escorted us. "Thank you for bringing us here. I'm sure you have other, more important things to attend to."

My two helpers looked ready to leave, but the lead guard seemed reluctant to leave us alone. His supposed hospitality very thinly veiled an eagerness to see us safely shut away. It honestly felt like he wouldn't be satisfied until he saw us actually enter my family's house. He probably wanted to make sure the door was locked before he left, too.

Movement in an upstairs window caught my eye. Someone had been peeking out at the street below, probably when Rhyss had started knocking. When the person saw that I had caught them looking, they stepped back and tweaked the white curtain shut.

"Oh! I think my family knows we're here," I said, turning a bright smile on the three guards. "I'm sure they'll be right down to let us in. Thank you, again, for your bravery in fighting off the Fae-touched and for seeing us safely here."

The lead guard reluctantly turned to go. "Of course, madam. Sir." He nodded at me, then Rhyss. "Have a good evening."

The three men started off, leaving Rhyss and me standing on the doorstep. When they were a good distance away, the door finally opened.

"Thank goodness! I thought those guards would never leave."

I smirked at my half-sister Halianna, one eyebrow raised. "We haven't seen each other in several years, and that's the first thing you say to me?"

Halianna laughed and pulled me into a hug. "It's always nice to see you, Farrah. Welcome! Come in, come in."

She ushered Rhyss and me into the shop's foyer. As my eyes adjusted to the dim light, my heart sank.

I surveyed the shop. "What happened here?"

The inside of the shop looked just as forlorn as the boarded windows outside. A pile of unclothed dressmakers' mannequins lay haphazardly in one corner. On the other side of the room sat the huge wooden loom my mother often spent hours weaving at, but it too was empty.

Halianna sighed. "For a while, it hadn't been safe to open up the shop. And now, there is hardly anyone left in Shonn to buy our wares. So we closed everything down."

I ran my finger across the frame. Black grime coated my fingertip, and I sneezed from the cloud of dust I had inadvertently stirred up.

"But ... this doesn't make sense." Mother and Halianna must have lost their household Fae, like everyone else. But even if the household Fae were gone, my mother's own tendency for cleanliness and her sense of pride would have kept the shop in pristine condition, regardless of whether or not the shop was still in business.

Halianna took my hand, heedless of the dirt on it. Squeezing it gently, she said, "It's probably for the best that the shop is closed. Mother hasn't had the strength lately to keep it up, and it's taken all I have to take care of her. Farrah ... she's dying."

10

– · –

CHAPTER TEN

MY MIND REELED, AND I swayed on my feet.

My bright, strong, beautiful mother ... dying?

Without thinking, I pulled my hand from Halianna's, turned and headed for the back of the shop, toward the partially concealed staircase that would lead upstairs to my family's apartment.

Halianna called out after me. "Farrah, wait! I need to—"

But I didn't answer her, just bounded up the stairs. At the top, I strode straight to my mother's room at the end of the hallway. The door was ajar, and I pushed it wide open to enter the room.

Halianna could have spent hours, or even days, trying to prepare me for what to expect, and I still wouldn't have been ready. Mother lay in bed with her eyes closed, propped up against some pillows, looking frail and worn. Her ebony skin was ashen, and I could detect a faint wheezing in her breathing as she slept.

Not wanting to disturb her, I began to back out of the room. But, still disturbed by the sight of my mother lying ill, I bumped into the doorframe.

My mother's eyes fluttered open and she saw me. "Farrah?"

"Hello, Mother." I crossed over to the bed and carefully sat down on the edge.

Mother reached out to hold my hand. It was thinner than I remembered, cold and clammy. I blinked back the sudden tears that threatened to spill.

A ghost of a smile crossed her face. "You got my message. Good. I'm so glad you came."

"Of course. It sounded urgent."

"It is." Her eyes lit up, and I realized she was looking at something behind me. Turning around, I saw Halianna and Rhyss now standing in the doorway. "And there's my future son-in-law! So happy you'll be an official part of our family at last, Rhyss."

Rhyss murmured, "Thank you," but remained standing awkwardly just inside the room.

Mother waved at some chairs on the other side of the room. "Come in, sit down. We have a lot to talk about. Halianna, could you bring up some tea?"

My sister nodded, then hurried away. As her footsteps receded, Rhyss grabbed a chair, bringing it closer to the bed before sitting down.

I rubbed my fingers over my mother's hand. "Mother, how are you feeling? Halianna said you're ..." My voice trailed off. I couldn't bring myself to say it out loud. *Dying*.

Mother waved away my concerns like dying wasn't such a big deal. "I've had better days, that's for sure. We can talk about that later. For now, there's something more pressing we need to discuss."

What could be more important to talk about than my mother's final days?

"But ... your health ... isn't that the reason you asked me to come here, in person?"

She squeezed my hand again. "Oh, no, dear. The primary reason is, we need to talk about your wedding."

Halianna returned then with a tea tray, loaded with a small pot, some cups, and several sandwiches. Rhyss jumped up to take it from her, then busied himself pouring cups and handing out sandwiches. Halianna seemed surprised—after all, she was the host, not him—but she let him serve while she also pulled up a chair next to Mother's bed. From his slow, drawn-out movements and downcast eyes, I guessed Rhyss just needed something to do to cover his awkwardness. I didn't blame him. We had expected a happy homecoming, but so far this trip to Shonn had been anything but.

Once everyone was settled, refreshments in hand, Mother spoke again. "Well, my darling, you know I couldn't be happier that you and Rhyss will be getting married. You definitely have my blessing on your upcoming wedding. But what you may not know is that Faerie tradition demands that you also get a blessing from your Fae parent, lest that blessing becomes a curse. Even though you are only part Fae, that tradition still applies to you. And you must do it soon, before you run out of time."

"Run out of time?" I wondered.

Mother sighed. "Like so many things related to magic and spells and the Fae, there is a time limit. I believe the blessing must be obtained within six months of engagement, or it changes into a curse."

I counted back mentally. Rhyss and I had become betrothed just after Samhain. Winter was nearly done. Soon it would be Ostara, the holiday celebrating the start of spring. Which meant ...

"We have two, maybe three weeks at the most, to get my father's blessing," I said. "But I'll be honest, I wouldn't even know where to start looking for him. I suppose we could start around Shonn first, then—"

"You have possibly less than that to find him." My mother spoke reluctantly. "Remember, time flows differently in Faerie."

"In Faerie? What do you mean?"

Mother sighed again. "When your father left, I knew exactly where he had gone. I just didn't tell you, because I didn't want you going after him."

She smiled ruefully. "Even though you did anyway. He had gone back to Faerie, back to his people. And that's where he is now, still."

The silence in the room was deafening.

Finally, I spoke. "So you're saying I may need to go into Faerie to find my estranged father to get a blessing on my upcoming marriage?"

"There's no maybe about it, Farrah. You have to go. Even if your Faerie side could deflect a marriage curse, your human side would never be able to. And as for your intended—" my mother leveled a look at Rhyss "—he would definitely get hurt, as he is fully human."

"Oh," Rhyss said in a small voice.

"And as part of receiving the blessing, the Fae child's betrothed must also present themself to the Faerie parent or parents. Or the blessing is denied. So—"

"So I guess we're both going to Faerie," Rhyss said. "All right, then. What do we have to do?"

I turned on him. "Are you crazy? Faerie is wild, dangerous. Humans wander in all the time and become slaves or transformed or go insane. And now, it's worse than ever. You saw those refugees. And those Fae-touched—"

Rhyss put his hand on my back, trying to calm me. "There's no help for it. It's what we have to do, if we want to get married."

"Can't we just elope?"

"No, dear," my mother put in. "Not without a Fae blessing, first. That would be a surefire way to bring a Faerie marriage curse down on your heads. You have to do it the traditional way."

"I hate tradition."

Rhyss grinned at me. "And that's why I love you."

11

CHAPTER ELEVEN

RHYSS AND I LEFT Mother alone soon after to rest, seeing that it took most of her strength to tell us about the Faerie marriage blessing. Halianna said she would bring down the dirty dishes, and we offered to help her clean up.

Once my sister entered the kitchen, I rounded on her. "What's this about Mother dying?"

Halianna carefully set the dishes down on the counter and reached for the bucket. She frowned, looking down into it. "Drat. I forgot to get more water."

Rhyss took the bucket from her. "I can get it."

"Are you sure? It's no bother, I—"

"I'd be happy to," Rhyss said firmly, already halfway to the back door. I suspected he just wanted to get away from a potentially emotional conversation.

"Well, thank you," my sister said. "The well is just outside, to the right."

"I'll find it," he promised, and then he was out the door.

Halianna and I stood there in the kitchen, staring silently at each other. I could tell she didn't want to talk about it, but I crossed my arms and pursed my lips pointedly.

Finally, Halianna sighed. "There's not much to tell, honestly. The doctor—before he left Shonn, like practically everyone else—said he wasn't sure what was wrong with her, just that she was getting weaker by the day. He didn't give her much past a month or two to live."

I let out a strangled sob. Halianna embraced me, holding me until my shaky tears had subsided somewhat. I pulled back, pushing the tendrils of purple hair that had escaped from my braid away from my face. "How long has this been going on? What are her symptoms? Are you sure she's dying?"

"Since just after Midwinter," my sister answered readily. "She suddenly collapsed, and from there she's grown progressively worse. Trouble breathing, coughing up blood. And yes, I'm sure. She's so thin and pale. She used to be able to walk around a little bit; now she can't even get out of bed." Her voice cracked, an echo of my own sadness.

I studied my sister's face, a younger—and fully human—version of mine. Same ebony skin as my mother and I, except where I had inherited my father's lavender hair, hers was dark brown with streaks of gold, like our mother's. I also knew—from hours of failed experiments when we were younger—that she lacked the innate magic I possessed. Halianna had no magical ability at all.

My half-sister was the union of a short marriage between Mother and a man of Orchwell, where Mother and I had moved after my father's abandonment. I had been very young—four, perhaps five years old?—when we had moved in an attempt for my mother to start a new life, away from Shonn and memories of my father.

Mother had remarried and had my baby sister, Halianna. But shortly after Halianna's birth, Mother's new husband died after being thrown off his horse while on a commission. We had lived off the money from the modest estate he had left behind, and when that ran out, I had hired myself out as help to any Orchwell Seekers.

Once I was self-sufficient, Mother felt it would be all right for her to move back to Shonn. I think she just wanted to get away from the unhappy memories in Orchwell, but still needed something familiar. So she and Halianna left, and I stayed in Orchwell to work.

"Since Midwinter," I mused. I looked around the kitchen, thinking. Just like the shop, the kitchen looked a little rough—cleaner than the shop up front, probably because Halianna used it frequently. But it wasn't sparkling and spotless, the way it usually looked when ... "I heard what happened to the household Fae."

Halianna nodded. "Yes. I've tried to keep up, but ..."

"When did it happen?"

"At Midwinter. Such a strange event. It's all the kingdom can talk about." She made a face. "Well, what's left of the kingdom."

So Mother had fallen ill around Midwinter. And, just a few weeks ago on Midwinter, all the household Fae in Shonn had mysteriously perished.

A widespread magical call could have lured the household Fae to abandon their posts in Shonn, despite their deep loyalty. I wondered if that same sort of call would have been able to decimate them as well.

But only the Great Ones of Faerie could put out such a call. And, as far as I knew, the Fae were still leaderless.

Now I dreaded the upcoming trip into Faerie even more.

Since Halianna didn't have any more information about Mother's condition, I changed the subject. "What's going on with the guards? They acted awfully suspicious of us, like they wanted to make sure we were securely locked away in here before they left Rhyss and me. And even though they saw we were under attack, they waited until the last possible moment to help us." I quickly filled her in on the morning's events.

"Well, when—"

Rhyss chose that moment to open the back door. "I've brought fresh water," he said unnecessarily. Seeing that my sister and I were more or less composed, he stepped into the kitchen, hefting the now-full bucket. "Where would you like this?"

Halianna pointed to a spot on the counter, and for a few moments the kitchen was a flurry of deciding who would do what chore. Once we were settled and working, Halianna finished her earlier thought.

"Once Mother fell ill, all of my focus was on caring for her," she said. "And when everyone started leaving, it was too late for us to go. Mother is too sick to move. There are so few people left in Shonn that anyone or anything new is regarded as part of the Terrors."

12

—·—

CHAPTER TWELVE

"THE TERRORS?" I GULPED. This didn't sound good.

Halianna shrugged and started scrubbing at a dish. "That's just the general term for it. But you know Valdonne's Treaty?"

Rhyss and I both nodded.

"Well, now it's like it never even existed," Halianna said. "On Midwinter, all the harmless Fae died. No one knows why, or how. And not before they completely destroyed the homes they used to take care of. And then different Fae started appearing all around the kingdom. The malevolent ones. Playing all their usual tricks—glamours and luring the unwary, seduction and shapeshifting. You can't be sure that the neighbors and friends you've known for years are truly themselves—they might be Fae in disguise. With less people in Shonn, it's easier to tell ... but then, we're less safe with fewer numbers."

My sister sighed. "That's probably why the guards delayed so long in helping you fight off the Fae-touched. They couldn't be sure if it was all an elaborate trap."

"That makes sense," Rhyss said. "It doesn't excuse them, but it makes sense."

Halianna continued to scrub at her now-spotless dish. "There's so few people left in Shonn. We can't afford to lose anyone."

I gently took the dish from her and began drying it with a clean towel. "If you scrub any harder, you'll break it."

She let out a frustrated sob. Tears streaked down her face. I put the dish down and pulled her into a hug.

Poor Rhyss stood to the side, looking like he wanted to be anywhere but in the kitchen with us. I looked at him over my sister's shoulder. "I just realized we left our bags on our horses. Could you go get them?"

Rhyss nodded so vigorously I thought his head would fall off. He opened the back door again, escaping into the sunshine. I chuckled as I watched him go. After a moment, Halianna also laughed a little with me.

"He doesn't handle emotion too well, does he?" my sister remarked, pulling back from our embrace to wipe at her face.

"He's gotten better recently," I said, thinking of how sentimental Rhyss could get over his new godson. I looked at my sister. "You all right?"

She sniffled. "Yes. It's nothing I'm not used to already. It's just ... I wish I could get out of here. I feel like I'm just waiting for some unknown doom to fall. But I can't leave our mother behind. And I don't want her to die just so I'm free to leave." Her tears started falling again. "I'm such a horrible daughter."

I shook my head, rubbing her arm to calm her. "No. No, don't say that. Hey, if anyone is a bad daughter, it's me. I've been in Orchwell this whole time, and rarely get back to Shonn to see you two."

Halianna giggled through her tears, producing a funny little hiccup. "When did this become a competition of who's the worst daughter?"

I smiled, shrugging. "You started it."

She sat down at the table and put her head in her hands. "I just want us to be safe. And right now this is the least safe place I can think of."

I sank down in a chair opposite her. "I have an idea."

Halianna looked up at me, eyebrows raised.

"I was planning on contacting my friend Jennica, back in Calia," I told my sister. "She'll want to know what's going on with the Fae. She might have some ideas on how to get you and Mother out of Shonn safely."

Halianna frowned. "Unless she can send an entire army, I don't know what good that will do. No one wants to travel this way right now. And I don't know why a Calian would care about what the Fae are doing right now, even if Calia *is* steeped in magic." She paused for a moment, thinking. "Jennica ... why is that name familiar?"

I grinned. "Well, if you ever meet her, make sure to call her 'Your Majesty', although 'Queen Jennica' also works."

Halianna's jaw dropped. "You're friends with the queen of Calia?"

"I'm sure I've told you before. In one of my letters to you, some time over the years." I frowned. "Didn't I?"

"No," Halianna said positively. "I would have remembered if you had. How do you know her?"

"It's a long story. The short version is, I met her through Beyan."

"If I had magic like you, I'd love to travel the way you do." Halianna sounded wistful. "And having magic right now would make things a lot easier."

"Maybe. Sometimes it just complicates things."

"Maybe. I still say it would make things better." Her eyes gleamed, but this time from excitement instead of tears. She clapped her hands, and for a moment all the cares that had worn her down fell away. "Call your friend. It would be so exciting to say a queen had rescued us!"

I laughed. "Hey, what about me?"

She smiled. "I thought that was obvious, silly." She stood up and kissed the top of my head, then went back to the stack of dirty dishes.

13

—·—

Chapter Thirteen

By the time Rhyss returned, Halianna and I had tidied up the kitchen and had moved on to the rest of the place.

A knock on the front door announced his presence. Halianna called out, "Come on in, it's open!"

The door cracked open a bit. Rhyss cautiously poked his head in the house. "Is it okay to come in?"

"Of course it is," Halianna said cheerfully. Hearing the change in her tone from earlier, Rhyss opened the door fully and stepped inside.

"I got our bags," he said, holding them up.

"Perfect," I said. "And you have perfect timing. You can leave the bags over there—" I pointed to the right of the staircase leading up to the apartment "—and help us clean."

Rhyss surveyed the dusty, shuttered workspace. "Are you planning on reopening the shop?"

"No. But we'll have to leave for Faerie soon, probably tomorrow morning. So we should help Halianna while we're here."

Rhyss shrugged. "Fair enough. Give me a rag, will you?"

Between the three of us, we made quick work of cleaning the shop. I supposed if Halianna and Mother eventually left the kingdom, it wouldn't really matter if the shop was clean or not, but seeing the happiness and relief on Halianna's face made the thankless chore worth doing.

When we were done, we sat around the now dust-free workspace and relaxed. Halianna turned to me. "So, about your friend—the queen. Do you think she really could help Mother and me?"

I laughed. I suspected that Halianna's excitement over meeting a queen was greater than the prospect of escaping Shonn.

"We may as well contact her now," I said. "Maybe she can give us some ideas on how to find my father in Faerie."

I opened my hand and spoke the spell that would call the queen. Soon, her image appeared above my palm. She broke into a smile.

"Farrah! Rhyss! I'm so glad to see you two are safe. Where are you? Are you in Shonn?"

"We are." I quickly recounted the events of the past few days.

She frowned. "We'd heard rumors of people leaving Shonn, but few of the refugees have come to Calia. I hope they'll be all right. The news of Fae unrest is even more disturbing. Are you sure you and Rhyss have to go into Faerie?"

I nodded. "It's not an ideal time, but Faerie is always perilous to traverse."

Jennica pursed her lips, thinking. "I wonder ... Tradition and protocol are important to the Fae, correct?"

"Very," I affirmed. "There are severe consequences for those who try to sidestep doing things the proper way."

"Then, if I send you as official envoys of the Calian crown, no Fae can harm you while you are there." She smiled. "If you happen to be searching for your father while you're there, that's no business of Calia's. Or Faerie's."

Rhyss and I looked at each other, then back at Jennica, answering grins on our faces. "Neat and clever. That will work nicely."

"Do we have to do anything to make it official?" She frowned. "I wish we had thought of this while you were here. I could have sent you with a signed letter, or something similar."

"We didn't know," I assured her. "And you don't need to do a formal ritual or anything. Just say the words, and the land of Faerie will recognize us as your representatives."

"Ah." She nodded. "Rhyss and Farrah, I am sending you as my personal representatives to the Faerie court, to establish relations with their new leadership for the betterment of both Faerie and Calia."

I felt the words settle around me as if Queen Jennica had indeed spoken a magic spell. Even Rhyss shivered a little. I smiled at the queen. "That should do it. Thank you."

"Thank *you*. I meant it, you know. If you have time, after finding your father, I would like it if you could visit the Faerie court and meet their new rulers on Calia's behalf."

"Your wish may come true. Starting at the Faerie court is as good a place to start the search as any."

With that settled, Jennica turned to look at my sister. "Forgive me for the delayed introduction, but we had to get the urgent business out of the way first. May I know your name?"

My sister gaped slightly at the queen. I think she was in awe—not only was she talking to a queen, but said queen was apologizing to her for a breach in manners! After opening and closing her mouth a few times, she finally stammered out, "H-H-Halianna, Your Majesty. My name is Halianna."

"My half-sister." I rested a hand on her shoulder.

Jennica studied us, taking in our resemblance. "I can see that. Well met, Halianna."

"Your Majesty," my sister murmured.

"We've got a bit of a problem, Jennica." My sister gasped at my familiarity, but I ignored it and continued talking. "It's not safe in Shonn right now, but with Mother so ill, and Rhyss and I leaving for Faerie tomorrow—"

"Say no more," Queen Jennica interrupted me. "Halianna, you and your mother are welcome to stay here in Castle Calia for as long as you need."

Even while Halianna mumbled her thanks, Jennica said, "Now, how to get you to Calia. I could send an armed escort, but it would still take them a few days to get there. And there's no guarantee they'll get there safely, not to mention the return trip. Not if the roads are as dangerous as Farrah says. And it doesn't sound like you should wait there any longer than need be." She thought for a minute. "I think the best thing is if I come and get you."

"Oh, thank you, Your Majesty, but that's not necessary," Halianna said, confused. "We've managed this long. Perhaps—"

"Nonsense," Jennica said. "Give me a few days to settle things here. I can get you in three days."

"You'll have to bring a litter of some sort to carry Mother," I said.

"Good point. I'll ask Beyan for help. And I'm sure someone here at the castle knows about that sort of thing."

"But ... pardon me, Your Majesty, but I don't understand," Halianna said. "How can you bring us to Calia, if you're not sending an escort?"

Jennica grinned. "I hope you don't mind riding on a dragon's back. I don't normally carry passengers when I fly, but in certain situations, I make an exception."

Halianna's eyes widened. She opened her mouth, then closed it again, speechless.

Rhyss, Jennica, and I laughed. "I'll create a calling stone for Halianna," I said. "That way you two can stay in contact even after Rhyss and I leave."

Jennica nodded. "Good idea. And have Halianna learn how to link to Taryn, just in case I'm not available." She turned thoughtful. "Speaking of calling—will you and Rhyss be able to contact any of us here in Calia while you're in Faerie?"

"I'm not sure. Not only does time run different there, but the magic between the Gifted Lands and Faerie isn't always compatible. But if we do meet with whoever is in charge of the Faerie court now, they might be able to help us contact you. If anyone can create that strong of magic, it's the Great Ones."

"I hope so. We'll be worried about your safety the whole time you're gone. Especially if we have no way of getting updates."

We said our goodbyes and ended the call. The rest of the day passed by in a flurry of activity. I created a calling stone for Halianna and showed her how to use it, testing it by calling Taryn, the Calian Royal Advisor.

The usually unflappable blonde woman showed a bit of dismay when I told her of Jennica's plan to come to Shonn. "How do we know the guards won't shoot her on sight? I know I would if I saw a large golden dragon flying over the gates. It's too late to send a message. Not that it sounds like there is any leadership left to send a message to. Oh, dear."

Rhyss went back out into the city to buy food and supplies for our journey into Faerie. We'd have to bring a lot of food and ration it well, as it was unwise to consume Faerie food or drink. Not unless we wanted to be enchanted, transformed, or permanently bound to live in Faerie.

By the time night fell, we had finished our preparations and gathered for an evening meal, exhausted but content. As we said our goodnights, my sister paused. "Do you really think we'll be okay? Mother and me, I mean. In Calia?"

"Of course. You'll be guests of King Beyan and Queen Jennica—it can't get much safer than that."

Halianna bit her lip. "I wish you could join us, instead of going into Faerie."

I embraced her. "We'll join you soon. And Rhyss and I will be fine in Faerie."

I hoped.

From the doubtful look on her face, I could tell Halianna was thinking the same thing.

14

CHAPTER FOURTEEN

THE NEXT DAY DAWNED cold and clear. We all—except for Mother—woke up early and went about our preparations, silent and subdued.

More than once I caught Halianna looking at me out of the corner of her eye, unshed tears threatening to fall. My heart felt just as heavy. I didn't want to leave my family so soon after arriving, but I felt better knowing we had a plan to get them out of Shonn safely.

We lingered over breakfast, but eventually we had to say our farewells. Upstairs, I gingerly hugged my frail mother.

"I'll see you again soon, in Calia," I told her. Earlier, we had briefed her on her upcoming journey with Halianna.

"It won't be soon enough," she said, smiling weakly. I smiled back and turned to go. She grabbed my hand suddenly, with surprising strength.

"If you find your father—" Mother began coughing. Rhyss rushed over with some water, but she waved the proffered glass away. She spoke again, stronger now. "If you find him, tell him ... tell him I never forgot. Please. Tell him that."

My heart broke as I saw the longing in my mother's eyes. I nodded slowly. "I'll tell him."

She leaned back against her pillows, satisfied. I leaned over and kissed her forehead. "We'll see you in Calia."

Downstairs, at the shop's front door, I embraced my sister. Neither of us tried to hide the free-flowing tears.

"We'll be together again soon," I said, but the reassurance may have been more for me than for her.

"I know," Halianna sniffled. She wiped at her eyes. "When you go through the gates, go northeast a bit, toward the forest. The Veil isn't far, although its position changes from time to time. But it will be in that general area. It should be about an hour's walk from here. If you haven't found it by midday, you've probably missed it and will have to try again tomorrow morning. You could go at night, but I don't recommend it." She shuddered. "Not with the creatures coming out of there lately."

"Thank you." I touched my forehead to my sister's. "We'll be together again soon, I promise."

More tears glistened in her eyes. "You'd better not break that promise."

I nodded, not trusting myself to say anything more. Nearby, Rhyss coughed discreetly. We both looked at him.

He nodded toward the growing daylight. "We should go."

I nodded again, then squeezed Halianna a final time. Stepping back, I gave a little wave and then turned, hoisting my pack a little higher on my back so it sat comfortably between my shoulders. I didn't look back. I knew if I did, I'd never want to leave.

We made it to the gates of Shonn without incident. From the distrustful looks of the guards as we passed, I think they were glad to see us go. We stopped briefly at the city stable to make arrangements for our horses. We couldn't take them into Faerie with us, and I doubted they would enjoy an aerial ride with Queen Jennica to Calia. For now, they would remain at the stable, but Halianna would sell them before she and Mother left.

We passed through the gates and headed in the direction my sister had instructed. I had forgotten to ask her if the Veil was in the forest, or just outside it, but it was too late now.

Rhyss broke the silence that had been hanging like a fog over us since we said goodbye to my family. "What's this Veil your sister was talking about?"

I surveyed the area. We could see trees in the distance, with a wide grassy area between us and the edge of the woods. The field looked normal enough, but we'd have to go over every part of it carefully to find the Veil.

I sighed. I hoped it wouldn't be a long, fruitless search. The thought of having to come back several mornings to crisscross the field was disheartening.

I started walking, Rhyss on my heels. "The Veil Between the Worlds. It's the unseen border between the land of Faerie and the Gifted Lands, and it's found within Shonn's boundaries. It's easiest to travel into Faerie on certain holidays, or in the morning or late at night, but the border closes around midday, reopens, and then closes again at midnight."

"Ah, so that's what Halianna meant."

I looked at him apologetically. "It's usually easier to wander into Faerie by accident. When you're trying to go there deliberately, it's like the border knows that and evades you on purpose. Stubborn thing."

Rhyss, now walking side-by-side with me, wandered a little off to the left. "Sounds like most things in life. But I'm sure we—"

I turned. Rhyss was gone.

I waved my hand experimentally in the direction I had last seen him. Nothing unusual happened. I took a few more steps to my left, waving my hand all the while. *It's probably a good thing most of Shonn has fled*, I thought sardonically. *Anyone watching me right now would wonder what in the Gifted Lands is wrong with me.*

And then I saw it, right in front of me.

An area about twice as tall and wide as me shimmered in the sunlight. A casual passerby might have thought it was the shimmer of sunlight reflecting off the day's heat. But as I stuck my arm through the shimmer, my hand and half of my arm disappeared.

I pulled my arm back. It was still there, along with my hand, whole and unharmed.

I stared at the shimmer. Here it was, then. The Veil Between the Worlds.

And Rhyss was on the other side of it.

In Faerie.

I took a deep breath and plunged through the Veil.

15

— · —

CHAPTER FIFTEEN

ONE STEP, THEN ANOTHER. My skin prickled, and I felt a little light-headed, like I was stepping outside myself.

The skin-crawling sensation stopped, and my two selves snapped back together. The hazy feeling faded, and I was very much aware of myself again.

I stared, awestruck, at the world around me.

Faerie.

As a healer-for-hire, I'd traveled extensively around the Gifted Lands. Each region had impressed me with its unique beauty—the gorgeous seasons in the northern kingdoms of Calia and Orchwell, the wildness of Bomora on the Aentin Sea in the west, the exotic glamour of Annlyn in the south.

But the land of Faerie, with its Otherworldly perfection, surpassed any of the beauty the Gifted Lands offered.

Unlike in the human realm, where winter was slowly releasing its hold on the Gifted Lands, Faerie's spring had already arrived. This magical world didn't have to bear gradual change; when it was time for the season to change, it happened in an instant. Perhaps this accounted for Faerie's unreal gorgeousness, where each perfectly formed petal and tree leaf boasted colors that were a little too vibrant.

But I knew, from the one time I had been in Faerie, long ago, that its citizens possessed the same unreal perfection that the land did. It was part of their charm, and also what made the Fae so dangerous.

My initial glimpse of Faerie had me so in wonder that I nearly forgot why I had stepped through the Veil. Fortunately, Rhyss was just on the other side of the Veil, also gaping, wide-eyed, at the world around him.

"This place ... it's incredible," he said.

I grabbed his hand. He looked down at me. I smiled. "Just so you remember what's real, and what's not."

He touched a bright silver rose, rubbing its velvet softness between his fingers before he leaned over to smell it. "Oh, wow. This would tempt any perfumer into a life of crime just to have a little bit of this."

Gently, I tugged him away. "While we're here, it's probably best to not take anything, even if it seems like it's wild, like these flowers. Everything belongs to the Faerie King and Queen, and what is of Faerie should stay in Faerie."

Reluctantly, Rhyss let go of the rose. He squeezed my hand. "Thanks." Looking around, he asked, "Where do we start?"

We were standing in a small clearing, surrounded by a ring of trees. Behind us was the Veil, which was bordered in silver-and-white vines and flowers, including the rose Rhyss had just been admiring. In one direction, just beyond the trees, I could see a pale white ribbon of a road.

I pointed at it. "There's a road over there. What do you think?"

Rhyss grinned and started pulling me that way. "I like roads. They always go somewhere. Let's go."

We walked through the trees and made it to the road. Once there, we looked both ways, but didn't see any important landmarks in the distance, in either direction.

"Which way?" Rhyss asked.

I looked to my left. "This way."

We started down the road. After we had been walking for awhile, Rhyss broke the silence. "Have you ever been here before?"

"To Faerie?"

"Yes."

"I have, just once, a long time ago." I waved back the way we had come. "It looked different the last time. When I came through the Veil before, I found myself in a Faerie village, just outside the royals' palace."

"Really? I wonder if the Faerie royals moved the Veil, so it wasn't disturbing anyone."

I shook my head. "The King and Queen don't have anything to do with it. Every year the Veil moves on its own. I understand it used to move all over the Gifted Lands, but in the last century or so it stayed within Shonn's borders, although it's not always in the same area."

"That's convenient, at least for the people of Shonn."

I grimaced. "Not everyone would call it convenient. Some might say it's dangerous, instead."

Rhyss chuckled. "A good point." He gave me a curious look. "You said you'd been here before, a long time ago? When?"

I blew out a breath. "Oh, I was really young. About three or four, I think."

I could feel the weight of Rhyss's eyes on me. "You were that little? Why? What were you doing in Faerie?"

I didn't respond right away. The only sound we could hear was the crunching of the small gravel underfoot as we continued down the white dirt road. I sneaked a look over at my betrothed. He just continued to stare at me, one eyebrow raised as he waited for my answer.

I looked down at my moving feet. One step, then another. I kept looking down as I answered. "I wanted to find my father."

"And did you?" Rhyss gently asked.

"I did." I sighed. "He had lived in Shonn with us for several years, but then one day he just went back to Faerie, with no warning. So I went in search of him. I wanted him to come home."

I smiled ruefully. "It didn't work, obviously. He told me to go back to Shonn, that he would be there soon. Like a fool, I believed him. But he never returned to Shonn. And I was too heartbroken to search for him again." I blinked back unexpected tears. Even after all these years, my father's abandonment still hurt. "Then Mother and I moved to Orchwell, and when she moved back to Shonn I stayed behind. And then I got busy working, and—"

"—And it was easier to just bury yourself in your work than to come back here and see him again."

"That wasn't what I was going to say."

"You didn't have to." Rhyss gave me a sympathetic smile. "I know you well."

I chuckled. "Maybe a little too well."

Rhyss looked down the road, shading his eyes from the sun. "So, where are we headed?"

I shrugged. "I have no idea."

Rhyss stopped. "Wait. You mean we could be going the wrong way?"

I stopped, too, turning around to face him. "In Faerie, there's really no wrong way."

"What do you mean?"

I gave Rhyss a gentle nudge, urging him to continue walking. He did so, but I could tell he was wary. "Faerie's not like the Gifted Lands.

It focuses more on intentions, wishes or fears, rather than absolutes. At least, for visitors like us, it does."

"What does that mean?"

I tilted my head slightly, thinking of the best way to explain it. "Back home, everything stays in one place, and it's where it's supposed to be. Certain things are always true. North is always north. If you go due south, you'll eventually reach Annlyn. The Aentin Sea is always on the western edge of the Gifted Lands."

"I'm following you. So far."

"While certain parts of the Gifted Lands have magic, overall the continent is not magical. The magic is a part of the people, or the creatures, and not necessarily the land itself. But Faerie is an inherently magical land. It's that magic that responds to the deepest desires of those who traverse Faerie."

Rhyss frowned in thought. "Kind of like how Jennica, and pretty much every other Calian mage, has to study and prepare in advance to cast their spells, but you can just sort of think things into existence?"

I nodded, pleased. "That's it exactly. I'm impressed."

He nudged my shoulder with his. "Just because I'm not magically inclined doesn't mean I haven't picked up a few things over the years, watching you and Jennica do magic."

I beamed up at him. "Sometimes I wish I could do magic the way Jennica can. If a spell goes wrong, it would be easier to pinpoint what part I messed up. When you do magic based on feelings and intentions, it's a lot harder to correct any mistakes. And 'try harder' is not a helpful correction."

"But you have to admit, your way of doing magic is a lot faster. No need for elaborate set ups, or to bring anything with you."

I laughed. "Handy in our line of work."

I looked down the road. Still nothing, except for a seemingly endless stretch of a white gravel road lined by trees on either side.

"So how much longer?" Rhyss asked.

I shrugged. "I guess it depends. We obviously haven't decided what we want to do first, so until we figure that out, the road will just lead us nowhere."

"Well, what are our options? We can look for your father. Or we can visit the Faerie court, deliver Jennica's message, and go from there."

I pondered Rhyss's words for a moment. "It's probably best if we meet their new leaders. If they even have a new king and queen yet. That will give us some insight into how things stand over here—how dangerous or welcoming the realm would be to us right now. And hopefully, they can help us start our search for my father."

"It's settled, then. To the Faerie court we go."

As Rhyss finished speaking, I felt something settle over us. Not a heavy feeling, but definitive. As if our course was now set and nothing could deviate us from it.

Rhyss shuddered, then shook himself like a dog shaking off water. "That was odd."

"You felt it too?"

He nodded. "I guess it's too late now to change our minds. Let's hope the Faerie court is friendly."

"From the stories I've heard, I'm not hoping too much." I paused. "I also hope we can finish our business here quickly. Time in Faerie flows differently than it does in the human world. It's not wise to stay too long. We could be here for a week, and return to the Gifted Lands to find that a year or more have gone by."

Rhyss shuddered. "Find your father, get his blessing, get out. Got it."

We continued on in companionable silence. We hadn't been walking long when Rhyss gave a small shout and pointed. I followed the direction of his finger.

There, in the distance, stood the shimmering white palace of Faerie.

16

——◦——

CHAPTER SIXTEEN

WE APPROACHED THE PALACE, wary and watchful.

From a distance, the Faerie palace had been impressive, a shining white beacon rising up above the lush green trees. From where Rhyss had spotted it on the road, we had been too far away to see any detail, other than the vague impression of multiple towers that rose into the sky and an overall majestic feeling.

Up close, the seat of Fae power was even more impressive. And intimidating.

Everywhere we looked, all we saw was white. White stone walls, white cobblestones, a white metal portcullis firmly closed against outsiders. Even the trees and shrubs lining the palace walkway were white, looking like life-sized sculptures made of ice. I reached out and touched one of the trees. The white bark, rough under my fingertips, was definitely not ice.

Rhyss whispered to me, "Do they not believe in color here?"

"White is the color of royalty, in Faerie," I replied. I giggled. "It's a good thing they have magic here. Can you imagine trying to keep all of this clean back home?"

Rhyss shook his head. "It would be enough to make all the mages in the Gifted Lands give up their magic."

We fell silent and looked up. I couldn't see anyone patrolling the walls, but I had a strong feeling that Rhyss and I were being watched.

"Well, we won't get anything done just standing here," I said. "Shall we?"

We stepped up to the gate. I called out, "Hello, the castle! Is anyone there?"

A small head popped over the battlement. "Hello, hello? Who's that?"

Perhaps it was a trick of where we stood on the ground in relation to whoever had called back, but I couldn't see them clearly. The top of the speaker's head barely cleared the crenel. All I saw was a shock of short grey hair and a pair of dark eyes staring at us from over the wall.

Next to me, Rhyss was trying not to snicker. I nudged him, worried that he'd offend the guard and we'd never gain entry.

"I am Lady Farrah, and my companion is Lord Rhyss. We're official representatives of King Beyan and Queen Jennica of the kingdom of Calia, in the Gifted Lands," I said. "We are here to convey their respects to the new king and queen, and establish a friendship between the two kingdoms."

The grey hair whipped back and forth. "Oh dear, oh dear. I suppose you're just in time, which is no time at all to be here." The hair stopped moving and the eyes stared down at us again. "We have no king and queen."

I blinked. "Oh."

"We have several."

I looked up at the diminutive guard. "What? What do you mean?"

The grey hair started bouncing up and down. Each time it traveled up, we could see a bit more of the guard's face—snub nose, round red cheeks. A hint of a grey beard on his chin, and I had a feeling if we could see all of the guard, that beard would be down to his feet. *A gnome. That'd be my guess.*

The guard said, "Since the death of the last king and queen, several have come forth to claim the crown. None have taken power yet, but they have all begun gathering supporters. But soon—oh soon!—they will all try to become the next rulers of the land of Faerie."

"Who is in charge right now, then? And why didn't he or she just become the next king or queen?"

"That would be Lord Chela. And he is forever ineligible to rule as king. When he became High Chancellor, he swore to always serve the Crown in that position, and never seek additional power, under pain of death."

"Smart move, whoever bound him thus," I murmured.

"What do you mean?" Rhyss asked me in a low voice.

"I'll tell you shortly," I said quietly. Raising my voice, I called up to the guard, "Can we meet with Lord Chela?"

The guard narrowed his eyes, then nodded. "I suppose, since you're on official business. I will go check." His grey head disappeared.

With the guard now out of earshot, I turned to Rhyss and explained my earlier statement. "The Fae aren't quite immortal, but they live so long that in human terms, they practically do live forever. And the Great Ones—the king and queen, and the lords and ladies of the Fae court—live longer than the general Fae do. Which means whoever rules Faerie wields an immense amount of power and influence over the entire land. Those in power could live for centuries. It's practically impossible to oust a bad ruler. Creating permanent bindings, like the High Chancellor's oath, encourages stability. And it means he might be a good ally—his vow means he's hard to corrupt."

Rhyss tilted his head thoughtfully. "I'm not sure about that. A near-immortal life might get boring after a while. And if the Fae are as long-lived as you say, this Lord Chela, or someone like him in a similar position, could nurse a grudge for a very, very long time. It might be worth risking death to stir things up a bit."

I blinked in surprise. "Huh. I had never thought of it that way."

In front of us, the shining white portcullis slowly started rising, grabbing our attention. A small, wizened man with grey hair and a long grey beard stumped toward us. "You are the Calian envoys?"

Recognizing his voice as that of the guard who spoke with us earlier, Rhyss and I both nodded. The guard waved a hand at us, beckoning us in. "Come along, then."

He turned on his heel and started walking away. Rhyss and I exchanged a look, then hurried after him.

Just like outside, mostly everything in the palace courtyard was white as well. To our right, an elf stablehand held on to the reins of two beautiful white horses, petting their noses and speaking calming words to them in a low voice. Two more elves polished a stately white carriage.

The all-white interior made the gathered courtiers, in their non-white dress, stand out. Elves and gnomes mingled, as did nymphs and selkies, recognizable by the animal pelts they wore on their belts. Several trows—known as trolls in the Gifted Lands, although in Faerie they preferred their Fae name—towered over the crowd, and I looked up, surprised that the sunlight hadn't turned them all into stone. Various lights blinked in and out among the crowd of courtiers, and I realized they were will-o'-the-wisps, another nighttime Fae like the trows.

I scrutinized the gleaming white stone walls around us. Perhaps the castle held some special magic that allowed Fae of any kind to be safe here, regardless of how the time of day or the environment usually affected them.

The guard threaded through the courtiers, hurrying through another doorway. Rhyss and I followed as best we could, but there was quite a crowd of Fae milling about in the courtyard, and our guide moved much faster than we did. We got several odd looks from the various courtiers as we passed, but no one stopped us.

The guard waited for us just inside a doorway. "Come on, come on now!"

Once we were just a few steps away, the guard started moving again. The interior of the castle was just as bright as the courtyard had been. Upon closer examination, I realized that the white walls glowed with some internal light. I wondered if the walls responded to the passage of time outside, and dimmed when night approached.

We followed our guide down a twisty path of hallways that ultimately led to a pair of closed, giant white doors. A pattern of silver-and-white flowers and vines, mirroring the ones that had outlined the Veil, formed an arch around the doors. In the door's center, the Seelie Court's heraldic symbol was displayed: a trio of white roses, their thorny stems twisted around each other.

My steps stopped as I took in what I presumed was the entrance to the Faerie palace's throne room. I licked my lips nervously, my throat suddenly dry. *Maybe we should have gone to look for my father first.*

Our diminutive guide noticed my reluctance. "Come on!" he repeated, sounding impatient.

I took one step forward.

The oversized doors flew open, seemingly of their own accord.

I jumped back, startled, and gave a little yelp.

The guard looked amused. He hadn't touched the doors, and he also didn't seem fazed at the doors opening on their own. No servants stood on the other side of the doors, either. So unless their servants were invisible—which I somehow doubted—magic was used liberally here. Even Queen Jennica, despite her magical prowess, didn't use magic so casually. Neither did I. Magic wasn't unlimited—every time you used it, it took something from you, be it energy or power reserves or, in some rare cases, something more sinister.

But here in the Faerie palace, that apparently wasn't an issue.

The magical doors distracted me enough that I didn't notice the figure at the other end of the room right away.

"My lord, may I present Lady Farrah and Lord Rhyss, envoys from the kingdom of Calia." The gnome guard's voice echoed off the stone walls. I blinked in surprise as my attention snapped to the man to whom we were being presented. I hadn't expected the guard to have such a booming voice, but I supposed it came with the job—in case he needed to alert his fellow guards to an attack, or something similar.

Rhyss bowed, and I sank into a curtsey. The man studied us silently for a few moments, then nodded. "Well met, officials of Calia. I am Lord Chela, High Chancellor of the Seelie Court."

17

—·—

CHAPTER SEVENTEEN

THE HIGH CHANCELLOR STOOD, waving our guide away. "You may go."

The guard bowed and scurried away, presumably back to his position at the castle wall. Lord Chela turned his attention back to us, stepping down from the dais where he had been sitting to the right of the twin white marble thrones.

Interesting, I noted. *Even though he's the interim ruler, he shows the proper respect to the Faerie thrones.* My estimation of him went up several notches.

The High Chancellor tucked a strand of his long, straight black hair behind his ears. In a pale blue fitted jacket and trousers that brought out his ice blue eyes, the tall, slim Lord Chela cut an imposing figure. Cords of silver threaded through his coat and in his hair, displaying his powerful status in the Seelie Court, second only to the king and queen.

"So, you are here on behalf of the rulers of Calia," he stated.

"That is correct, my lord," Rhyss said. With my intended standing at his full height, I noticed the two men, Fae and human, were nearly eye-to-eye.

"Who are the rulers there, again?"

"King Beyan and Queen Jennica."

Lord Chela frowned. "I thought the current ruler of Calia was King Eedrann?"

I said, "Eedrann has not been king of Calia for several generations, my lord. I believe he was their second king? The water mage who designed the beautiful Castle Calia."

Rhyss raised an eyebrow, but wisely didn't say anything. Such as the fact that Eedrann's reign had been so long ago, he had practically passed into Calian legend by now. I could tell what Rhyss was thinking, though. *Just how old is Lord Chela?*

"Is that so." Lord Chela seemed lost in thought. "I will admit, it has been a long time since I've paid attention to the state of affairs in the Gifted Lands."

A long time. That was an understatement.

He frowned, his gaze sharpening as he regarded us. "Although recent events have changed that. When we focused too much on our own affairs, and disregarded those of the mortal world, we paid for it with the lives of King Finvarra and Queen Oona. We will not be so foolish again."

I met his steely, accusing eyes without flinching. "Lord Rhyss and I share your realm's sorrow over the loss of two such fine rulers. The man responsible for their deaths has been brought to justice, and steps have been taken to ensure no such breach will ever happen again."

"Let us hope so." Lord Chela's tone implied that he didn't quite believe me. I bit my tongue, nearly drawing blood. But better that than saying what was on the tip of it: *If your king and queen hadn't engaged in acts that violated Valdonne's Treaty, perhaps they wouldn't have been killed.*

"So, these new Calian rulers," Lord Chela continued. Neither Rhyss nor I bothered to correct him. "They sent you here? For what purpose?"

"They wish to send their condolences over the loss of your king and queen, and to establish a friendship between the kingdom of Calia and the Seelie Court," I said.

"You do realize we do not have a new king and queen yet?"

"We learned that when we arrived in Faerie," Rhyss said. "Unfortunately, we had no way of knowing that before we came. We thought, since time flows differently between the Gifted Lands and Faerie, that perhaps your new rulers had been appointed already."

The High Chancellor smiled unpleasantly, as if he had bit into something sour or rotten. "Pretty words, indeed. But I suspect that is not the true reason you are here. I want the truth, or I'll have my guards escort you to the Veil immediately, and you will forever be barred from re-entering Faerie."

I gulped. Next to me, I could see Rhyss just as visibly shaken. But I suppose it was to be expected. Compared to us, Lord Chela had had lifetimes to learn human behavior and see through our lies and excuses. Not to mention his experience in the Faerie court. Fae trickery was legendary, after all, and Lord Chela had held his position as High Chancellor for a very, very long time.

"My companion speaks truth," I said. "We *are* here to establish a friendship between our two kingdoms. But you are right, there is more to it than that."

I recounted the stories of the refugees, about the deaths of the Shonn household Fae and the growing Unseelie encounters, and our own meetings with the boggart and Fae-touched on our way to Shonn.

Lord Chela's face darkened at my tale. "We are not responsible for the actions of the Unseelie Court."

"We understand that, my lord." I spoke carefully, worried about offending our potential ally. "But with the death of your court's rulers, it seems the Fae of the Unseelie Court have been getting bolder of late. Or do you not agree?"

The High Chancellor's face tightened in anger, and I cringed inwardly, thinking I had overstepped. But then Lord Chela sighed. "It's true, and while the Seelie Court cannot control the actions of our more ... wicked ... brethren, our strong former rulers kept them in line, if only indirectly. But it was enough."

He started pacing. Rhyss and I stood still, only our eyes following him. The High Chancellor seemed worried, and if someone this powerful and experienced was worried—well, I hoped our faces didn't betray our own surprise and worry.

"Our late rulers were not only beloved, but strong leaders. They had also ruled for a long time—since before your King Eedrann ever ruled Calia."

Oh, my. That was indeed a very long time.

"While I admit that they engaged in activities that were, shall we say, unwise—" Lord Chela grimaced, and Rhyss and I exchanged a glance, thinking of the "unwise activity" that had gotten the former Faerie King and Queen killed—circumventing Valdonne's Treaty by taking human children.

In typical sneaky Fae fashion, King Finvarra and Queen Oona hadn't outright violated the terms of the treaty by abducting the children. Someone else had done that for them. They had just accepted the kidnapped children if someone happened to be offering them. Which someone had been.

"—they still had a big influence over both courts, and all of Faerie. Upon their death, the Seelie Court went into shock, and mourning. The Unseelie took advantage of that to start causing havoc."

He sighed again, and suddenly looked worn and defeated, as if all the years of his existence had fallen upon him. "I've enough to do, trying to sort through the potential contenders for the throne. Of which there are many. Added to that is the Unseelie Court acting up. And ..."

He looked beyond Rhyss and me, at the doors to the throne room that were still open. He then turned back to us, his gaze assessing. "Envoys of Calia, I wonder ... you might be just what I needed, at a time I need it most. But can I trust you?"

Rhyss and I stayed silent, wondering what Lord Chela was getting at. He seemed to be talking to himself, anyway.

"But what if you're spies? The timing of your visit is quite convenient. Still ..."

Rhyss looked at me, unsure of what to say. I took a deep breath and chose my words carefully. When making a promise in Faerie, you had to word things just right, or risk being beholden to more than you offered initially. But it also worked in reverse—a particularly clever human could sometimes trick one of the Fae into making a promise that entrapped them into a bigger bargain than the Fae wanted.

"High Chancellor, we would be happy to help you and the Seelie Court, to the best of our ability, so long as it brings no harm to the kingdom of Calia, its rulers, and its people."

Lord Chela's eyes narrowed. Then, in one swift motion, he snapped his fingers and the doors slammed shut behind us.

18

—·—

CHAPTER EIGHTEEN

"So BE IT," HE said, sighing. "And thank you."

He gestured at the now closed doors. "What I have to say is for your ears only. The doors are spelled so that none can listen in on conversations in this room when they are shut. You will also be unable to speak of our conversation to anyone who was not present in this room when it happened."

Rhyss and I nodded in understanding.

The High Chancellor stepped back onto the dais and sank down in his chair. He waved a hand, and two more chairs appeared for Rhyss and me.

Lord Chela ran a hand through his long black hair, looking agitated. "As I said earlier, there are many contenders for the Seelie Court throne. Some have stronger claims than others, either through lineage or popularity. As our next rulers are, hopefully, going to rule for a long time, I must make sure the best possible candidate is crowned.

"However, lately some odd things have been happening that make me believe we have Unseelie Fae in our midst, vying for the throne. If King Finvarra and Queen Oona were still alive, their magic would uncover the imposter immediately, but without them ... I lack that kind of power. Once we crown our new king or queen, they will inherit the magical power that comes with overseeing the Seelie Court. And the title and power, once conferred, cannot be taken away, unless through death. And, as I'm sure you've realized, the Fae are long-lived, and hard to kill."

He sighed, running a loving, respectful hand over the arm of one of the thrones. "Not that I would want to kill my liege. Even if my oath as High Chancellor didn't bind me against doing so. But if a disguised Unseelie Fae becomes our court's next ruler ... there's no telling how much destruction they could unleash on us, and on all of Faerie."

Rhyss leaned forward in his chair. "That's unsettling news. What kind of odd things have you noticed?"

Lord Chela blew out a breath. "At first, I just saw little things. Withered plants, some dead animals in the forest."

"But isn't that the natural order of things?"

"Yes, but not in the way you mean. We do not have a slow transition between seasons—our winter transforms into full spring overnight. Finding those dead plants meant the season hadn't fully taken hold, which never happens. And while the animals here can die, as they can in your world, the wildlife I found had been killed, completely drained of blood, mutilated, some headless. Only the Faerie King and Queen, who own all the flora and fauna in our realm, are allowed to hunt the animals of the forest. And they would never have desecrated the bodies in such a manner."

Feeling sick, I glanced at Rhyss. He looked just as unsettled. The High Chancellor didn't seem to notice as he continued speaking.

"And then, more recently, I have heard reports similar to your tales of the Fae-touched and Fae shapeshifters in the Gifted Lands. Valdonne's Treaty was supposed to keep your people safe from incidents like those. And while the former king and queen liked to, shall we say, bend the Treaty to suit their needs from time to time, they would never have allowed outright action against the human realm. Their deaths loosened the hold the Seelie Court had over all of Faerie, so our unsavory cousins can wander freely into your world."

I frowned. "So the Unseelie Fae are running amok, thanks to the untimely death of the Seelie Court rulers. I still don't see how that means one of the Unseelie is vying for the throne."

Lord Chela folded his hands in his lap, sorrow etched on his face. "Because, when the period of mourning was over and the Seelie Court announced the crowning of a new monarch, that Fae—Lord Yaxen, the one with the best claim to the throne—was found dead shortly thereafter. Murdered."

My eyes widened. Rhyss leaned back, letting out a long whistle. "How can you be sure it was one of the Unseelie Fae that did it, and not someone from your own court?"

"I can't," Lord Chela admitted. "But Lord Yaxen had been well-loved by all, and it had long been common knowledge that, should something happen to King Finvarra and Queen Oona, he would have been the next in line. Also, he died by magical means that felt distinctly Unseelie in origin."

He paused, frowning. Almost to himself, he added, "Although there was an element to it that was unfamiliar as well. Perhaps human magic? But I don't see how a human mage could be that powerful. And there are not that many in Faerie."

The High Chancellor sighed again. "And because of Lord Yaxen's unexpected death, not only are we without a new ruler, but it's created such chaos that only an Unseelie would enjoy."

I nodded in understanding, but Rhyss looked confused. Lord Chela didn't seem inclined to explain, so I did. "In Faerie, words have weight. Some things may be more binding than others—such as the High Chancellor's oath to serve the Seelie Court's king and queen."

Rhyss nodded. "You've mentioned that before."

"If King Finvarra had pledged that Lord Yaxen would be the next ruler in his place, then that vow would be practically unbreakable. Meaning that nothing, short of death, would have stopped Lord Yaxen from taking the throne. Even if Yaxen himself decided he didn't want to be king anymore, he still would have had to accept the crown. It would take very strong, very dark magic to overcome that vow."

"Oh." Rhyss looked thoughtful.

"With Yaxen gone, we don't have a clear heir to the throne," Lord Chela said. "Finvarra didn't name a successor beyond Yaxen. The others who have come forth all have equal claims, when you weigh power against political savvy, wisdom against popularity."

"Isn't there some sort of plan in place for this kind of situation?" I said.

"There is." Lord Chela touched the throne again, and the sadness for his fallen lieges was written plainly on his face. "In the event that there are multiple claims to the throne, each claimant must undergo the Trials to prove they are worthy to rule."

"The Trials? What's that?" Rhyss asked.

"It's a test for all potential rulers to undergo, to see who is fit to be the new king or queen."

"What do these Trials entail?"

Lord Chela stroked his chin thoughtfully. "It varies. When King Finvarra underwent the Trials, many years ago, he had to be recognized by all the realms of Faerie. Not the citizens, mind you, but the elements themselves. This time around ... I'm not sure. The exact nature of the current Trials is up to my discretion."

A smile spread across his face. It should have been a pleasant sight, but instead it chilled my blood. "I think, for these current Trials, the royal contenders should find and unmask the imposter."

Eyebrows raised, Rhyss asked, "What would you have Farrah and I do to help you in this task? Please don't ask us to undergo your Trials."

Lord Chela shook his head, horrified. "No, no, definitely not. A human could never rule over the Fae."

He paused, studying me. He seemed fascinated by my face. No, my hair.

He sniffed the air, like a bloodhound picking up a fugitive's scent. "But one of you is not fully human."

I nodded in acknowledgement. "You are correct, Lord Chela. Although I hail from the human world, I also have Faerie blood."

The High Chancellor sniffed again, a smile blooming across his face. "Ah, how could I not have noticed right away? How perfect!"

Rhyss and I exchanged guarded looks. "Perfect, my lord?" I echoed warily.

Lord Chela ignored my comment as he muttered to himself. "Yes, yes, that will do nicely. Perhaps, as a newcomer with fresh eyes, you will see something that I cannot."

He raised his voice and looked at me. "We will let it be known that you, as an official envoy from Calia, yet one of our kin, would like to get to know the different candidates. After all, you will need to establish a friendship with our future ruler, but as you have no way of knowing who it will be, you will need to get to know all of them. My dear Lady Farrah, you will be the official Seelie Court judge for the upcoming Trials."

Our travels all over the Gifted Lands had given Rhyss and me a wide variety of experiences. Very few things can surprise me.

Except this.

My jaw dropped open. I gaped soundlessly at the serene Lord Chela, who seemed quite pleased with himself.

"If something should happen to Lady Farrah while she is visiting your realm, and especially while she is observing your Trials, King Beyan and Queen Jennica might take that amiss." Although Rhyss spoke evenly and politely, the threat underneath his words was clear.

"Understandable," Lord Chela said. "Which is why I assume you will accompany her, to make sure she stays safe."

"Of course I'll be with her," Rhyss said. "But as I have no magic, I can hardly—"

"The royal hopefuls are all accomplished mages or warriors. It would be in their best interests to make sure no harm comes to Lady Farrah. And, of course, I will cover any expenses you may incur while in Faerie, on my official business."

"That is quite generous, but—"

"But if you decide to deny assistance to the Seelie Court, as is your right, then it is our right to deny the kingdom of Calia any assistance as well, should they need it in the future."

Rhyss crossed his arms, his lips flattening into a thin, angry line. I could practically hear his teeth grinding together. He was outmaneuvered, and he knew it.

I sighed, giving in to the inevitable. "When do your Trials start? And what should we expect?"

"It starts in two days. As for what will happen, that will be up to those vying for the throne. But since all of Faerie has been touched by these mysterious doings, I expect that you will be traveling all over Faerie as the group investigates.

"Which, for two humans, should be a fascinating trip. If you go to each contender's home regions, then you will get to see the deep forests of the elves and centaurs, the Fire Mountains of the giants, the wild sea of the selkies, and the mysterious stillwater of the nymphs.

"In the meantime, you will stay here at the palace."

"Oh, we don't want to—" I began.

"You'll be safer here than if you camped or tried to find other lodging, and the potential kings and queens are staying in the palace as well, so you'll have a chance to meet them and get to know them."

It sounded like a good plan, even though I knew we were outmaneuvered again.

The High Chancellor snapped his fingers. A white circular brooch appeared in the air, then fell into his outstretched palm. Holding it up, I could see the Seelie Court symbol etched on it, the three roses pure and deadly in their beauty.

But I didn't see beauty. I saw twining stems strong enough to bind, and thorns deadly enough to kill.

Lord Chela held the brooch out to me. Reluctantly, I took it and fastened it to my bodice. Now all of Faerie could see where my loyalties lay.

The High Chancellor nodded, satisfied. "Also, I give you my word that anything you eat or drink while you are in the Faerie palace will not harm, enchant, or bind you in any way. I'll also make sure your provisions for the road are just as safe."

That took care of that. Which, honestly, was a huge relief. But still ...

"I sense that there is something else you require of me?" Lord Chela said. "What is it? I would grant it, if I can. After all, you are doing me a great service."

Rhyss nudged me. I sighed. "We're not here only as envoys of Calia. We are here on personal business as well."

"Oh?"

"We came to find my Fae father, to get his blessing on our upcoming marriage."

"Oh! My congratulations!" Lord Chela smiled. "Who is your father? As High Chancellor, I know most of the citizens of Faerie. And if I don't know him, I will know someone who can find him for you."

"His name is Hyrinn," I said. "Lord Hyrinn, I should say. Last I recall, he oversees the region of—"

Next to me, I heard Rhyss's small, surprised gasp, but I was focused on the High Chancellor, whose face had darkened at my father's name. "Hyrinn. I know him. That traitorous knave will never see the light of day again."

My eyes widened. "You know him? What do you mean, he'll never see the light of day again? Is he—" my voice dropped to a whisper "—dead?"

Lord Chela gave a short, unpleasant laugh. "He is not, although I'm sure he longs for it. No, he is a permanent guest in the palace dungeon, fitting for the criminal he is."

Of all the ways I would have described my father, *criminal* was not one of them. "What did he do?"

In a clipped, angry voice, the High Chancellor said, "He tried to kill King Finvarra and Queen Oona."

19

—·—

CHAPTER NINETEEN

WHAT? MY FATHER TRIED to kill the king and queen?

My mind, blank just moments before, now filled with questions. When? Where? Why?

And, really? Perhaps the High Chancellor was mistaken.

Was Lord Chela sure that my father had attempted murder?

I grasped at the first question that made sense to ask. "When? When did this happen?"

The High Chancellor pursed his lips as he thought. "About a year ago? I don't know how you count your human years, exactly."

"C-Can I see him?"

Lord Chela shrugged. "I don't know why you'd want to visit with a known traitor, but I suppose we can't help who we're related to."

He smirked and stood. "At least fulfilling your request was easy. Let us hope that your investigation goes just as easily."

We followed the High Chancellor out of the throne room, down an empty white hallway, and then down several flights of stairs, deep underneath the castle.

Underground, the intense pure white of the Faerie castle gave way to cold grey rock walls and hard-packed dirt floors. The walls had an inner glow, just as the upstairs ones did, but the whole area lacked the beauty of the rest of the palace. Fae magic might be near limitless, but it would just be wasted down here. There was no need to impress the prisoners with the palace's majesty.

But besides the white stone, the other thing missing was—

"There are no guards posted?" I asked Lord Chela.

"No need." He indicated a Corrigan cowering in the corner of her cell. Her once-beautiful hair hung in limp locks around her weary face, and as she turned her dull red eyes upon our group, I saw a flash of dark silver at her neck. She shifted her weight, creating a clanking sound, and I saw a long, dark silver band around her ankle, with a chain the same color tethering her to the wall.

"Iron?" I said.

"Yes. It guards the prisoners better than any Fae could."

"But, how—"

"—do we get the prisoners chained in their cells, if the touch of iron is anathema to the Fae?"

I nodded.

He smiled grimly. "Years ago—most likely centuries, to you—a human mage designed these prisons as payment to our king and queen. The mage brought in the iron chains from your land, then enspelled them so only three Fae—the king, the queen, and the High Chancellor—could lock and unlock them magically, without having to physically touch them. As the first two positions are currently vacant, I am the only one in the land who can free these poor souls. Not that I want to."

We had reached a cell in the middle of the prison corridor. In this cell sat a lone human-shaped prisoner, his back to us as he stared at the wall.

Lord Chela rapped on the cell bars. "Lord Hyrinn." I could hear the sneer in his voice as he placed an ironic emphasis on the honorific. "You have visitors."

The prisoner didn't move. I thought perhaps he hadn't heard us, but then he shifted, ever so slightly, a mess of rags and thin limbs. He turned to face us, his eyes flat and uninterested as they slowly swept over our group, taking in Lord Chela, Rhyss, and then me.

His eyes kindled as he stared at me.

I stared back, mouth suddenly dry, any words or thoughts completely gone.

Even though it had been over two decades since I had last seen him, even though the man before me was emaciated and worn, I would have recognized him anywhere.

"Father."

My voice broke the charged silence that held us in thrall.

The thin man moved faster than I would have expected, for one chained and malnourished. He rushed toward us, ignoring Lord Chela's slight flinch and hand raised in warning. At the bars of his cell, we stood, practically nose to nose.

My father reached out a withered hand, but the iron shackle around his wrist yanked his hand back before he could touch me.

"Farrah?"

Rough and cracked, his voice sounded as if he hadn't used it in years. Hearing him speak my name, my heart broke. Tears ran unbidden down my cheeks.

Next to me, the High Chancellor coughed discreetly. "You should be safe, with Hyrinn chained and locked away in his cell. I ... I will give you a few moments of privacy to visit."

I blinked, wiping the tears from my face with the back of my hand. I swallowed, trying to find my voice around the lump that had suddenly appeared in my throat. When I could finally speak, my voice sounded just as rough as my father's. "Thank you."

Lord Chela nodded in acknowledgement. "Come join us when you are ready."

Putting a hand on Rhyss's shoulder, he steered my betrothed back down the hallway the way we had come. "Now, my friend. Let us discuss the upcoming Trials."

Through watery eyes, I stared at the man who had broken both my mother's and my heart oh so many years ago. An adult Fae's appearance rarely reflected their true age, but my father's weakened condition made him seem older than he would have normally looked.

Beyond the broken shell he had become, I could see the shadow of the man I remembered. Pale skin, near translucent due to being hidden away in a cell. The pronounced nose I had inherited, unlike my half-sister's cute stub nose, reminiscent of our mother's. And my father's lavender hair, the true color muddy under months of accumulated dirt.

Now that we faced each other, I didn't know what to say. *Hello, how are you?* seemed incredibly inane. On the other hand, *I heard you tried to kill the Great Ones of Faerie* was probably a bit strong for a conversation starter.

I settled on, "It's been a long time."

Father stared at me, as if he couldn't believe what he was seeing. "Farrah? Is that really you? It can't be."

"I know it's been a while—about twenty years—but—"

"Twenty years? My daughter, what do you mean? I only left you and your mother a year ago. You were barely knee-high. I meant to go back—"

"A year ago? But—" I stopped, remembering what I had told Rhyss upon our arrival in Faerie. *Time in Faerie flows differently than it does in the human world.* It was quite possible that, upon his return to Faerie and subsequent imprisonment, he had missed my entire childhood back in the Gifted Lands.

Father dipped his head. "Oh, Farrah. We've lost so much time."

He reached a hand out to touch my cheek. "You've grown into such a beauty. You look just like your mother."

His voice broke in pain. "How is she?"

"She's ... well. Enough. She never stopped loving you. Father ..."

"I can't believe you're here. I don't know where to begin. I—"

"Why don't we start with, why didn't you come home?" I couldn't keep the hurt and disbelief out of my voice. "And why did you try to kill King Finvarra and Queen Oona?"

His head shot back up. "No, no, my daughter. I never tried to kill them."

"But, Lord Chela said—"

He shook his head vehemently, then winced from the quick movement. "I would never have tried to harm the royals. Although I had stayed away from Faerie for a while, to be with you and your mother, I swear I didn't try to kill them."

With wild, wide eyes, he gripped the cell bars. The shackles would let him move that far, at least.

"Farrah. I was framed."

20

CHAPTER TWENTY

I GLANCED OVER MY shoulder. Lord Chela and Rhyss were, thankfully, deep in conversation at the end of the hallway, and not looking our way. I turned back to my father.

"What do you mean, you were framed?" I hissed.

He slumped against the bars of his cell. "I hadn't planned on returning to Faerie. Once your mother and I met, and especially after you were born, I was quite content to stay in Shonn. But a message came to me, urging me to return to take care of ... something."

He craned his neck, looking down the hallway to where Lord Chela and Rhyss stood talking. Gesturing for me to come closer—I stepped so close my cheek mashed up against the metal bars of my father's jail cell—he lowered his voice and spoke rapidly. "I never told your mother this, but I wasn't supposed to stay in the Gifted Lands as long as I did. The former king had sent me on a diplomatic mission, first to Annlyn and then to Graenir. I had finished my task and was ready to return to Faerie, when I met Staela."

He sighed, his face softening as he remembered. "Compared to cold Faerie perfection, Staela's humanity was refreshing. And she was beautiful, and kind. I was instantly smitten. I know, I know, I should have reported back to the king, and then returned to Shonn. That would have been the smart thing to do. But if I went back, the king would have had more tasks for me, tasks that would keep me in Faerie. And I was afraid if I left Shonn, even if it was just for a Faerie year, too much time would go by. I might return to find your mother married to someone else, or worse, dead from old age."

He smiled sadly. "As we can see for ourselves, a Faerie year means something quite different to you humans."

I sniffed and swallowed, willing myself not to cry over the unfairness of it all.

Father continued, "I sent a message to the king, convinced him I needed more time. The difference between the flow of time in human and Faerie worked to my advantage. In time, the king forgot I was still in the Gifted Lands.

"But then I received a letter, saying that someone back in Faerie knew I had abandoned my commission. If I didn't return, just for a short time to do them a 'favor', then they would expose me to the king. If I did this favor, then they would smooth things over with the king, allowing me to live in Shonn permanently and without fear."

He shook his head. "When you came to visit me—that's what I was in the midst of doing. Trying to locate the mysterious messenger. That's why I couldn't go back with you at that time, though I wanted to, with all my heart."

I gripped the bars of the cell so hard my knuckles began to turn white. "Who? Who was it, Father?"

My father opened his mouth to speak, then his eyes grew wide and he shut his mouth against whatever he had been about to say. I heard footsteps approaching, and looked over to see Lord Chela walking toward us, Rhyss on his heels.

Behind the High Chancellor, Rhyss mouthed, *I'm sorry*, as he nodded toward the other man. I shrugged, releasing the bars. Lord Chela would only stay away so long. My father and I probably had had more time together than the High Chancellor allowed most prisoners and their visitors.

"Is all well here?" Lord Chela asked, noting the wild look in my father's eyes and my own intensity.

I nodded.

"Good. Then let us go back aboveground."

I met Father's eyes. Even though he didn't physically look any better than he had when we first came down here, his face looked a little lighter.

With hope.

Because of me.

I reached out and touched his face. He reached up with both shackled hands to cup mine.

"I'll try to come back again soon and visit," I said.

He didn't say anything, just nodded as he continued to grasp my hand. I kept my hand at his face for another moment, then reluctantly withdrew it.

Next to me, Lord Chela coughed, not even trying to hide his annoyance. He turned and started walking down the hallway.

"Goodbye, Father," I said. Tears pricked my eyes again and I turned and headed after Lord Chela. Rhyss reached over and took my hand, squeezing it in sympathy.

We had only taken a few steps when I stopped, remembering. "Wait!"

Next to me, Rhyss also stopped walking. Just ahead of us, Lord Chela paused and looked back at us. "What is it?"

I looked at Rhyss, then back at my father. "Our marriage blessing! It's the whole reason we're here!"

I had taken two steps toward Father's cell when Lord Chela's voice stopped me. "Oh, that's right. It won't matter, my dear."

"What do you mean?"

Lord Chela stayed where he was, but his eyes were sympathetic as he regarded Rhyss and me. "Your father is in prison for his crime against the Faerie Crown. As a disgraced Fae, he has been stripped of his title, his lands, and even his magic. In some respects, he is no better than a human, although he will still have his long life to regret his crime."

"His magic?" I looked at Father in horror. He looked down at the floor, unwilling to meet my eyes. "But—what about the marriage blessing? Or does this mean there's no danger of it becoming a curse?"

"Oh, you do still have to worry about that," Lord Chela said. "But your father cannot avert it for you, for a blessing from him now means nothing. Perhaps if the two of you prove successful in helping me, then I can look into helping you. It's hard to say; Fae tradition can be quite tricky to get around. We'll see."

With that, the High Chancellor disappeared up the stairs.

Fuming, I followed after him. Rhyss, worried, came after me. We caught up with Lord Chela at the top of the stairs, and he serenely led the way back to the main hall.

We were halfway there when I realized I had forgotten to give my mother's message to Father. *But then again*, I thought as I glared at Lord Chela's back, *I wasn't the only one who had forgotten to relay important information.*

And, thinking about the upcoming Trials and my investigation, I wondered what else Lord Chela had conveniently forgot to mention.

21

CHAPTER TWENTY-ONE

WHEN RHYSS KNOCKED ON my door later that evening, I was still fuming.

The poor bewildered man stepped into my room, watching me pace back and forth. "He knew! He had to have known! The minute he learned who my father was, he could have said something. Instead, we're now trapped in this investigation—and even if we do figure out who the Unseelie imposter is, there's no guarantee he can do anything about the marriage blessing. Curse. Whatever."

Rhyss crossed his arms. "Still upset about Lord Chela, I see."

I stopped pacing long enough to stamp a slippered foot. "I was so careful about how I worded that promise, and we still got tricked."

"I meant to ask you about that, actually. We might have been doomed from the minute you finished speaking."

Now *I* crossed my arms. I threw in a glare for good measure. "What do you mean?"

"Well, you made the High Chancellor promise no harm would come to Calia, its rulers, or its people. But you forgot to include us."

"What are you talking about? Or course I—" I flopped down on my bed as Rhyss's meaning hit me. "Oh, my."

"Yes, I wasn't sure how specific you had to be in a binding promise. We're from Orchwell, not Calia. If you really want to get particular, then I'm originally from Bomora and originally, you're from Shonn. So ... does that mean we're outside his protection?"

Frustrated, I grabbed part of my bed's coverlet, balling it in my fists. "I can't believe I didn't think that through." My poor bed got more rumpled in my agitation. "We'll just have to be extra careful, I suppose. And make sure we don't fail."

I sighed. "Correction. Make sure *I* don't fail."

Rhyss smiled. "You won't. When have you ever failed?"

I smiled back. "I can think of a few times I've come pretty close. Anyway. Why did you knock?"

Rhyss held up a strip of silk. "Do you mind tying this for me?"

"Of course not." I stood, holding out my hand for the length of fabric. Rhyss gave it to me, and I busied myself in tying the cream-colored silk around his neck. I giggled. "You know, you'll have to learn how to tie one of these soon. For the wedding."

Rhyss groaned. "Formal wear. Maybe I can get Beyan to tie it for me."

The image of the king of Calia tying a mercenary's cravat—even if we had both known him for most of his life—made me giggle even harder. "He's got servants for that. He'll probably just get one of them to do it for him."

Rhyss laughed. "No, no. If he's going to be my best man, king or not, he has to tie my tie."

Laughing along with my betrothed helped ease my agitation. Rhyss noticed, and, placing his hands on my shoulders, leaned down and kissed me on my forehead. "I'm glad to see you smiling. Are you nervous?"

I blew out a breath. "Yes. You?"

He raised his eyebrows at me. "What do you think?"

I grimaced. "I suppose tonight's celebration is a good thing. No time like the present, and all that. Still, a little more warning would have been nice."

"I completely agree."

After visiting the dungeon and returning to the main hallways of the palace, Lord Chela had announced that, even though the Trials wouldn't officially start for another two days, tonight—*tonight!*—there was going to be a formal dinner to commence the event as a whole. All of the contenders for the Crown of Faerie would be present, of course, as well as their chief advisors or supporters. It would be a great way, the High Chancellor pointed out delicately, to meet everyone and start taking their measure.

When I had pointed out—just as delicately—that Rhyss and I had not brought any formal clothing, as we were travelers who had come to Faerie for an entirely different purpose, Lord Chela had said that was no issue. This *was* Faerie, after all. Our evening attire would be ready for us shortly.

And so now Rhyss stood before me, in a black brocade fitted jacket with matching pants. I finished tying his cravat and stepped back to admire my handiwork. I grinned, admiring the view as well.

"You clean up nicely," I said. "I haven't seen you looking this fancy since Jennica's wedding."

"The first one? Or the second one?"

"Both. Although you can't count the first one. I mean, it wasn't even really her getting married."

"Still." Rhyss smiled, remembering. "That was a fun day."

"If you call nearly getting killed by a power-mad king fun."

"It can be, depending on how you look at it."

I swatted him on the arm. "There will be no fights-to-the-death at our wedding, are we clear?"

"But there will be fights, is what you're saying?"

I swatted him again. "You're incorrigible. Let's go."

I started to move toward my bedroom door, but Rhyss grabbed my hand, stopping me. "Wait."

I looked at him, confused. "What is it?"

He spread my arm wide so he could get a good look at me. "I haven't told you yet how beautiful you look."

I blushed, looking down at my own formal outfit. If money and imagination had been no limit, this would have been the dress of my dreams. Uncanny, how whoever created this dress—in record time, and with absolutely no input from me—had just known, somehow, that this was what I wanted.

When I had first laid eyes on my gown for the evening, I cried. Not a lot, and not for long—I am nothing if not practical—but the Faerie creation was truly a vision in cream and green and gold. Something I could never afford, even if I could find a seamstress willing to take on such an intricate project. If I could get married in any dress, it would be this one.

Made of a pale cream organza, the fitted bodice was trimmed in a delicate gold lace that twinkled like candlelight. The bodice gave way to a simple, full skirt, covered by a pale green overskirt that was also trimmed in the gold lace. A sprinkling of small pearls covered the dress. Sheer cream fitted sleeves, with the pearls threaded throughout and the gold lace at the wrists, completed the outfit.

Correction, I thought, as I fastened the Seelie Court symbol to my dress. *Now my outfit is complete.*

Rhyss tilted his head thoughtfully. "I thought only Faerie royalty could wear white?"

"White is the color of Fae royalty, true. But others can wear white. Just not all white. And these—" I gestured at the off-white parts of our outfits "—are actually cream, not white."

"What would happen if we did wear white?"

"If someone wore all white, especially right now while there is no recognized ruler, it would be seen as presumptuous and arrogant, at best. More likely, it would be taken as a challenge to all who are vying for the Faerie throne right now."

"Hmm." Rhyss tapped his chin. "So if we see anyone wearing a bunch of white ..."

"We'll definitely want to keep an eye on them, yes."

Rhyss leaned over and gave me a light kiss. "Beauty and brains. Everything I ever wanted."

I grinned, even as I gave him a playful shove. "Come on. We're already late."

"Fashionably late," Rhyss corrected me, crooking his arm. "May I escort you to dinner, Lady Farrah?"

I giggled, remembering that back in Calia, we were titled. Even if we rarely used them. I took his arm. "You may, Lord Rhyss."

Together, we left my room and headed to the dining hall of the Faerie palace.

22

Chapter Twenty-Two

Once we reached the dining hall and got a good look at the scene before us, our mirth faded. The High Chancellor sat at the head of the table, which was occupied by a diverse group of Fae talking amongst themselves. In the seats closest to Lord Chela, a pair of elves conversed with a burly centaur, who remained standing. I noticed the centaur's place setting was propped up with two little boxes, so he could eat comfortably. At the other end of a table, a selkie and a nymph chatted with a giant, who towered over his slender and slight companions. An oversized chair had been brought in to accommodate the giant, and his dinner dishes looked suspiciously like serving platters.

Rhyss raised a worried eyebrow at me. I squeezed his arm. He placed a hand over mine, squeezing back.

"I suppose it's too late to ask Lord Chela to send plates up to our rooms?" Rhyss muttered.

"Unfortunately." I sighed. "Shall we?"

Rhyss took a deep breath. "All right."

He guided me into the room. I had worried that we would end up sitting in the wrong spots—a major faux pas—but our tardiness had the unexpected benefit of revealing our seats, the only two unoccupied places. We hurried over to the empty chairs.

Lord Chela had placed us in a strategic spot. Instead of giving us the guests-of-honor spots near the head of the table, we sat in the middle, where we could observe and interact with the majority of the other dinner guests. The ambiguity would also make the other guests unclear on who we were and what our purpose was, I realized. I looked down the length of the table to where the Head Chancellor sat. *Very clever, Lord Chela.*

He caught my eye and nodded, holding up his glass of wine. To the others, it looked like a greeting. But to me, it felt like he had heard my thoughts, and was saluting me for figuring out his game.

Rhyss and I had barely settled into our seats when Lord Chela rose. The rest of the table quieted down as we all turned expectant faces to him.

"Welcome, all of you, to tonight's dinner. In your honor." He chuckled, spreading his arms wide to indicate everyone at the table. Around me, answering laughs arose.

"This is indeed a momentous occasion," Lord Chela continued. "Even as we mourn the deaths of our beloved King Finvarra and Queen Oona, we must look ahead to find the new ruler of the Seelie Court, and of the Fae. To that end, the Trials to determine who that will be shall commence two days hence."

He paused, looking around the table. "That will be one of you, once you prove yourself worthier than the others."

Low murmuring arose amongst the guests. Lord Chela continued speaking, and the group grew quiet again. "Lately, there have been some strange occurrences happening in our beloved land. Animals found mysteriously slaughtered, plants dying when they should be flourishing. Lord Yaxen's murder. And rumors of the Unseelie running unchecked in our world and the human realm.

"I believe there is an Unseelie Fae in our midst, masquerading as one of our own, creating havoc wherever they go."

The murmuring started up again. The giant said, "That's impossible!"

The centaur commented, "What proof do you have, Lord Chela?"

The pair of elves cast suspicious looks around the table. The selkie shrank into herself, and the nymph sniffed, acting as if this horrible news was beneath her.

"I do not have definitive proof," Lord Chela admitted. "So, then, this is what your purpose in the Trials will be: find this imposter, and bring them back here for justice. Do this, and you will be named the next ruler of the Seelie Fae. Traveling around Faerie under the pretense of seeking the recognition of each of your home regions will be a good way to keep your investigation secret."

Rhyss whispered to me, "It will be fascinating to see all the different regions of Faerie."

I nodded, shushing him as Lord Chela continued, "Also, there is one more thing to note."

The High Chancellor pointed at Rhyss and me. Seven pairs of eyes suddenly focused on us, and I tried desperately not to fidget under their collective assessment. Some seemed friendly, others curious. One gaze was downright hostile.

Fumbling under the table, I blindly reached out for Rhyss's hand. It wasn't far—he was already reaching for mine. We clasped hands and squeezed tight, our nervousness hidden from the others at the table.

I hoped.

"We have with us some guests from beyond the Veil. Please welcome Lord Rhyss and Lady Farrah, envoys from the kingdom of Calia in the Gifted Lands."

A smattering of polite applause sounded from the other dinner guests. Lord Chela continued, "I have appointed Lady Farrah as my official representative in the Trials. She is uniquely qualified, as she is of both the Fae realm and the mortal world. Her intended, Lord Rhyss, will accompany her as another observer, advisor, and protector. I trust that you will welcome them both and not hinder Lady Farrah in any way as she judges the Trials."

Dead silence. And then the room burst into noise.

"Well, that's certainly a ... choice," one of the elves said snidely.

"But—what—a human? To oversee the Trials?" the giant sputtered.

"I think it's a brilliant idea," the centaur said.

"It's unheard of," the nymph countered, flipping her long blue-green hair over one shoulder. "Humans getting involved in Fae affairs, especially in something as important as the Trials? Never!"

The selkie didn't say anything, just looked around the table with nervous, darting eyes.

The Fae continued to argue amongst themselves.

Rhyss whispered, "I think Lord Chela is enjoying himself a little too much up there."

I silently agreed as I eyed the High Chancellor, who was watching the other dinner guests argue without jumping into the conversation himself. Was that a smirk playing at the corner of his lips? Yes, he was definitely enjoying the chaos he had just created.

As the talking around us grew louder and more heated, I whispered back, "You have to admit, it's a smart move. It gives us a reason to be there and ensures they won't hurt us."

Rhyss muttered, "Something tells me he's playing at something much, much deeper."

Before the arguing Fae could come to blows with each other, Lord Chela raised one hand and spoke. "I thank you for your thoughts. I shall certainly consider them." His offhand tone suggested he would do nothing of the sort.

The others knew it, too, but couldn't really do anything about it. The grumbling around the room subsided into an uneasy silence. Lord Chela waved his hands and a feast appeared on the table.

As we began eating, awkward small talk started between various pairs of guests. At the head of the table, the High Chancellor ate serenely, his keen dark eyes missing nothing. No one spoke to Rhyss or me, despite our best efforts to draw our dinner companions into conversation.

I chewed morosely. Next to me, I caught Rhyss's expression, a reflection of my own apprehension. Inwardly, I sighed.

This was going to be a long dinner.

23

CHAPTER TWENTY-THREE

I WAS RIGHT. IT was a long, silent, and awkward dinner.

Well, for Rhyss and me. Maybe not so for the others, who eventually settled into random, if somewhat stilted, conversations. But, I supposed, since they were all in competition with each other, they couldn't get too friendly. With each other, or with us—the supposedly impartial judge and her advisor.

Finally—*finally!*—the dessert course appeared. *Thank the gods*, I thought, knowing the evening would soon be over and Rhyss and I could escape to the relative safety of our rooms.

I frowned, a bite of marzipan cake halfway to my mouth. *Thank the gods? Rhyss is becoming a bad influence on me.* My betrothed frequently invoked the gods, something which never failed to amuse me. I didn't doubt his sincerity in his faith; it was just that, as part-Fae, I knew that some people in the Gifted Lands also worshipped Faeries. So did that make me part goddess? I'd like to think so. But, funny, whenever I teased Rhyss with that, he didn't find it nearly as amusing.

At the head of the table, Lord Chela clapped his hands twice to get our attention. "After dinner, we will retire to the courtyard for some entertainment."

I stifled the groan that threatened to escape. Apparently, the night wasn't over just yet.

The giant finished his dessert first, scraping his chair back from the table. He stood up and held his hand out to the nymph, who had also finished eating. Together, they headed to the doorway.

The selkie also headed toward the entryway, her nervous eyes darting everywhere. The selkie bumped into the nymph, who bristled. "Watch where you're going, Bettan!"

The giant frowned down at the nymph, but didn't say anything. He escorted the nymph out the door, the selkie skulking several paces behind them.

The two elves left shortly after, conversing quietly.

The centaur came around the table and stopped where Rhyss and I were sitting. He winked. "Don't worry, they'll come around."

"I hope so," Rhyss said, standing and holding out his hand toward the centaur. "I'm Rhyss. Er, Lord Rhyss. It's a pleasure to meet you, Lord ...?"

The centaur clasped Rhyss's hand in a hearty handshake. "Paxen. But I'm not a lord."

"Oh? But I thought ..."

Paxen laughed. "Not everyone vying for the throne is nobility. Or at least, officially holds the title. I have been a long-standing member of the Fairwood's Council—my home region. Now I want to serve Faerie on a larger level."

"Ah, I see. Thank you for that information." Rhyss turned to me. "This is Lady Farrah."

Paxen bowed over my hand. "Well met, Lord Rhyss, Lady Farrah. I look forward to talking with you more in the courtyard." With that, he left the dining hall.

That left Lord Chela, Rhyss, and me in the dining hall. Rhyss held his hand out, helping me stand. We nodded at Lord Chela and were about to leave when—

"I hope you don't mind your new position as judge for the Trials." His smooth voice grated on my nerves.

I turned slowly to face him, my back stiff. "I didn't have much of a choice."

"True. But it will be the perfect way for you to figure out what's really going on. You would earn the favor of the Seelie Court for Calia, and you would earn the favor of the High Chancellor for your upcoming marriage. Really, it is perfect."

Perfect for whom? Unthinking, I took a deep breath and opened my mouth.

Rhyss placed a warning hand on my shoulder. I gritted my teeth. The High Chancellor was insufferable, but he was right, and I hated knowing that.

I pasted a smile on my face. "It's a good idea, my lord. If you'll excuse us, we'd like to go meet the contenders in the courtyard."

He waved a languid hand at the door. "By all means. I'll be along shortly."

Rhyss and I hurried out of the room. I could feel the High Chancellor's eyes boring into our backs as we went. Once we were out of earshot, Rhyss asked, "What was all that about?"

I shook my head in disgust. "The nerve! We're on his side, and he still has to try to get the upper hand. Spare me from the Fae and their power plays."

"I hope that's all it is."

My steps slowed as I shot Rhyss a look. "What do you mean?"

He stopped walking and looked up and down the hallway, ensuring that we were alone. He lowered his voice. "We've heard countless times about how the Fae like to play the long game. What if ... what if Lord Chela is trying to entrap us in some way?"

I shrugged uncomfortably, remembering my vocal misstep earlier in the day. "I've already messed up in neglecting to be thorough in our promise to help him. What else could he get us with?"

Rhyss frowned. "Let's say something goes wrong during the Trials, and one of us gets hurt, or killed. We're here as official representatives of Calia. While the Seelie Court can't take direct action against Calia, if something should happen to either one of us while we're on business for Calia ... that could be construed as an act of war. And if Calia attacked first—"

"Then the Fae would be within their rights to defend themselves." My frown mirrored Rhyss's. "You're right. I didn't think of that. But what would be the purpose in inciting a war with Calia?"

"Who knows? Domination? Distraction? And the other kingdoms might get involved, too. Calia has several allies it could call upon, if needed. There's Bomora, thanks to Calia's aid in dismantling the Emerald Order. Orchwell and Calia have always been on decent terms. Also Annlyn, through former Royal Consort Joichan's ties to that country. Rothschan's leadership is in shambles, but there are people in positions of influence who could sway the Rothschan people to help. And now even Graenir, if things go well with Joichan and Melandria's ambassadorship."

I blew out a breath. "When you put it so plainly ... I guess we'll just have to make sure we don't get hurt, killed, or fail as judge or ambassadors."

Rhyss snorted. "Of course, it's so easy. Silly me."

I laughed and let him lead me into the courtyard.

24

CHAPTER TWENTY-FOUR

THE WHITE STONE OF the open courtyard glowed under the softness of moonlight. In one corner, a quartet of gnome musicians played on stringed instruments. Little lights flickered in the semi-darkness. Back home I would have thought they were fireflies, but here, if I concentrated hard enough, I could hear faint sighs and whispers in the air, from the general direction of the lights. *Will-o'-the-wisps*, I realized.

The will-o'-the-wisps weren't the only new Fae in the courtyard. Looking around, I saw another giant, a few dryads, and some pixies mingling with the dinner guests.

"Where did all these other Fae come from?" Rhyss murmured in my ear, echoing my own thoughts.

"I'm not sure." I scrutinized the newcomers. "My guess is, perhaps they're advisors or supporters of each of the candidates."

"This will be fun," Rhyss said.

Paxen, the centaur who had introduced himself inside the palace, approached us. At his side was a dryad, her long greenish-blonde locks falling over her tan skin. An extensive tattoo of sorts covered her legs and arms, and I realized it was the pattern of her tree bark.

"Ah, my new friends from the human realm." Paxen greeted us with a big smile. "I'd like you to meet Lilliana. She is serving as my advisor during the Trials."

Rhyss bowed over Lilliana's hand, while I dipped into a curtsey. Lilliana giggled. "There's no need for that. I'm not a fine lady, to be bowed and curtseyed to."

"Yet."

Lilliana gave Paxen a fond look. "Even when you do win the throne, I don't know that I'd want to move into the palace. Too stifling for me."

Paxen's smile grew wider. "When. I like the sound of that."

"Does everyone here have an advisor?" I waved at the group before us.

Paxen nodded. "All except the selkie. Selkies tend to be solitary creatures, but very loyal to their kind."

"Are the advisors also going to be accompanying you on the Trials?" Rhyss asked.

Lilliana shook her head, then nodded. At my thoroughly confused look, she laughed. "Sort of. There may be certain tasks that our candidates must do alone, and we must let them. Like you, we are allowed to observe the competition, give advice to our candidates, and—most importantly, try to solicit support for them. Sometimes having the good will of the majority in Faerie is more important than being the most competent ruler."

"Although the latter is still important," Paxen put in. "If you can have both, that's the best thing of all."

Lilliana sighed. "King Finvarra and Queen Oona were that rare combination of both—well-loved, and good rulers. They'd ruled for so long, I think we got complacent, thinking their rule would never end. Losing them is a definite blow to the Seelie Court."

Lilliana's comment provided the perfect opening. "Lord Chela mentioned that there have been some strange occurrences happening around Faerie lately. Withered plants, animals found dead of unnatural causes. And in our own world, we were attacked by the Fae-touched just outside of Shonn."

The centaur and the dryad both nodded gravely.

"It's because of the strange happenings that I decided to try for the kingship," Paxen said. "Even if my claim isn't as strong as some." He nodded toward the pair of elves from dinner, who mostly seemed to keep to themselves.

Rhyss put a thoughtful finger to his chin. "Speaking of which—and pardon me if this is an impertinent question—but why didn't King Finvarra and Queen Oona ever have children? Having a legitimate heir would be a lot easier than going through all this, wouldn't it?" He waved a hand, indicating the royal hopefuls in the courtyard.

"The Fae do not have as many children, or as frequently, as humans do," Lilliana said. "Because we are so long-lived, we're considered fortunate if we have one child every century or so. When King Finvarra had—" she paused, her discomfort evident on her face "—a child that wasn't Queen Oona's, before they were able to have one of their own, he was unable to sire another child for some time. According to rumor, Queen Oona was so incensed she refused to ever lay with the King, even after his indiscretions had been supposedly forgiven."

"Ah, I see." Rhyss fell silent, mulling over Lilliana's words. It not only explained why Faerie was now looking for a new leader, but also why King Finvarra and Queen Oona—widely considered good and wise rulers—had been willing to break Valdonne's Treaty to gain human children.

"Mistakes had been made," Paxen said, as if he knew what we were thinking. "Which is why I'm part of the Trials. My desire to make things better in Faerie is stronger than most."

"Which is why I threw my support behind Paxen," Lilliana said.

"Yes, instead of with her sister, where her support should truly lie," a new voice said.

25

CHAPTER TWENTY-FIVE

WE ALL LOOKED UP to see a beautiful young woman approaching us.

Well, she looked young, perhaps in her mid-twenties, like Rhyss and me. But there was no mistaking the shrewdness in her turquoise blue eyes, and she carried herself with a maturity that belied her age. Like a queen.

Which, I suppose, was appropriate, considering I recognized her as the nymph from our earlier dinner. Her pale skin, practically translucent, glowed like the white stone walls around us. Her long blue-green hair fell in gentle waves around her face, making me think of flowing rivers, or ripples on the sea. Her dress, which had an odd, scaly pattern to it, changed color in the moonlight, starting as a pale pink, deepening to a rich rose, and then ending in a deep purple.

"Sister?" I asked, looking from the dryad to the nymph.

"Through our shared bond of nature," the nymph said.

Lilliana sighed. "Aryn, friends though we may be, you know my thoughts on this. Being mistress of multiple elements does not mean you are the best one to be our next ruler."

I gave the newcomer—Aryn—an appraising look. She must be an apsara, a rare type of nymph who controlled more than one element. From her appearance, I guessed maybe air and water. Although—now that I looked a bit closer—she also had the look of a celestial nymph about her. If that was true, then she was indeed a rare creature.

Aryn's pretty face twisted into a sneer. "And what power does Paxen command, that he is more suitable than I am? He has none. And he will have no hope of ruling our realm with no power at his disposal." Her eyes narrowed. "I do know your thoughts on the matter, sister, but I daresay it is your heart that is leading you."

Lilliana colored at the dig, but didn't respond. Heavy footsteps sounded nearby, drawing our attention away and stopping any further arguments between the nymph and the dryad.

A deep voice boomed, "If power is the criteria to be the next king, then why waste our time? Crown me now and be done with it!"

The giant chortled, his laughter reverberating through our bones. Unlike Aryn, he was dressed simply in leather pants stitched from animal skins, and a tunic made of leaves woven together.

He leaned down slightly and peered into first Rhyss's face, then mine with earnest dark brown eyes. His brown hair flopped in his eyes, and he pushed it back with one hand before offering that same hand to me. "I'm afraid we didn't get off on the best foot at dinner, earlier. I was just so surprised, I didn't know what to say. But that's no reason to be rude. Sorry about that."

"It's all right. To be honest, I was just as surprised to be named judge." I put my hand in his as a peace offering. "I'm Lady Farrah. Pleased to meet you."

The giant bowed over my hand. "Itan. Pleased to meet you." He turned to Rhyss, shaking his hand, then straightened up.

Aryn had stiffened, looking uncomfortable and wary, when Itan had approached our group. Now, she cut in icily, "As I was saying, power is important to be a good ruler. But not necessarily brute strength. I meant *magical* power."

Aryn, Lilliana, Paxen, and Itan fell into a discussion about the most important attributes the future king or queen of Faerie should have. I half-followed the conversation, my eyes wandering around the courtyard. Rhyss looked positively lost, as magic wasn't his strong suit.

Of our dinner companions, the only ones not to join us were the two elves and the selkie. I caught the elves watching us, but when my gaze fell on them, they turned their noses up and walked away, back into the palace. The selkie had been in conversation with one of the pixies, but when the pixie left to talk to someone else, the selkie stayed in the corner, avoiding eye contact with anyone else.

And I thought I couldn't wait for this evening to be over, I thought. But it did make me wonder—how could a creature so obviously uncomfortable to be here possibly hope to be the next Fae ruler?

I whispered in Rhyss's ear, "What do you think is their story?"

Aryn, Lilliana, and Paxen were still talking—although now it sounded more like arguing—and had moved a little away from Rhyss and me. But Itan turned toward us, and in a surprisingly quiet voice, said, "Ah, ol' Bettan's not so bad once you get to know her. She's just shy, is all. But she's got a keen mind, one that would be very good for the realm."

I grimaced, embarrassed at being caught gossiping. Rhyss blushed so hard his face matched his red hair.

"And what of the two elves who were at dinner with us?" I asked Itan.

"Ah. That's Fionn and his mother, Hahna."

"Just Fionn? No title? I thought most, if not all, of the elves are nobility."

Itan shook his head. "Hahna was at one point. But she was stripped of her title quite some time ago. It was the least King Finvarra could do."

Rhyss furrowed his brow. "What do you mean?"

Itan motioned for us to come closer. Lowering his voice further, he said, "King Finvarra had an affair with her, back when she was still Lady Hahna. Fionn was the result. Queen Oona was incensed when the king's indiscretion came to light. But instead of leaving the king—and losing her position of power—she took out her ire on the king's mistress. Made sure Hahna lost her lands, her fortune, and her status. She even hired an assassin to kill the baby, but King Finvarra intervened, and cast a spell on Fionn."

"A protection spell?" I asked.

"Of sorts. If Fionn dies of anything other than natural causes, then a curse will fall on his killer. What could the queen do? The king had outsmarted her." Itan clicked his tongue. "It was quite the scandal."

"Interesting." Rhyss turned a thoughtful look toward the doorway where the two elves had disappeared. "So, based on birth, Fionn has the best claim to the throne."

"Yes," Itan confirmed. "And, if the rumors are true, he also has the magical skill to match. But Hahna has mostly kept him hidden from public view. It was only after King Finvarra and Queen Oona died that we started to see more of him."

"And how about you, Itan?" I asked. "What is your claim to the throne?"

Itan shrugged. "Not as strong as some others, honestly. I've a cousin twice removed who married into the minor nobility. But, between you and me—" he looked around and lowered his voice "—the real reason I'm here is to figure out who's behind the weird deaths."

"Weird deaths? You mean of the wildlife?"

"The wildlife, but also of the Fae. Where I'm from, in the region of the Fire Mountains, we've been having some mysterious deaths lately. Healthy giants, in the prime of their lives, found dead in their homes with no explanation why. No sign of break-ins, but they're found with odd markings on their faces or bodies. I volunteered for the Trials, mostly because I hoped the High Chancellor might know what's going on."

The giant sighed. "Bettan mentioned there have been similar things happening along the coast of the Lonely Sea, where she's from."

"Ah, interesting. I suppose it's good that your goals align with the High Chancellor's, then. If you're successful, you'll not only stop the deaths, but you'll also gain a crown."

Itan shrugged. "I'm fine without the crown, to be honest. That kind of thing can be more trouble than it's worth."

Across the courtyard, the other giant called out to Itan. Itan waved, then turned back to Rhyss and me. "Excuse me." He lumbered away.

"What do you think?" I asked Rhyss. "Do we have a sheltered prince, unused to politics and court intrigue? Or a calculated move by a shrewd mother who's potentially looking to get some of her own back?"

"Or possibly both?" Rhyss countered. "And while we're at it, let's throw in some mysterious deaths to boot."

"Who—or what—do you think is behind those?"

He sighed. "I guess we'll find out soon enough."

26

CHAPTER TWENTY-SIX

SLEEP ELUDED ME THAT night. After spending several hours tossing and turning, I finally drifted off.

I dreamed that I woke up, at some point during the night. Moonlight shone through the open curtains of my window, and, feeling restless, I walked over to my bedroom's balcony to get some fresh air.

Standing at the railing, I marveled at how beautiful the night sky was, as if the stars here glowed brighter than the ones in the Gifted Lands. Which was a silly thought, of course—weren't the stars the same in either realm? Looking up, though, it sure didn't seem like it.

I lowered my eyes to look over the castle grounds.

And found myself staring into a pair of bright crimson eyes.

I wanted to scream. But I felt paralyzed, whether by fear or by magic, I wasn't sure. I couldn't do anything but stare at the red eyes, surrounded by a hazy darkness, as an equally dark arm reached out toward me. It touched my lavender hair, which hung in a loose halo around my face, and twisted a thin, grotesque finger around a curl. Its knifelike nail sliced through the lock of hair, before that same finger moved up, ever so slowly, to graze my right cheek. An icy chill bloomed where its finger touched my face.

Self-preservation kicked in, and I brought my right hand up as I shouted a shielding spell. The unknown creature in front of me shrieked as well, and I felt myself falling backward ...

I woke up, my heart pounding as my breaths came in shallow gasps. The morning sunlight shone weakly through my bedroom windows. I groaned, turning over in my bed. Last night's dream left me feeling groggy, with a dull headache, like I hadn't really slept. The temptation to close my eyes and go back to bed was strong, but I also didn't want to oversleep on the one day Rhyss and I had to make preparations before we joined the Trials. I groaned again and sat up.

Blinking in the growing sunlight, I tried to shake off the remnants of last night's dream. I ran a hand through my hair, but stopped short when I realized that one lock of hair was shorter than the others.

I stared at the balcony doors. It couldn't be ...

I got out of bed and made my unsteady way to the balcony. Everything seemed to be in order, but when I put my hand to the door handle, I saw the door was slightly open. Hands shaking, I opened the door wider and stepped onto the balcony.

On the floor was a curl of light purple hair.

I doubled over, gagging, although thankfully nothing came up. Once I had gotten myself under control, I snatched up the curl and rushed back into my bedroom. I went straight to the full-length mirror that stood in one corner of the room. Moving as close as I could to the glass, I examined my right cheek, the one the dream spectre had touched.

From the middle of my ear to just before my mouth was a faint, pale line against my ebony skin. I ran my finger down its length. My skin was intact and uncut, and when I examined the line closer I noticed it had an unusual glow, something a regular scar wouldn't have.

A magical mark, then. That *thing* from last night had marked me. I shuddered. I didn't think it had been for benevolent reasons.

But why had it marked me?

And more importantly, *what* had marked me?

Rhyss was already in the dining hall when I entered, his plate piled high with bread rolls, cheese, and meat for breakfast. He grinned when I walked in. "Good morning, sleepyhead. This is a first."

I yawned, still not fully awake. After the adrenaline of finding out last night's dream wasn't a dream had worn off, I felt even more tired. "That's pretty impressive, considering we've been traveling together for what—ten years? more? I don't think I've ever slept in later than you."

"Well, there was that one time, when we were on Kaernan's commission ..."

"That's not fair. Someone used a sleeping powder on us. We *both* overslept."

Rhyss just chuckled and waved at the sideboard, where plates of cold food sat. "Make yourself a plate and come join me."

I did as he suggested. Looking around the room, I asked, "Where is everyone?"

Rhyss and I were the only two people in the room. I supposed Lord Chela had already come and gone, but what about the others? After how late last night's party went, I didn't expect anyone would wake up early.

"Lord Chela already ate," Rhyss said, confirming my guess. "Paxen and Lilliana were also here earlier. So were Aryn, Fionn, and Hahna, although they kept to themselves. I haven't seen Itan or Bettan."

"How long have you been here?" I asked, sitting down next to Rhyss with my own full plate of food.

"A while. This is my—" Rhyss's face scrunched up in thought "—third plate. I think? Maybe it's my fourth."

I eyed his plate. "Hmm. Maybe you should pace yourself."

"Oh, don't worry. I am."

I chuckled. Then, turning serious, I asked, "Do I look any different to you?"

Rhyss opened his mouth to speak, then paused. "This is a test, isn't it?"

"No, no. I'm just wondering if there's anything about me that's unusual." I smiled to show him he had nothing to worry about, angling my right cheek toward him. The magical scar was so prominent, he was sure to notice it.

Rhyss looked me up and down carefully. "You look the same to me. Beautiful as ever."

I frowned. "Really? You mean you don't—"

My words died in my throat. I tried again, eager to tell Rhyss about my unsettling nightmare.

But nothing came out. No matter what I wanted to say, I couldn't tell him about my dream that wasn't a dream, or about how the spectre had left its mark on my cheek. Even trying to point to it wouldn't work. I was well and truly silenced.

What was going on?

"Are you all right, Farrah?" Rhyss asked, sounding concerned. "You seem a little—"

Aryn burst into the room.

"Oh, goodness. Finally, someone! Have either of you seen Lord Chela?"

Although I didn't know Aryn that well, my impression of her from last night was that she was always cool and in control. But she wasn't in control now.

She was frantic.

I shook my head, but Rhyss said, "I believe he's outside."

Aryn made a strangled cry and turned on her heel, presumably to go find the High Chancellor.

"Wait!" Rhyss called after her. "What's wrong?"

Aryn faced us, a wild, haunted look in her eyes. Her dress, a simple one of green and blue that matched her hair, swirled around her feet.

"Itan is dead."

27

— · —

CHAPTER TWENTY-SEVEN

ARYN DISAPPEARED DOWN THE hallway, moving faster than I would have expected from her languid movements at last night's party.

Rhyss and I were out of our chairs and after her without a second thought.

She passed the throne room, not bothering to check inside to see if Lord Chela was there. *I suppose that was the first place she checked*, I thought.

Although various servants were around, she didn't ask any of them to confirm where the High Chancellor was. It was a smart move, I conceded begrudgingly. The servants would have noted her distress, and started gossiping the minute she left the area.

Which made me wonder ... "Do you think anyone else knows?" I whispered to Rhyss as we hurried after Aryn.

"It doesn't seem like it," Rhyss whispered back. "Yet. It's only a matter of time. We'd better find Lord Chela soon."

We emerged into the palace courtyard, squinting from the glare. With the morning sun shining down on the white palace walls, the area was blindingly bright. When my eyes adjusted, I saw Aryn at one end, deep in conference with Lord Chela. Brow furrowed, he looked thunderous.

Aryn was gesturing wildly as we approached. "... And he was just lying there, eyes and mouth wide open."

Lord Chela looked up, nodding at Rhyss and me, but his focus was on Aryn. "Does anyone else know?"

Aryn's mouth flapped up and down in surprise. "Ah ... no? Maybe? I don't know?"

"Come." Lord Chela strode off without another word, back into the cool interior of the palace.

Aryn, still flustered, ran off after him. Rhyss and I exchanged a glance. Sighing, I said, "I guess we follow."

We hurried after Aryn and Lord Chela, catching up to them in short order. The High Chancellor was heading toward the palace wing that housed the guest suites, walking at a quick pace. A servant snapped to attention as we passed, asking, "My lord? Do you require—" but Lord Chela waved him away and kept going.

We had just entered the hallway with the guest bedrooms, when a shrill scream pierced the air ahead of us, followed by a loud crash. About halfway down the hallway, one of the bedroom doors was open, the morning sunlight spilling onto the stone floor. Behind us, we could hear footsteps coming, as other parts of the palace stirred at the scream.

"So much for keeping things quiet," Rhyss murmured to me, as the four of us broke into a run.

We reached the open doorway, crowding into the room to see what was happening.

Itan the giant lay sprawled on the floor near his oversized bed, his eyes and mouth open wide in a frozen, horrified expression, as Aryn had described. A thin trickle of blood trailed from his mouth down his cheek. A terrified gnomess stood nearby, shaking uncontrollably with her hands covering her mouth. At her feet lay broken dishes and a wooden tray.

When the gnomess saw the High Chancellor, she began babbling. "L-Lord Chela! Forgive me, sir, I-I didn't mean to drop the dishes, I was just so startled. I swear, my lord, he was like this when I got here. H-He's not breathing, sir, I-I didn't know what to do—"

"It's all right, Keeley, anyone would have been frightened," Lord Chela said, his voice gentle. "Why don't you head down to the kitchen and get yourself a drink to calm your nerves."

Keeley dropped to her knees, trying to pick up broken crockery with still shaking hands. After dropping the dishes twice, Lord Chela said, "Don't worry about the dishes for now."

"Yes, my lord. Thank you, my lord." Keeley curtsied, then rushed out of the room.

Lord Chela rubbed his temples briefly, the first time I'd ever seen his tight veneer of self-control crack. "And now everyone in the palace will know about Itan within moments. So there's no need to rush while we take a look around."

He knelt down beside Itan, feeling the giant's neck for a pulse, even though we already knew it was a pointless gesture. Sure enough, Lord Chela looked over at Aryn, Rhyss, and me, nodding his head in confirmation. Aryn gave a little sob and fanned herself, looking faint.

"Here." Rhyss sprang to the nymph's side, guiding her to a chair and gently helping her sit down. "Do you need anything?"

Aryn shook her head, waving at Itan's body. "This is more important right now."

Lord Chela was studying the giant's frozen face, frowning as he examined the body and the surrounding area. "I see no wounds, and no blood other than this line on his face. It doesn't look like he was attacked, at least not physically."

"Is it possible his heart just gave out?" Rhyss asked doubtfully.

Aryn said, "Itan was in his prime, stronger than any of us. No, this has to be the work of evil magic."

The High Chancellor spread his hands wide, hovering just above Itan's body. Closing his eyes, he concentrated as he mouthed a spell.

The rest of us watched, wide-eyed and barely breathing, as Itan's body began to glow. First white, like the stone of the palace around us, then melting into a pale ice blue. Frost began to form over Itan's deepening blue lips. It made the trickle of blood on Itan's face more prominent, a dark ribbon against the rest of his now unnaturally pale skin.

Aryn let out a small sob that threatened to turn into something louder. Rhyss put a steadying hand on her shoulder—partly to calm her, but also ready to clamp a hand over her mouth if need be. Everyone knew it wasn't a good idea to startle a magician in the middle of a spell, but Aryn seemed beyond caring.

Fascinated, I studied Lord Chela's spell while trying to maintain a respectful distance. The frost now completely covered Itan's mouth.

And then, inexplicably, Itan blinked. His eyes, which had been sightless in death just moments ago, now held a modicum of recognition.

And hatred.

28

CHAPTER TWENTY-EIGHT

BUT WAIT. I THOUGHT he was dead?

I had barely finished my thought when Itan lunged, his meaty hands ready to strangle Lord Chela. The High Chancellor broke off his spell and shouted another, throwing his hands in front of him like a shield. His ward went up just in time. Aryn cried out, and even Rhyss made a strangled sound.

Itan bounced off the ward and fell back.

My right cheek flared, a streak of cold traveling down the length of my magical mark. I hissed at the sudden pain, but my discomfort went unnoticed in the room's chaos.

The glow around Itan had faded. Lord Chela cautiously dismantled his ward, noting Itan's stillness. Itan's face had settled back into its unseeing stare, and his body didn't move again.

In the stunned silence, Aryn asked, "Is he dead?"

The High Chancellor nodded grimly. "Yes, but we'll have to burn the body instead of sending it back to his people for a proper burial." He sighed. "Burning Itan's body will ensure that it can't be possessed again."

Aryn gasped, and Rhyss and I exchanged a look over her head. *Do you know what we're dealing with?* his look seemed to ask.

The trouble was, I didn't.

While the Unseelie Fae were a lot of things—cruel, vindictive, chaotic—I had never heard of any who could possess another's body. It might be something the Great Ones of Faerie could do, but I wasn't sure. I made a mental note to ask Lord Chela about the powers of the Great Ones, and hoped he wouldn't find the question offensive.

There was one other, equally disturbing, implication. In order for another being to possess Itan's body after death, it meant it had stolen Itan's soul. While I had never delved into dark magic, I understood there needed to be a life anchor to allow a black magician to possess a body—which is why a possession usually happened while the host was still alive. After the host was dead and the soul had gone to its final rest, the body could be reanimated, but not possessed, unless the soul was tethered somewhere. So the creature that had killed Itan was powerful, more than the average Fae, whether Seelie or Unseelie.

I rubbed my cheek. The icy feeling had faded, but I still felt self-conscious, like the whole room could see how my scar had responded when Itan came back to false life.

"What now, Lord Chela?" Rhyss seemed to be the only level-headed one among us. Aryn sat collapsed in the chair Rhyss had helped her to earlier, quietly sobbing into her hands. Meanwhile, I surreptitiously moved my jaw, willing the stiffness from the cold shock out of my face.

"We carry on with our day, I suppose. I'm sure the entire palace will know of Itan's death by now," the High Chancellor said. "But the servants will give this room a wide berth until they're ordered to come in here."

He looked at Itan sadly. "Such a fine Fae, and undeserving of such a fate. We'll have his funeral tonight, and I'll keep this room locked and warded until then to make sure there are no more unpleasant occurrences."

"I'll head back to my room," Aryn said. "If I am not needed for anything today, I'd like to be left alone until Itan's funeral."

"Of course, Aryn." Lord Chela looked at Rhyss and me. "And for you two? What are your plans?"

"We wanted to take today to prepare for the Trials," Rhyss answered for both of us.

"A wise decision." Lord Chela looked thoughtful. "There is a village nearby where you should be able to pick up any supplies you will need for your travels. If you like, I can send my steward with you, and he can advise you on your purchases. And, of course, any expenses you incur will be paid for by the Crown. I authorize it as Regent."

"Thank you."

The four of us left the room, Rhyss supporting the unsteady Aryn. He continued on with the nymph to her room, which was just two doors down from Itan's.

Torn, I hesitated between following Rhyss and Aryn, and staying behind to talk to Lord Chela. The High Chancellor solved my problem by asking, "Lady Farrah, I don't mean to impose, but would you be wiling to add your magic to mine as I seal this door?"

I tried to hide my surprise at the unusual request. "Oh, of course. What do you need me to do?"

Lord Chela put his hand on the handle of the now closed door. "Just place your hand over mine, if you would."

I did as he requested, doing my best to hold still while he murmured a quick spell. Our layered hands glowed blue, as did the area surrounding them. A brief tingle ran through my hand, and I fought the urge to flex it, forcing myself to ignore the sensation.

A faint click sounded from under his hand, as of a key being turned in a lock, and he looked up. "That should do it."

I removed my hand and shook it, wiggling my fingers until the tingling feeling wore off. "Why did you need my magic?"

"You are an unusual case, Lady Farrah. Half Fae, half human? I may be a powerful magician, but even my spells may be subject to corruption, like any mage's. But with your heritage, our magic is somewhat compatible, and yet your human side should alter this spell enough that no Fae would be able to undo it—besides me, as the creator." He waved at the magically sealed bedroom. "Unless, of course, they had a human mage to help them. Just an added precaution."

"Ah. Smart." I paused. "Before I go, Lord Chela. A question for you ..."

"Please."

I sighed. "After seeing Itan ... I wonder at how powerful this Unseelie is. Most minor Fae wouldn't be able to kill a giant, much less steal his soul and take over his body. Could this be the work of one of the Great Ones?"

Lord Chela frowned. "It's possible. But even the Great Ones have their limitations. King Finvarra was one of the mightiest mages in the realm, and I don't know if even he could have done this."

Hmm. Not good to hear.

"And now I have a question for you, Lady Farrah." Lord Chela looked down the hall to the room where Rhyss had escorted Aryn. The nymph had been safely settled in her room, and Rhyss was now headed back toward us. "I understand Aryn found you and Lord Rhyss in the dining hall before she came to the courtyard, yes?"

I nodded.

He continued, "Did she say why she was in Itan's room?"

I paused, thinking. "No, she didn't. Maybe she wanted Itan to escort her to breakfast?"

"She had already eaten," Rhyss said as he reached us, having over-heard part of our conversation. "Remember? I mentioned that to Lady Farrah when she arrived in the dining hall. Aryn, Lilliana and Paxen had already come through. Itan and Bettan were the only ones I didn't see."

"Perhaps they had come and gone before you arrived," Lord Chela said.

"No, that's not possible." Rhyss looked sheepish. "I woke up really early because I was hungry, and I got to the dining hall before the food was even served."

Despite the seriousness of the situation, I smirked. That was Rhyss for you.

"Hmm." A worry line snaked between Lord Chela's brows, marring his otherwise unworldly perfect face. "I will respect Aryn's wishes to be left alone, for now. She is obviously distraught. But I do find it interesting that she was the one to discover Itan, and not Keeley or another servant."

"Especially since it looked like Keeley was bringing him breakfast," I said. "He must have requested it the night before or early in the morning."

"Exactly," Lord Chela agreed. "It's something we will need to look into further."

Rhyss smirked. "And I suppose by 'we', you mean Lady Farrah and me?"

The High Chancellor gave us a grave smile. "Welcome to the Trials."

29

—·—

CHAPTER TWENTY-NINE

THE THREE OF US headed back to the throne room, where Lord Chela introduced us to his steward, Henry.

"But—you're human!" Rhyss blurted out.

The lean, muscled man in front of us was, indeed, human. He looked to be in his late thirties or early forties, with startling green eyes and black hair that was just beginning to turn grey.

"I am," Henry confirmed. "I've served as steward to the Seelie Court for, oh, a century at least. Perhaps a little longer? After a while here, you lose track of time."

"Wait," I said. "Do you mean to say you witnessed the Great War?"

"Oh, no," Steward Henry said. "That happened before my time. But I did come to Faerie of my own free will."

A rapturous look fell over his face as he reminisced. "I was in Shonn for a week, visiting a cousin. Each night, I would hear the most beautiful music, but I never saw who was playing it. On my last night, determined to find the musician, I wandered the fields outside Shonn, and wandered into Faerie. I suppose, under Valdonne's Treaty, I could have returned to the Gifted Lands and my home kingdom. But this place called to me in a way that nothing else in my life ever had. So I stayed, and I've never regretted it."

"That's wonderful," I said, and I truly meant it. The majority of humans in Faerie weren't as fortunate as Henry, having been tricked, enspelled, or kidnapped into coming here. Which was the exact reason the Treaty had been enacted—even if it wasn't always enforced.

"Steward Henry has been invaluable in his unwavering commitment to the Seelie Court," Lord Chela said. "And speaking of service—I know I promised his services to you while shopping, but I'm going to need his help with the preparations for Itan's funeral first."

"That's all right," Rhyss said. "We'll head to the village first and look around. Henry can join us when he is able."

"Perfect," Lord Chela said. He turned to the steward. "Please give them directions to the village, then come find me. We have much to do before tonight."

"Yes, my lord," Henry said.

The High Chancellor left. Rhyss, Henry, and I walked outside, through the courtyard and under the portcullis, just outside the castle walls. Henry pointed down the road, shading his eyes against the sun's brightness. "When you come to a crossroads, turn left. The village should be under an hour's walk from there. Since you're under the official protection of the High Chancellor, no one should bother you, but keep a wary eye out nonetheless.

"There's several shops that can outfit you, but I suggest talking to Larres. He'll give you the fairest deal, especially once he sees you wearing that." The Steward pointed at my brooch.

"I'll meet you soon. I shouldn't be too long; I've had some recent experience organizing a funeral, after all." He chuckled at his grim humor, prompting sympathetic smiles from both Rhyss and me.

We said our farewells, then Rhyss and I started down the road while Steward Henry headed back into the palace.

"You know, we should have asked Henry for suggestions on what to buy," Rhyss said. "I have no idea what we'll face as we head to the Trials with the others."

"We can ask at the various shops," I said. "Although it sounds like it's been a long, long time since they've had to select a new king or queen. The shopkeepers might not even know."

"I guess we'll just start with the basics. Food, water, shelter." Rhyss brightened. "And we can try whatever food we want, and not have to worry about any enchantments."

"That *is* a bonus." The food in Faerie was rumored to be unparalleled in flavor, so exquisite that the greatest chef in the Gifted Lands would spill all their cooking secrets if they could just have one more bite. Which explained why humans were so easily captivated by it when in Faerie. Then again, pretty much everything about the realm of Faerie was captivating.

I sent a silent thank you to Lord Chela, and his foresight in offering us his protection. It would make navigating Faerie much easier.

"I'm glad we have some time to ourselves," I said. "I'm curious—did Aryn say anything when you escorted her to her room?"

Rhyss laughed. "You mean like, 'If I just keep crying, no one will suspect I murdered Itan'? No, nothing so helpful as that."

I nudged him playfully. "If she had, it would make our job much easier."

"It would." He sobered, thinking. "She mostly just cried nonstop. Although—she did say something about it being too late, now that he was dead."

I frowned. "What does that mean? What was too late?"

"She didn't say. Trust me, if she had said anything interesting, I would have told you right away."

"I know you would," I said. Rhyss and I had practically grown up together, having known each other since we were teenagers, and then working together as mercenaries into adulthood. We had no secrets between us. And even if we tried, we knew each other too well to keep them for long.

We walked in silence for a while, the white gravel of the road crunching underneath our feet.

We hadn't gone far when we reached the crossroads Henry had mentioned. Although the paths weren't marked, we picked the left-hand road and continued on.

"I'm glad Steward Henry gave us such detailed directions," I said as we headed down the new road. At Rhyss's raised eyebrows, I elaborated. "It's too easy to get lost in Faerie. If you don't follow directions exactly, for example. Or if you need help, there's plenty of Fae who'd be willing to take advantage of you."

Rhyss nodded in understanding. "Let's hope we don't run into any creatures like that boggart near Shonn. That was a nasty sort."

"We should be fine," I said. "Anyone who harms us will have to answer to the High Chancellor, and ultimately the Faerie Crown."

"True, but I doubt that protection extends to the Unseelie," Rhyss pointed out. "I didn't get the impression they followed the rules of the Seelie Court."

"No, you're right." I shivered, despite the warm spring sun overhead. "Whatever we came across in the Gifted Lands, it's bound to be worse here, where they're connected to their power."

"You mean we might encounter worse than the Fae-touched?" Rhyss said. He gave an ironic snort. "How bad do we need that marriage blessing again? Oh, that's right. We can't get it, at least not from your father. Maybe from the High Chancellor, if all goes well and he's so inclined. Honestly, it might be better to take chances with a marriage curse. What's the worst that could happen?"

"You say that now, but you've never seen the effects of a Faerie curse," I pointed out. "It's not as simple as normal misfortune, like being perpetually poor or having a debilitating injury or illness—"

"Both of those sound pretty bad to me."

"True, those are hard to deal with. But those are things that could happen to anyone, and people learn to rise above it. Imagine falling asleep and waking up a hundred years later, to find out everyone you love is dead and your kingdom is completely different. Being transformed into an animal, forced to live beyond the span of a normal beast's life with your human memories. Dancing until you die, or are desperate enough to cut off your feet. And also—"

"Okay, okay, I get it. We don't want a Faerie curse over our heads, and especially not over our marriage." Rhyss sighed. "But it's gotten even more complicated than just making sure the Trials are done fairly. Who's the imposter? Who killed Itan?"

"And who framed my father, and why?" I sighed too. "We know the questions. I just hope we find the answers, and soon."

30

Chapter Thirty

The trip to the nearby village was thankfully uneventful, but I couldn't shake the feeling that we were being watched. I kept a wary eye out as we walked, but I didn't see anything unusual. That is, more unusual than what one would find in Faerie. Perhaps I was just jumpy from Itan's death and the upcoming Trials?

Since I couldn't say with certainty what was bothering me, I didn't say anything to Rhyss. But still, I couldn't shake the feeling.

We had barely set foot in the village when something small and fast darted at our faces, nearly running straight into Rhyss's nose. His eyes crossed as he tried to focus on the diminutive figure—a rather startled pixie—and I giggled. So did she.

"Oops! Sorry about that!" The pixie shook herself all over, resembling a dog shaking off water.

"I should apologize, for startling you, Miss—?" Rhyss began.

Behind the pixie, a nasally voice yelled out, "Stop that pixie!"

A gnome in a bright green cap, with a white beard that skimmed his toes, stumped down the cobblestone street toward us. He reached up in the air, trying to grab at the pixie.

"Gotta go!" The pixie giggled again and flew away, out of the village.

"Blast it!" The gnome said, as he accidentally bopped Rhyss on the nose. "That's the third time she's evaded payment! If her parents hadn't been such dear friends of mine ..."

Rhyss rubbed his nose. "Had we known, we would have tried harder to detain her."

"Oh, well. She'll be back, I'm sure." The gnome pointed at Rhyss's nose. "Sorry about that."

"It's all right, Mister—?"

"Larres," the gnome said. "But no Mister. Just Larres. And you are?"

"Oh!" Rhyss brightened. "I'm Lord Rhyss, and this is Lady Farrah. And you're the one Steward Henry sent us to see."

"Henry? From up at the castle?" Larres looked Rhyss and me over. "Henry's a good sort. Always pays his bills on time." He tapped his chin thoughtfully. "But I don't remember him putting in an order recently."

"He didn't," I said. "Or at least, I don't think he did. We're here to shop for ourselves. Steward Henry said your shop had the fairest prices."

The gnome puffed up with pride. "That I do. But why don't you take a look for yourselves? Come, come."

He turned and started back across the village square, toward a shop with a bright spring green door, the same color as Larres's pointed cap. The door hung slightly open, betraying Larres's haste to catch the pixie.

Rhyss and I followed after the gnome into a tidy shop with floor-to-ceiling wooden shelves filled with all sorts of fabrics, jars, papers, and other items. A wooden ladder leaned against one wall, and a staircase on the far side of the shop led to a second floor with more overflowing shelves. I looked around, impressed at the number of goods on display. The shop had seemed much smaller from the outside. But then again, this was Faerie. I was sure magic was involved to help Larres maximize his store's space.

Larres stood in the center, hands on his hips as he surveyed his domain. "Welcome to Larres's Esoteric Emporium."

"It's amazing," I said. "I wouldn't know where to start looking. Although, I'm also not really sure what we need."

"I can help you with that. What, exactly, are you shopping for? A celebration? A journey? Or do you just want some souvenirs of your time in Faerie?"

"A journey, I suppose. I'm supposed to judge the Trials, which start tomorrow."

Larres's jaw dropped. "A *human* is overseeing the Trials? Oh my, oh my, oh my! I don't think I've ever heard of humans being involved in the Trials since ..." He paused. "Actually, I've never heard of humans being involved in the Trials. Unless the task was to enchant them or entrap them or something similar. But to *judge* them? No, no indeed."

He stopped, head cocked to one side as he scrutinized me. "But wait a moment—you're not human, are you? Or am I mistaken?"

"I'm part human," I said. "My Father is Fae."

"Ah, that's it, that's it." Larres nodded, pleased with himself. "I thought so."

I smiled. I liked this high-strung gnome. "Since you're familiar with the Trials, perhaps you know what we might encounter? Although the High Chancellor has pledged his protection. So we should be safe, even if those participating are not."

Larres shook his head. "The Trials aren't safe, not for anyone. If Lord Chela has promised to ensure your safety, then that means any Fae that tries to harm you will face the consequences. So no one will hurt you, at least not directly. But that doesn't mean you can't get hurt or killed by accident."

He turned to a nearby shelf, surveying its contents. "Let's see. You'll probably need this ... maybe a few of these. Oh, and some of this can't hurt."

He began pulling items off the shelves. Soon his arms were full, and he dumped the lot on the polished wooden countertop, then went back to the shelves for more. He even made a few trips to the second floor to get some things. Rhyss and I stood by, watching with amusement. Whenever either of us tried to approach a shelf to browse, or offered to help Larres, the gnome waved us away.

Larres put the last item on top of the countertop pile and stepped back, crossing his arms in satisfaction to survey his work. "There! That should do it!"

"I'll say," Rhyss commented. "What is all this stuff?" He poked at the pile. "And do we need all of it?"

Larres frowned. "I may have gotten a bit carried away. It's just so hard to know what you'll need. Better to be prepared than not."

31

CHAPTER THIRTY-ONE

HE PICKED UP A thin envelope, the paper hand-dyed a lovely robin's-egg blue. He shook it, and I could hear the sound of something soft, like powder, settling inside.

"Take this, for example. As humans in Faerie, you're susceptible to the magic in our food and drink. Why do you think so many humans end up staying in Faerie after eating our food? Sprinkle a little of this on whatever you're going to consume before you do, and it will keep those enchantments from touching you."

I reached out my hand to take the envelope. My guess had been correct—when I opened the envelope, a sparkly white powder winked up at me. I quickly sealed it, afraid of spilling the contents. "That's handy. We'll take as many as you have."

As Larres pulled more envelopes from the shelf, I asked, "But what's the catch?"

He wagged a finger at me. "Smart girl. You'll do just fine in Faerie. You're right—being enchanted is not the same as being harmed by mundane means. If someone poisons your drink, or serves you spoiled food, this powder won't help you."

Rhyss held up a plain white square of fabric. He turned it this way and that, trying to uncover its secrets. "What's this for? It's too small to be a tablecloth or a blanket. But it's too big to be a handkerchief." He rubbed the fabric between his fingers. "And it's kind of scratchy."

"Ah, that's one of my favorites," Larres said. He took the fabric square from Rhyss. "Tell me, on your travels so far, was there anything you wish you had packed that you didn't? Any clothing that you found yourself in need of?"

"Well, we hadn't planned on staying in Faerie long. The other night we needed formal clothing, but obviously we hadn't planned for that."

Rhyss barely finished speaking when Larres threw the coarse white fabric into the air. The fabric floated down, transforming into a black brocade fitted jacket and trousers, similar in style to what Rhyss had worn at the dinner with the Trials contenders.

Larres caught the fine outfit, handing the coat to Rhyss. Rhyss shook out the jacket, admiring it.

"Very nice." He held it up to his chest, frowning. "But it seems a bit small for me."

Larres laughed, holding the pants against his body. "Yes, they did come out gnome-sized, didn't they? It works better if the person who desires the clothing is the one throwing the cloth. But as you can see, it's real clothing, and not an illusion."

"Still, it's impressive. How long does the magic clothing last? Or is it a one use only item?"

"No, no limit as to how many times you can create something from the cloth. As for the outfits it creates, those only last for a day. These fabric squares are quite rare, and don't come cheap. But they're remarkably handy. You can make most any type of clothing from it, including armor."

"And the exceptions?"

Larres laughed. "You're just as quick as Lady Farrah, here. It can only make non-magical clothing. Nor can you enhance it with any enchantments. Magic won't stick to it."

"We'll take two, one for each of us," I said.

Rhyss and I sorted through the pile, and with suggestions from Larres, we whittled our purchases down to something manageable. The bundles were still fairly heavy, but not so much that we couldn't carry them in our packs. And some things—like the enchantment-blocking powder—would eventually get used up, so we wouldn't be hauling a huge load of stuff forever.

Still, when Steward Henry arrived as we were finishing our selections, both of us breathed sighs of relief.

"Hello there, Henry," Larres greeted the newcomer. "Thanks for recommending these two to my shop." He waved at us, and then at our large purchase.

"Of course, old friend," Henry said. "Have they paid yet?"

"No, we were just getting to that part."

Henry tossed a small velvet purse on the counter. From the heavy thud it made upon landing, I knew it was stuffed with coins. So did Larres. His eyes widened, and an equally wide smile spread across his face. He picked up the purse and hefted it experimentally. "Hmm."

"If it's not enough, just bill the remainder to Lord Chela, High Chancellor of the Seelie Court," Henry said.

"That's the way of it, huh?" Larres loosened the drawstring holding the velvet purse closed and peeked inside. He whistled. "I think this will be enough to cover their payment, and then some."

"If you're sure."

"I am." The gnome shopkeep nodded at Rhyss and me. "It must be nice to have rich friends."

"A very generous patron," I corrected. "Indeed, without his pledge of protection, and his promise to take care of our expenses, we wouldn't be able to stay in Faerie."

"Hmm," Larres said again, sizing us up silently. Although the gnome seemed a good sort, I wondered how long it would be before our business was known throughout the entire land.

"If you're done, we should get going," Steward Henry said, looking at Rhyss and me. At our nod, he picked up some of the bundles on the counter. "I have a mule tied up outside."

Larres waved goodbye as the three of us exited his shop, our arms laden with packages.

Outside, Rhyss and Henry secured our purchases to the mule, then Henry turned to us. "I have a few errands to run while I'm in town. If you'd like to go back to the palace, you're welcome to, or you can stay here and look around while I take care of some things."

"I think we'll head back," I said. "Not that I wouldn't like to stay and shop some more. It's not often we get to visit a Faerie village."

"But I don't think we can carry any more things," Rhyss said, eyeing the pack mule. The poor beast seemed shrunken under the weight of all our purchases. "This is plenty."

"Very well, then. I'll be back at the palace in a few hours, if you need anything. Itan's funeral will be held at sundown in the courtyard."

"We'll be there," I promised. "I take it everything's been arranged?"

"As much as can be," Henry said. "The first thing I did was send word to his family. Fortunately—although I am loathe to use that word in this situation—the region where Itan was from is close enough that his family should be here in time for the funeral. That will give them some closure, at least. But I need to pick up a few, rare magical components for the spells Lord Chela needs to do tonight."

He sighed. "I hope I'll be able to find them, or there might be trouble."

"If you need assistance—" I began, but Henry waved away my offer.

"Head on back. You two will need to get ready for the Trials anyway, so don't waste any more time here."

With that, we said goodbye and went our separate ways, Henry further into the village, and Rhyss and me leading the pack mule down the white stone road, back toward the palace.

As we walked, my skin prickled. I looked around, but still didn't see anything out of the ordinary.

A hand touched my arm. I yelped.

"Why so jumpy?" Rhyss said. "Are you okay? You were just so quiet, I wondered what you were thinking."

I shook my head, wishing I could shake the unsettled feeling from my skin. "Do you sense anyone watching us?"

Rhyss slowed his steps, concentrating on the area around us as we continued walking. After a few moments, he said, "No. But this is Faerie. I would think something is always watching, right? Even if we can't see them?"

"Possibly. But I don't know. This feels ... different. Active curiosity, as opposed to just noticing us passing by. Someone—or some *thing*—is targeting us, specifically."

Rhyss looked around again. He put a hand on the hilt of his sword. "If anything attacks us, we'll be ready."

But nothing revealed itself as we continued walking back to the palace. And the uneasy feeling stayed with me the entire way.

32

—·—

CHAPTER THIRTY-TWO

A FLURRY OF ACTIVITY met us the moment we entered the palace grounds.

Even if Henry hadn't mentioned the site of tonight's funeral, we would have known it right away.

An overly large pyre, big enough to hold a giant's body, stood half-built in the center of the courtyard. Servants ran to and fro with materials for the pyre, or readying the area. I saw the faint outlines of various sigils carved into the pyre or painted around it on the ground, and recognized the symbols for protection and containment.

Rhyss sighed. "Such a sad business. I know we didn't know Itan long, but he seemed like a good fellow."

I nodded. "We'll just have to figure out what happened to him, and fast."

I started to unload my bundles from the pack mule. Soon my arms were fairly full, and I still hadn't gotten all my purchases, or Rhyss's.

"Don't worry about those," Rhyss said, swatting my hand away. "I'll take the mule to the stable and bring the rest of the things. You've got enough to carry as it is."

"If you're sure—"

"I am."

"Thank you," I said. "I'll be in my room, then."

"Go." Rhyss shooed me away. "I'll come by later with your stuff. And don't spend too much time working—we're going to be working nonstop pretty soon."

I reached up on my tiptoes to kiss Rhyss on the cheek, trying not to drop anything, then headed inside the palace.

Back in the guest wing of the palace, I tried not to stare at the closed door to Itan's room, but it was hard to ignore. I could feel the strong sealing magic emanating from the area; the air practically throbbed with all the magic floating around. Well, after tonight that uncomfortable pulsation would be gone. As would Itan, and the threat from his possessed body.

I sighed, fumbling with the doorknob to my room. Once I got it to turn—no easy feat with the pile of purchases in my arms—I pushed open the door with my hip, backing into the room until I could drop everything on my bed.

I blew out a breath, happy to be relieved of my burden. A floorboard creaked behind me.

"That was fast," I said, turning around to greet Rhyss. "Just add my things to the pile—"

My words died in my throat. It wasn't Rhyss in the doorway.

Instead, the selkie Bettan stood there, framed in the doorway, silently staring at me.

"Oh!" I said. "Forgive me, I thought you were someone else."

Bettan didn't speak, didn't move. Her dark, unfathomable eyes followed my movements, the only thing that betrayed her stillness.

"It's Bettan, right?" My voice seemed overly loud in the room. "I'm sorry we didn't formally meet each other at the dinner. Please, come in."

I waved at an empty chair near the bed. The selkie glided into the room, her footsteps just as quiet as her demeanor.

Up close, I noted that she was a few inches shorter than me, with big brown eyes set in a round, childlike face. Unlike most of the other Fae courtiers, who favored elaborate hairstyles and jeweled adornments, Bettan let her straight silver-grey hair flow freely down her back, where it hung to her waist. Her spotted grey-and-white pelt, a reflection of her hair, was attached firmly to her belt.

Bettan gracefully sank into the offered chair. I cleared a space on the bed and sat as well, folding my hands in my lap. Bettan and I stared at each other, the silence stretching out between us. I stayed as still as I could, feeling that any sudden move or sound from me would send the skittish selkie running.

Just when I thought I would burst from the heavy quiet in the air, Bettan spoke. "I—I've been wanting to talk to you all morning. I just ... wasn't sure how. I followed you to the village—"

That was her? I thought. Out loud, I said, "Why didn't you approach Lord Rhyss and I on the road, then?"

Bettan hung her head. "I—I wasn't sure I should come forward. But ... Itan's death was no accident."

Oh, really? I couldn't tell from the possessed dead man that tried to attack the High Chancellor.

But I refrained from saying my thoughts aloud. Instead, I said, "Do you know who or what caused it?"

"I saw Aryn leaving Itan's room early this morning, when I was on my way to breakfast," Bettan said.

"Aryn was the one who reported his death," I pointed out. "She said they were to have breakfast together, when she found his body in his room."

"Of course she would have found him. She was in his room all night."

I gave Bettan a sharp look. "How do you know?"

"She went to his room sometime after midnight," Bettan said matter-of-factly. "I was coming back from the baths, and when I turned the corner, I saw her slip into his room and then the door closed."

"Midnight? That's rather late to take a bath, don't you think?" I tried to keep my tone as neutral as Bettan's.

The selkie shrugged. "I needed to unwind after the stress of the evening. I like the water, and I lose track of time when I'm in it."

Fair enough, considering her other form was a seal.

"Perhaps she visited Itan late at night, then returned to her own bedroom, and went back in the morning?" I suggested.

"Perhaps," Bettan said. "But like I said, it was early. No one else was up yet—I was surprised to see Lord Rhyss in the dining room. And Aryn was wearing the same dress in the morning that she had worn to the dinner and courtyard concert the night before."

I paused, thinking of how Aryn had looked this morning. Lovely and ethereal, of course. But—last night she had worn a shimmery creation of pink and purple. This morning's dress was blue and green.

If Bettan was telling the truth, then Aryn had spent the night in Itan's room.

And if that was true, then sometime during the night or upon waking in the morning, Aryn would have known that he was dead. But instead of reporting it immediately, she had returned to her room to freshen up and change first, before seeking help.

Then I remembered the run-in Aryn and Bettan had last night, as both Fae were leaving the dining room. Obviously there was no love lost between the two women. Wouldn't it serve Bettan to discredit her rival for the throne?

But Itan had seemed to think highly of the selkie. So, was it in Bettan's nature to lie?

I shook my head, as if that could help my jumbled thoughts make sense. "Thank you for telling me, Bettan. I'll look into it."

"Please do." Bettan stood and moved to the doorway, sidestepping at the last moment to allow Rhyss, carrying the remainder of my packages, to enter.

"Greetings—Bettan, is it?" Rhyss said.

"Yes. Goodbye," the selkie said, and slipped out of my bedroom.

"Goodbye," Rhyss echoed, a puzzled look crossing his face. He dropped the bundles at the foot of the bed near me, and shut the door. "Did I offend her?"

"No," I sighed. "I think she's just a woman of few words."

Seeing the look on my face, Rhyss sank down in the chair Bettan had occupied earlier and took my hands in his. "Is everything all right?"

"No," I said again. I recounted my conversation with Bettan.

Rhyss leaned back in his chair and whistled. "Interesting. But it raises more questions than it answers."

"Yes, it does. And don't forget Fionn and his mother Hahna. They were less than friendly last night."

"From what Itan said, it sounds like Fionn has the best claim to the throne. And probably the most to lose if he can't complete the Trials successfully."

"So, what now? Gather everyone together and question them? Corner Aryn and ask her why she omitted crucial information?"

Rhyss tapped his chin in thought. "You're probably better suited than I am to question everyone. I wouldn't be able to hide what I'm thinking."

I smirked. That was true. My intended had many wonderful qualities, but subtlety was not one of them. Rhyss tended to be a bit brash, an in the moment and in your face kind of person.

"Honestly, I'm not sure what I'd ask, just yet," I admitted. "I think, at tonight's funeral, it would be best to just observe everyone, and see what their reactions are."

"Good idea." Rhyss nodded and then stood. Leaning forward, he kissed the top of my head. "I'll let you get packing, then. I've got to get my own things together, anyway. I'll see you tonight."

He left, closing the door behind him. I picked up one of the bundles and half-heartedly picked at the string holding the items together. I sighed. A long afternoon of packing followed by a funeral. What a day.

33

— · —

CHAPTER THIRTY-THREE

BY THE TIME THE sky had started to turn pink with the setting sun, I had finally finished my packing. I had assumed I would have to leave some things behind in the palace, but either I was a better packer than I thought, or—more likely—Faerie items somehow magically conformed to their owner's needs.

I fingered the magic cloth square, figuring tonight was a good time to try it out. I threw the white fabric in the air, and when it fell back down, I held a dark grey dress in my outstretched hands. Although Lord Chela hadn't informed Rhyss and me about Faerie mourning customs, I thought it best to pay my respects to the late Itan in the Gifted Lands tradition.

I left my bedroom. In the hallway, I met Rhyss, clad in black-and-grey in a similar modest fashion.

"Well, we know they work," he said, gesturing to our outfits.

"Too bad this is how they make their debut."

He crooked his arm, offering it to me. "The next time we use them, we'll make sure it's a happy occasion."

I smiled gently and took his arm, letting him escort me outside.

A sizeable crowd had gathered in the castle courtyard. I found that surprising; I had thought only the High Chancellor and Itan's immediate family would be allowed entry to his funeral. Partly because a smaller funeral would help quell more rumors from starting, and also to keep potential injury to a minimum if whatever inhabited Itan's body broke free, despite Lord Chela's protective measures.

But it seemed the entire palace—and then some—had turned up for the funeral. The pyre, now completed, took up the center of the courtyard. Fae courtiers milled around, with servants on standby, doing their best to blend into the background.

Steward Henry followed Lord Chela as the High Chancellor sprinkled some powder over the ground, murmuring a spell under his breath. I spotted Fionn and his mother Hahna near the pyre, openly curious about the magic worked into the wood.

Across the way, Paxen and Lilliana quietly talked, with Aryn standing nearby. Her normally haughty features held a tinge of sadness. As Rhyss and I approached, she turned red-rimmed eyes on us, sniffled, and then turned away, obviously not wanting to engage in conversation.

I didn't see Bettan in the area. Perhaps she would be along later? But the sun had nearly set, and the funeral would begin soon.

Paxen and Lilliana broke off their discussion to greet us. "A bad business," Paxen said, gesturing at the pyre.

"Do you—" Lilliana began, but at that moment a single, mournful note pierced the air. We all looked toward the castle entrance.

A bagpiper slowly strode into the courtyard, playing a slow, melancholy funeral song. He moved to a far corner, continuing to play, as a group of giants emerged from the castle interior.

Two male giants, their faces drawn down in sorrow, carried Itan's body on a litter. They both looked like younger versions of Itan—his brothers, I presumed. Itan's body glowed purple and silver with several layers of containment magic—most likely Lord Chela's doing.

Two more giants, a man and a woman, walked behind the pair of giants that bore Itan's body. Their dark brown hair had begun to fade into grey, and the lines around their eyes and mouths had deepened in their grief.

The man opened his mouth, releasing a loud, keening wail that drowned out the music of the bagpipe in the courtyard's corner. The musician gently faded out his music. Meanwhile, the woman joined the other giant in his mourning, her voice a haunting counterpart to the man's wail.

The two brothers gently moved Itan from the litter to the center of the pyre. As the body touched the pyre, the wood glowed purple and silver, engulfing Itan for a moment before fading away.

Some in the gathered crowd gasped, while others murmured to each other. If those present hadn't been aware that there was a spell on Itan's body and the funeral pyre, they now knew, and it had ignited their curiosity.

Their sorry task finished, the two brothers stood back and joined their parents in the wordless mourning cry.

No, not wordless.

I couldn't understand the words—the four giants were speaking in a language unfamiliar to my ears—but I knew, instinctively, they were singing a funeral song for their loved one. I could feel their love, the pain and the longing in their lament. I bowed my head, letting their song of farewell wash over me.

Their last sorrowful note hung in the air, then faded away. The giants' loud wails settled into soft sniffles as they leaned on each other for comfort.

Lord Chela stepped forward, hands outstretched toward the pyre as he strengthened the wards around Itan's body. So far, everything seemed to be fine; there was no movement from the dead giant, so the High Chancellor's containment magic must be working.

Either that, or whatever had killed and possessed Itan had moved from its former host.

Satisfied with his spell casting, Lord Chela turned to address the crowd in the courtyard.

"My dear friends, we are here to remember the all too brief life of Itan. A beloved son and brother, he was a shining example of ..."

As Lord Chela continued his eulogy, I surreptitiously surveyed the Fae around me. My gaze slid past Itan's family, dismissing them as possible suspects. They had just arrived this afternoon for the funeral, and, although I hadn't been introduced to any of them, their grief seemed genuine. Besides, with Itan gone they had lost their best possible connection to the Seelie Court kingship.

But, with Itan's death, that only left four contenders for the throne—Fionn, Bettan, Aryn, and Paxen.

34

— ◆ —

CHAPTER THIRTY-FOUR

ACROSS THE WAY, FIONN and his mother stood watching the proceedings with disinterested looks. Hahna even yawned, although she tried to daintily hide it. Next to me, Paxen and his advisor Lilliana both dabbed at their eyes, their heads bowed in respect. I hated to think Paxen could have possibly killed Itan, but as direct competitors, he would have a good reason to want Itan dead.

Meanwhile, tears streamed unchecked down Aryn's face as she stared, unblinking, at Itan's body on the pyre. It seemed like she was trying to memorize every last detail about Itan, before he was gone forever. I would have pegged her for a noisy, showy crier, the kind of person who would want others to know she was grieving, but she surprised me with her self-control. Aside from her silent tears and her hands, clasped together so tightly they were turning white, no one would have guessed she was upset.

Bettan was still nowhere to be seen.

Lord Chela finished his speech. Steward Henry stepped forward, two lit torches in his hands. He held one out to each of the older giants, but the woman sniffled and shook her head, refusing to take hers. One of Itan's brothers patted his mother on the shoulder, then reached out to take the offered torch in his mother's stead. Together, father and son moved to opposite sides of the pyre, and, at the same time, slowly lowered their flames to ignite the wood.

The pyre caught fire, the flames licking up the sides and quickly engulfing Itan's body. Only the crackle of the fire, punctuated by the occasional sniffle from someone in the crowd, filled the night air.

After a few moments of reverent silence, the crowd began thinning out. Most of the courtiers left through the palace's front gates, headed for their own homes, although a few went inside the castle. With a final choked sob, Aryn turned on her heel and started toward the palace. Lilliana and Paxen exchanged a worried glance and hurried after Aryn, but the nymph brushed them off and only walked faster.

Eventually, the only ones left watching the burning pyre were Itan's parents and brothers, Lord Chela, Steward Henry, Rhyss, and me. Lord Chela spoke quietly to the family of giants before disappearing into the castle.

A light touch on my arm startled me, and I looked over to see Henry nodding his head toward the palace where Lord Chela had gone. With one last glance at the grieving family, Rhyss and I followed Henry inside and through the castle hallways.

When we were safely out of earshot, Henry said, "The pyre will burn all night. According to Fae tradition, only the deceased's family is expected to keep a vigil during that time."

"Such a sorry business," Rhyss murmured, and I nodded my head in agreement.

The three of us stopped at the junction where the main corridor met the hallway that led to the private suites. "I need to help Lord Chela with maintaining the pyre wards, and oversee the servants as we close the castle for the night. But before I leave, is there anything either of you require?"

Rhyss shook his head, but I said, "With all the ... recent excitement, we forgot to ask. Are you or Lord Chela going to join us during the Trials?"

Steward Henry sighed. "Alas, no. Lord Chela has to stay here at the palace and continue running the day-to-day of the Seelie Court. I'm needed here to assist Lord Chela, and especially with the mystery surrounding Itan's death, he'll need an extra pair of hands and eyes. So it's quite fortuitous that you two showed up when you did, to oversee the Trials."

"Fortuitous indeed," I murmured, and Rhyss smirked.

Fortunately, Henry didn't notice. "You'll each have a horse, and if you choose to stay at any of the area inns, all of your expenses will be covered. You can also camp with the contenders, although I'm sure you'd be more comfortable in some cozy beds with a good meal in your bellies." He smiled. "Well, if neither of you need anything, I'll say goodnight here. I'll see you in the morning, before you and the rest of the guests leave."

"Wait. Can I see my father one more time before we go?"

Henry paused. "I-I'm not sure."

"Please."

The steward pursed his lips. He leaned back a little, looking down the hallway. I held my breath, anticipating his negative response. So I was taken off guard when he turned back to me and said, "All right. Come with me. And hurry, please."

Henry started down the main corridor, moving quickly. Rhyss and I followed him through the hallways, into the palace's underground dungeon. At the entrance, the Steward stopped, waving me forward. "Don't take too long. I can only give you a few moments."

I nodded and hurried to my father's cell, leaving Rhyss and Henry at the entryway. Father was slumped against the wall, dozing, but when he heard my footsteps he began stirring. By the time I stood in front of his cell, he was fully awake and standing at the bars, waiting for me.

"Farrah! What are you doing down here, so late at night?" Father got a good look at my outfit. "And why are you dressed like that?"

"Rhyss and I leave in the morning to judge the Trials. I don't know when we'll be back, so I wanted to say goodbye first. There was a funeral tonight," I said, and quickly filled him in on the events surrounding Itan's death.

As I told my tale, my father had gone very still. At the mention of the shadowy being that had haunted my dreams and had possibly killed Itan, my father hissed between his teeth.

"Be careful, daughter," he said. "You asked me earlier who framed me. I do not know, but I do remember the creature they sent to do their dirty work: a figure shrouded in shadows, much like you describe, with piercing red eyes. It seems like they have returned to interfere once more with the Seelie Court, when it is vulnerable."

"I'll be careful," I said, although I knew we were both wondering how I could keep such a promise.

I reached through the bars and squeezed my father's outstretched hand. He leaned forward, as much as he could through the bars, and kissed the top of my head. The stench of his unwashed, grimy clothes and body washed over me, and tears pricked my eyes at the sorry state he was in. *I'll clear your name, somehow*, I promised myself.

Steward Henry ushered Rhyss and me back upstairs, and escorted us back to the hallway that led to the guest suites. We said goodnight to Henry and continued down the hallway to our bedrooms. Quietly, I said to Rhyss, "Did you notice anything unusual at tonight's funeral?"

"Besides the magic sigils on the funeral pyre and the giant who died under mysterious circumstances? What did I miss?"

"Aryn looked extremely distraught, more than I would have expected. And Bettan never showed up at the funeral."

Rhyss frowned. "Maybe Bettan can't handle things like funerals and strong emotions. And Aryn did find Itan's body. I'm sure she's still feeling the stress of it all."

"Maybe." But I didn't think it was that simple.

We had reached the hallway's end, and the group of doors that led to the guest suites. Rhyss started to open his door, then noticed my hesitation. "Aren't you going to bed?"

I stood outside Aryn's room, hand poised to knock. "Soon. I'm just going to check on Aryn, make sure she's okay."

I knocked, and was surprised when the door gave way under my light touch. Although it had looked closed, it had apparently been slightly ajar, and the force of my knock caused the door to open inward.

"Aryn?"

The room was empty. Aryn wasn't there.

Rustling sounded behind me. Rhyss's voice sounded low in my ear. "Where is she?"

"That's what I want to know."

"Should we go look for her?"

A massive yawn escaped my lips. "As much as I'd like to, it's late, and we have a busy day ahead of us. Days, really. We'll just add this to the list of mysteries we have to unravel."

Rhyss yawned in response. "That list is growing longer by the minute."

We left Aryn's empty room, closing the door behind us. Rhyss gave me a quick kiss on the forehead before I entered my room.

Inside, I changed into my nightclothes, crawling into bed and drawing the covers up to my chin. I settled in and waited for sleep to overtake me.

But it didn't, at least not right away. Perhaps it was the flickering light dancing on the wall from the funeral pyre in the courtyard that kept me awake. Or the occasional keening wail from one of Itan's family members that pierced the night air. Regardless of the reason, true sleep eluded me, and I spent a fitful, restless night drifting in and out of hazy nightmares featuring red-eyed smoke creatures, fire, and heart-rendering cries.

35

—·—

CHAPTER THIRTY-FIVE

MORNING DAWNED GREY AND cold.

Rather fitting for the day after a funeral, I thought. *But not auspicious for the start of the Trials to determine the next Seelie Court ruler.*

The early hours were filled with subdued activity. After breakfast and some last minute preparations, we were ready to leave. The fire had burned out sometime after midnight, allowing Itan's family to retire for the night as guests of the High Chancellor's. The charred shell of the funeral pyre was empty, and the area around it had been swept clean of the magic sigils and ashes. I didn't envy the servants whose thankless task it had been to wake up early and take care of the burned remains before the rest of the castle stirred.

Rhyss and I joined the eclectic group of travelers gathered at one end of the courtyard. Paxen and Lilliana cast worried glances at Aryn, who stared, unblinking, at the pyre. Aryn seemed to have her emotions under tight control now, but her eyes still shone with unshed tears. She also looked a bit disheveled, and I wondered if she had kept her own vigil for Itan last night.

Fionn and his mother Hahna attended their horses, acting like they were going for a routine ride in the countryside and pointedly ignoring the pyre and the rest of the group.

Steward Henry gave orders to a group of servants who were running around fulfilling final requests, while Lord Chela talked quietly with each of the royal hopefuls.

Just as things were winding down, and we were ready to go, Bettan slipped into the courtyard. I wondered how she would ready her horse in time, but she just sidled up to it, pulling its head close to hers in a short, whispered conversation. The horse snorted and dipped its head, and Bettan mounted it in a graceful, fluid motion.

I mounted my own horse, understanding washing over me. Bettan, being part animal herself, would naturally be able to converse with other beasts, and didn't need a saddle or bridle to ride. She just needed permission.

Lord Chela said a few words to Bettan, who nodded. He then approached Rhyss and me.

"Be well and safe travels. There's always a little bit of danger associated with the Trials, but nothing that should touch you, as my official representative. However, if something should go awry, please contact me immediately. Do you know how to create a calling spell?"

I nodded.

"Good. But I doubt you'll need to use it. And remember, your judgment is definitive and final. If you decide to disqualify someone, for whatever reason you deem fit, it cannot be contested."

I smirked. "That'll make me real popular, I'm sure."

Lord Chela missed my sarcasm. "Quite. They'll all be on their best behavior."

The High Chancellor waved us off, as our group of eight passed through the palace gates. Fionn and Hahna took the lead, their bearing suggesting that they already considered themselves the new rulers, and were just tolerating the Trials for show. Bettan and Aryn were next, riding side-by-side in an uncomfortable silence. Paxen and Lilliana were third in line, ever alert and occasionally whispering things to each other. I guessed they were worried about Aryn and her deep grief over Itan's death.

Rhyss and I took up the rear, trying to keep an eye on our companions and our surroundings all at the same time. I was glad we were so far back, where we could—for the most part—talk without being overheard by the others. Still, Rhyss slowed his horse's pace, and motioned for me to do the same.

"What would be grounds for disqualification?" Rhyss asked me in a low voice. "Cheating? Stealing? Lying?"

I snorted. Softly, I said, "Those are practically considered Faerie pastimes. At least when it comes to how they deal with humans. But I suppose, in regards to how the Fae treat each other, those would be frowned upon."

"As is murder."

"Indeed." I surveyed the riders in front of us. "I hope we have a chance to question everyone individually."

"We may have to create that chance, if it doesn't come up naturally."

I nodded, frowning. Down the road, Paxen turned around, realizing Rhyss and I weren't following close behind. "Lord Rhyss! Lady Farrah! Is everything all right?"

"Yes! Yes, we're fine," I said, and spurred my horse forward.

"Make sure you stay close by," Paxen said as Rhyss and I rejoined the others. "It's not safe for humans on their own in Faerie."

"Even if you do have the protection of the High Chancellor," Lilliana said.

"Where are we headed first, do you know?" Rhyss asked.

"To my home region," Paxen said proudly. "The Fairwood."

"Ah. You'll have the advantage, then."

"As will Fionn," Paxen pointed out fairly. "And the elves are of a higher caste than the centaurs, so he'll be in a much better position than I."

Even though it didn't seem like Fionn or his mother were paying attention to our conversation, I thought I caught a faint smirk on both of their faces. Or maybe that was just their usual expressions.

"What's the Fairwood like?" I asked.

"Now you've done it." Lilliana laughed before Paxen could speak. "Get ready for an earful. Good thing we've got hours and hours on the road."

"I can't help it if the Fairwood is the most beautiful place in all of Faerie," Paxen said. "Lush, majestic trees. Colorful flora and charming fauna, the likes of which many have never seen. I mean, it's even in the name. *Fair*wood. What do you expect?"

An unexpected voice sounded nearby.

"The Fairwood is home to many creatures of Faerie," Fionn drawled in his smooth, languid tone. I grimaced, then quickly smoothed my face to show no emotion. I was trying my best to remain neutral, but I couldn't deny that I had taken an instant dislike to Fionn and his mother.

"The elves—who I daresay put the 'fair' in 'Fair Folk'—have the distinction of being the oldest residents of the forest, stewards of the land and its ancient earth magic. Newer residents, such as the centaurs and the nymphs—" he nodded at Paxen, Lilliana and Aryn "—also have access to some of the Fairwood's magic, but not to the same extent as the elves."

"Newer residents?" Rhyss echoed.

Fionn laughed. Even his laugh grated on me—I could feel the condescension dripping from that quick sound. "I suppose, by human standards, all of Faerie would be considered ancient. But yes, some Fae races are older than the others."

Fionn turned in his seat and spurred his horse forward so he was once more riding side-by-side with his mother in the front. Eyeing his back with obvious distaste, Paxen lowered his voice and said, "*Older* doesn't necessarily mean *better*."

Lilliana snorted in smothered laughter, turning it into a cough when Fionn and Hahna glanced over their shoulders at her. The pair of elves turned back around, and Lilliana rolled her eyes.

"How long until we reach the Fairwood?" I asked.

"A few days," Paxen said. "It's straight south of the palace. If we veer east right now, we'd find ourselves in the Fire Mountain region, where Itan was from. Past the Fairwood is the Lonely Sea, the home of the selkies."

"What about the lake that Aryn hails from?"

Aryn sniffed, turning her head slightly to join in the conversation. "Lake? What lake? I don't know where you got the idea that I was a water nymph."

"Oh." I blinked, taken aback. "Lord Chela said your home was stillwater. I just thought—"

"I am a celestial nymph," Aryn said proudly. "The High Chancellor probably said my home was stillwater because only the reflection of my star in a perfectly still body of water can bring me to earth, and only at night." She looked around at our group with disdain. "I doubt anyone here will be able to travel to my home region. Perhaps I will be the only one to gain the approval of the heavens, if that is the case."

So, Aryn was a celestial nymph. *That explains a lot*, I thought. Aryn had an otherworldly beauty—more than usual for the Fae, who were renowned for their exquisite features—and the cold, detached demeanor to match.

But now that I knew Aryn's background, I cast an appraising eye skyward, where a few billowy clouds floated in a calm blue sky. Aryn was right—how would the other royal hopefuls reach her home region to be tested?

I shook off the thought. That was a problem for the would-be royals to figure out, not Rhyss and me. I could practically hear Rhyss's voice in my head: *Thank the gods.* I chuckled.

"What's so funny?" Rhyss asked, looking at me.

"I'll tell you later," I said.

We fell silent, letting the sound of our horses' hooves mark our time on the road.

36

— · —

CHAPTER THIRTY-SIX

ONCE THE SKY BEGAN to turn pink and orange with the approaching sunset, Paxen announced that we should think about setting up camp. Rhyss and I chose to camp with the group, mostly because there didn't seem to be any signs of civilization nearby. Traveling through the Faerie wilds at night by ourselves didn't appeal to us. Fortunately, we were used to the rigors of travel and sleeping in less-than-ideal conditions, so we weren't bothered.

Not that there was anything "less-than-ideal" about our group's overnight provisions.

Once we found a good spot, Fionn and his mother Hahna immediately saw to their own comfort, ignoring the pointed inquiries from the rest of us about making a fire or cooking food. After they tied their horses to a nearby tree, they combined their magical efforts together to create their sleeping quarters.

Rhyss eyed the elves' tent. Although one could hardly call it that.

"I understand that magic makes things easier, but isn't that going a bit overboard?" Rhyss whispered to me, eyeing the building, so obviously out of place in the middle of the Fae wilderness. Their "tent" looked more like a small cottage, complete with ivy climbing up over one of its faux stone walls. It could have easily fit our entire group, and maybe a few extras, but once Fionn and Hahna had finished their magical creation, they had gone inside and firmly shut the wooden door against the oncoming night. And the rest of us.

I shook my head in disbelief. "If this is how lavish they are just camping in the wilderness, imagine how power reckless they would be as rulers," I said, pitching my voice low enough for only Rhyss to hear.

He waggled his eyebrows at me, then turned his attention to shaking out our bedrolls and placing them near the fire which he, along with Paxen, had built. Lilliana had helped by gathering wood. Aryn couldn't be bothered to get her hands dirty, and Bettan had disappeared for a time, only to reappear to tell us she was leaving.

Oddly, no one except Rhyss and me seemed concerned about this.

"Nightfall is coming. Where are you going? You'll be safer with the group," I said.

"Nightfall is coming. That's exactly why I'm leaving," Bettan said. She lifted her head and sniffed the air, turning her head sharply to the left, then the right. She looked as alert as a dog on the hunt. "I can sense water nearby, and I sleep better next to water."

"I'll go with you," Aryn said. "I'd like to find a still body of water and get back to my sisters in the sky, even if it's just for a night. I've been gone several days now, and I miss them."

"Ah, all right," I said. "I'm glad you'll be together. We'll see you in the morning, then."

"Goodnight," Bettan said, before she turned and headed into the trees that lined the road. Aryn didn't bother saying anything, just turned her head haughtily and followed Bettan into the darkening trees that lined the side of the road.

Lilliana came up next to me, putting her hand on my shoulder. "Do not take offense at Aryn. She is actually much sweeter than she seems."

I snorted. "Not to be rude, but I find that hard to believe."

"No, really, she is. But she is under a lot of pressure right now, with the Trials. When she announced she was going to participate, her star sisters disowned her."

I looked at Lilliana sharply. "Disowned her? Why?"

Lilliana sighed. "The celestial Fae tend to take a disinterested view in the affairs of the earthly Fae. They view themselves as above—literally and figuratively—our petty little concerns. I understand Aryn was also betrothed to another one of the celestial Fae, an ancient air being, and her father was furious when she broke off the engagement."

"She broke off the engagement? What was her reason?"

Lilliana shrugged. "She never told me, so I don't really know. But she's a passionate sort. My guess is she fell in love with someone else. She's too aware of her heritage and duty to go against tradition otherwise."

Lilliana turned away to talk to Paxen, and I sat down next to the fire, mulling over our conversation. Something about Lilliana's statement bothered me, but whatever I was on the verge of piecing together remained just out of reach.

I heard a rustling nearby, and I looked up in time to see Lilliana melt into the tree line. I blinked as I looked again. "Did Lilliana just blend into a tree?"

Paxen laughed. "Yes. Just as Aryn wanted to be back with her people for a short while, Lilliana felt the same. We'll see her in the morning."

"You're not leaving too, are you?" I asked Paxen.

"And be away from your fine company, and that of Lord Rhyss?" Paxen smiled. "When we reach the Fairwood, I'll head home, for as long as the Trials take place there. And of course, you and Lord Rhyss are welcome to stay in my home. But I don't mind camping. Besides—" his eyes twinkled as he nodded toward the silent stone cottage "—someone's got to watch out for those two."

Rhyss and I laughed, and for a few moments, I actually thought officiating the Trials might not be so bad.

37

CHAPTER THIRTY-SEVEN

I COULDN'T SLEEP AGAIN that night.

Perhaps it was the worry over my father, left behind in a Faerie dungeon, or the fact that the Trials had now officially started. Perhaps it was knowing that Rhyss and I were no closer to having a curse-free marriage, and, at the rate things were going, should probably just accept this inevitability instead of hoping the High Chancellor would be able to give us a blessing instead of my father. Most likely it was a combination of all of those things. But as I tossed and turned in my bedroll, I sighed and sat up, exasperated at myself for my racing thoughts and knowing sleep wouldn't come easily because of them.

Our camp's fire had died down, giving off just enough light and warmth to touch Rhyss, Paxen, and me curled up next it. But the light didn't penetrate beyond where we lay. I gasped and rubbed at my eyes, unsure if they were playing tricks on me.

A shadowy, wraith-like figure floated on the edge of our camp, its tattered, dark grey misty robes swirling around where its feet would be. It faced the tree line.

At my gasp, the creature turned to face me. In the dark of night, its crimson eyes glowed. My eyes widened. It was the nightmare figure from a few nights ago.

The night Itan had died.

And although I had no concrete proof, I just knew that it was tied to Itan's death somehow.

And I also knew, with unerring certainty, its presence meant another death was coming.

I stood up. Or, I tried. With my legs still tangled up in my bedroll, and my movements slow from being in a not-quite-sleeping-but-not-quite-awake state, I started to stand and tripped over myself, landing heavily on my hands and knees. And still trapped in my bedroll.

I turned to Rhyss, shaking him. But except for a little groan, he didn't stir. On the other side of the dim fire, Paxen also remained fast asleep. How could they sleep through all this commotion?

"Rhyss, wake up," I said. "There's a—I see—"

But I couldn't finish my warning. I wanted to say, *There's a phantom here*, or *I see a ghost*, but I kept choking on the words.

The mark on my cheek flared to life, like an icy finger traced its way down the near-invisible scar. I shivered.

The wraith's red eyes kindled once more, and I cowered, suddenly paralyzed with fear. The phantom hissed and then darted into the trees.

I sat back heavily. Putting my shaking hand to my chest did nothing to calm my frenzied heartbeat or slow my frantic breathing.

I reached out again to touch Rhyss's shoulder, but all he did was snore and turn on his side.

The paralysis I had felt moments ago left me as quickly as it had overtaken me. Now all I felt was a deep weariness. Maybe I was just imagining things.

Although the glow of the campfire seemed like the eyes of the wraith, watching my every move, and the occasional pops from the fire morphed into an angry phantom hiss.

I settled into my bedroll and closed my eyes, willing much needed sleep to claim me.

And then a scream pierced the night air.

I sat up, sleep completely forgotten. Nearby, Rhyss and Paxen also woke up.

Fionn appeared in the doorway of the cottage, his normally unreadable face frantic. "Mother? Where's Mother?"

"She's not with you?" I asked.

"No—I woke up when I heard that scream—she's not here—"

Another scream pierced the air. I scrambled to my feet as I looked toward the trees, debating the wisdom of running into the dark forest. Rhyss hastily grabbed his sword and belted it around his waist.

A wild crashing through the trees caught all our attention. As one, we turned to face whatever was coming.

Hahna stumbled out of the trees, wild-eyed. Fionn rushed to his mother, catching her just as she tripped over a tree root and fell, sobbing, into his arms.

Fionn helped Hahna over to the fire pit, while Paxen threw some new logs on the flames. Hahna sank down on a log by the fire, still crying uncontrollably.

"Hahna?" I said gently. "What's happened?"

Hahna didn't answer me, unable to control herself.

Fionn stepped back, horrified as he got a good look at his arms—and his mother—in the firelight.

Fresh, bright red blood coated Fionn's bare arms.

The same blood that completely drenched the bodice of Hahna's nightdress.

38

— ◦ —

CHAPTER THIRTY-EIGHT

WE EXPLODED IN A flurry of questions.

"What's happened?" Rhyss put his hand on his sword hilt, ready to fight.

"Mother, are you hurt?" Fionn dropped to his knees in front of Hahna. "Have you been attacked? Who attacked you?"

In between hysterical sobs, Hahna choked out, "I-I'm fine. Th-This is not my b-blood."

"Then, who—?"

Hahna pointed toward the forest, her voice coming out in breathless gasps. "A-Aryn. Bettan. At the ... at the lake. It may be ... too late."

I straightened. Rhyss drew his sword, stepping to my side to accompany me into the woods. Fionn and Paxen both looked ready for action, but they didn't move. Instead, they just looked at me.

Oh! I realized. *They're waiting for orders ... from me.*

"Fionn," I said. "Do you want to stay with your mother, or—"

The elf bared his teeth in a menacing snarl. "Whatever or whoever did this to my mother must pay. I'll go with you and Lord Rhyss."

"All right, then." I turned to the centaur. "Paxen, stay here and watch over Hahna."

Paxen nodded.

"Let's go." I headed into the dark forest, Rhyss and Fionn on my heels. We didn't bother trying to be quiet as we made our way, figuring speed was more important. Besides, any advantage of surprise we might have had would have been ruined by Hahna's earlier screaming.

Once we were a few steps in, I stopped, looking up to find the moon overhead so I could get my bearings. I wished I had thought to ask Hahna how to find the lake, but it was too late now.

"Look!" Rhyss pointed.

I saw a dark shadow on the base of a nearby tree, at about my shoulder height. "*Illumine*," I whispered. A cold, silver ball of light appeared above my hand. I sent it toward the tree, curious to see what Rhyss had noticed.

Part of me wished he hadn't seen anything.

It was a handprint, perfectly outlined in fresh blood.

"Did Hahna do this?" Rhyss wondered, peering at the handprint over my shoulder.

"I'm not sure. Maybe?" I thought of the grey wraith I had seen—or maybe imagined—earlier in the evening.

"No, I don't think so," Fionn said. A little of his characteristic haughtiness had crept back into his voice, now that he was away from the shocking sight of his mother covered in blood. "This handprint is too big to be hers."

We continued on, but hadn't gone far when Rhyss grabbed my arm. "Over there!"

Another bloody handprint, similar to the first, appeared on a tree to our left. And then, a few steps later, another one on a tree to our right.

Studying them, I noticed that the hands were oriented in a rather specific way....

"Rhyss," I said. "Look at these prints. Does it seem to you—"

"Like they're pointing at something?" Rhyss finished. He shuddered. "Yes. Whether or not that's a good thing, I don't know."

"It's almost like they're showing us the path to take. I'm not sure I like this."

"Me neither, but what choice do we have?"

A good point. But still, the idea of following a trail marked by bloody handprints did not sit well with me.

It didn't seem to sit well with my companions, either. By unspoken agreement, we drew closer together, walking just a bit quieter than before.

The silence suited me. I could feel a headache starting to form. Lack of sleep always affected my spell casting, although I was skilled enough now to work through my exhaustion. I just paid for it in other ways that my body let me know about. I sighed soundlessly, knowing there was little I could do about it.

I sent my light ahead to find other handprints. They didn't always follow a straight line, and there was a time or two when we had to backtrack because we lost the trail.

And yet, even if we did get a little lost, a new handprint would appear before us to point us in the right direction. So we never strayed off the path too much. Which, in a strange way, was comforting. I didn't want to be lost—but I also didn't want to wander the dark woods with an invisible presence guiding me via bloody handprints.

I had been so intent on following the gruesome trail that I nearly missed the change in the forest.

But Rhyss didn't. He whispered, "The trees are thinning up ahead. And the air smells different."

He was right—the air had that cool tang that signaled we were near water.

We quickened our pace. Rhyss, in the lead, stopped suddenly and then gave a low whistle.

The moon shone overhead in the open area, providing enough light that we could see the deep, calm water of a lake stretching out before us. The water lapped at a pale, sandy shore, mostly barren except for some driftwood.

And the outstretched body of a woman, lying facedown. Her blue-green hair was fanned out around her head, so her features were hidden.

Rhyss gently turned the lifeless woman over, pushing her hair out of the way. Even without Rhyss's quick intake of breath, I would have known who it was.

Aryn.

39

—·—

CHAPTER THIRTY-NINE

HER UNMATCHED BEAUTY HAD been marred by deep marks that ran the length of each side of her face, from ear to chin. Two long marks, just far apart as if someone had taken their index and middle finger and scratched her pale cheeks with their obscenely long fingernails. The blood drying on her face was turning black, as if she had been dead for hours, although the blood on Hahna had been relatively fresh.

With her long hair to one side, we could see a bright red puddle underneath Aryn's head and neck. Her sightless eyes stared up at the moonlit sky overhead, never to take in another sunrise.

I turned around and stumbled away a few paces before I threw up in the scrub that bordered the lakeshore.

Rhyss immediately knelt by my side, holding me steady and pushing my lavender braid out of the way so I wouldn't accidentally throw up on the ends of my hair. He pulled out his waterskin. "Here."

Gratefully, I took the offered waterskin and opened it, tipping a bit of water into my mouth. I swished it around and spat to the side, trying to get rid of the taste of vomit. My stomach roiled, and I fought another wave of nausea that threatened to come up. When I thought I had things under control, I took a deep swallow and then passed the waterskin back to Rhyss. "Thanks."

I stood on shaky legs and looked at where Aryn lay. "We've seen dead bodies before. I don't know why this got to me so much."

Rhyss stood, looking grim as he steadied me. "Because usually they're other mercenaries who fell in a fair fight. Sometimes they're people who've done much evil, and deserved what was coming to them. This is neither."

Fionn looked up and down the length of the moonlit beach. "But where is—"

From the direction of the darkened woods, a twig snapped.

The three of us were on instant alert. Rhyss stepped in front of me, raising his sword.

Bettan stumbled out of the forest, near the area where Fionn, Rhyss, and I had emerged just a few moments ago. *Had we passed her in the darkness? But how?*

The selkie made her shaky way toward us, holding her hands out in front of her. For balance? She had never shown such a need before. But tonight she definitely seemed disoriented, like she had just transformed into her human form for the first time.

I sent my spell light toward Bettan. Coupled with the moon's glow that lit our little beach, it revealed the selkie's blood-stained hands. Similar red slashes decorated her formerly demure grey dress.

"Oh my gods," Rhyss breathed.

Part of me wanted to run to the selkie, to see if she was okay. But caution held me back. Something about her seemed off....

"Bettan?" I said uncertainly.

The selkie opened her mouth to speak. But instead of words, an inhuman shriek tumbled out of her. Her eyes flashed red briefly, an eerie imitation of what had happened when we had found Itan dead just a day ago.

Rhyss and Fionn both stepped in front of me, swords ready. I threw up my right hand and shouted a warding spell, bracing myself in case I needed to throw more power into our shield or conjure magical attacks of my own.

But Bettan didn't try to attack us. Instead, she kept wailing. And perhaps my eyes deceived me, but I thought I saw a thin line of grey smoke trail from her mouth into the air. When the last of the smoke had disappeared, Bettan stopped shrieking.

The selkie stiffened, then crumpled to the sand.

We waited, apprehensive, but Bettan didn't stir. Fionn put his sword away. "Is she—?"

I lowered my ward. "I'm not sure."

I sketched a quick spell at Bettan, reluctant to approach her without some reassurance. I breathed a sigh of relief. "She's not dead ... and she's not dangerous."

"I hope," Rhyss muttered. His sword was still in his hand.

The three of us walked over to where the selkie lay. I started to reach out, but Fionn stopped me and shook his head. "Stay back, Lady Farrah. I will see to her."

He knelt down and touched Bettan's shoulder. She groaned and shifted, then opened her eyes. "Where am I?"

Fionn frowned. "You don't know?"

The selkie groaned again. "I ... I'm not sure." She started to sit up.

"Here. Let me help you."

"Thank you." Bettan coughed, then pushed her hair back from her face. She froze as she got a good look at her hands. "Oh my ... oh my ..."

"Did something attack you?" I asked gently.

"I—I don't remember."

"What do you remember?"

"I ..." Her eyes widened in horror. "I was standing on the shore ... Aryn was coming back down from the stars ... and then I don't remember anything after that except for a brief moment, when she was bleeding on the shore. I ... I think I did it."

"What?!" The question was overly loud coming from all three of us, and Bettan winced.

"I—I didn't mean to. I don't know ... what came over me ..."

"It was you?" Fionn looked ready to strangle Bettan, and she shied away from him. "You killed Aryn ... did you kill Itan as well? Did you attack my mother?"

"I—no! I didn't kill Itan!" Bettan put a hand to her head, massaging her temple as if a headache had suddenly blossomed there. "I .. I don't think I did. No, no, I'm sure I didn't. As for your mother ... I don't know? I can't remember. Why can't I remember?"

"You don't sound sure," Fionn accused. He turned to me. "By her own admittance, she killed Aryn. She most likely tried to kill my mother. I demand justice. Immediately."

"What would you have me do?" I asked.

"Justice, my lady. Execute her."

He grabbed the selkie by her long hair and pulled her to him. She yelped, instantly falling silent when a sharp dagger appeared at her throat.

"Or better yet, Lady Farrah. Let me."

40

Chapter Forty

Bettan's eyes grew wide as she stared at us in a silent plea. Fionn twisted his knife ever so slightly, and a small bead of blood formed at one edge.

I put out a hand, trying to placate the elf. "I admit it looks suspicious, Fionn, but—"

"If we don't take action now, this selkie will murder us all in our beds before the Trials are even truly underway!"

Fionn had a point. But I didn't want to agree to a decision so final, even if the surrounding evidence did look bad for Bettan. Beside me, Rhyss stirred uncomfortably, and I knew he was thinking the same thing.

"Fionn, think," Rhyss said. "Killing Bettan here won't bring Aryn back. And we won't be any closer to answers, either."

Fionn gave me a hard stare. "Well?"

I glanced at Rhyss. His brow was furrowed and his lips had thinned into a hard line, but he shook his head at me, as if to say, *This is completely your decision.*

And, unfortunately, he was right.

I pressed my lips together, thinking. Slowly, I said, "Lord Rhyss is right, we have more questions than answers right now, and killing Bettan won't help us find those answers."

Fionn's face twisted into an ugly frown. But before he could argue with me, I continued speaking.

"But Fionn, you are also correct. Bettan's story is questionable, at best. And if she is guilty, it would be foolish to let her run free."

Bettan gave an involuntary cry, and Fionn's frown changed into a smirk of triumph.

"So, what I propose is this: Bettan is no longer eligible to participate in the Trials. I will contact Lord Chela so she can be imprisoned in the palace dungeon, where her true judgment will await until after the Trials are over."

Rhyss nodded. "A wise decision, Lady Farrah."

Fionn ground his teeth. "I have no choice but to agree, my lady. I just hope we don't regret this decision later."

I hoped so too.

A feeling of finality settled over me, as if some unseen force had witnessed our speech and had locked something into place. Looking around the group, I could tell they all felt it too. Now that it was settled, Fionn pushed Bettan away from him and strode over to the lake edge, looking over the calm water with a stormy expression. Bettan hunched over, weeping.

"If you could keep an eye on things here for a bit," I said to Rhyss, "I'll call Lord Chela."

Rhyss nodded, and I turned away to look for a quiet spot to cast my spell.

A hand gripped my ankle, holding me in place. I looked down to see Bettan staring up at me, her free hand reaching toward me in supplication.

"Please," she whispered. "You must understand. Even though I loved him too, I would never have killed her."

Rhyss leaned down and gently pulled the weeping selkie away from me. Holding her firmly, he said, "Go on, make your call. I've got things under control here."

I nodded and moved away from the group, and away from where Aryn lay. I conjured a calling spell and waited. Fortunately, I didn't have to wait long until Steward Henry's face appeared, floating above my outstretched hand.

"Lady Farrah! Good to see you." Henry frowned. "Although it's rather late to be calling, don't you think?"

I sighed. "I wish I didn't have to call. Here's what's happening ..."

I quickly outlined the details of Aryn's death, leaving out my nighttime vision of the grey spectre. I still wasn't sure it hadn't been a trick of my eyes, or an odd dream.

Henry's frown grew deeper as I relayed my tale. "Another death? This is not good."

"Lord Chela did say the Trials were dangerous."

"Dangerous, yes. Lethal, rarely. It takes a lot to kill a Fae. And the Trials have barely begun."

"I'm not sure how we're supposed to get Aryn back to her people. And we probably can't move on until Bettan has been collected and taken back to the palace."

Steward Henry paused. "Have you had a chance to examine the body, Lady Farrah? Do you think ... do you think whatever killed Itan also killed Aryn?"

I hesitated, not wanting to talk about my night visions. And, from experience, I knew I wouldn't be able to talk about them anyway. "I haven't looked her over in-depth, but I suspect her death and Itan's might be linked."

The steward sighed. "If you think that, even in the slightest, then the best thing to do would be to burn the body. I'll send word to her family in the celestial region. As for Bettan, I will arrange to have someone get her. You and the others should be able to get on the road in the morning without worrying about what to do with her."

"Thank you, Henry."

The steward scrubbed a hand across his face, looking like all the centuries he had kept at bay by living in Faerie had fallen on him all at once. "With Itan and Aryn both dead, and Bettan disqualified, that only leaves Paxen and Fionn as potentials for the throne. Of the two, Fionn has the better claim to the crown."

"Should we call off the Trials?"

"No, no. Once underway, it must be seen to completion. But I do wonder if something else might happen soon."

I shuddered. "Let's hope not. But Rhyss and I will keep our eyes and ears open."

Henry sighed. "That's all the High Chancellor and I can hope for. Thank you."

We said our goodbyes, and I ended the calling spell. I rejoined Rhyss, who still held a tight grip on Bettan. The poor selkie. Personally, I believed her when she said she hadn't been responsible for Aryn's death. But we also couldn't take a chance on her unless we were entirely sure of her innocence.

Once she was safely locked away in the palace, I wondered if the grey spectre that kept haunting my dreams would continue following me, or go after Bettan.

"What now?" Rhyss asked me.

I sighed. "We burn the body. Then we head back to camp, where Steward Henry said he would arrange for someone to come get Bettan and deliver her to the palace."

At my words, Bettan let out a loud wail and began sobbing harder. Her noise nearly distracted me from what was happening nearby.

41

— · —

CHAPTER FORTY-ONE

JUST A FEW PACES from where we stood, one of Aryn's hands twitched. Her fingers twisted, claw-like, and began scratching at the sand. Her other hand twitched and swiped against the ground.

My right cheek throbbed with sudden cold.

"Look!" Rhyss's horrified voice drew everyone's attention to the dead nymph, impossibly coming back to life. Already Aryn was half-propped up on the ground, using slow, jerky movements.

Fionn cursed and drew his sword. Rhyss looked torn, knowing if he grabbed his weapon, he'd have to let go of Bettan.

I shouted a spell, and a ball of purple-blue flame shot from my hand toward Aryn. No, not Aryn. Whatever grotesque creature had taken over her body.

My magic hit the creature square in the chest, spreading quickly to become a violet bloom of fire. I conjured another fireball and sent it after the first, where it hit Aryn's long, beautiful blue-green hair. Flames licked up her tresses, and she snarled at me, her eyes glowing red.

"Fionn!" I yelled. "Cut off her head!"

Even though she was half-engulfed in purple fire, Aryn still managed to stand. Fionn ran forward from where he had been standing

behind Rhyss, Bettan, and me. I stepped in front of Rhyss and
Bettan, readying yet another ball of fire.

Aryn snarled again and lunged at me. I threw the fireball at
Aryn even as I covered my face with my free hand. Behind me,
Rhyss yelled, and I heard a swish as he drew his sword. Bettan
cried out, and then her wailing subsided into muted sobs.

Aryn's fingers swiped at my arm. I braced myself for the feel of
nails scraping down my skin, but all I felt was a light, short scratch
before her arm fell away.

I lowered my arm and looked up. A headless body burned at my
feet. A few paces away, Aryn's head lay on the sand, where it had
landed when Fionn neatly removed it from her neck.

I shuddered. "Thanks," I said to Fionn.

The normally indifferent elf looked shaken. "Don't mention
it." He glanced down at Aryn's severed head, now sightless again,
covered in blood and sand and surrounded by a cloud of tangled
blue-green hair. "Really, please don't."

Rhyss hugged me from behind. "Are you all right?"

I leaned into him, drawing strength from his presence. "Yes."

I stayed in his arms for a moment more, then untangled myself
so I could look around. Rhyss resheathed his sword. Bettan still
wept uncontrollably, too shaken to even think of running away.

Fionn knelt down, wiping his blade on the grass nearby.

I turned to Rhyss. "Why don't you take the others back to the
camp, and wait for whoever Steward Henry is sending? I'll take
care of things here and meet you in a bit."

Rhyss hesitated. "Are you sure? If she ... that thing ... should
suddenly 'wake up' again—"

"Thanks to Fionn's quick actions, I don't think she will." I made sure to pitch my voice a little louder so the elf could hear me. I couldn't be sure, but I thought I saw his chest swell with pride. "I'll be fine."

Rhyss nodded reluctantly. He turned to Fionn and Bettan. "All right, everyone. Let's head back."

Fionn stood up and sheathed his now-clean sword. He took a firm grip on one of Bettan's unresisting arms. Rhyss took a deep breath and raised his eyebrows at me before taking Bettan's other arm. The three of them disappeared into the dark woods.

Alone now with Aryn—or, more accurately, what was left of her—I sketched a few quick symbols of containment and protection over the area. I lowered my head briefly in respect. "May your soul find the stars again, lady."

I conjured more magical fire, sending it to gently cover Aryn's head and body. While I was confident my protection spells would hold, I forced myself to watch the fire burn until nothing was left but ash, which blew away in the breeze. With a final sigh, I left the lake, so deceptively peaceful, to join the others.

I returned to the camp to find everyone awake and alert. Hahna had gotten herself under control, and was sipping some tea from a battered tin cup that Paxen had produced from his pack. Rhyss and Fionn were conversing quietly with each other. Bettan slumped against a nearby tree, her hands tied behind her back.

"I thought Steward Henry's messenger would have arrived by now," I said, looking around the camp.

Rhyss shrugged. "We haven't seen anybody yet."

"Hmm." I frowned as I called the Steward. His face appeared above my outstretched hand almost immediately.

"Ah, Lady Farrah. I am glad you called again."

"What's wrong?"

Steward Henry sighed. "I put a message out, but no one wanted to go. Since the former king and queen died, no one's been able to keep the Unseelie Fae in check ... and nighttime is particularly perilous for those of the Seelie Court."

I ground my teeth in frustration. "I understand. But what are we to do with Bettan? We can't leave her here, but I also don't want to keep her with us."

"I can send someone in the morning, but they won't reach you until at least the afternoon."

Footsteps sounded behind me. Rhyss said, "If you can do that, I will wait here with Bettan, and then catch up with Lady Farrah after."

"Are you sure?" Henry and I asked at the same time.

Rhyss nodded. "That's fine. Lady Farrah will be with Paxen and Fionn, both of whom can protect her. I'll leave immediately after Bettan is picked up, even if it means traveling at night."

"Oh, Rhyss—" I started.

"I'll be vigilant, I promise."

Henry stroked his chin thoughtfully. "This will work, then. I'll dispatch someone at first light. Thank you, Lord Rhyss."

"Of course." Rhyss inclined his head toward the Steward.

We ended the call soon after, but none of us felt like sleeping. Fionn and Hahna talked quietly, just outside their fancy tent-cottage. Why they didn't go inside to talk, I wasn't sure. Paxen bustled about the camp, wanting to keep busy. Bettan stared into the fire, her face blank. Rhyss leaned against a tree and closed his eyes, but I knew he wasn't asleep.

I sat next to Bettan. "What did you mean, back at the lake? Even though you loved him—loved who? What were you talking about?"

Silent tears streamed down Bettan's face. "Didn't you know? Itan and I were betrothed, before he left me to be with Aryn. I was hurt by his betrayal, but I never would have wished death on either one of them. I loved him. I love him still."

For a few moments, only her sniffles and the crackle of the fire in the camp behind me punctuated the night air.

"What were you doing at the lake, anyway?"

Bettan wiped at her eyes. "I'm a selkie. I like to sleep in the sight of water. So I was sleeping on the shore, when a splashing sound woke me up."

She touched her temples and winced. "The rest ... it's a bit fuzzy. I—I think Aryn was drowning. Which doesn't make sense, as a nymph of two elements. But she was ... fighting something. I couldn't see what. She was ... screaming. I ... changed into my selkie form and swam out to save her.

"I grabbed her with my teeth and held on ... and the next thing I knew, we were on the shore. She was bleeding, and I had her blood all over me."

Hmm, interesting. "To carry a full grown Fae from deep water to shore in your seal form would be near impossible," I said.

"I—I suppose? I don't know, I just know I needed to help her ..."

"What was Aryn doing out there, anyway?"

"She's a celestial nymph. I'm sure she wanted to go home for a bit, to be with her sisters in the stars."

"Wait. You said she was a nymph of two elements. What was the other one?"

"Water." Bettan frowned. "So she shouldn't have been drowning."

Before I could ponder that fully, Hahna walked over. "Lady Farrah, with your permission, I would like to go back with Bettan."

I looked up at the elf, who now seemed fully composed and in control of herself. "Are you sure? Wouldn't you rather stay with your son?" I frowned, thinking. "I believe we are headed to your home region, eventually."

"We are, but the Seelie Court palace is closer. As my son has repeatedly reminded me." She sniffed. "My dear boy is just worried about his mother's safety, like a good son should be."

"If you wish, then you're welcome to go back," I said. "But before you do, I would know one thing."

"Of course, Lady Farrah. If I can help you in any way ..."

"What were you doing at the lake, earlier tonight?"

Hahna blushed, and I could see a hint of the younger woman that had captivated King Finvarra at one point. "It's going to sound so silly, Lady Farrah."

"Go ahead."

She sighed. "When I can't sleep, I like to walk under the stars. It's so peaceful. I was wandering along the lakeshore when I saw Aryn fall from the sky."

"So you witnessed Aryn drowning? And Bettan swimming out to save her?"

Hahna frowned. "I don't know about that. I was on the far side of the lake. By the time I reached them, Aryn was dead and Bettan tried to attack me."

Bettan didn't argue, just sniffed and turned away.

"Then what happened?" I asked.

"Bettan was crazy, snarling and clawing at me like some enraged cat, but I fought her off. She ran into the woods. I hurried back to the camp to find all of you and get help."

I nodded grimly, remembering what happened after that.

"Is there anything else, Lady Farrah?"

I sighed. "No. Get some sleep." I looked at the nighttime sky, which was now decidedly lighter. "Although it doesn't seem like there's much left of the night to sleep in."

"I suppose not. Good night."

Hahna went back to the tent-cottage, and I sighed again, thinking over the night's events. A light touch on my shoulder startled me.

"Forgive me, Lady Farrah," Paxen said. "But if you would like to get some rest, I'd be happy to continue watching Bet—the prisoner."

Bettan still sat turned away from me, but the slump in her shoulders suggested she was still crying. Over at the tree, Rhyss didn't stir, and I wondered if he had actually fallen asleep.

"Thank you, Paxen," I said, standing up. I settled into my bedroll and closed my eyes. But my thoughts continued to race, and I knew that sleep would not come easy. If it came at all.

42

—·—

CHAPTER FORTY-TWO

LILLIANA STEPPED OUT FROM the trunk of a stately oak at the road's edge. "Good morning, everyone."

I groaned, blearily opening my eyes against the weak morning sun. I poked Rhyss, who snored next to me. When had he moved from the tree to his bedroll?

His snore stopped halfway, and he cracked open one eye. "Just a few more hours?"

"I wish," I smirked. "Time to get up."

Paxen was moving about the camp, rather slowly. The poor centaur. He had made good on his promise to watch Bettan, but now paid for it with lack of sleep.

I sat up and stretched, wincing at how loud my back cracked.

Lilliana looked at the three of us, confused. "Did none of you get any sleep? I must say, sleeping in the oak last night was the best sleep I've had since going to the palace."

"It wasn't your tree, was it?" I thought Lilliana was from the Fairwood, same as Paxen and the elves.

"Oh, no," she laughed. "It was just a courtesy, from one dryad to another, to allow me to stay for the night."

"Getting back to your roots, as it were," Rhyss put in, more awake now, and we all groaned at the pun.

"I think I liked it better when you were still snoring away," I joked, smiling at Rhyss. He smirked at me.

My smile faded as I regarded Lilliana. "But to answer your question—no, we didn't get much sleep."

I outlined the night's events for the dryad, minus Bettan's comments about her broken engagement to Itan. Lilliana's cheerful countenance turned dark as I talked.

"So both Aryn and Itan are gone," Lilliana said. She sighed, tears shining in her eyes. "Poor Aryn. She didn't deserve to die in such a fashion. And I find it hard to believe that Bettan could be capable of such an act, but you never know what's truly in someone's heart."

I nodded, keeping my thoughts to myself.

A sudden slam startled us all. The door to the magicked cottage had been flung open, and Hahna stood in the doorway, blinking in the sunlight. Fionn appeared behind her, then moved past her to untie their horses.

"Ah, I see everyone is awake." She turned and fussed over Fionn. "Be careful out there, my son. Although perhaps I am in more danger, as I'll be waiting here with a murderer."

"I can break down the camp, since we'll be here all day anyway," Rhyss said, ignoring Hahna's pointed comments about *waiting with a murderer.* "Just take your things, I'll clean up the rest."

"That's easy enough." Hahna stepped away from the cottage door, then snapped her fingers. The building shimmered, then quickly collapsed in on itself, becoming the two packs she and her son had been carrying. She picked them up and held them out to Fionn, who secured them to the horses. "You were saying?"

Liliana turned her head slightly so Hahna and Fionn couldn't see her face, and rolled her eyes at me. I stifled a snort of laughter. Paxen raised his eyebrows. "Perfect. Let's get on the road, then."

While everyone else packed away their things, Rhyss pulled me aside. "Be safe out there."

"You as well. I hope Steward Henry's messenger gets here quickly."

"Me too. But don't worry. I'll be back with you before you know it."

He kissed the top of my forehead and then hugged me. I held on tightly, trying to fight the uneasy feeling that had settled over my heart.

From our original group of eight—nine, if you counted Itan—we were now down to seven. And of that seven, three were staying behind. That knowledge weighed on all of us; our entire group was rather subdued as we set out.

We settled into mostly the same lineup as yesterday—Fionn in the front, Lilliana and Paxen in the middle, and me bringing up the rear. I turned in my saddle to look back at the camp one last time.

Bettan hadn't moved from her position by the fire pit. Her eyes were closed and she sat extremely still; exhaustion must have finally overtaken her and she had fallen asleep. *I suppose there are worse ways to spend the day while you wait to be locked away*, I thought.

Hahna and Rhyss bustled about the remnants of our camp, cleaning, although it didn't look like Hahna was helping much. As if he felt me watching, Rhyss looked up, saw me, and waved cheerfully. Hahna straightened up, but didn't wave. She turned a thoughtful look on Rhyss.

And then my group turned a corner and the camp was out of sight.

I turned around in my seat, shivering. What was wrong with me? I resisted the urge to turn around and ride back to the camp. Rhyss would be fine. Steward Henry's messenger would reach them soon, and then Rhyss would join us. Everything would be fine.

"Are you well, Lady Farrah?" Lilliana had noticed my apprehension.

"Yes, thank you. I'm fine." Maybe if I kept saying I was fine, I would be.

"You've nothing to fear, Lady Farrah," Fionn said. Could he read my thoughts? I hoped not.

"Soon Steward Henry's messenger will take Bettan away, my mother will have an escort to get her safely back to the palace, and Lord Rhyss will rejoin us," Fionn continued. "We'll hardly notice their absence."

I nodded, more to reassure myself than because I agreed with Fionn's succinct assessment. We rode in silence for a bit. I found myself riding in front with Fionn, which suited me just fine now that his normally disagreeable mother was not traveling with us.

Which reminded me....

"Why didn't you go with your mother last night, to walk around the lake?" I asked.

"Hmm." Fionn looked thoughtful. "I suppose it was because I didn't hear her get up. Although I was sleeping right by her. I must have been more tired than I thought. I wonder why she didn't wake me to accompany her? I certainly wouldn't have let her go out in the Fae wilds at night by herself."

"Does she do that often? Take walks at night by herself?"

The elf frowned. "Not that I can remember. Perhaps before I was born, but not now."

Paxen came up to us. "Fionn, I know Bettan had mentioned some odd deaths among her people in the Lonely Sea, but without her with us, I'm not sure how we can approach them."

Fionn looked thoughtful. "That's a good point. Wasn't there a selkie who relocated to the Fairwood a while back?"

"Jahna? Do you think we should ask him?"

"It's a thought. Since it's official business ..."

I stopped listening to their conversation, mulling over my own thoughts. Why *hadn't* Hahna woken up her son to accompany her on a midnight walk around the lake? Especially since we were in wild country, with the Unseelie running around unchecked. Hadn't she been worried about her safety?

Or had she been lying to me?

43

—·—

Chapter Forty-Three

Paxen took a deep breath, enjoying the earthy tang of the woods around him. "Ah. It's good to be back home."

Fionn drew his horse beside Paxen, sharing a rare smile with the centaur. "In that, we are in agreement."

After a day and a half of traveling, we had reached the ancient Faerie wood known as the Fairwood. Fionn, Paxen, and Lilliana seemed lighter, more at ease now that they were home. I openly marveled at the stately, gorgeous forest that surrounded us.

As helpers-for-hire, Rhyss and I had traveled all over the Gifted Lands, and had seen our fair share of forests. But the Fairwood, with its home in the otherworldly land of Faerie and its roots literally—and liberally—steeped in magic, surpassed anything I had seen before.

The majestic trees stretched high into the sky, taller than our eyes could see. Any birds nesting in their branches would have been safe from hunters—I doubted arrows could have flown that high. Not that you could see their nests from where we stood, anyway. Each massive trunk would have taken at least two or three of us, holding hands, to encircle.

Each leaf and flower was exquisite in its perfection. There were no holes from bug bites, no damage from drought or rot. And the rich colors were so vivid, a master painter would weep to know the secrets of their creation. We'd seen such uncanny beauty in another forest back in the Gifted Lands—an area called the Hwisprian Woods that bordered Rhyss's home country of Bomora, which held an ancient magic of its own—but that forest's beauty was a pale shadow of what a true Faerie wood looked like.

"Glad to see you like it." Paxen smiled at me.

"It's beautiful," I said, still looking around. "And so peaceful."

"We consider ourselves the caretakers of the forest." Paxen indicated Lilliana, Fionn, and himself. "As we, and our people, have a deep connection with nature, certain things are considered taboo. Like hunting."

"But—I thought at the dinner the other night—" I stopped, unsure of how to continue.

"That we ate meat?" Paxen laughed. "Sometimes we do, depending on the circumstances. At the High Chancellor's dinner, we could hardly say no to the food presented to us. And when we are not in the Fairwood, we hunt like any other travelers would. But here, the animals are under our care, and are nearly as intelligent as us. In the Fairwood, we do not hunt, and we only eat meat if the animal died peacefully."

"Ah, good to know." I was grateful for the warning. I might have committed a major faux pas in the Fairwood without it.

We fell silent as we traveled further into the forest, soaking up the beauty that surrounded us.

A shout at the front of our group caught my attention. "Welcome back!"

An elf close to Fionn's age greeted us. Her long silver-white hair was looped in a braid-ring around her head, and a smile spread across her face as she jumped down from her perch and ran toward us. She had been sitting atop a pile of rocks on one side of the road. On the other side, two elven archers put down their bows and stood watching us. I swallowed hard, realizing I had been so distracted I hadn't even noticed them.

The woman stopped in front of Fionn's horse, reaching out to grab one of his hands with hers. "Cousin, you're back! Does this mean you return with good news?"

Fionn shook his head, another rare smile on his face. Two smiles in less than an hour! The Fairwood must be magical indeed, to elicit such a reaction from the normally cold and aloof Fionn.

"I'm afraid not, Genevieve," Fionn said to his cousin. "The Trials have barely begun, and we already have bad news. Two of those competing have died, and one has been disqualified."

Genevieve's aquamarine eyes grew wide. "Really? You'll have many stories to share at tonight's dinner, then."

Fionn raised an eyebrow. "I suppose I will. But a celebratory homecoming, already? We haven't even completed the Trials yet."

Genevieve giggled. "You know we in the Fairwood welcome any excuse to celebrate. Besides, it will be a great place to give and get gossip."

She squeezed her cousin's hand, then let go as she turned to the rest of us. "Well met, Lilliana, Paxen. Who is this you've brought with you?"

"Meet Lady Farrah," Paxen said. "Lord Chela, the High Chancellor, has appointed her the official judge of the Trials."

Genevieve raised an eyebrow. "Really? A human?" She looked me up and down. "Although—perhaps not all human?"

I nodded.

Genevieve turned to the others. "Has Lord Chela gone mad, sending an unknown, even if she is part Fae? Why could he not come himself? Or send Steward Henry in his place, who's been here so long he's practically Fae?"

"I believe Lord Chela is busy running the realm," Paxen said, a hint of admonishment in his voice. "And with two very violent and unexpected potential murders, in addition to other unsettling things happening around Faerie, I think both the High Chancellor and his Steward need to focus on other things right now."

Genevieve's mouth had dropped open when Paxen mentioned *murders*. She closed it abruptly, trying to hide her surprise. "Well. It will be a very interesting dinner tonight, indeed."

"Indeed."

Genevieve took in a deep breath. "Well, then. It is good to see you all. Rest, and I'll see you in a few hours."

Paxen nodded as Genevieve stepped back and waved us on. Fionn didn't move, letting the rest of us pass them. I figured he probably wanted to stay behind and catch up with his kin.

Lilliana said, "I'm going to find my sisters. I'll find you later tonight." She turned and blended into the deeper forest.

Paxen said, "Come with me. You can rest in my home until it's time to attend the dinner."

"About that," I said as I followed Paxen. "What is this dinner that Genevieve kept talking about?"

Paxen stopped, looking over his shoulder at me. "My apologies, I forgot that as a newcomer to the Fairwood, you wouldn't be used to our ways. When one of the Fairwood comes home from an extended trip, it is customary to host a community-wide dinner upon their return. Partly to celebrate their safe homecoming, and partly to get news from the outside. With the Trials underway, the residents of the Fairwood are going to be quite curious about what's happening. And about you."

The centaur continued walking. Fortunately, with his back to me he couldn't see my apprehensive glance. I sighed, hurrying after him.

As if meeting the original five royal hopefuls hadn't been scary enough. Now I had to undergo the scrutiny of the entire Fae community of the ancient Fairwood.

Alone.

Lovely.

44

—·—

CHAPTER FORTY-FOUR

EVEN THOUGH THE THOUGHT of being paraded in front of the entire Fairwood community later that night had me feeling unsettled, it didn't stop me from falling into a deep slumber once Paxen and I reached his home.

I woke up in semi-darkness. The shadows in my room had considerably grown darker, and I guessed it was now at least late afternoon.

I yawned and rolled out of the very comfortable—and surprisingly human-sized—bed. Paxen had given me a guest room made for non-centaurs, saying he preferred the large, plush rug in his own room that was devoid of any other furniture.

Opening the door, I blinked against the onslaught of fading sunlight that hit my eyes. The window was in just the right spot that the setting sun shone right into my open bedroom door.

"Ah, you're awake!"

I could hear Paxen's voice, but with that darn light in my eyes I couldn't see him. I stepped away from the door, willing my eyes to adjust.

My centaur host solidified in front of me, wearing a formal-looking silver and purple velvet vest over his lean torso. The vest bore a lone silver leaf on the left side, affixed to the fabric above his heart. Paxen had braided his long black hair back, threading it with ribbons that matched his clothing.

I nodded appreciatively. "Fancy."

Paxen blushed and ducked his head. "Thank you. It's always a big occasion when the Fairwood community gathers."

"What does that mean? Or is it just a decoration?" I pointed at the silver leaf.

Paxen looked down at the leaf, then back up at me, beaming. "It's a sign of my standing in the centaur community. As I grow older, and do more for the good of my fellow Fae, I will gain more symbols of my accomplishments."

"Older? How old are you, if you don't mind my asking?" The centaur didn't look much older than me.

"Oh, I'm only 112 years old. Practically a child, in the eyes of my peers."

I blinked in surprise. 'Only' 112?

"Well, I hope I look as good as you when I reach your age." I surveyed my host again. "Do I need to dress up, too?"

"You don't have to, but it might help you feel more at ease with everyone else." He eyed my traveling clothes, now wrinkled from my nap. "Since you are the High Chancellor's representative, and all."

I smirked. "Point taken."

I ducked back into the bedroom. I called forth a spell light, sending it above my head so I could illuminate the entire room.

Rummaging around in my pack, I found one of the magic cloths Rhyss and I had purchased from Larres. Throwing it up in the air, I willed it to become something suitable for the Fairwood celebration.

The white fabric square floated down in front of me, turning into a simple but elegant gown that shimmered brown and gold and green. Flashes of white showed in the skirt when I shook it out, twisting it in my mage light to look at it. The earth tones must be in deference to our Fairwood hosts, I realized, and the white showed I was a representative of the Seelie Court.

I changed into the new outfit, admiring its perfect fit on my body. I was glad there were no limits to the fabric's use. I could get used to this handy little bit of magic.

Two more things left to do. I affixed the triple roses brooch to my dress, hoping it would cut down on the amount of questions I was sure to face at the party. I chuckled to myself. Or it might create more.

As for the other thing I couldn't forget—I rummaged through my pack once more until I found what I wanted, tucked away near the bottom. I shook out one of the thin blue envelopes, making sure it was still sealed tightly, and tucked it away in a pocket of my dress.

When I exited the room, Paxen took my hand, bowed over it, and kissed it. "Lady Farrah. You look stunning."

I smiled. "Thank you. Faerie magic does wonders."

"That it does."

Paxen opened the door, waving for me to go first. "If you're ready, Lady Farrah?"

"I'm not, but something tells me that doesn't really matter."

Paxen grinned wryly. "Unfortunately, duty rarely cares if we truly are ready for it or not. It makes life rather interesting, don't you think?"

I laughed and stepped over the threshold. Paxen followed, closing the door behind him and making a small gesture with his hands. The air before the door shimmered briefly before settling back to normal, an indication of a magical ward being raised.

Paxen held his arm out to me and I took it. We strolled down a rough dirt path lined with tall trees.

The path opened out into a large clearing bathed in the growing moonlight, punctuated by the purple haze of twilight. Small devas danced around our heads and then dashed away, their lights providing additional magical illumination.

What seemed like the entire population of the Fairwood had turned out for the occasion, filling the clearing with otherworldly creatures of all kinds. Lilliana and her sister dryads mingled with pixies, gnomes, and centaurs. Meanwhile, Fionn held court with some of his fellow elves, who were obviously hoping to gain favor with him should he become the next King of the Seelie Court.

To one side of the clearing, mage lights bobbed above a large table laden with exquisite-looking dishes. And up close, they smelled even better. Paxen pointed some of them out as we walked by. "Rose-and-nectar pie, roasted wild boar, honeyed berries ..."

He looked up to see another centaur waving at him. "Oh, excuse me. It looks like my friend wants to talk to me. Will you be all right here?"

I nodded, and Paxen left.

I can see why humans would want to stay in Faerie, I thought as I surveyed the table. *This all looks delicious.*

My joy at seeing the buffet faded a bit as I thought of Rhyss. He would have loved this. One quality of Faerie food was that humans could eat large amounts of it without getting sick, unlike regular food back in the Gifted Lands. Of course, the tradeoff was that once a human ate Faerie food, they lost their appetite for regular food. I withdrew the blue envelope from my pocket. With the powder inside it, I would be able to partake in the celebration without any permanent effects.

I sighed. Yes, Rhyss definitely would have loved this.

I piled a plate high with Faerie food—making sure to sprinkle the enchantment-neutralizing powder over it—and then turned from the buffet to look for a comfortable place to balance my plate. I hadn't taken two steps when a small table appeared in front of me.

Oh, good. How convenient. And I was glad I hadn't bumped into it and spilled my food, which would have been quite embarrassing. I placed my plate on the tabletop, which was at just the right height for me to stand and eat at the same time.

As I ate, I idly wondered, *Since this table is a Faerie construct due to my need, and will most likely disappear when I'm done with it, if I* had *bumped into it, would that magic leave a bruise?*

A voice interrupted my musings. "A human! In the Fairwood? We should kill her now, before it's too late!"

45

CHAPTER FORTY-FIVE

I SWALLOWED HARD AS I looked up to see who had spoken.

A centaur, his dark brown hair liberally laced with streaks of white, approached the table where I stood. He also wore a purple and silver vest, similar to Paxen's, but the vest had additional braids and adornments that Paxen's lacked.

The centaur drew his sword, holding the tip just inches from my nose. Startled, I dropped the slice of rose-and-nectar pie I had been holding. It fell with an ungraceful *plop* back on the side of my plate, losing form as it landed. The sweet contents oozed out, some falling on the table. *What a waste of a good pie,* I thought inanely.

"Now, then. Give me one reason why I shouldn't kill you right this second," the centaur growled.

Around us, the other Fae of the Fairwood stood frozen, watching to see what would happen next.

Paxen hurried toward us. "Because, Saan! She's the High Chancellor's representative for the Trials! Can't you see, she's wearing the official crest of the Seelie Court? Now put down your sword, you fool!"

Saan glared at Paxen, then at me. I held my breath, but met Saan's gaze without blinking.

Finally, Saan lowered his sword.

Paxen took the weapon from Saan. "Are you insane? Threatening Lady Farrah like that? We can only hope Lord Chela will be merciful, when word of this gets back to him!"

Saan clenched his jaw, but he got the hint. He turned to me, his right eye twitching. "Forgive me, Lady Farrah. I ... misunderstood the situation."

I'll say, I thought. Out loud, I said, "What exactly did you think the situation was? My forgiveness awaits upon your explanation."

Saan looked around the moonlit clearing. Now that things had settled, the other Fae had gone back to their conversations.

"The Fairwood has had ... issues ... lately," Saan said reluctantly. "There are several areas in Faerie where it's easy to pass through the Veil between our world and the Gifted Lands. The Fairwood is one of them. We had a good amount of humans who resided in the Fairwood. But recently, they all disappeared."

"Really?" I couldn't help but remember the Fae-touched that had attacked Rhyss and me outside of Shonn.

Saan nodded. Now that he had begun his story, the words came pouring out, as if he was relieved to be able to share them.

"Many of those missing humans have lived in Faerie for decades. Some even longer. At this point, they're like family to us." He looked over his shoulder at the group of elves conversing with Fionn. "Well, like family to *most* of us."

"Some will never accept outsiders, no matter how much time has gone by," Paxen commented. I noticed he still kept Saan's sword away from him.

Saan nodded. "And then, about two weeks ago, we started finding the bodies."

"Bodies?" Paxen looked at Saan sharply. "What? How? This is the first I've heard of this."

Saan sighed heavily. "I didn't want to ruin your homecoming right away, although I knew eventually you'd hear about it. But yes, there have been several deaths in the Fairwood. The gnome Tenken, an entire pixie family of five, Khana—"

Paxen gave a strangled cry. The sword dropped from his hand, falling onto the grass with a soft thud.

Saan put a sympathetic hand on Paxen's shoulder. "Yes, Paxen. I'm sorry."

Tears pricked Paxen's eyes. He turned to me, trying to hold back his emotions. "Khana is—was—a dear friend of mine. We grew up together."

"Oh, my. I'm so sorry," I said.

"What happened?" Paxen asked Saan. "How did she die? How did any of them die?"

Saan shook his head sadly. "That's the thing. No one knows for sure. After the humans disappeared, our community's been on edge. We set up a watch. Tenken was found just outside the Fairwood, where he had been on guard duty. The pixie family was found inside their home by a neighbor. Mother, father, and their three children, all dead in their beds. As for Khana, her case was the strangest."

"Strange? How so?"

Saan nodded at Genevieve, the elf who had greeted us upon our entry into the forest. She caught his eye and started to make her way over to us.

"There was a witness to it. Khana was visiting Genevieve the night she died."

Genevieve reached our group, overhearing Saan's statement. She nodded, her face sad. "That's correct. It was nighttime, and we were in my home, having tea. Khana stepped outside for a moment, just for some fresh air. I gathered our dishes and had brought them to the kitchen. I heard a scream, so I dropped everything and ran to the front of the house. When I opened the door, Khana was lying on the doorstep."

Genevieve looked at Paxen, her eyes just as watery as his. "I tried everything, but I couldn't get her to wake up. I realized later she was already gone from the moment I found her."

"I understand," Paxen said. Genevieve reached out to him. Their tears flowed freely as they hugged in their shared grief.

Saan and I looked away to give them a moment of privacy, before I cleared my throat. "So, the Fairwood's human residents disappeared. Some of the Fae have been dying in mysterious ways. Are the deaths still happening?"

Saan shook his head. "It's hard to say. Khana's was the most recent, but it's been a few days since her death. It's possible whoever or whatever killed her will strike again."

"Similar occurrences have been happening around Faerie. One of the other royal hopefuls, Itan, mentioned that some strange deaths had happened near the Lonely Sea, and around the Fire Mountains."

Saan looked around. "Where is this Itan? I would be interested in discussing this with him."

"Ah ..." I looked down at my hands. "He is dead, unfortunately."

Saan's face darkened as I outlined the events of the last few days. "This is distressing to hear. Especially since it doesn't sound like you are any closer to knowing who is behind these deaths."

I shook my head. "It looked bad for Bettan. Although I'll be honest—I didn't quite believe she had hurt Aryn. But we didn't have many other options for her."

"Letting her stay and compete, with her innocence in question, would have cast a pall over all of the Trials."

I nodded, glad he understood.

Saan sighed. "Well, all we can do is be watchful. For tonight, I suggest we enjoy ourselves. I truly am sorry for threatening you. I thought any stranger to the Fairwood was a threat, but I realize now you are not my enemy. Although we have a common one."

He held his hand out to me. "Let us work together to find this unknown foe who threatens all of Faerie."

I looked the grizzled centaur in the eye, then dropped my gaze down to his outstretched hand for a long moment. Finally, I placed my hand in his. "Agreed."

He bowed over my hand. Straightening, he then glanced at the table, where my dessert had congealed into an unappetizing mess. "And let me get you another slice of pie."

I felt a wide, genuine grin spread across my face. "Sounds good, my friend."

After finishing my new piece of pie, I decided it was time to return back to Paxen's to sleep.

"It's been an eventful last few days, and the Trials haven't even really started yet," Paxen said understandingly. "The Fairwood revels will go late into the night, and I haven't seen many of these Fae in a while. So don't worry about waiting up for me."

I nodded. "Of course. Oh, before I go—how do I undo your house ward?"

"Ah, yes." Paxen sketched a quick figure in the air, sending his spell to encompass me. I felt the weight of his magic settle on me before dissipating. "There. The house ward should now recognize you and allow you entry."

"Thank you." I turned and headed down the path, away from the clearing and the party.

I had nearly reached Paxen's house when the sky overhead darkened. It was like someone had drawn a dark cloth over the stars and moon; instead of moving clouds slowly blotting out the nighttime sky, everything around me went pitch black quite suddenly.

Is it going to rain? I wondered. But that didn't seem right. It had been clear all day, with no clouds in sight. And this was Faerie. Even the weather could be influenced by magic, given enough power. I doubted the residents of the Fairwood would want to chance a storm ruining their party.

Thunder boomed overhead, causing me to jump. Lightning split the sky, and I cursed under my breath. The storm promised to be a nasty one. I needed to get back to Paxen's quickly.

I hurried down the dirt path. Surely Paxen would be following along behind me any minute now. He wouldn't want to stay in the open clearing when a storm let loose. None of the Fae would, I was sure.

But no one joined me as I made my way back to Paxen's home, and as I cleared the path, the sky opened up. Hard rain pelted down, so quickly that my shoes soon stuck to the fast-growing muddy ground. I stumbled the rest of the way to the house, barely able to see where I was going.

I reached the porch, throwing out a hand to find Paxen's front door. The instant my hand touched the handle, I felt a little tingle as the house ward recognized me. There was a slight click as the door unlocked itself, and I tumbled inside the dark, but dry, interior.

I stood at the door for a few moments, letting the rainwater drip off me. I called forth a spell light to chase away the darkness, then removed my muddy shoes. Poor Paxen would have enough of a mess to clean up without me trailing mud all over his house.

Fortunately, I didn't have to worry about cleaning the mud and leaves from my Faerie-made dress. Ending the magic that had created it took care of that. But it still took me some time to dry off, change, and take care of my dirty shoes. A look around the front room and my bedroom showed me that, for all my caution, I had tracked some dirt through the house. Feeling guilty, I cleaned up the floor—which also took a while.

The storm continued to rage outside.

And in all that time, Paxen still hadn't returned.

Perhaps he had sought shelter at another friend's place, I reasoned. After all, it had been a while since he had been back in the Fairwood. Even if the storm had ended the party, he could have just gone somewhere else to continue the festivities.

It didn't really matter. And I was tired. I snuffed out my spell light and climbed into bed. Sometime during the night I thought I heard the front door open and shut, but since there was no noise after that brief moment, I fell right back to sleep.

What *did* wake me up, however, was the sound of heavy pounding on the front door.

46

CHAPTER FORTY-SIX

"OPEN UP! NOW!"

The pounding on the door started up again. Groaning, I rolled over and opened my eyes. I saw the tiniest sliver of sunlight slicing through the mostly drawn curtains at the window.

The pounding grew louder and more insistent. Pretty soon whoever was outside would break the door down. I groaned again and felt around on my bedside table for the magic cloth. I had been too tired last night to put it away, and now I was actually thankful for my uncharacteristic sloppiness. Frequent travel had taught me to pack light and stay organized—usually.

I threw the cloth in the air and caught the lavender-colored linen dressing gown that fell back toward me. I shoved my right arm through a sleeve, then my left, before flinging open my bedroom door.

As I hastily tied the gown closed, Paxen approached from the back of the house.

"What's going on?" I asked him.

"I don't know," he replied. He opened the front door, revealing Saan and a dryad I didn't recognize standing in the morning sunlight.

"Saan? What's this about?" Paxen said.

Saan's face was sad. "We're here to take you away, Paxen."

"What?!" Both Paxen and I spoke at the same time.

The unknown dryad cleared her throat. "Paxen of the Silver Leaf Clan, you are officially under arrest for breaking into a Fairwood residence and for assaulting the elf Fionn. If you would come with us, please."

I stepped forward. "I don't understand. Whose residence? And can you be sure it was Paxen?"

"Last night, sometime during the community celebration, Fionn returned home to find an intruder in the home he shares with his mother, Hahna. The intruder had already ransacked the front room, and upon being discovered, attacked Fionn and made their escape. Unfortunately, Fionn was injured in the process."

"Injured?" I repeated, my stomach sinking.

"Fionn fell unconscious due to his injuries, and is currently in the Fairwood infirmary," the dryad said. "But before he did, he was able to name his attacker."

Paxen shook his head. "I didn't do it. I swear I didn't do it."

"Then how do you explain that Fionn named you as the intruder? And two witnesses saw you leaving his house."

"I don't know. The storm happened, and then—" Paxen stopped, blinking. "Then I remember coming home, sopping wet, and going straight to bed. I—I don't remember what happened in between."

The dryad snorted. "A likely story. You can tell it to the Council, and see if they buy it. Come on, then." A wand appeared in her hand, and Saan put a hand on the hilt of his sword, which hung around his torso. "Or we will take you by force."

Paxen slumped, deflated. "No, I'll come peacefully."

"Very well." The dryad moved to the side to allow Paxen room to leave.

Paxen took two steps forward, then turned to look at me. "Lady Farrah. Please find Lilliana. She'll know what to do."

I nodded.

And then the three of them were gone.

I closed the front door, then turned and leaned against it. What to do now? Every single candidate for the Seelie Court throne was now out of commission. The threat to Faerie was still at large, and I was no closer to figuring out what was going on.

Panic started to rise up. I doubled over, forcing myself to take deep breaths to calm myself. Rhyss would be here soon—by nightfall, if not sooner. His presence would be very welcome, and he could give me advice before I contacted Lord Chela. After all, Paxen's arrest and the news of Fionn's comatose state had just happened. I didn't have to tell the High Chancellor anything.

Yet.

I blew out a breath and headed back to my bedroom to get dressed. I needed to find Lilliana, check on Fionn, and uncover the truth of Paxen's supposed break-in, and I couldn't afford to waste a single minute more.

"I don't believe it. I can't believe it. Paxen would never do such a thing!"

The dryad wrung her hands, clearly agitated by my news.

"I don't think so either, but I will also admit that I don't know him—or, really, any of the royal hopefuls—that well," I said, trying to be fair.

Tears threatened to spill from Lilliana's big brown eyes. "But I know him, and I know—I just *know*—that he wouldn't have broken into Fionn's house. Or anyone's house! What would he even gain from it?"

"That's what I need to find out," I said. "I left the party early, and I thought I heard him come in sometime during the storm. But since I had already gone to bed, I don't know exactly when he returned. Were you with him, after I left?"

Lilliana sniffled. "No, not really. We did talk a little bit during the party, but when the storm rolled in, everyone scattered. I thought he was going back to Saan's to catch up."

I frowned. "Maybe he did, but if so, it can't have been for very long. Saan was one of the Fae that came to arrest him."

"I'll head to the Council chambers to talk to Saan," Lilliana said. "What will you do?"

"I do want to hear what Saan has to say. But I'd like to check on Fionn, see how he's doing. I think that takes priority. After that, I'll stop by Fionn's house. Maybe I can figure out why Paxen—or whoever—wanted to get in so badly."

Lilliana nodded. "I can relay what Saan has to say to you later."

"Thank you, that will help."

Lilliana dabbed at her eyes. "I just don't like this idea, that Fae would turn on Fae. That's an Unseelie thing. We Seelie, and especially those of us in the Fairwood, look out for each other."

You used to, at any rate, I thought. But I wisely kept that thought to myself, not wanting to upset the dryad further.

Lilliana gave me instructions on how to find the infirmary, and from there, Fionn's house. "The Council chamber is easy to reach—when you're ready to go there, just head in any direction. It's your intention to find it that helps you reach it, rather than going to a specific place."

It sounded rather confusing to me, but then I realized that perhaps the Fairwood Council chamber didn't exist in the Faerie realm on a permanent basis. Or maybe the Council had good reason to keep their building hidden.

We said our goodbyes and headed off in different directions. A short walk brought me to the Fairwood's infirmary, a modest grey-and-white stone building ringed by trees.

As I approached, several pixies fluttered around me. They moved so fast, I could barely make out what they were wearing—miniature aprons and crisp nurses' caps.

One of the pixie nurses hovered in front of my face. "State your business," she said in a high-pitched voice as equally crisp as her cap.

"I'm here to visit Fionn," I said.

She hummed disapprovingly. "We only allow family to visit. So, unless you are here in an official capacity—"

I drew myself up to my full height and put on the most haughty manner I could. Pointing at my brooch, I said, "I am Lady Farrah, the official judge of the Trials, of which the elf Fionn is taking part in. High Chancellor Lord Chela appointed me."

The pixie nurse blinked. "Oh. Oh, my. That changes things. Pardon me, Lady Farrah. Give me one moment, please." She bobbed a little curtsey before flitting inside.

I didn't have to wait too long. The pixie reappeared within moments, dipping into another mid-air curtsey. "Lady Farrah, you have been cleared to enter. I am Nurse Edanna. Please, come with me."

She disappeared into the infirmary again. I followed her inside. Nurse Edanna hovered at the end of the austere hallway, waiting for me to see her, before turning the corner. I hurried after. She kept such a quick pace, turning down multiple hallways, that I had no time to take in the area, just getting a vague sense of grey-and-white stone walls and spartan surroundings.

Finally, she stopped in front of a plain door that matched the other plain doors we had passed. "Here is the patient's room. He is still unconscious. We are unable to get a hold of his mother to let her know what happened."

I blinked in confusion. "Really? You can't reach her?"

The pixie nurse frowned. "We've tried, but for some reason we cannot connect with her using our magic."

"Hmm. I know she's headed back to the Seelie Court palace, and should even be there now. If you like, I can contact the palace—and Hahna—for you. I need to call them later anyway, once I have more information for them."

Nurse Edanna brightened. "That would be very helpful, thank you."

She opened the door to Fionn's room and waved me in. "We do ask that you limit your visit. I'll come back and check on you when the time is up."

I nodded. "Of course. Thank you."

The pixie disappeared down the hallway as I quietly closed the door behind me. Turning, I surveyed the still figure on the bed.

Fionn lay on the pristine bed, his long blond hair fanned out on the pillow underneath his head. His breathing came slow, but even. I stood there awkwardly, not sure what to say or do. Fionn and I barely knew each other—it was unlikely that a visit from me would aid in his recovery in any way. Even a visit from Paxen, unwelcome though it might be at this time, would elicit more of a reaction. But still, I had come, hoping for—what? A clue of some sort? A sign?

I coughed a little. "Hello, Fionn? It's Lady Farrah. I—I just wanted to make sure you were well."

No response. But I hadn't really expected one.

A few minutes ticked by as I stood there, uncomfortable.

I sighed and turned back to the closed door, already ready to leave. I had reassured myself that Fionn was alive, at least.

Behind me, I heard a stirring on the bed. Startled, I glanced over my shoulder to see Fionn sitting up in the bed, his eyes huge and focused as he stared and pointed straight at me.

47

CHAPTER FORTY-SEVEN

"FIONN!" ASTONISHED, MY HANDS flew to my mouth. "You're awake!"

"Don't—" Fionn croaked, his voice hoarse from disuse. "Don't let her—"

I flung open the door and called down the hallway, hoping the pixie nurse who had escorted me—or really, anyone—would be nearby to hear me. "Can anyone hear me? Please come, quick!"

A fluttering of little wings responded to my statement. I whirled around, words tumbling out of my mouth as I did so. "Fionn? Don't let—?"

But my unfinished question fell on deaf ears. Fionn had fallen back on the bed, unmoving.

Nurse Edanna rushed into the room. "What's going on? Is everything okay?"

I pointed at the figure in the bed. "Fionn—he was awake just now."

She flew over to Fionn, while other pixies swarmed into the room. A cloud of diminutive nurses surrounded the elf, looking him over.

Nurse Edanna glared at me, a ferocious frown on her face. "Lady Farrah, the patient's condition remains the same. If anything, he seems more agitated than he was before your visit."

"Nurse Edanna, I am not lying to you," I said. "He was sitting up in bed not even a minute ago—"

"Lady Farrah, your visit is now over," the pixie said sternly. "Please leave."

"But—"

"One of our orderlies will escort you out of the building."

I sighed and nodded. One pixie detached himself from the group and beckoned to me. I followed him through the twisty hallways back outside.

I looked up, assessing the position of the sun in the sky. About mid-morning. Rhyss couldn't get to the Fairwood fast enough. It would be nice to have a familiar, trusted face here, in a place where my tenuous authority as Trials judge was the only thing that garnered the barest amount of assistance.

Now, which way to Fionn's house? What had Lilliana said? Oh, yes. Through the trees, turn left at the giant boulder, then follow the path until I started seeing a cluster of homes built into the trees.

I sighed again and started toward the elf's residence.

I found the cluster of homes easily enough. How to gain entry was the true challenge.

As Lilliana had told me, the majority of the elves' homes were built into the trees. Way, way up—I could see the buildings nestled in the tree branches above me. But I didn't see any ladders or even handholds on the trees that allowed people to climb up.

There had to be some magical means to reach the upper level, then. It made perfect sense—this was Faerie, after all. Magic flowed here as abundantly as air.

I frowned as I studied the houses above me. If Paxen felt it necessary to ward his home, then the ones above me were probably warded as well. So how did Paxen get past Fionn's ward? And, if there were no bridges or ladders, how did Paxen even get up to Fionn's house?

A pointed cough drew my attention.

A dark-haired elf glared at me. His long hair was pulled back, and he wore an official-looking grey-and-black uniform. He held a wickedly sharp spear in his right hand.

"State your business, human." He practically spat the last word at me, like it was a curse.

"I'm Lady Farrah, and I'm here on behalf of High Chancellor Lord Chela." I subtly angled myself so the sunlight would catch on the triple roses brooch. "I'd like to take a look at Fionn's place, so I can give the High Chancellor a complete report about what happened."

"A likely story," the elf growled. He pointed at my brooch. "And that's probably fake."

He used his spear to wave in the direction I'd come from. I tried my best not to flinch, even though the sharp tip was just mere inches from my cheek. "Be on your way."

"Now, Chasta, is that any way to talk to an honored guest?" Fionn's cousin Genevieve appeared, gently pushing the guard's spear away from me.

Chasta frowned. "Do you mean to say this human is telling the truth?"

"Yes. She arrived with Fionn, Lilliana, and Paxen last night. Do be careful where you point that thing, please."

"Will you vouch for her?" Chasta wasn't willing to let things go that easily.

Genevieve sighed. "Yes. Does that make you happy?"

"Fine. But if she murders us all in our sleep, then the blood of the Fairwood will be on your head." Chasta stalked away, grumbling to himself.

"I'm sorry about that," Genevieve said, not even caring if Chasta was out of earshot. "Everyone's been on edge since the deaths I told you about, and then when Fionn was attacked last night ..."

"Yes, about that," I said, seizing the opening. "I'd like to visit Fionn's home. Perhaps I can get some idea of why the break-in occurred."

"Of course, Lady Farrah." She held a hand out to me. "Please, take my hand. I warn you, this might be a bit jarring."

Cautiously, I took Genevieve's outstretched hand. She murmured a few words. A shimmery slit of vertical light appeared in front of us. With a slight tug on my hand, Genevieve walked forward, leading me through the magical gateway.

As soon as I passed through the light, the air around me grew foggy, and I felt heady, like I was about to faint. Around me, all I could see was an endless white plane. Genevieve's voice floated back to me.

"Just hold on to me, Lady Farrah. It'll pass quite quickly, you'll see."

She still had a firm grip on my hand, for which I was grateful. I concentrated on the feeling of my hand in hers, using that bit of reality to anchor me in this odd magical area. She tugged at my hand, and I obediently followed.

We stepped out of the white zone onto a narrow wooden porch that wrapped partway around a wide oak. I swayed slightly, and Genevieve reached out another hand to steady me. Again, I was glad for her assistance—when I gained my footing, I took a cautious look over the edge. The open porch was a long way from the ground.

"What was that? Where were we?" I asked Genevieve.

Satisfied that I wasn't going to fall over the edge, the elf let go of my hand. "*That* is how we elves travel from our part of the forest to other parts of the Fairwood. Some may consider it a waste of magic, but it does keep us safe." She spread her arms wide, encompassing the tree homes around us. "Since you need permission to be able to access someone's home, we don't even bother to lock our doors or set wards."

I raised an eyebrow. "Are the elves really that worried that their Fairwood neighbors would betray their trust?"

Genevieve shook her head. "We've always preferred the higher area, but before we had easier ways to access our homes. The trouble wasn't necessarily from our neighbors, but from the Unseelie. They've always been a nuisance, but now they're quite bold." Her face fell. "Although, in light of recent events, it's possible we can't trust the Seelie of the Fairwood, either."

She turned mournful eyes on me. "Paxen's arrest—it's all anyone can talk about right now. I hate to think he could be capable of such a thing. Despite the Trials, he and Fionn are—were—good friends. But it all looks so bad."

"I know. Hopefully we can figure things out soon. Speaking of Paxen, though—how would he have gained entry to Fionn's? Since I needed your help to get up here, I would assume it would be the same for him?"

Genevieve shook her head. "No. Once you're marked as a friend, you're allowed access, although it can be tricky for those with lower magical ability to pass through. Those without magic would need an escort, every time."

I nodded, trying not to show my frustration. So it would have been easy enough for Paxen to enter Fionn's house. That explained the how. Now I needed to understand why.

I put my hand on the door handle. "Do I have permission to enter, then?"

Genevieve nodded. "Yes. In Fionn's absence, as his closest kin, I can—and have—granted you that permission. And if you don't mind, Lady Farrah, I will stay out here and wait for you. No one has touched anything since Fionn went to the infirmary. I suppose I should clean it soon—especially since Hahna's away—but I just can't bring myself to. Not yet."

"I understand. Thank you, Genevieve."

The elf turned away, looking out over the trees. I took a deep breath and opened the door.

48

─ · ─

Chapter Forty-Eight

My hand tingled slightly, almost as if I had been shocked, as I turned the door handle.

Odd.

I shook off the sensation and walked in, closing the door behind me.

Although it was still mid-morning, the curtains had been drawn shut, and little light filtered in. Which made sense—if Paxen or whoever had broken in was busy tearing through the place, they wouldn't want anyone outside to be able to see in. I debated opening the curtains, then decided against it. Best to leave things as they were, just in case. And besides, I shouldn't let Genevieve see me rummaging through Fionn's things.

Unsure of where Fionn might have left a lantern, I called up a spell light. "*Illumine.*"

A small ball of silver light flared above my hands. I sent it upwards so I could see the rest of the room.

I gasped.

"Oh, my," I breathed. "What happened here?"

Fionn's home looked as if the storm from last night had blown through, although all the windows and doors had been firmly shut against the elements. Papers were strewn everywhere, and the furniture had been overturned. Several breakable items lay shattered on the wooden floor, including a purple vase that had been filled with daisies, and a lantern.

I picked up the lantern. Half of its glass casing had broken, but it seemed otherwise intact. I righted a small table that had been tipped over by the front door. Lighting the lantern, I placed it on the table, glad to have more light in the room.

I blew out a breath as I assessed the damage. Although nearly everything in the main room had been upended, it didn't look like it had been done out of destructive malice. Otherwise they could have just set fire to everything and been done with it. No, I guessed the intruder had been searching for something specific.

As I stood in the middle of the room, I found my gaze drawn to the room's entry points—the windows, and the front door. Remembering the tingling sensation I had felt when I first entered, I frowned, trying to make sense of why it bothered me so.

And then it hit me.

Genevieve had granted me permission to enter just a few moments ago. Any house wards shouldn't have bothered me. Paxen's had recognized me, and the sensation had been quick and painless. But Fionn's ward had felt unpleasant.

Wait. Genevieve said the elves' homes had no house wards.

Now on the alert, I trailed a hand just a few inches above a windowsill, testing. Nothing. Searching the other window turned up nothing, either.

Turning to the front door, I knelt down so I was eye level with the door handle. A worn brass knob, it looked like, well, a door handle.

I reached out toward the handle, my hand just hovering near it. Concentrating, I muttered, "*Revelare.*" The quick spell would reveal any recent magic used in the area.

The door handle glowed a fiery reddish-black. A small, strange symbol showed faintly in the glow.

Interesting. That wasn't a house ward. But what exactly was it?

Just to the left of the door, another red-black glow caught my eye. My spell had caused it to light up as well. I picked it up, then straightened.

The object in my hand was a small twig, about the size of my index finger. When I held it, I didn't feel anything particularly magical. But its color matched the door handle. And it also bore that odd symbol, same as the door.

Well, then. A bit of a dead end. If there had been magic stored in it, the spell had already been used.

One end looked burnt, and didn't glow. The other end—now that was interesting. I raised my eyebrows in surprise.

Whoever had dropped this twig had used its magic to gain entry into Fionn's house. Which meant that, for some reason, the elf had put a protective spell on his house, despite what Genevieve had thought. With Fionn being a participant in the Trials, the extra precaution made sense.

Maybe.

Or maybe it made sense if the elf had something to hide.

I looked around. Aside from the destruction left behind, nothing important stood out to me.

Except for the formerly spelled twig in my hand.

I shoved it in my pocket, vowing to study it later. I looked around again, halfheartedly sifting through the items strewn about the room.

There was a big pile of books to one side, suggesting that Fionn had a fairly sizable library.

I picked up a book of poetry, then put it aside to pick up another book. This one was an elven romance novel. I smirked. It didn't seem like Fionn's type of reading. Perhaps it belonged to his mother. I set it back down.

My hand brushed against a leather-bound tome with a title etched in gold writing on the front. Curious, I read the title.

The Gods of the Gifted Lands: A Fae Perspective.

And underneath were two more books on the same subject. I recognized one as a primer from my grade school days. The legends about the gods had been written in an easy-to-understand format, only highlighting the positives about each kingdom and glossing over the complicated politics that had led to the gods' disappearance.

Now this was interesting. And unexpected.

Gifted Lands tradition held that our continent was created by seven gods, each of whom possessed their own unique powers or ideals. While they agreed on creating the continent, they could not agree on what the land's seat of power should be like, or where it should be located. So instead, they each fashioned a kingdom that reflected the one thing they each championed.

By the time the seven kingdoms had been created, the seven gods, once so united, were now at odds with one another. Each believed their kingdom to be the most superior.

Blinded by their pride, six of the gods prepared for war, meeting in the middle of the continent. But just before the first attack would have commenced, the seventh god, founder of the kingdom of Graenir, distracted his fellow gods and goddesses. Luring them away from the battlefield, he brought them to his kingdom and sealed them away. Knowing that staying in the Gifted Lands would endanger this newly created world, the seventh god joined the others in their confinement. The near-battle and its aftermath came to be known as the Six Gods' War.

Whether or not this was true, I didn't know. Rhyss believed, but not every person in the Gifted Lands shared his devotion to the long-gone gods.

The realm of Faerie was much, much older than the Gifted Lands. It was easy for any of us in the Gifted Lands to believe in Faerie. Unlike our mythical creator-gods, our Fae neighbors were still involved in the lives of us mortals. I was proof enough of that. But there was no such proof that the gods were anything but stories and legends.

So why would one of the Fae care about the ancient gods?

49

CHAPTER FORTY-NINE

I POKED AROUND THE mess on the floor a little more, but nothing else looked interesting. And I still had to meet Lilliana at the Council chamber.

I picked up the three books, wanting to study them later. An empty sling hung on the wall, one of the few things that hadn't been touched. I grabbed it and threw the books into it, placing the bag around my body.

As I opened the door, Genevieve raised her eyebrows at me. "Done already?"

"For now," I said. "I might come back tomorrow. For now, I need to meet with the Fairwood Council."

"I see." The elf pointed at my newfound bag. "What's in there?"

"Just some books that looked interesting. Don't worry, I'll bring them back soon."

Genevieve shrugged as she held out her hand. "Take your time. I doubt that Fionn will care that you have them. He's not much of a reader."

I frowned, hesitating before I placed my hand in hers. "He's not? But there were so many books in there."

"Oh, those aren't Fionn's. Those are Hahna's." Before I could ask anything else, her hand closed around mine, and she pulled me into that strange, disorienting portal that transported us from Fionn's house in the trees back to the forest floor.

As before, I stumbled out of the blank white area back into the lush green of the Fairwood. I blinked, trying to get my bearings. Did anyone ever get used to such jarring travel?

Satisfied I was now able to stand steady, I turned to Genevieve. I still had so many questions. But she dropped my hand and pointed. "You wanted to go to the Council chamber? Here it is."

My gaze followed where she pointed.

A majestic dome loomed ahead of us in a large clearing. Covered in vines, leaves, and snaking branches, it looked like the building had just grown out of the ground.

I looked around wonderingly. "How big is the Fairwood, anyway?"

Genevieve laughed. "As big as we need it to be. But the Council exists in its own unique place, both within and outside of the Fairwood."

I chuckled. "Say no more. If I try to think about it, it just makes my head hurt."

"Yes, some things about magic are better to take on faith than reason."

I shifted the bag on my shoulder. "Well, I should get in there. Thank you, Genevieve."

"Happy to be of assistance, Lady Farrah. Will you be able to find your way back?"

"I think so. I'm to meet Lilliana, and I'm sure we'll have plenty to discuss after."

"Very well, then." With a small wave, Genevieve turned and headed into the forest. I headed toward the wooded dome.

At the entrance, vines dotted with small red and white flowers—and wicked-looking thorns—covered the doorway. I didn't see a door handle, or any holes in the entryway, and unlike at the infirmary, no one stood guard outside.

I stared at the door. A very solid mass of thorny vines met my gaze.

Was it acceptable to contact Lilliana while she was in there? Did magic even work inside? I craned my neck, wondering if I could see into the building at all. No such luck.

My hand accidentally grazed one of the vines. "Ouch!"

I pulled my hand back, but the damage was already done. A small bright red bead of blood formed on the tip of my index finger. A similar smear appeared on a thorn at about my eye-level.

I sighed as I looked down at my finger. Frowning, I pressed my index finger and thumb together to stanch the flow of blood.

A swishing sound made me look up.

The vine curtain that had been blocking my way now pulled back to permit me entry. I eyed the thorn that had pricked my finger. The red smear of blood sank into the vine, and soon the only spots of red were from the vines' flowers.

Although there was plenty of room for me to walk through, I hesitated. The vines rustled at me, somehow sounding impatient. Wary, I passed through the curtain, just clearing it before it swished shut behind me.

"Hey!"

The vine curtain rustled again. Could vines be sentient? I supposed in Faerie, that could happen. I glared at the curtain, sure it was laughing at me.

Just inside, I could hear Lilliana's pleading voice. "But, sir. Surely you can at least place him under house arrest for the time being, until things can be confirmed. To this point, Paxen has an impeccable record—"

"Is this that human we've been hearing so much about?"

I looked over. The human-looking speaker stood at the far end of the room, along with Saan and Lilliana. Paxen was nearby, his hands shackled behind him and his hind ankles bound to the wall.

Poor Paxen. This didn't look good.

I approached the group, studying the speaker as I walked. I couldn't tell from his carefully blank expression what he might be thinking. Once I was close, I began to dip into a curtsy.

The man stopped me. "No, Lady Farrah. It is I who should be bowing to you."

He made good on his word, immediately giving me a deep bow. I blinked, surprised at this sudden show of respect from one of the Fae when everyone else in the Fairwood had either acted scared or disdainful toward me.

"This is Warin, the head of the Council," Lilliana explained to me. "He's led the Council for quite some time—even before I was a sapling."

"I was chosen for my position about halfway through King Finvarra and Queen Oona's reign," Warin said. His eyes twinkled. "Despite my rather progressive ways."

"Warin has long been known as a champion of the hapless humans that wander into Faerie," Saan said.

"How could I not be? When my own lineage includes mortals."

"You mean you're not Fae?" I asked Warin.

"I am, in part," he said. "Just one quarter. But there's enough in my blood to allow me to live in Faerie."

I raised my eyebrows. "How does a human—even one with a quarter Fae in them—become the leader of a vast Faerie region?"

Warin shrugged. "When I was born, my Fae grandmother came to claim me. She had lost her Fae daughter to a human man, and didn't want me to be lost to her as well. I've lived my entire life in Faerie, and consider myself more Fae than human."

I smirked. "I doubt it was so easy as that."

Warin grinned. "True. There was a bit of trickery from both my grandmother and my father. My father bargained to keep both my mother and me in the human realm, but in the end, had to reach a compromise."

"And you've never been back to see them?"

Warin shook his head, his eyes sad. "That was over one hundred years ago. They're long gone by now, I'm sure."

"I'm sorry."

"Don't be. I barely knew them, and my grandmother and I are very close. I enjoy my life in Faerie."

I nodded, but still felt a bit sad for him. At least his story of being taken to Faerie ended somewhat happily, unlike the majority of humans-in-Faerie tales.

"And now to the unfortunate business at hand," Warin said. "Lilliana told me you would be coming by, but the Council has already reached a decision. After hearing Saan's report, as well as Paxen's rather muddled recollections, we will put Paxen—"

"Please," Lilliana burst in. "Don't send him to the Underground."

Warin frowned. "It's absolutely shameful behavior from such an esteemed member of the Council." His frown deepened as he looked over the shackled Paxen. "*Former* member of the Council."

"Until you have definitive proof," Lilliana pleaded. "Please."

Warin sighed. "All right, Lilliana. Paxen will be placed under house arrest, instead of being sent to the Underground."

"Thank you." Lilliana's eyes shone with unshed tears.

At Warin's words, Paxen looked up, a spark of hope in his eyes as he murmured his own thanks.

"Lady Farrah," Warin said. "I understand you are staying at Paxen's during your time here in the Fairwood? Would you want to move? We can find you alternate lodging."

"No, I'm fine where I am," I said. "Unless the Council would prefer I stay elsewhere?"

"I would never harm Lady Farrah," Paxen said roughly.

"I would have thought that true of you and anyone in the Fairwood, yet here we are," Warin said pointedly, and Paxen hung his head.

"I will be fine," I said hastily. "I am not without my own means of defending myself, and my companion, Lord Rhyss, will be here tonight."

"Very well." Warin motioned at Paxen, and the chains that held the centaur's back legs to the wall fell away. "Saan, please escort Paxen to his home. I trust you can perform the necessary spells of binding?"

Saan nodded.

"Good. If there's nothing else?" No one said anything. "Then I think we are done here."

Lilliana moved to Paxen's side, murmuring words of comfort to him. Saan went to his other side, grabbing his arm to escort him.

Paxen shrugged him off. "There's no need to treat me like a criminal, Saan. I came here willingly, I'll leave the same way."

"Let's get going, then," Saan said. The trio began walking toward the exit.

"Lady Farrah, may I have a quick word with you before you go?" Warin asked. He lowered his voice. "If there's anything you need, if you feel unsafe at any point, contact me right away. With the recent killings in the Fairwood—and I understand in all of Faerie—I don't want to chance your safety."

"I appreciate that, Warin. But I doubt that I am in any danger—"

"You are also part Fae, are you not?"

"Yes. How did you know?"

Warin smirked. "It's all anyone in the Fairwood can talk about since you arrived. It's your Fae half that keeps them civil, as well as the High Chancellor's favor." His smirk faded. "But be careful. Right now anti-human sentiment is running high. Even with your Fae blood and Lord Chela's favor, you might not be safe."

"What do you mean? Why not?"

"So far, all the deaths have been Fae. When they started happening, many of the humans started disappearing."

I frowned, thinking of the Fae-touched that Rhyss and I had encountered outside of Shonn. "Whatever is killing the Fae might also be harming the humans."

"Perhaps. Or perhaps the humans are behind it. That's what many of the Fae around here think, anyway."

"The High Chancellor thought the Unseelie were responsible."

Warin's frown matched my own. "We've had our issues with the Unseelie, for sure. But the attacks—while they are magical in nature, they do not have the mark of the Unseelie. Since human magic is so different than that of Faerie, it seemed a logical conclusion.

"For those of us humans who have lived lifetimes here in Faerie, we are safe, for we are known and trusted. But since you are new here—just be careful, Lady Farrah."

50

CHAPTER FIFTY

THE WALK BACK TO Paxen's was quiet, our group's mood somber, as each of us were lost in our own thoughts.

For my part, my mind raced as I tried to make sense of the day's events. I needed to hear Saan's account of the break-in. I wanted to study the books I had picked up from Fionn's—no, Hahna's—library. And I was curious about why the residents of the Fairwood were so adamant that humans, and not Unseelie Fae, were behind the deaths happening all around their realm.

My goodness. I would have a lot to tell Rhyss when he got here.

Speaking of which ... I eyed the position of the sun. It was a bit hard to tell through the trees, but I estimated it was probably midday, or perhaps a little later. My stomach growled, and the three Fae looked at me.

I smiled sheepishly. "I suppose it's time for lunch."

"I won't take long at Paxen's," Saan said. "Although, Lady Farrah, you don't have to be present. My spell casting won't affect you."

"It's okay, I'd like to be there. I find watching other mages at work rather fascinating."

Saan nodded and we all fell silent. We were soon back at Paxen's. Once there, Saan spoke the words of binding that would keep Paxen imprisoned in his home. The centaur could not leave, under penalty of death, and none could help him escape, or they would face the same fate. Only Saan, Warin, or one of the Great Ones of Faerie could release Paxen from his binding.

Saan then spoke a second spell, one of peace. "No thoughts of violence, either magical or mundane, will enter the minds of any under this roof."

Satisfied, Saan took his leave. Lilliana, Paxen, and I watched him go, then Lilliana said, "I probably should go as well. Paxen, I'm so sorry this is happening to you. If there's anything you need—"

"I'll be fine, Lilliana," Paxen said gently. "Thank you for ... everything."

"Of course. Lady Farrah, is there anything you require before I go?"

"Lord Rhyss should be here soon, if he's not already at the Fairwood's border," I said. "When he arrives, could someone bring him here?"

"I'd be happy to escort him here," Lilliana said. "I'll keep an eye on the border myself."

"Thank you."

The dryad disappeared into the forest, and Paxen and I were left alone at his home.

Now his prison.

My stomach growled again. Paxen chuckled. "Come, Lady Farrah. I'll prepare a meal for us."

I laughed. "Now, that's the best thing I've heard all day."

I dropped off Fionn's sling in my room, then joined Paxen in his kitchen. Over his protests, I insisted on helping make our lunch.

As I peeled some potatoes, Paxen worked on lighting a fire in the hearth.

"Paxen?" I tried to keep my tone light.

"Mmm?"

"If it's not too difficult to talk about—what did Saan say happened?"

The logs in the hearth caught fire. Paxen straightened, turning to face me. He sighed. "Just the same as you heard when he came to arrest me. Someone—me, according to the reports—broke into Fionn's house during the storm. Fionn happened upon the intruder, and was injured in the intruder's flight from his home."

"And they're certain it was you?"

"Apparently there were witnesses. One of Fionn's neighbors, and a passerby in the area. And also—only certain Fae have access to Fionn's house."

"Really? I would have thought, since the Fairwood seems so open and trusting, that most Fae would be able to come and go from each other's homes as they please."

Paxen shook his head. "Not in the elven community. There's a reason they built their homes high up, in the trees—they like to keep to themselves. If they want to interact with the rest of the Fairwood, they come down to the forest floor. Besides, it's a bit—complex—to access their homes, if they even grant you that privilege."

Remembering how Genevieve transported me up to Fionn's home, I nodded. "So, the witnesses, and your special access, pinned you to the scene."

He hung his head. "Yes. But—I don't recall going there at all. Which is what I told the Council."

"What do you remember?"

Slowly, Paxen said, "After you left the party, Lady Farrah, I was talking to Saan and Genevieve. Then a storm came in, strong and unexpected. Everything in the clearing went dark—quite surprising, really. A natural storm should have no effect on our magic. Then—"

Paxen winced, putting a hand to his forehead. "Forgive me, I seem to have a headache. Let me think. Then ... I ..."

His breathing started coming in shallow gasps. "I—I don't know. Oh!"

He put his other hand to his head, shutting his eyes against another wave of pain. "I ... I think—I must have—"

I hastily put the potato I was peeling and my knife to the side. "Paxen! Are you all right?"

He started to shake his head, then stopped when more pain came. "This happened earlier ... at the Council chambers. When I ... tried to remember ... what happened ... during the storm."

"Oh, dear. We can stop talking about it, then, if—"

"No." He took a deep, shuddering breath. "No, it's okay. I want to talk about it, I want to remember so I can clear my name."

He looked at me, then, and I could see the confusion in his eyes. "It's the strangest thing, Lady Farrah. If I try to think about what happened during the storm, my head hurts something fierce. And I can't remember anything, anyway. But ... I do remember coming home, late at night, once the storm was done."

"Does your head hurt now, recalling that?" But looking at him, I already knew the answer, even before he shook his head no. The color had quickly returned to his face, his breathing was even, and the sudden, sharp headache that had plagued him just moments ago seemed like it had never existed.

"Well, I'm sure it will come back to you," I said reassuringly. "Let's eat, and then rest. It's been quite a morning."

"A good plan," Paxen agreed, and went back to his meal preparations.

I picked up the potato and knife I had put aside.

We worked for a while in silence, and then I recalled Warin's earlier words. "Paxen?"

"Hmm?"

"Warin mentioned that many in the Fairwood don't trust humans right now. That they're blaming the recent deaths on human mages, and not Unseelie Fae. Do you know why?"

Paxen paused in his work. "While they were interrogating me, it did come up—I think because the traces of magic found on those who died were rather unusual. If magic is used, the Seelie Fae can determine if it was cast by a fellow Seelie, or an Unseelie. Foreign magic would most likely be a human's—who else has magical ability? The magic remnants on the bodies felt somewhat familiar, and yet, had a very wild element to it. The Council thought perhaps a human mage had corrupted Faerie magic somehow."

He went back to his preparations. I frowned, thinking.

Mages could often sense another's work, and the "flavor" of human magic and Fae magic tasted quite different from each other. In that, Paxen was correct. I was a rare magician with the ability to work magic like the Fae—from instinct, with little training—but with a human feel to it. In theory, the two types of magic were anathema to each other and couldn't mix, unless—like me—you were the result of an interrealm union.

And yet—the magic I had felt at Fionn's—it hadn't felt like wholly Fae or wholly human magic. It had a little bit of Fae magic, but like Paxen said, there was a wild, unknown element to it.

And if I couldn't even recognize the type of magic, then what could it be?

While Paxen bustled around the kitchen, I cast a silent spell, sending it after the centaur.

And stifled the gasp that threatened to spill out.

Paxen's form was outlined in a hazy red-black, a similar hue to what I had seen earlier on the twig. That same red-black glow arced a line through the air toward me.

Linking Paxen to the spelled twig in my pocket.

I waved away the spell before Paxen could see it. Eventually, I would probably have to tell him, but I wanted to have more, definitive information before I mentioned it. But knowing that Paxen and the spelled stick were linked brought up more questions.

What was the purpose of the spell?

And more importantly, who was behind it?

51

CHAPTER FIFTY-ONE

AFTER A PLEASANT LUNCH—IN which Paxen and I talked about everything but his house arrest—the centaur announced he was going to take a nap.

"I had a late night—and it's been quite a day. And, frankly, I can't think of what else I could do right now," he said wryly.

I chuckled.

"Will you be able to find something to occupy yourself, Lady Farrah?" Paxen asked.

"I did have some reading I wanted to do," I said. "That should keep me busy until Lord Rhyss arrives."

"Oh. Well, you are welcome to avail yourself of anything in my modest library, if you like. The light in my study is good, and the whole room is quite comfortable."

"Thank you."

Paxen pointed out the study to me, then retired to his room to rest. I grabbed Fionn's bag from my room, then headed into Paxen's study.

I looked around appreciatively. A large bay window let a flood of light in, and a bookshelf with knickknacks and three rows of books graced one windowless wall. Two plush chairs and a long couch were in one corner of the room for visitors, with a wooden desk—taller than a regular desk, and sans chair—on the opposite side.

I plucked a cushion from one of the chairs and crawled onto the bay window, settling in to look over the three books I had taken from Fionn's house.

The first book I picked up was the grade school primer, which was pretty much as I remembered it from my childhood. Flipping through it brought a fond smile to my face. I hadn't taken the legends of the Gifted Lands gods to heart as much as Rhyss had, but I had enjoyed this book for all the fanciful stories it contained.

Looking at it a bit closer, however, I realized something. While the book acknowledged that seven gods had created the Gifted Lands, the stories only focused on the six who had created the kingdoms of Calia, Bomora, Orchwell, Shonn, Rothschan, and Annlyn. Not much was said about the kingdom of Graenir or its creator.

Frowning, I examined another book. It was similar to the primer, containing stories about the gods, penned by a human from the Gifted Lands. This text was written for an older audience, so the stories had a little more depth to them, but not much more. And still nothing really about Graenir or its founder.

I set it aside and picked up the last book. This was the one that had caught my eye at Fionn's—*The Gods of the Gifted Lands: A Fae Perspective.*

It was considerably weightier than the other books, which was promising. But that wasn't the main thing that intrigued me about it.

As the supposed gods of Gifted Lands lore had, in theory, created our land and kingdoms, the topic understandably was of interest to those who inhabited those areas. All the histories had been written by human scholars. To my knowledge, the citizens of Faerie didn't know or care about the mortals' gods. The author of *The Gods of the Gifted*

Lands: A Fae Perspective claimed to have been an eyewitness to the events described in his book.

A memory sparked in my mind, from when I was about two or three. I had asked my father about the gods, after learning about them in a history lesson at school. He had laughed and picked me up, setting me on his knee.

"Humans, with their short lives, want to know their beginnings and endings," he had said. "It gives them comfort to believe in something bigger than themselves."

"But is it true?" I had asked. "You're from Faerie. Wouldn't you remember?"

He had shrugged. "I may be long-lived, but if gods did indeed once walk this world, that's beyond even my lifetime."

I blinked, the rest of the memory fading away. The Fae were long-lived, but they were not immortal. They could die, or be killed. Because of their long lifespan, they tended not to have many children, unlike their human counterparts. It was quite possible that there were hardly any Fae left alive who remembered the gods and witnessed the creation of the Gifted Lands.

And if that was true, then that meant the book in my hands was very old.

And very rare.

Reverently, I opened the book and started reading. Then I paused, swinging my legs over the side and jumping down the short distance from the windowsill.

I hurried over to the desk in the corner, rummaging around in its various drawers as I searched for something to take notes with. Paxen did say I could help myself to whatever I needed. Finding some blank paper, a quill, and a half-full bottle of ink, I headed back to the bay window.

Now, I was ready to read.

I put *The Gods of the Gifted Lands: A Fae Perspective* to one side and reached my arms above my head. The stretch felt good. How long had I been sitting in the window, reading?

Looking around, I realized the sunlight in the room had faded. I hadn't noticed because the wall sconces had magically lit themselves once the room started to darken. *That's a handy spell. I should look into doing that back home.*

I flipped through the pages of notes I had taken during my reading. Much of what the Fae author had written echoed things I had learned previously, about the creation of the Gifted Lands, the seven gods and their kingdoms, and the Six Gods' War.

But the author also mentioned something I had never heard before.

What we had been taught in the Gifted Lands was that, in the aftermath of the Six Gods' War, the seventh god sealed away his kin and then joined them in their eternal confinement. And that was that—the story ended there.

But the writer of *The Gods of the Gifted Lands: A Fae Perspective* claimed to be an eyewitness to the events. And, according to him, the seventh god had allowed for a provision for the gods to be set free, in case there was ever a need for their power and presence in the Gifted Lands.

The gods had been imprisoned somewhere near Graenir, but each god could, in theory, be called forth from the kingdom they had specifically founded.

Although the author had noted what one was to do to free a god, I didn't understand any of it. It seemed that a potion of some sort needed to be made, and poured over the site where the gods had been sealed in Graenir, or over a Secondary Seal in one of the other kingdoms. But much of the spell language was archaic and forgotten. And I was fairly sure that most of the ingredients needed for the potion didn't even exist anymore. If the gods had indeed walked among us, that was centuries ago. Language changed and evolved, as did flora and fauna.

Finding the site of a Secondary Seal wasn't easy. There, the author stated, the magic flowed free and wild, in a place where two worlds touched. He didn't elaborate on what, exactly, the "two worlds" were. I assumed Faerie and the land of the gods, although how anyone would know what the land of the gods looked like was beyond me.

There was one more section that caught my eye. Along with the potion, the author stated that "two worlds" needed to be combined. Something about a binding red thread. A long spell in a long-dead language followed. I put the book down and massaged my temples. I had been reading for a while at that point, and the author's flowery words made my head spin.

I hopped off the window seat, stretching once more before putting the books and notes in my bag. After returning the quill, ink, and pillow back to their original places, I left the study.

I found Paxen in the main room, wiping the fireplace mantle with a rag. The room, which had been in fairly good shape when I had arrived yesterday, now looked spotless.

"I didn't want to disturb you," the centaur said.

I put my hand on his wrist, stopping his cleaning. Gently, I turned his hand over. The rag was just as spotless as the rest of the room.

Paxen smiled sheepishly at me. "I may have gone over this room several times. There's not much else to do."

I smirked. "I understand. But it's only been the first day. Not even a full one. You're going to go mad by the end of the week at this rate."

"I agree. But there's nothing I can do about it." He sighed. "At least you and Lord Rhyss will be here, for a little bit. Having company—and news of the outside world—will be nice."

"Speaking of which, has Lord Rhyss arrived? Lilliana was going to bring him here once he reached the Fairwood."

The centaur shook his head. "She hasn't been by."

I frowned, eyeing the windows. The sunlight was nearly gone, the purple of twilight taking over the forest outside. "That's not right. He should have been here by now."

At that moment, an insistent knocking started at Paxen's door.

The centaur and I exchanged a look. My stomach dropped, even as Paxen quipped, "Well, I've been here all day, so I'm not sure what they can arrest me for again."

He opened the door. Lilliana stood outside.

"Lilliana!" I rushed to greet her. "We were just talking about you. Is Lord Rhyss with you?"

She shook her head, worry lining her face. "No, Lady Farrah. His horse arrived. But without him."

52

— • —

CHAPTER FIFTY-TWO

LILLIANA AND I HURRIED to the border of the Fairwood, with the dryad giving me the scant details as we went.

"It seemed odd that a horse had wandered in with a saddle but no rider. I thought you might be able to identify the items in the saddlebags, whether they belong to Lord Rhyss or not."

At the forest's border, my heart sank. A guard elf was holding the reins of the horse that I instantly recognized as Rhyss's mount. A quick search through the saddlebags confirmed that the horse was, indeed, the one Rhyss had been riding.

"But then where is Rhyss?" I muttered, going through the bags again. But they didn't hold any clues as to where he could have gone.

"Did you contact Steward Henry?" I turned to Lilliana. "If something attacked Lord Rhyss on the road, then perhaps Hahna and Bettan were also in danger?"

"No, Lady Farrah. When the horse arrived, I went to get you right away."

I nodded absentmindedly, searching through the bags a third time. I wasn't sure why. It wasn't like a third round would suddenly produce information when the first two checks hadn't.

But then I realized that my searches hadn't turned up one thing: the spell stone I had given Rhyss so we could call each other magically. If it wasn't in his saddlebags, then hopefully he was carrying it on his person.

Usually, only mages could connect with each other through a magical calling spell. But a while back, Queen Jennica of Calia and I had experimented with infusing objects with the calling spell. It had come in handy several times, as our non-mage friends and allies could now contact us directly, with no need for magical knowledge.

I held out my hand and concentrated, willing Rhyss to appear.

Nothing.

Closing my eyes, I focused more intently. I blocked out all the extraneous sounds—the horse's snuffing, the wind blowing through the trees, the breathing of the elf and the dryad near me. Instead, I tried to hear Rhyss's voice in my head—his excited goofy lilt, his quiet intensity.

"F-Farrah?" A rough voice cut through my concentration.

"Rhyss!" My intended appeared, finally, in front of me. But—

"What's happened?" I asked. "You don't look so good."

Rhyss lay on his side, one cheek against a dirt floor. His head was at an odd angle, and I realized he must have fished the calling stone from his pocket, but for whatever reason hadn't brought his hand up to the level of his face.

He groaned. "I don't ... have ... much time."

"What? What do you mean?"

"Be back ... any minute." He groaned again, trying to sit up, then collapsed again from the effort. I gasped as I got a better look at his face. A bruise bloomed on one cheek, and dried blood showed at the corner of his mouth. "Farrah. After you ... left. Killed ... messenger. Tried to run ... overpowered me. Took us ... both. Locked ... up."

"What? Bettan did this to you and Hahna?"

"No." He coughed, and my heart wrenched to see a trickle of new blood trail from his mouth. "Hahna ... did this."

Next to me, Lilliana gasped. My eyes widened. "Where is Hahna now? Where are you and Bettan?"

Rhyss took in a shallow breath. I could tell it hurt him to breathe, and I wondered at the extent of his injuries. "Hahna ... soon. We ... not sure. Dark. Dirty. She said ... open ... rift."

There was a scuffling sound, and Rhyss said, "Gotta ... she ..." He stopped, panting for air. "Love you."

Abruptly, he disappeared.

I stared at the empty air above my hand, not wanting to believe he was gone. "Rhyss? Rhyss!"

Frantically, I tried reaching out with the calling spell again. But a dark hand decorated with a swirling pattern stopped me.

"Lady Farrah. Don't. It sounds like contacting him again might endanger him."

I turned unseeing eyes on the dryad.

"Don't worry. We will find him, Lady Farrah," she soothed.

I took a shuddering breath. "Yes. We will find him. And Bettan." My voice hardened. "And Hahna."

"Yes." The dryad looked at me curiously. "But how?"

I looked up at the now nighttime sky, which I could see unhindered at the Fairwood's border. While part of me wanted to just ride off into the night to find Rhyss, I knew that would be foolish. What I needed were answers.

But unfortunately, there were no more to be had here.

"I'll need to leave the Fairwood soon, but I don't know where to go," I said, defeated. "Do you think Paxen might have an idea?"

Lilliana nodded encouragingly. "I think so. And I'll go get Warin. The four of us together should come up with something."

"I wish Fionn wasn't unconscious," I burst out. "He's got answers, I'm sure of it, but I don't know what. I don't even know what questions to ask."

We walked back in silence. I was so lost in thought that I didn't notice the figure standing at Paxen's door, waiting for us, until we were nearly upon him.

"Oh! Good evening, Saan," I said, surprised. What would the grizzled centaur be doing here? I doubted Paxen had suddenly been pardoned. "Are you here to see Paxen?"

"No, actually. I came to find you, Lady Farrah," Saan said. "Fionn is awake."

— ele —

Again, I hurried through the woods, this time accompanied by both Lilliana and Saan. My heart hammered in my chest, keeping time with my footsteps. I was determined to find out whatever Fionn knew.

At the infirmary, a pixie nurse tried to stop us from entering. "It's after hours. Come back in the daytime."

"We're here to talk to Fionn." My tone brooked no argument.

The pixie nurse's eyes darted from me, to Lilliana, to Saan, then back to me again. "All right," she said, sounding nervous. "But one at a time. All of you together might be overwhelming for him. He's been under enough stress already."

"I'll go in his room alone," I said. "But they stay outside. I want witnesses."

The pixie nurse waved us in, seeing that we would not be dissuaded. I flew down the hallway to Fionn's room, Lilliana and Saan on my heels, and opened the door. The elf was sitting up in bed, sipping at a bowl of pale green soup.

"Fionn. I'm glad to see you looking so much better."

"Lady Farrah." Fionn set the bowl down on his lap tray.

"Here, let me help you." I picked up the tray and put it on a side table, then pulled up a chair next to the bed and sat down. "Now that you're awake, I have some questions for you."

"Yes?" The elf shifted uncomfortably.

"Yes." My eyes and my voice were hard, and Fionn swallowed nervously. "I believe you have information that could have helped with our investigations into the recent deaths around Faerie. And that you've been holding that information back this whole time. Something to do with your mother?"

Fionn's eyes widened. "How did you know?"

"She decided it was time to make her move." My jaw twitched. "She killed Steward Henry's messenger, and is holding Bettan and Lord Rhyss somewhere. So. Talk."

Fionn stayed silent.

I opened my hand, and a shimmer appeared above it. "The High Chancellor is just a call away. I'm sure he'll find whatever you have to say *fascinating*. Two of your Fairwood neighbors are outside this room, and have heard you betray yourself just now. And if you decide not to tell me what I need to know, I will make sure you rot in Lord Chela's dungeon for the rest of your unnaturally long life. I am his official representative, after all. My decisions during the Trial are beyond contestation. And they are final."

There was a long pause while we stared at each other.

Finally, Fionn sighed. "I'll cooperate. Please don't imprison me—at least, until after I help my mother."

I closed my fist, shutting down the calling spell.

Fionn hung his head, ashamed. "My whole life, Mother's always been a bit unhappy. I know losing her title hurt her deeply. She's always been content to stay at home, reading her books. She loves history—the more obscure, the better.

"One of our neighbors, many centuries older than my mother, passed away a few years ago. She was one of the few elves who had stayed friends with my mother, even after King Finvarra took Mother's noble status away. A very lovely woman, a fellow history lover with quite the collection of books. When she died, my mother inherited her collection.

"The woman was fascinated by the human world and its lore. It was something she and Mother talked about often. Mother would tell me about it sometimes, something about the old gods still being alive, but I never really paid attention. But Mother was quite intrigued by the notion. And when King Finvarra and Queen Oona were killed recently in the Gifted Lands, and the High Chancellor announced the Trials were to take place, Mother became obsessed. She wants her title to be restored."

"But that can't happen," I said. Then it dawned on me. "Unless the new ruler—"

"Yes." Fionn looked embarrassed. "It wasn't my idea to enter the Trials, even though I have the strongest claim to the throne."

"So your mother is ambitious. She wouldn't be the first. Why are you telling me this now?"

"You have to understand." Fionn gripped the coverlet on his bed so hard his knuckles turned white. "She uncovered some information from that lady's library, and it became her obsession to reach the locked-away gods. She formed an alliance with an odd evil creature, a walking shadow, that does her bidding. I fear that the more she relies on it, the more it corrupts her.

"A while ago, she tried to kill King Finvarra and Queen Oona, but failed. Some other poor noble took the blame. But then the royal couple died, and she saw her chance to put me on the throne. Now she'll stop at nothing. When Itan died, I suspected my mother was behind it. When Aryn died, I was sure of it."

He took a deep breath. "That's why I sent her back to the palace. I told her it was for her safety, but I planned on contacting Steward Henry to have him imprison her. I was going to bow out of the Trials, and stay here in the Fairwood. But then, the night of the party, my mother took over Paxen's body. She sent him to my house, spoke to me through him. I confronted her about the deaths of Itan and Aryn, and told her I couldn't look the other way anymore. She flew into a rage, destroying the house and injuring me. When I finally awoke, the nurses were abuzz with the rumor that Lord Rhyss's horse had arrived without him, and I knew it was too late to call Steward Henry."

He looked over at me, tears in his eyes. "I don't care if you disqualify me from the Trials. I just want my mother back, the way she used to be."

I didn't say anything for a long moment. Then: "Help me find them, and I'll do what I can. Fionn, do you know where your mother might be?"

He swallowed hard. "My guess is—the Underground."

53

–·–

CHAPTER FIFTY-THREE

By the time the sun peeked over the horizon, I was standing at the Fairwood border with Fionn, Lilliana, Saan, Paxen, and Warin.

Upon hearing Fionn's confession, Saan had immediately contacted Warin, who called an emergency meeting with the rest of the Fairwood Council despite the late hour. The Council pardoned Paxen and released him from the house binding.

The centaur had been kind enough to bring the books from Fionn's library that I had been studying earlier, as Fionn wanted to look through my notes. Fionn, Paxen, Lilliana, Saan, and I had talked late into the night, making plans.

Now, I cast a worried eye on the elf, pale and weak-looking in the morning light. "Are you sure you're well enough to travel?"

Fionn nodded. "She's my mother. I have to be there—no matter what happens."

The rest of us stared at him, waiting.

Fionn hastily added, "And I swear to aid any and all of you, even though it be against my own kin. If I betray any of you, my life is instantly forfeit."

I nodded, satisfied, as I felt the magic of his vow binding him to protect us.

Warin cleared his throat. "Saan and I will escort you to the Underground entrance, where I will unseal it for you to enter. I'm afraid I'll have to reseal it behind you, or risk that the Unseelie could come aboveground." He looked grim. "They have their ways, but I don't need to make it easier."

"I understand," I said. "And thank you."

"If you run into any Unseelie down there, you won't be thanking me, Lady Farrah," Warin warned. "Please be careful."

"We will be." *I hope.*

The six of us began our silent, solemn trek to the Underground entrance, about a half hour's walk beyond the border of the Fairwood.

While we walked, my thoughts went back to last night's conversation with Fionn.

Hahna had become obsessed with the idea of releasing the gods, he had said. While the gods were imprisoned near Graenir, there was another place that one could possibly reach their prison—the Underground.

Just as the Veil in Shonn was the place where the human world and the realm of Faerie met, pockets of the Underground held the most ancient magic, uncorrupted by time and frequent use. But the wild magic wasn't the only danger of the Underground. It was also where the heart of the Unseelie Court lay, and there would be no help for any Seelie Fae who found themselves in their lawless domain.

After Fionn's explanation, I had understood why Lilliana had been so passionate in her quest to keep Paxen from the Underground.

"It sounds like a horrible place," I had said.

"It is," he had agreed. "If you're unfortunate enough to be sent there, you'll most likely never be heard from again."

Now, as we stood at the entrance to the Underground, all my apprehension flooded back.

Before us lay a small mound of earth, covered in vines and thorns and flowers in a similar fashion to the Fairwood Council's chambers. But an odd, foul smell permeated the air, a tangy, earthy smell tinged with decay. A sense of despair and dread hung about the place.

I looked around the group. "Are we ready, then?"

Lilliana, Paxen, and Fionn all gave me solemn nods.

Saan drew his sword, ready for anything that might come forth.

Saan said, "Warin will cast a spell of protection and containment, but something of this magnitude will quickly drain his energy. The sooner he can seal this place up, the better."

Warin spread his hands wide, murmuring a spell under his breath.

The vines glowed a bright green, snaking around each other before withdrawing into the ground. The mound split in the center, following the vines' path before dissolving, leaving a gaping black hole before us.

The head of a small, green-skinned creature popped up and looked around. "Oh, what's this, what's this?"

Then the little goblin noticed the sun shining overhead. "Ah! Cursed light! How it—"

Before it could finish its thought, Saan's sword pierced through its neck. The centaur held up the skewered goblin, flinging its limp body from his weapon.

"Go now, and quickly," Saan said. "Before more of these creatures appear."

Paxen sprang forward, disappearing into the hole with no hesitation. His voice floated back up. "It's not that deep."

Lilliana went next. Fionn turned to me. "Don't fret, Lady Farrah. I'll catch you."

"Thank you." I turned to Saan and Warin. "And thank you both."

Warin could do no more than nod slightly, still mouthing his spell. Saan said, "Good luck."

I jumped into the dark hole after the others. "Oh!"

True to his word, Fionn caught me before I could hit the ground, setting me gently back on my feet. I looked up. The sunlight was rapidly disappearing as the mound of earth closed above our heads. Soon we were in the cool dark. I swallowed hard, trying to fight the panicked feeling that I was buried alive.

"Illumine." A silver ball of light appeared above my hand.

"What now?" Lilliana asked.

"I don't know." Looking up, I saw only darkness from the hold we'd fallen through. The cramped cave we were in had a single tunnel leading out. "I guess there's only one way we can go, for now."

Paxen muttered to Lilliana, "You tried so hard to keep me from here, yet here I am. Thanks anyway."

The dryad snorted in quiet laughter.

"Shall we?" I asked.

We headed down the tunnel, with my mage light floating in front of us to light the way. Fionn and I were in front, with Lilliana and Paxen following behind. By unspoken agreement, we all kept quiet, feeling on edge.

In the confining dark, it was hard to tell how long we had been walking. Suddenly Fionn threw a hand out in front of me, stopping me from moving forward.

"What—" I started to ask, but the elf shushed me.

I strained to hear—the Fae had keener hearing than I did—but then I caught the sound Fionn already had heard echoing down the tunnel: the low murmur of voices, and footsteps.

The voices were coming from somewhere to the right, just ahead of us, and were growing louder. There was an odd scraping noise, like something big and heavy was being dragged along the ground, a syncopated rhythm to the sound of the steps.

Hastily, I extinguished my spell light. And just in time.

"Gods, this one weighs a ton," a raspy voice complained. The steps and the scraping noise stopped.

A wheezy laugh met his words. "Lazy bones. Show some respect! And don't let His Excellency hear you say that. If the alliance with the gods goes through—"

Now it was Raspy's turn to laugh. "You really believe those old tales are true? You've been in the Underground too long! Or maybe you're a softie for elves? Ha, the king's not the only one with odd taste in women!" There was a smacking sound, then, "Ow!"

"That's what you get for making fun of me. And for being so disrespectful to His Excellency. He has his reasons for keeping that Lady Hahna around. And if believing in those gods means we get to run topside, not having to worry about the daylight hurting us, and finally getting the better of the high-and-mighty Seelie Court, then I'll be the strongest believer you ever did see." Wheezy started walking again, then stopped. "Come on, or we'll be late."

"But it's so heavy," Raspy whined.

Another smack sounded.

"Ugh, fine," Raspy said. Both sets of footsteps started up again, along with the scraping sound of whatever-it-was Raspy was dragging behind him.

We waited several moments to make sure the two Unseelie were gone, and that no one else was coming towards us. When I was sure we were alone, I breathed, "Should we follow them?"

"Yes," Paxen said. "But carefully."

I called forth another spell light, and we started moving forward. We came across the right hand tunnel that the two Unseelie had come from, but passed it by.

Soon a faint glow appeared. It steadily grew brighter as we continued, so I put out my mage light.

And then we were at the tunnel's end.

I gasped at the small city that unfolded before us.

An imitation of a nighttime sky dotted the dirt and rock of the enormous cavern overhead.

That's what caused the glow we had seen, I realized.

The fake stars shone down on a spiral network of hard dirt streets and squat buildings that encircled the black stone palace that rose up in their midst. Dark holes haphazardly spotted the cavern walls. Other tunnels, perhaps, or smaller caves for the Unseelie to live in?

A hand grabbed my arm and drew me back.

"Forgive me, Lady Farrah," Fionn said in a low voice. "But we are now in the heart of the Unseelie Court. We must be careful."

I nodded, realizing I had been foolishly standing in the tunnel entrance for all of the Underground to see.

"We are fortunate it is their night," Fionn continued. "Since many of them cannot go aboveground during the day, they run their time opposite to ours. So this is a good time to sneak into their city."

What if we can't find Rhyss and Bettan before their day begins? But I didn't voice my concerns aloud.

"Where do we start?" I asked instead.

"The palace. If what we overheard was true—" Fionn looked over the sleeping city, at the dark palace in its center "—then my mother is working with the King of the Unseelie Court."

54

CHAPTER FIFTY-FOUR

UNDER THE COVER OF the Underground's false night, we snuck into the Unseelie city.

It felt like the windows of the darkened homes stared at us as we walked by, unable to avoid their sightless eyes. The empty streets did nothing to calm my nerves; instead, I felt like every shadow hid an unknown threat, just biding its time.

The city's circular layout meant we were, quite literally, walking in circles. I ground my teeth, frustrated at how long it would take to reach the town center and the palace.

We passed a house with a chipped barrel to the side of its front door. Down the way, on the left, a laundry line hung out the window, several items of clothing hanging like limp ghosts from it.

Fionn touched my arm. I looked at him. He nodded his head at an alley to our right.

I shrugged, looking at Lilliana and Paxen. They shrugged too—but trying it seemed better than walking this endless circle. I nodded at Fionn.

The elf took the lead, darting across the quiet street to blend into a pool of shadows. A second later, he disappeared into the alley.

I took a deep breath and followed him. I expected to hear voices cry out and footsteps coming after us, but fortunately nothing happened. Soon Paxen and Lilliana joined us, and we took a moment to calm our nerves before continuing.

"Where is everyone?" I whispered to Fionn. "I know it's their night, but ..."

"You forget, it's daylight above," Fionn whispered back. "I'd estimate it's close to midday. They'll be at their weakest now, so many of them will be sleeping soundly. Which is good for us. But still, we must be cautious."

With that, he turned and headed down the alley. The rest of us followed.

The alley opened onto another circular street with squat houses similar looking to those on the first street. Fionn, ever the leader, turned left. We continued on until we saw another alley.

We followed the alley and the new street it had deposited us on. But after a few minutes' walk down the new street, I realized something—we were back on the street we had originally started on.

I immediately stopped walking. Paxen and Lilliana, who noticed I had stopped, also halted. Fionn continued on a few more steps before realizing that none of us were following. Turning around, he stalked back to us.

"What are you doing?" he whispered furiously. "We need to keep going!"

"We're back where we started," I whispered. "Can't you tell?"

I pointed at the chipped barrel. "I recognize that from when we were here before. As well as the laundry line hanging from that window."

Lilliana nodded slowly. "She's right. I remember those things too, but not from the second street."

"How did we get turned around?" Paxen wondered.

"I don't know, but we can't afford to waste time," I said. "It will be their daylight before we know it."

"There's no help for it," Fionn said. "We'll just have to try our luck and hope we don't have to backtrack too much."

Unfortunately, he was right. I ground my teeth in frustration and headed down the right-hand alley.

On the second ring of streets, we bypassed the alley that had led us back to the first street, looking for an alternate route to take. Our gamble paid off—we found ourselves on the third ring of streets, one circle closer to the palace.

But our next shortcut brought us back to the outermost circle.

This is taking forever, I thought. *We'll never get there in time.*

I eyed the starry sky overhead. Nothing in the false night had changed position, making it hard to gauge the true passage of time. For the first time in my life, I cursed the existence of magic.

Before we headed to the second street again, I halted the group. "There has to be a better way of going about this," I hissed. "If we keep at it this way, we'll be doing this all night."

Fionn frowned. Slowly, he said, "Perhaps I could ... try a spell that would reveal the correct path?"

"You can do that?" Lilliana said. "Why didn't you do that earlier?"

"I wasn't sure I was fully recovered enough to try it," the elf said. "But I feel much better now. However, I should warn you—"

"If you're well enough to do magic, then that spell is a good idea," I said.

"But, Lady Farrah, you must understand—"

"We'll cover any additional spell casting that needs to be done. Please, cast the spell."

Fionn pursed his lips and nodded. "All right."

He closed his eyes and concentrated. Nearby, the entrance to the alley began to glow, a purple outline clearly marking it as the way to go. Oh, good. Since we knew this particular alley was the correct one—having gone down it several times already—I breathed a silent sigh of relief. Fionn's spell had worked.

We started toward the now glowing alleyway entrance.

A muted thump sounded behind us. Lilliana paused, but Paxen gave her a gentle push, urging her to keep moving.

We heard another thump, closer this time.

Paxen, at the rear of our group, turned around. He gasped. "Everyone, hurry. We're being followed. Ogres."

Great. Ogres behind us. And then in front of us, a few feet from the alley, several boneless, pale figures with beady red eyes appeared. They moved as one, sluggish and relentless, and the mere sight of them immediately chilled my body.

"Sluagh!" Fionn hissed. "Let's go!"

Sluagh. The restless dead, who would steal our souls if they could get close enough. We'd never be able to fight them off. Our only hope was to outrun them.

We bolted for the alley.

55

Chapter Fifty-Five

Now that the Unseelie Fae were aware of our presence, we didn't bother trying to be quiet as we ran. We exited onto the second ring of streets and hurried along, looking for the purple glow that would signal Fionn's spell and the correct alley to take.

Around us, windows were flying open as more Unseelie peered out of their homes to see what the commotion was about.

We found the side street that would take us to the third circle and sprinted down it.

"How did they know we were here?" I asked, panting slightly. "Were we not quiet enough?"

"I tried to warn you," Fionn said. He didn't sound out of breath at all, just a bit annoyed. "Doing my magic in an Unseelie den such as this is tantamount to setting off fireworks in the nighttime sky. Any Unseelie within a fifty mile radius would know that a Seelie Fae was in their midst."

Oh. I closed my eyes briefly, mentally chastising myself for not allowing Fionn to finish his statements earlier. I had been so worried about Rhyss, and the city's daylight arriving soon, that I had let those fears override my usual good sense.

"I'm so sorry," I said. We were now running down the third street, frantically looking left and right for a purple glow.

Our group of pursuers had grown. The clamor from the original group had attracted the attention of others. The shuffling sluagh and the lumbering ogres had picked up some friends—goblins and boggarts, who moved considerably faster. Our energy was flagging, but we didn't dare stop to rest. One wrong move and the Unseelie Fae would be upon us.

"Where is it, where is it?" Lilliana said frantically. We had run halfway around the circular street and still hadn't seen any purple light.

"Fionn, did your spell wear off?" I asked, huffing for breath.

"No, it should last for a full day," he said. Even the unflagging elf now sounded winded.

"Then where *is* it?" Lilliana shrieked.

"There!" Fionn pointed.

I would have missed it completely if he hadn't seen it. On this third street, Fionn's spell illuminated not an alleyway, but a ladder attached to the wall of one of the buildings. Apparently the way to the next circle of streets was up, across a rooftop.

We put on a fresh burst of speed. Fionn reached the ladder first, but instead of scrambling up it, he motioned for me to go first. "Lady Farrah! Lilliana! Get up there, and we'll follow!"

I began climbing, but Lilliana paused. "What about Paxen? How is he going to get up there?"

"Don't worry about me," Paxen said. "Go, go!"

I reached the top and leaned down to grab Lilliana's hand. The force of hauling the dryad up caused us both to sprawl across the roof.

A shout below made me look over the roof again.

The goblins and boggarts were upon our companions. Paxen had drawn his bow, picking off the small Unseelie at a distance. Fionn's sword sliced down the few that had slipped through their guard. But the rest of the Unseelie Fae would catch up soon, and we would not be able to fight their large numbers.

I raised my hands and shouted, shooting fire at the advancing Unseelie. Squeals and high-pitched cries filled the night as the Unseelie Fae caught on fire and ran, panicked, through their ranks. I nodded, satisfied at the small amount of time I had bought for my friends.

"Fionn! Paxen! Hurry!"

Fionn jammed his sword back in its sheath and began climbing the ladder.

Meanwhile, I stretched out my arms, murmuring a levitation spell as I did so. I'd used the spell before, notably to help Rhyss get back into an inn we were staying at when he got locked out late at night. But back then it was quiet. And Rhyss hadn't been moving around as much as Paxen, who was again shooting arrows at the oncoming Unseelie.

Fionn reached the top of the ladder and crawled onto the rooftop, aided by Lilliana.

Ah, there. My spell was complete, and only awaited the trigger word that would start Paxen's ascent. I started to say it—

Paxen screamed.

My concentration broken, I blinked rapidly, trying to fight off the headache that instantly bloomed from the magical backlash. Peering over the side of the roof again, I saw Paxen had thrown his bow to the side and was now fighting the Unseelie in close combat.

I tried to focus again so I could restart the spell, but my head hurt too much. Fionn and Lilliana were shouting. "Paxen! Paxen, come on!"

He glanced up briefly, and in that moment, I knew he wasn't going to be joining us.

He kicked the ladder with his hind legs, causing it to break away from the wall. The ladder fell to the side with a loud crash, conveniently taking out a few goblins in the process.

Loud thuds told us the ogres had arrived.

Fionn turned away. "Come. We must go. Now."

Lilliana sobbed, "But we can't leave Paxen."

I swallowed hard, my throat thick. "We have to. Come on, Lilliana."

I grabbed the dryad's hand and tugged her across the rooftop. Fionn had already reached the other ladder, but didn't descend.

Skidding to a stop, I saw why.

We were two more circle streets away from reaching the center—and the palace. But below us—on what would be the fourth street—our path was blocked by a sea of Unseelie creatures. There were too many to fight our way through, even if we had wanted to.

A clang behind us made us turn and look. The fallen ladder had been righted, and a swarm of goblins scaled the ladder. Meanwhile, boggarts from the fourth circle street clambered up that ladder.

Fionn drew his sword. Lilliana, looking afraid but determined, stood ready for a fight, although away from the forest she was at a severe disadvantage. As the Unseelie city was made primarily of stone and metal, she had little wood to work with—the primary material she could manipulate with her nature magic.

For my part, my head was splitting. Spell casting in this state could do me harm, but I had to try, even though I was swaying on my feet and my eyes refused to focus.

It wouldn't have mattered. We were soon surrounded. A sneering goblin plucked Fionn's sword from his unresisting hands.

The ground shook as an ogre on the fourth circle street lurched toward our roof. He shook his lank, greasy hair back from his face and laughed, his evil chuckle vibrating through my body.

"New playthings for His Excellency." Even from here I could smell his rotten breath. His gap-toothed smile revealed jagged, yellowed teeth. "Perhaps as a reward we'll get to play with you too, when he's done with you."

Two meaty hands reached out. Grasping Lilliana and me in one huge, grimy hand, and Fionn in the other, the ogre proceeded to parade us through the street, heading toward the palace.

"Lady Farrah!" Lilliana's voice cut through the fog in my pounding skull. "Are you alright?"

I groaned, on the brink of passing out. Being jounced around in the ogre's fist as he waved his living trophies about was not helping me feel better.

"Try to hold on," the dryad encouraged me.

I tried to follow her advice, but her voice came from so far away. I could barely hold on to consciousness—and, frankly, I didn't want to.

Blessed black nothingness threatened to take over me. I willingly gave in.

56

CHAPTER FIFTY-SIX

WHEN I CAME TO, I was mostly lying on cold, hard ground. Someone cradled my head in their lap, but the rest of me was rather uncomfortable.

I groaned and opened my eyes.

I was, indeed, lying on a cold, hard floor—the smooth marble of what looked to be a fancy, large room. Lilliana's concerned face hovered above me, breaking into a relieved smile when she saw I was awake. The smile didn't quite reach her eyes, wide with worry and fear.

"How are you feeling, Lady Farrah?" Lilliana murmured. "Are you able to sit up?"

"I'll try," I said, even though my head and body ached as if two dragons had batted me around like a ball mid-air. Slowly, I suited my actions to my words.

And promptly wished I hadn't.

We were in the middle of a large room, all right—the throne room of the Unseelie palace. Nearby, Fionn was also on the ground, kneeling, slightly bent over with the obsidian-tipped spears of two Unseelie guards trained on him.

Two more weapons were fixed on Lilliana and me.

In front of us, a man lounged on a twisted, black marble throne. Darkly beautiful, he wore his long golden hair free, accentuated by two black highlights that framed his delicate face. The dark greys and blacks of his tunic and pants set off the unusual necklace he wore—a long leather cord, at the end of which was a fist-sized, spherical bone pendant of perfect creamy ivory.

"Ah, our final guest is awake." Even his voice was gorgeous and melodic. "I warned Chantuk to be careful when bringing prisoners in, but he does get so excited."

The figure stood, descending the dais to stand over Lilliana. His necklace twisted, and I saw a thin black seam across one side of the pendant.

The seam fluttered, and a thin sliver of white showed against the black and ivory before disappearing. I recoiled in horror. Were those ... eyelashes?

"Welcome to my home. I hope you enjoy your stay here." His voice dripped with irony. "Although I suppose the pleasure is truly all mine. But where are my manners? Allow me to introduce myself. I am King Balor, ruler of all the Unseelie." He pointed to the spiky silver crown that lay atop his shining tresses. "But perhaps you already knew that."

"Bow before His Excellency." One of the goblins poked me with the tip of his spear. I hastily dipped my head. Next to me, Lilliana did the same.

"How fun," King Balor said. "A dryad. We haven't seen one of your kind down here in decades. Centuries, perhaps. Trees don't really grow in the Underground, you know."

Lilliana shuddered, refusing to look up at the Unseelie King.

He turned to me. A long, painted black fingernail reached out to touch my chin, forcing my head to look up. King Balor's piercing emerald eyes met mine. "But you're not of Faerie." He sniffed the air, testing. "Not entirely. Fascinating."

He eyed my white brooch with distaste. "You wear the talisman of the Seelie Court. Which, my dear, makes us instant enemies. Pity. I do find you ... intriguing."

He started to run that long fingernail down the side of my face. My cheek flared at his touch, and I flinched. He stopped halfway, his eyes growing wide. "And yet you bear my mark. Fascinating, indeed. Especially since that other one who had my mark is now dead. Pity, that. I'm sure he would have been useful, had he stayed alive." He laughed. "At least, until I had the chance to kill him myself."

I bore his mark? I thought back to how I had gotten that invisible mark, from the night phantom's visit to the Seelie Court palace. *Is he related to that spectre, somehow? And why would he want to mark me?*

I also recalled how, whenever I tried to tell Rhyss about my night visions, I couldn't. *Was the king's mark the reason why I had been unable to speak of what I saw?*

Lilliana focused on the last part of King Balor's statement. "What other one? Who's dead?"

When the king spoke, his eyes focused only on me, as if we were the only two people in the room. "Marking people is quite handy. It makes them mine, so I can return to their bodies after death. And it prevents them from acting out against me."

At my hiss of understanding, the king smirked. "Don't worry, I only pick the best. The giant, then that celestial nymph. The centaur, too, although I had to do it through an indirect spell instead of a direct mark. Perhaps that's why he fell so easily when my people overtook him. I told them to leave him alive, but the Unseelie aren't always known for being careful—or following directions." He laughed again.

Lilliana, realizing "the centaur" the king spoke of must be Paxen, let out a choked sob. Tears sprang to my eyes. Poor Paxen. He didn't deserve such an ending.

King Balor touched my chin, using his pointy nail to force me to look up at him. "But you, my dear, seem to be beyond my reach. Why is that?"

I met his gaze, refusing to show weakness.

He sniffed as he let me go, then strolled over to Fionn. "And you ... you look familiar. What is your name, elf?"

Fionn set his jaw and refused to speak, not meeting the king's gaze.

King Balor clapped in delight. "Ah, yes. I know who you remind me of. A lovely woman who is a frequent guest in my court. Her name is Lady Hahna, I believe." He emphasized Hahna's title with a slight sneer.

Upon hearing his mother's name, Fionn looked up.

"Oh, you know her? Yes, you do look a lot alike. And she's mentioned her beloved son oh, so many times. Why, I feel like I practically know you."

The king smirked at Fionn. "Well, I could hardly turn away the son of such an esteemed visitor. I'll be happy to host all of you tonight. For as long as need be."

He clapped his hands again, and the goblin guards snapped to attention. "Take our guests to their rooms, if you would."

King Balor turned away, ascending the dais to sit on his throne again. The guards grabbed Fionn, Lilliana, and me, dragging us from the throne room. The last thing I saw before the heavy wooden doors closed was the king lounging on his black throne again, idly twisting his leather cord around one long painted black fingernail, a sinister smile on his face.

The goblin guards escorted us to a cold block of cells in a lower wing of the palace. Flickering torches lit the walls every few feet, providing a minimal amount of light. I could hear scrambling and scratching sounds coming from various cells, but the torchlight didn't extend far enough for me to see who—or what—was hidden in the shadowy corners.

The guards stopped at a set of adjoining cells. They threw Fionn into one, and Lilliana and me into the other.

"Have a good stay," one of them mocked. I could hear the definitive click of a key being turned in the cell door's lock, punctuated by the guards' cackling. Their laughter echoed off the stone walls as they left.

I sank down onto the cold stone floor. The light from the opposite wall went just far enough that I could see Lilliana, hunched against the wall. I moved closer to her. "It will be okay. We'll find a way out of here." *Maybe.*

The dryad sniffled, trying to control her tears. The sound had a weird, off-rhythm echo.

My eyes were drawn to the darkest corner of our cell, directly opposite from where Lilliana and I were sitting, where the other sniffling sounds were coming from.

"Who's there?" I fought to keep the trembling from my voice.

The sniffling grew louder as we heard a soft scraping sound. A dark lump detached itself from the corner shadows and came toward us. Lilliana and I clutched each other, frozen.

The dark lump reached the edge of the torchlight, solidifying itself into a familiar figure.

"Bettan!" I gasped.

The selkie turned big, mournful eyes on me, still sniffling. Her eyes were watery, but her face was unnaturally flushed, and she was shivering. "L-Lady Farrah! And Lilliana? What are you doing here?" Her voice was thick with a cold.

"Looking for you! And Lord Rhyss," I said. Although our rescue mission certainly had gone sideways.

Bettan sniffled again. "Lord Rhyss is in the cell next to us. We've been here—a few days, I think? I've lost track."

I heard rustling in the other cell. Through the wall, Fionn said in a low voice, "She's right. Lord Rhyss is here, with me. I—I think he's sleeping. Should I wake him?"

I blew out a breath. "No, let him sleep, Fionn. Thank you for letting me know."

"Of course, Lady Farrah."

Lilliana reached a comforting hand out to Bettan, pulling her closer. "What happened? How did you and Lord Rhyss get in here? And where is Hahna?"

Bettan settled in next to Lilliana. She leaned against the dryad, her fatigue evident. "Shortly after you left, Steward Henry's messenger arrived. We left the camp and started heading north, back to the Seelie Court palace."

She coughed. It quickly turned into a rattling wheeze, and Lilliana and I exchanged a glance. While the Fae were long-lived, they could still get sick and die like mortals could. Bettan's cold worried me. If she was ill after just a few days in here, how bad was Rhyss's condition?

"We hadn't been on the road for very long when we were set upon by boggarts. They attacked the royal messenger. Lord Rhyss got injured when he tried to help the poor man. I was still shackled, unable to wield a weapon. Not that I would have been much help. And Lady Hahna just stood nearby, watching the whole thing happen.

"The boggarts left the messenger on the side of the road. Dead or alive, I do not know."

I bowed my head, remembering what Rhyss had said about the messenger's fate.

"They bound Lord Rhyss's hands and took us both down here, to the Underground. Lady Hahna—she's a 'Lady' down here—" even in Bettan's weakened condition, I could hear the sneer in her voice when she used Hahna's former title "—came with us, but disappeared when they threw us in the prison. We haven't seen her since."

Lilliana patted Bettan's hand. "She'll pay for her treachery. Somehow. But first, we must get out of here."

But no brilliant ideas came to mind, and the three of us fell silent. Bettan's breathing soon evened out, indicating that the selkie had fallen asleep.

I sat in the semi-darkness, glad for the quiet and knowing that I, too, should probably rest. I still felt queasy from my earlier failed magical exertion. If only I could have raised Paxen in time. Guilt and worry gnawed at me.

Footsteps sounded in the stone corridor outside our cell. Perhaps it was the goblin guards returning?

I stood up and peered through the bars on the cell's wooden doors.

A lone, cloaked figure made their careful way down the hallway. A pale white mage light bobbed above their head, giving them a touch more illumination than what the wall sconces provided.

The figure stopped in front of my cell. The mage light shone directly on my face, causing me to squint in the sudden onslaught of brightness. The person standing outside my cell pushed their hood back.

I gasped. "Lady Hahna?"

57

— · —

CHAPTER FIFTY-SEVEN

THE ELF STARED AT me for a few long moments, as if she couldn't quite place me. Then: "Lady Farrah? But where is my son?"

In the cell next door, Fionn called out, "Here I am, Mother."

Hahna moved to the other door, taking her bright spell light with her. I turned away, willing my eyes to adjust back to the prison's original darkness. When I turned back, Hahna was reaching her hand through the bars to caress her son's cheek.

"Oh, my darling. If only I had known you were coming, I would have made sure you would have had the regal welcome you deserve. Well, don't worry. I'll talk to King Balor, and soon you'll be free again."

"Mother." Fionn was barely controlling his anger. "What's this about you working with the King of the Unseelie? How did this happen?"

Hahna laughed, sounding unhinged instead of haughty. A wild look crept into her eyes. "I do what I need to, my darling. King Balor and I met when I was exploring the Underground, looking for the Secondary Seal that marks the eternal prison of Shonn's founder. His Excellency found the whole endeavor quite intriguing, as he has his own reasons to want to meet the legendary gods of the Gifted Lands. He offered his assistance if I could find a way to release Shonn's god, and eventually all seven. In return, he will ensure you get your rightful place as the next ruler of the Seelie Court. And then I will be restored to my rightful place as well."

Fionn gripped his mother's wrist. "Are you mad? You've promised King Balor an alliance with the ancient gods? How can you guarantee that? How do you even know they're still alive?"

"Oh, they're alive, my darling. And there have been signs that the seal on their eternal prison is weakening—for those who know how to look for such signs, and interpret them correctly. As you know, it's always been an area of special interest to me—"

"—Long forgotten legends, Mother. Nothing more."

"Not legend," Hahna said. Her voice dropped to a whisper. "Not anymore. Not for much longer."

"You can't be certain that Shonn's god will even want to ally with you or King Balor." Fionn's voice was hard. "And you don't know that King Balor will keep his word."

"Of course he will," Hahna said, but a flicker of uncertainty laced her voice. "He's invested so much in helping me—in helping us. And Shonn's god will gladly become an ally—who wouldn't, after being locked away all those centuries?"

"What are you talking about?"

"You're hurting me," Hahna whined, but Fionn tightened his grip. "Oh, fine. King Balor is a powerful mage, as any Fae ruler should be. He's able to split himself for short periods of time, to carry out tasks above ground. So his Shadow took care of Itan, and Aryn—"

The pieces fell into place. "And possessed Paxen," I whispered, horrified.

Hahna ignored me, fully focused on her son. "Perhaps when you become king of the Seelie, King Balor can show you how to send forth your Shadow."

"I would never willingly participate in such dark magic as soul splitting," Fionn spat out.

Hahna's madness suddenly disappeared, replaced by something hard and resolute. "You will do what I require of you, my son. My sacrifices will not be negated by your ungratefulness."

She yanked her wrist away from Fionn's now unresisting grasp. "Hmm. That will leave a bruise."

"What sacrifices, Mother? As far as I can tell, I'm the one in prison while you're walking around, consorting with dark Fae."

Hahna crossed her arms, surveying her son's face pressed up against the cell door. "And if wasn't for the dark Fae, I would be in prison myself. Or worse. Fortunately, the evidence against Lord Hyrinn that King Balor's servants planted was quite convincing. Otherwise, the High Chancellor would have traced the attempted murder of King Finvarra and Queen Oona to me, and then you would never be able to take the throne of the Seelie Court."

I gasped at Hahna's confession. She turned to me, smug.

"And then you arrived, and the Seelie Court was abuzz with the gossip that the traitor's daughter was judging the Trials." She smirked. "Your father was the perfect patsy. Rarely around in Faerie, his duties practically neglected because he'd rather spend his time in the mortal lands. He was already in a bit of disgrace with the Faerie nobles. We just helped the nobles convince themselves that their sentiments were well-founded. Even though my original plan failed, I was sure I would be able to turn things around. Just in case my son wasn't able to win the throne on his own merit."

Fionn's eyes grew sad. "Have you such little faith in me, Mother?"

Hahna looked back at her son, eyes narrowed. "I do what I need to," she repeated, her voice hard. "You will understand in time."

"I doubt that," Fionn muttered.

Hahna ignored his comment. "I must leave now, my son. When the time comes, be ready. Or be crushed."

She started to walk away.

"Wait!" Fionn called after her. "What do you mean, be ready? What are you going to do?"

Hahna turned, and the look on her face sent chills lancing down my spine. "You will see, my son. Soon enough. You will see."

58

Chapter Fifty-Eight

We waited, but Hahna did not return.

I must have dozed off, because I startled awake when I heard more footsteps coming down the hallway. Next to me, Lilliana and Bettan stirred.

A key turned in the lock of our cell door. When the door opened, the sharp tip of an obsidian spear met my face.

"Don't try anything," a goblin guard snarled. "Just stand up, slow-like, and come with us."

The guard moved back to allow me to exit the cell. Lilliana and Bettan followed after. The guard bound my hands behind me, doing the same to my companions.

Even if my hands were free, a quick glance down the hallway told me there would be no hope of escape. Besides the two guards at our door, there were two guards at each end of the corridor. The hallway was too narrow to cast spells or fight without possibly hitting one of my friends. Although I felt better from my brief nap—no more magically-induced headache—I didn't think I was well enough to take out six guards. Lilliana might have been able to help, but Bettan was in no condition to fight.

The two guards that had unlocked our door pushed us toward the end of the hallway, toward another waiting pair of goblins. Meanwhile, they turned and unlocked Rhyss and Fionn's cell.

Glancing back, my heart sank. Fionn's and Rhyss's hands had also been bound, and Rhyss stumbled as he left the cell. He still had a bit of dried blood at the corner of his mouth, and his hair and clothes were horribly disheveled. But when he saw me looking, his cracked lips split into a wide grin. Despite our situation, I found myself smiling back.

The goblins marched us back upstairs. But instead of heading to the throne room, they nudged us in a different direction.

"Where are we going?" Fionn asked.

As an answer, one of the goblins hit him with the flat of his spear. "Be quiet and keep walking."

We found ourselves outside the palace, under a murky copy of daytime. The "sun" was up, but didn't shine as bright as the true sun in day aboveground would have. Instead, the Underground looked as if someone had thrown a somewhat transparent dark grey veil over the world, and the sun was doing its best to pierce it.

King Balor and Lady Hahna waited in the circular courtyard. Upon our arrival, the king gave our group a chilly smile. "Ah, now we're all here. Let's not waste time, shall we?"

The two guards corralled us closer together. The king spread his arms wide, blanketing us all with a spell, then clapped his hands together once.

Air rushed past my ears as King Balor's transport spell moved us to a new location. We landed in another large cavern, about the same size as the one that housed the Underground Unseelie city. However, this one was quite different.

Instead of being surrounded by a Fae-built city, we were in a partially enclosed Underground grotto. Water cascaded down from an open rock above, ending in a deep, blue-green pool. Plants peeked out between the cracks in the rocks, which glowed pink and purple on one wall, blue and gold and green on another.

From a darkened corner, King Balor's Shadow stepped out, blending back into the Fae's body. I shuddered. So that's how the king knew where to transport us—he has sent his Shadow ahead of him, and then reached out to his Shadow to reunite. While I didn't condone the use of dark magic—and splitting your soul from yourself was definitely dark magic—I also had to admit it was rather convenient.

"Where are we?" Lilliana wondered aloud. But instead of being reprimanded by the guards, King Balor answered her.

"Illor's Grotto," he said. A hint of reverence colored his velvet voice. "There are not many places where the Underground and the World Above collide, but when they do, the magic in that area is raw, wild, and extremely powerful. But it is usually untamable, and so no Fae—Seelie or Unseelie—would ever consider trying to harness it."

He laughed—a velvet, melodious, and evil sound. "But I have harnessed it. That, combined with my Shadow, has made me near invincible."

I reached out mentally, trying to place the familiar feel of the grotto. And then it hit me.

The spelled twig. How Warin said the Fairwood Fae thought that humans were behind the deaths, rather than the Unseelie. By combining his Unseelie Fae magic with that of Illor's Grotto, King Balor had found a way to not only give more power to his magic, but also—as an unintended side effect—to mask the "taste" of his magic. That's why the magic on Itan, Aryn, and all the other deaths in Faerie felt odd to the Fae—because it was mixed with something they'd never encountered before.

"It's places such as these where the Secondary Seals are located," Hahna said. "Places that belong to no Fae, or human, but to something more feral and ancient."

She reached into her pocket and withdrew a small glass bottle. She held it up, showing off the dark, shimmery liquid sloshing around inside.

"Is that—?" I breathed, remembering my reading.

"Going to open the Secondary Seal in this grotto? Yes," Hahna said smugly. She uncorked the bottle, and a strong earthy smell mixed with decaying leaves and a metallic undercurrent wafted out. I flinched from the smell. Around me, the others also wrinkled their noses or put their sleeves to their faces to block the smell.

Hahna stepped over to the pool. Holding the bottle above the water, she upended it and poured the contents out. When the dark red-black liquid touched the beautiful blue-green water, it spread and stained the water, turning it the same red-black color as the potion. The water thickened and bubbled, then parted slightly.

As if it was waiting for something.

Hahna turned back to us. "That's the first part done."

She pulled a long, sharp dagger from her sleeve. "Now, for the second."

King Balor laughed. "Oh, Lady Hahna. I do so love your spirit. Quite entertaining."

Lady Hahna smirked. "Why, thank you, Your Excellency. But shall we get on with it?"

She pointed her dagger at one of the goblin guards standing near Lilliana and me. "Bring the prisoner over here."

The goblin started to push Lilliana forward.

"Not that one. The other one." She gestured at me.

"Oh, my lady. Wait a moment. Let me. Why, she'll practically throw herself in." King Balor turned to me, an evil grin on his face. He waved his black fingernails at me, and the mark on my right cheek kindled with cold.

"Into the pool with you."

59

CHAPTER FIFTY-NINE

A CHILL RAN DOWN the length of my cheek, spreading all over me. An odd numbness took over me, and I felt like my spirit was—well, not quite leaving my body. More like, stepping to the side as another presence started to take over.

But it didn't. The outside presence wanted to get in, and if it did, I would be unable to resist. But although it tried to sink its claws into me, it couldn't gain purchase. Its shapeless grey mist form hovered near my body, and its beady red eyes stared into my own brown ones as if it could bore its way through my eyes and into my body.

King Balor frowned. "Shadow! Why are you not possessing her, as I have commanded you to?"

The Unseelie King's other self continued to float nearby, probing, testing for a weak spot, and unable to find it. Something in me was able to resist it. Something foreign and familiar to the creature all at once.

It gnashed its pointy yellow fangs at me, frustrated that it could not accomplish its dark purpose.

Beads of sweat formed on King Balor's forehead. "Shadow! I. Command. You."

The King's Shadow tried once more to gain entry, but could not. With a loud scream, it launched itself at me, then bounced off my skin. It fled back to King Balor, wailing as it went.

The Unseelie King lurched as his Shadow reentered his body, then settled in. He glared at me. "I don't know how you resisted my Shadow, but you will pay for it. For now, we will have to do this the longer way."

He snapped his fingers at the goblin guard standing near Rhyss and Fionn. "Bring the human prisoner over to Lady Hahna."

Hahna turned to King Balor. "Speaking of prisoners—you could at least free Fionn, yes? He's my son; he shouldn't be shackled like that."

"My dear, until I can be sure of where your son's loyalties lay, it would be unwise for him to go unbound."

"But—he's my son—you promised—"

King Balor rolled his eyes. "He may be your son, but he's also Seelie. I have no guarantee that ..."

While the king talked, I became aware of a presence in the grotto. And I could feel its curiosity.

About me.

Magic in the Gifted Lands, as well as in Faerie, tended to just float around, a neutral, unfeeling thing, waiting for a mage to shape it to its will and use it. But in this place between the Fae and human worlds, the magic here was a wild, living *thing*.

And it bowed to now one.

Child. Who are you, who is so like us?

—My name is Farrah. I am a lot like you—part Fae, part human. Of both worlds, yet not completely belonging to either.

Ah. We do not see your kind often in this place. Welcome.

—Thank you.

"... and so, my dear Lady Hahna, I'm sure you understand," King Balor finished. Although his words were sweet, there was no mistaking the steel underneath. Hahna would cross him at her peril.

And she clearly understood his unspoken message. She pouted, but didn't say anything.

Rhyss now stood at the edge of the red-black pool, with the guard nearby. Hahna looked up at him. Although she was tall, Rhyss still towered over her by a few inches. She frowned. "How about—yes. On your knees, mortal. That will make killing you so much more satisfying."

I gasped and moved forward, only to be stopped by an obsidian spear.

The first goblin guard forced Rhyss to kneel, then grabbed his hair and pulled his head back, exposing his throat.

Lady Hahna started to chant, the words vaguely familiar yet not quite right. With a start, I realized she was reciting the spell I had read in *The Gods of the Gifted Lands: A Fae Perspective.*

The spell ... the potion ... and the need for the Two Worlds to combine.

Rhyss had said something about opening a rift ...

My eyes grew wide. I already knew what Lady Hahna and King Balor intended to do—unleash a god.

But now I knew how they meant to do it.

Lady Hahna faltered in her spell casting, then stopped, confused. Shaking her head, she restarted her spell.

I felt the rope binding my wrists, willing heat into my hands, trying to burn the ropes off. Once I started my own silent spell casting, I understood why Hahna was having trouble.

The wild, sentient magic refused to bend its will to Hahna. It was already angry that King Balor had bent it to his will, and it would not succumb to Lady Hahna.

Seeing that Hahna was having problems, King Balor frowned. His Shadow peeled from his body and stepped into Lady Hahna's form. She straightened, bolstered by the king's power boost to her magic.

Soon, through brute force, the two of them would be able to overcome the grotto's resistance and cast their unsealing spell.

Frantic, I poured more power into my own spell.

Child. Stop fighting against me. What is it you need?

I jerked my head up so abruptly that Lilliana, standing next to me, startled. —Oh, Wild One. Please—allow me to use my magic here—my intended is in trouble—my friends—

Granted.

A surge of magical power flowed through me. The fire I had tried to conjure earlier came easily to my fingertips, and the rope around my wrists burned to ash in an instant.

By the pool, Lady Hahna had finally completed her spell. She raised the dagger, ready to slash Rhyss's throat and spill his blood into the pool.

"No!" I shouted, flinging my hand out.

Lady Hahna screamed as a bolt of air shot out, hitting her square in the chest. She staggered back and fell to the ground, dropping the dagger as she flailed about. One of her hands hit the dagger's hilt mid-air, and it flew over Rhyss's head, lodging in the eye of the goblin guard who was holding his hair.

The guard let go of Rhyss and clutched his eye. Screaming, he slipped on the slick edge of the pool, and fell backward into the water. The thick red-black liquid closed over him, swallowing the goblin whole.

The pool bubbled again, the split in the pool growing wider as the water glowed and pulsed. It started to swirl, a hungry whirlpool.

King Balor was clutching his own chest, wheezing as if he had been punched himself. "Hah ... na. So ... close. Finish it."

Staring between him and Lady Hahna, I realized his Shadow was still with her—and it linked them both magically and physically.

Lady Hahna got to her feet, a bit unsteady. She fished around in her pocket, pulling out a second knife. It was smaller than the one she had lost to the pool, but no less lethal.

Of course she'd have to come prepared. Why can't evil mages not *have a backup plan?*

The grotto's magic still coursed through me, although it was beginning to ebb. I snapped my fingers, and the bonds of my friends fell from their wrists.

Bettan, still weak, sagged against the remaining goblin guard. Flustered, he dropped his obsidian spear as he tried to catch her. Lilliana grabbed up the spear and tossed it to Fionn. Bettan, who was unhelpfully sprawled over the guard in a tangle of limbs, winked at me.

Rhyss had picked up the spear the first guard had left behind, using it to keep Lady Hahna at bay. He backed away from the pool, towards where Lilliana and I were standing. Once he reached us, I pulled him to me in a big hug, burying my face in his chest briefly.

Fionn brandished his own spear at King Balor. The Unseelie King gave him a sideways glance, idly examining a long black nail. "I wouldn't, if I were you."

Fionn growled, pushing the spear point closer to the king, who just yawned, unimpressed. "I warned you."

Lady Hahna's eyes bulged as she suddenly gasped for air. She dropped her knife and grabbed at her throat, clawing at something unseen in the air.

Fionn whipped his head to look back and forth between his mother and King Balor. "What are you doing to her? Stop it this instant!"

The king gave him a nasty smile. "I could. Although I see no point in keeping her around, now that she's fulfilled her purpose."

King Balor languidly waved his fingers at Lady Hahna. She began walking backwards, toward the red-black whirlpool. Her eyes grew horrified as she realized that she couldn't stop herself from moving, no matter how hard she fought against it. If King Balor wanted her to throw herself into the swirling water, she would.

Fionn dropped his spear and held his hands out, pleading. "No! Please, Your Excellency. Please stop her. I'll—I'll do whatever you ask."

"Ooh, how lovely," King Balor said. "Swear fealty to me, now and always. And when you take the throne of the Seelie Court, remember your vow."

Fionn swallowed. "I do so swear."

"Perfect." The king flicked his fingers again, and Lady Hahna stopped moving. She doubled over, breathing heavily. She straightened slowly, her breathing more even as the effects of King Balor's spell faded away.

Fionn closed his eyes and hung his head, the finality of his new vow settling over him.

A slight rustling sound was the only warning we had. With murder in her eyes, a snarling Lady Hahna launched herself at us.

60

CHAPTER SIXTY

I HELD MY HANDS up, hastily crafting a shield.

The attack I had anticipated didn't come.

Lady Hahna had thrown herself at King Balor, not at Rhyss and me. But the king reacted quickly, throwing up a ward of his own. Lady Hahna bounced harmlessly off the Unseelie King's shield.

King Balor flung his arm out, and Lady Hahna flew back. She hit the stone wall at the far end of the grotto with considerable force, sliding down until a jutting boulder stopped her descent. A trail of blood followed her down. She lay across the rock, semi-conscious, an arm and one leg just inches away from the angry red-black whirlpool.

The King's Shadow detached itself from Lady Hahna and walked across the swirling water back toward us, where it melted back into King Balor's body.

The King frowned. "I didn't mean to send her that far. I forget how potent the magic is in this place. Umar!"

The remaining goblin guard managed to extricate himself from Bettan and stood at attention. "Your Excellency!"

The king waved at the far wall. "Go fetch Lady Hahna, would you?"

The guard eyed the whirlpool with trepidation, then began carefully picking his way to the other side.

King Balor eyed Rhyss. "Now, then. I suppose I'll have to finish the spell."

He lifted his hand. I tensed as I strengthened my shield.

The King's Shadow stepped forth again, walking straight toward where I was protecting Rhyss, Lilliana, Bettan, and me. The Shadow stopped in front of my ward, head tilted as it looked the shield over.

The Shadow reached out a long grey finger and touched my ward.

I screamed, feeling like a fire was spreading over my body as my magic dissolved. The intense pain made it hard to concentrate, making my shield fall that much faster.

Through the rushing in my ears, I could hear Rhyss calling my name. "Farrah? Farrah!"

And then another voice spoke.

Child. Let us help you.

—Please.

Mentally, I stepped aside, letting the grotto work through me. The hole in my magical shield stopped growing, then began to shrink. The Shadow's finger got caught in the now closed hole. It shrieked in pain.

An answering shriek sounded across the grotto. I turned in time to see the second goblin guard slip and fall into the whirlpool. The water accepted the new offering, swirling even faster as it swallowed the goblin's screams.

A rumbling sound reverberated through the grotto. The ground started to shake.

"What's happening?" Rhyss asked, close to my ear.

King Balor swore, his voice barely audible over the rumbling. "That idiot! Now the spell is unbalanced. It called for 'one of Fae, one of mortal flesh.' Even if I did throw you in—" he glared at Rhyss, then me "—it wouldn't work. I'll have to try something else."

He clapped his hands, and his Shadow flowed back to him. I dropped my shield, and Rhyss and I ran toward him. But he clapped his hands once more, and disappeared, no doubt headed back to the Unseelie city.

The shaking intensified. Small rocks and dirt began to fall from the ceiling and walls.

"We need to get out of here," Rhyss said. "But how?"

Look up.

I did as the voice instructed. Light filtered in from where the waterfall trickled from the ceiling, suggesting daylight was just above us.

"We're near the surface," I said, pointing. "We can get out there."

"Let's go," Lilliana said. She helped Bettan to her feet, putting an arm around her waist to help steady the selkie.

Rhyss and I led the way to the waterfall, surveying the best path up. There was a very narrow lip around the once calm pool, which was what the unfortunate guard had tried to follow to reach Lady Hahna. We could follow the edge about halfway, and climb up the wall behind the waterfall. If we were lucky enough to find handholds in the rock wall.

"I have an idea," Lilliana said, running her hands over the plants growing out of the grotto's walls. The greenery shivered under her touch. She plunged her hand in one of the crevices. When she pulled her hand out, she also tugged at one of the protruding plants—and then kept pulling. In her hand, the stem grew impossibly long, until a green rope dotted with leaves and flowers fell at her feet. "I'll go first. It should be easy for me to climb up, the plants will hold on to my hands as I go. I'll secure the rope when I reach the top and drop it back down."

The ground shook again.

"Sounds good," I said. "Hurry!"

Lilliana began to climb, jamming her fist in one dirt-and-plant filled crevice, then another. She scaled the wall quickly, and soon the plant rope tumbled back down into the grotto.

"Bettan, it's your turn. Rhyss, you go next." I ushered them into place. Bettan started up the rope.

"What about you?" Rhyss turned to me, panicked. "You should go, then me."

"You're in worse shape than me," I pointed out gently. Bettan was about halfway up the rope. "If something should happen to you back here while I was already aboveground, I'd never be able to forgive myself."

Rhyss nodded, unhappy. "You're right, as usual."

I smirked. "Thanks for noticing. Now get going."

Rhyss gave me a quick kiss on the forehead, then shimmied up the rope. The rumbling in the grotto grew louder. More rocks and dirt fell all around us.

"Fionn, do you—" I stopped, confused. The elf, who had been standing with the others, was now nowhere near me.

I spotted him moving cautiously along the edge of the pool, trying to reach Lady Hahna. She wasn't too far, but the constant ground shaking forced Fionn to go slowly, or risk falling into the whirlpool.

I held on to the rope, frantically waving at Fionn to come back. "Fionn! We need to get going!"

"No!" he yelled. "Not without my mother!"

Lady Hahna's eyes fluttered open. Her breathing came in ragged gasps. "My son ... leave me."

"No!" Fionn stretched out his arm, trying to reach his mother. She didn't move, or try to reach out to him.

"It's too late ... for me. Need to ... stop Balor. Watch out ... his eye."

She slumped over, falling unconscious. A bright red smear of blood trailed down the rock from where her head had rested to where it had fallen.

Lady Hahna continued to fall, tumbling into the red-black whirlpool. It sucked her down greedily, the water becoming even more violent. The ground shook even harder, and cracks began to show in the rock walls.

Fionn screamed. "Mother!"

"Fionn!" I shrieked. "We need to leave. Now!"

Fionn turned to me, his gaze unfocused. For a heart-stopping second, the elf didn't move, and I feared I would have to leave him behind.

The rock lip he was standing on began to break apart, bits of it falling into the swirling water. It galvanized him into action—he leapt toward me, barely clearing the crumbling path as the rest of it fell into the water.

I scrambled up the rope. A tug below told me Fionn was climbing up after me.

I focused on the light and the faces of my friends above me. Several hands reached down and pulled me up, helping me over the side. I crawled a bit away from the edge, trying to catch my breath.

Turning, I saw Fionn climbing over the edge. The ground shook once more, and the hole we had just climbed out of caved in, partially sealing off the grotto.

I peered down through the rocks and dirt. I could just see the pink and purple glow of one of the rock walls, before it dimmed and went out.

Remember us, child.

Closing my eyes, I placed my hand on top of the newly filled-in hole. —Thank you.

I sat up and looked around. We were on a stream bank, where the barest trickle of water disappeared into the ground. The grotto wasn't completely cut off, although it would be harder now for someone aboveground to access it. If they could even find it—the entrance wouldn't be obvious to a casual observer.

"What do we do now?" Lilliana wondered.

"I don't know about you, but I want to go home," a deep, familiar voice said.

As one, we stared at the speaker.

"Paxen!"

61

CHAPTER SIXTY-ONE

THE CENTAUR SURVEYED OUR group, hands on his hips and a wide grin on his slightly sunburned face. "Unless you want to just stand around here all day?"

Lilliana burst into tears. "Paxen!" She threw herself at the centaur, who grabbed her into a big hug.

When Lilliana finally let him go, the rest of us greeted Paxen with hugs and hearty handshakes.

"How did you get away?" I asked.

Paxen grimaced. "I didn't. While that ogre took all of you away, I was swarmed by the Unseelie on the other side of the building. The sheer number overwhelmed me, and I was knocked unconscious."

He touched his forehead, which sported a makeshift bandage. "But it worked to my advantage. When I came to, I could hear some of the boggarts arguing over me. They thought I was dead, and couldn't agree what to do with my body. I figured the best thing to do was to continue to play dead. So I did, and eventually they dragged me aboveground so some poor Seelie Fae could find me and have to deal with me.

"I contacted Saan and Warin, who wanted me to return to the Fairwood and get reinforcements. But I stayed in the area, hoping to

find a way to sneak back into the Underground. But fortunately—"
he nodded at all of us "—you figured a way to leave without my help."

I clasped the centaur's hand in gratitude. "Even so, thank you for
trying to get back to us. I'm so glad you're all right."

"Likewise." He sighed, eyeing the sun's position in the sky. "But if
we don't need to stick around, let's head back to the Fairwood. It will
take us a few hours, walking, so we should leave now. This area crawls
with Unseelie once the sun goes down."

"Wait!" Rhyss said. "What about King Balor?"

"He did get away," I said ruefully. "But at least he's also sealed away.
And perhaps he's weakened somewhat, since he relied so much on the
Grotto's magic, and now that's been taken from him."

"I hope so." Rhyss sounded doubtful, but there wasn't much any of
us could do. None of us knew where King Balor had gone, nor did we
want to return to the Underground to find him.

With that settled, Paxen took the lead on our journey back to the
Fairwood. A relieved and happy Lilliana stayed by his side. Bettan
still needed assistance, so Paxen and Lilliana took turns helping her
walk. Rhyss and I followed. Fionn took up the rear, brooding in his
thoughts.

Between Bettan and Lilliana, Paxen soon had the story of what
happened in the Underground. When Lilliana mentioned Lady Hahna, she paused, then dropped her voice. Fionn sniffed, but didn't
contribute to the conversation.

By the time we reached the edge of the Fairwood, the sun had
begun peeking over the horizon. The guards greeted us, somewhat
astonished—had they not expected us to return?—and one ran to
inform Saan and Warin of our arrival.

Saan came to meet us. "You don't know how relieved I am to see all
of you."

"Same, Saan," I said. "Although some of us are a little worse for wear."

I indicated Paxen, Rhyss, and Bettan. "These three will definitely need to be looked over by a healer. The others might want that, as well. For my part, I just want to sleep. Even if it is day out."

"Of course," Saan said. "But I'm afraid all that will have to wait a bit longer. Warin is waiting for you at the Council hall, with High Chancellor Lord Chela."

"Lord Chela is here?" I asked. The others shifted nervously.

"Yes. After you entered the Underground, we contacted him to let him know. After all, we were risking the future potential ruler of the Seelie Court, as well as the High Chancellor's representative. He needed to know. He left for the Fairwood immediately, and just arrived today."

I blew out a breath. "I understand. Well, let's go see Lord Chela."

Light filtered through the vines-and-flowers lattice that covered the dome of the Council chamber. In one of the pools of light stood High Chancellor Lord Chela, who turned to face us as our group entered the hall. Warin stood next to him, looking worried.

"Lady Farrah." Lord Chela bowed over my hand. "I am glad to see that you—all of you—are well."

"Thank you, Lord Chela," I said. "Unfortunately, not all of us made it back."

He frowned as he realized who was missing. "Where is Hahna?"

I outlined the events that had occurred since we had reached the Fairwood, and what had happened in the Underground. Lord Chela didn't interrupt, but his eyes grew darker as my tale unfolded. I kept to a strict recounting of the events, leaving out Fionn's swearing fealty to the Unseelie King, and carefully staying neutral when I talked about Lady Hahna's actions.

Lord Chela didn't say anything for a long moment after I finished. Then:

"Well. It seems that all of you, in your own way, accomplished the task of the Trials: to find out who was behind the murders." He raised an eyebrow at me. "Although I suppose it could be argued that you, Lady Farrah, did the bulk of the work."

I smirked. "Even if that were true, High Chancellor, I would not be named the next ruler of the Fae."

He smirked back. "It is not an easy job, to be sure. However, a ruler must be chosen."

"Before that happens, Lord Chela, I must request a complete pardon for Bettan. My accusations, as you heard, were wrong, and her innocence has been firmly established."

"Of course, Lady Farrah. Bettan, you are no longer considered guilty of Aryn's murder."

Bettan turned shining eyes on us. "Thank you, High Chancellor."

Lord Chela nodded in acknowledgment, then turned to Fionn. "Fionn of the Fairwood. For completing the Trials successfully, and because you have the closest claim to the crown, would you accept the kingship of the Seelie Court?"

Pride and sadness warred on Fionn's face. He swallowed, then sighed. "My lord, a few days ago, nothing would have made me happier. But—my circumstances have changed. I am no longer fit to be King. Respectfully, I must decline."

Lord Chela looked taken aback, but recovered quickly. "Well, of course. It is your decision, after all. But, if you decline, that is final."

"I understand. And I choose not to be the next Seelie King."

"Very well, then."

I glanced at Fionn. He was gazing at the ground, his face drawn, but as if he could feel the weight of my stare, he looked over at me. A sad smile crept across his face. I nodded back, proud of him and his decision. He had chosen to put the realm above his own personal desires, knowing that his vow to the Unseelie King meant he was forever compromised.

Lord Chela cleared his throat. "Bettan. Paxen. Both of you have also successfully completed the Trials, and after Fionn, you both have equal claims to the throne." He shook his head. "This has never happened before. I'm loathe to have you undergo another Trial, but—"

"Pardon me, my lord," I said. "But—what if they just share the throne?"

Paxen blinked, his brow furrowed as he processed this thought.

Bettan spoke up, sounding embarrassed. "Forgive me, Lady Farrah, but I do not want to marry Paxen."

I laughed. "I don't mean you two have to get married, unless you wanted to. But you could split the ruling duties between you, with Paxen as King and Bettan as Queen. They're just the titles for the job, after all."

Now Bettan fell silent as she pondered this concept.

Lord Chela chuckled. "Lady Farrah, you would make an excellent advisor. What a novel idea—and a good solution. If Bettan and Paxen are amenable to it, that is?"

The selkie and the centaur looked at each other, then back at us. As one, they said, "Yes. We accept."

Everyone laughed, then moved to Bettan and Paxen to congratulate them.

Lord Chela said, "Now that that is settled, I believe the infirmary is waiting for the arrival of some of you."

Paxen, Bettan, and Rhyss stepped forward. Warin did as well. "I will take you there."

Lord Chela and Lilliana followed the four of them to the exit, discussing coronations and advisory duties.

Fionn made to follow, but I stopped him. "Fionn. That was very noble of you. I know that must have been difficult, to give up the throne."

The elf sighed. "I never really wanted to rule. That was my mother's wish for me. With her gone, it hardly matters anymore. So, it wasn't really a hardship. Excuse me."

He hurried outside. Sighing, I did as well, where I found Lord Chela and Lilliana. Fionn stood nearby awkwardly, having been detained by the pair.

"Ah, Lady Farrah," Lord Chela said when he saw me. "I did want to discuss one more thing with you."

"Of course, Lord Chela," I said. "I am at your disposal. And I, too, had something I wished to discuss with you."

Lilliana said, "I'm going on to the infirmary with the others. Fionn, are you coming?"

Fionn shook his head. "I probably should, but I'd rather go home."

The two of them said their goodbyes and departed, leaving me alone with the High Chancellor. He turned to me. "Where are you headed, Lady Farrah?"

"Back to Paxen's to get some things to bring to Lord Rhyss, then on to the infirmary."

"Allow me to escort you to Paxen's, then."

We began walking down the tree-lined dirt path that would take us to Paxen's house. Neither of us spoke at first. Then, Lord Chela said, "I believe what you would like to discuss and what I have to say are much the same."

I smiled. "I believe so. Lord Chela, now that the truth has been uncovered, what will happen to my father?"

"Lord Hyrinn will be granted a full pardon and be set free. His title and holdings will be reinstated." Lord Chela glanced sideways at me. "And his powers will be restored."

"Thank you, Lord Chela."

"Thank *you*, Lady Farrah. I must admit, I didn't think having two humans wandering around in Faerie—even if one was part Fae—was the best idea, especially in light of the recent deaths of King Finvarra and Queen Oona. I appointed you as judge mostly to keep an eye on you—"

"Really?" My tone was dry. "I hadn't noticed."

The High Chancellor chuckled. "I am glad my fears were unfounded."

We turned a corner, and Paxen's home was at the end of the path. "This is the place, yes?" Lord Chela asked.

"Yes, it is, thank you." I paused. "What happens now?"

"If the others aren't injured too badly, we can probably leave for the palace in a few days. We have a coronation to plan, and your father to pardon."

"And then Lord Rhyss and I can get back to our own planning," I said with a smile. "I'll send you an invitation to our wedding."

The High Chancellor smiled as well. "I'd like that."

62

———

Chapter Sixty-Two

Three days later, Paxen, Rhyss, Bettan, Lord Chela, and I set out for the Seelie Court palace. The healers had given my friends medicines to help them recover quickly; after that, it was just a matter of time before they felt completely better.

Fionn had decided to stay in the Fairwood. He would accompany Lilliana later on for the coronation.

I leaned over the railing to wave to Fionn and Lilliana, who were rapidly growing into little specks on the ground. Rhyss pulled me back. "Woah, be careful, or you'll fall right out of this thing."

This thing was Lord Chela's gold-and-white chariot. Pulled by six majestic white swans across the blue sky, it was a lovely means of transportation, although—as Rhyss had just pointed out—perhaps not the safest.

I sat back down, settling into the plush white cushions. I ran my hand over the bright velvet. "This must be a pain to clean."

"Fortunately, there's magic," Lord Chela called from the front of the chariot, where he expertly handled the swans' reins.

I giggled. This chariot really was amazing. Perhaps I should suggest Queen Jennica get one? Or maybe—would the High Chancellor loan it to Rhyss and me for our wedding?

"You know, I'm kind of sad we uncovered the true murderer so easily."

I glared at him. "You thought that was *easy*? And why would you say that?"

"Don't get me wrong, I'm not happy that so many people died. But ... I was looking forward to sightseeing all around Faerie. And with no foul, out-to-get-humans kind of magic to worry about, either."

I chuckled. "Maybe we can come back after the wedding."

"A honeymoon in Faerie? Now that would be incredible."

Contented, I leaned back into Rhyss and watched the clouds go by.

The minute the chariot landed at the palace, I jumped out, heedless of the servants hovering nearby to help us.

Steward Henry greeted me at the door. "Lady Farrah! Welcome back."

"Henry," I said. "I'd like to visit my father immediately. Please."

A smile played at the steward's lips. "But, my lady, wouldn't you rather gather in the throne room with everyone else?"

"No, I need to talk to Lord Hyrinn right away."

Henry gently took my arm and led me inside. "Soon enough, Lady Farrah. But first, your presence is required elsewhere."

I sighed, but allowed the steward to lead me to the throne room.

Two gnome guards threw open the doors as we approached. And, standing by one wall examining a tapestry, was—

"Father!"

My father held his arms wide, and I fell into them, weeping. Enfolding me in a big hug, I could hear him sniffling as well.

After a long moment, I pulled back, holding Father at arm's length. He gave me a watery smile as tears streaked down his face, unchecked. He swiped them away. "Farrah. I never thought this day would actually come. And I have you to thank for it."

I started to wave away his thanks, and then I realized something. "You're wearing different clothes!"

My father stepped back a little more so I could see his whole outfit. Gone were the rags he had worn while a prisoner. Instead, he looked lordly in a purple and pale green ensemble. His hair had been washed and neatly tied back, and his face and hands were shiny and clean.

"Oh, Father," I breathed. As if my father's presence in the throne room wasn't enough, seeing him in a better state proved that Lord Chela had kept his promise.

Footsteps sounded behind me. Father immediately straightened, then bowed low. "Lord Chela."

The High Chancellor clapped Father on the back. "Welcome back, Lord Hyrinn. The new king and queen are eager to meet you. And I—I must apologize for how badly we misjudged you."

The two men locked eyes. I held my breath, afraid of what might happen.

Then Father stuck his hand out to Lord Chela, who grasped it and shook heartily. "All is forgiven, Lord Chela. Let us leave the past behind us."

More footsteps spilled into the room. Turning, I saw Rhyss, Bettan, and Paxen had joined us. Lord Chela and Steward Henry pulled the new royals aside, while Rhyss approached Father and me.

"Hello, sir," Rhyss said. Was he nervous? "It's a pleasure to meet you. Again. Again? I mean, we didn't really get a chance to talk last time. When you were in the dungeon. Uh. I mean—"

His voice cracked. Oh, yes. He was definitely nervous. I giggled. Rhyss blushed, his face nearly the same shade as his bright red hair.

Father placed a reassuring hand on Rhyss's shoulder. "I'm looking forward to getting to know you better, son. But in the meantime, I think there was something specific you two came here for?"

He took my hand and joined it with Rhyss's. Placing a kiss on my forehead, he said, "Farrah, Rhyss, you have my blessing to marry. May your union be as resourceful and strong as you have shown yourselves to be."

Our conjoined hands began to glow, first purple and pale green—the colors of Father's house—and then white, the blessing of Faerie.

All around us, our friends broke into applause.

Two days later, Rhyss, Father and I stood at the Veil's entrance, ready to go back to the Gifted Lands. Bettan and Paxen were there to see us off, along with a small group of royal guards standing at a discreet distance.

"You'll come back for the coronation, yes?" Paxen asked us.

"Of course," I said. "And you'll have to come to our wedding."

Bettan beamed as she gave me a hug goodbye. "Gladly."

Father fussed with his wrinkle-free, spotless outfit. "Do I look alright?"

I grinned and kissed him on the cheek. "You look wonderful. You look like a true noble."

Father continued to fret. "Perhaps I should stay here. I'll come for the wedding, of course. But it's been so long—"

"Don't be silly. Mother will be so happy to see you."

"If you say so." But he still looked worried.

With a wave to Paxen and Bettan, Rhyss stepped through the Veil, disappearing through the shimmery portal. I gave the new royals one last hug goodbye, then walked through the Veil as well, firmly holding on to my father's hand.

On the other side, two familiar faces greeted us. The first was Halianna. "You're back! Oh my, you're back!"

"Halianna!" I grabbed my sister up in a big hug. "It's so good to see you!"

The second was Queen Jennica, majestic in her golden dragon form. We had contacted the Queen to let her know we were returning to the Gifted Lands, and she had promised to get us in Shonn and bring us back to Calia. I had thought just Jennica would be meeting the three of us, and was surprised that Halianna had returned to Shonn.

"Thank you, Jennica," I said to the dragon. "I hope it won't be too much trouble, bringing four of us back to Calia."

She snorted, a whiff of hot air just grazing the tops of our heads.

"We're not headed back to Calia," Halianna corrected me. "Not yet, anyway. Mother wanted to come back to Shonn."

"What? Why?"

Halianna looked down. "She's taken a turn for the worse since you left. She wanted to be in her home country at the end of her days. The flight back was hard on her. I worried you wouldn't get back in time—"

I didn't wait for her to finish. Instead, I took off running toward Shonn's gates, not caring that my braid was coming undone and hair was flying in my face.

By some miracle, I passed through the gates unchallenged. Perhaps the guards were so shocked at the sight of a purple blur moving by that they didn't react fast enough. Or maybe they knew better than to mess with a woman who had a dragon, quite literally, at her back. Regardless, I ran to the house, climbing the stairs two at a time to make sure my mother was still alive.

Mother lay in bed, eyes closed, her chest barely rising and falling. The noise I made with my arrival woke her up, and her eyelids fluttered open. "F-Farrah?"

I rushed to her bedside, grabbing her hand. "Mother, I'm back. I'm here. And—there's something else—"

A commotion at the door caused Mother to crane her head to look around me. Her eyes widened. "Hyrinn?"

I stood and stepped to the side, allowing Father to take my place. He knelt down, gently touching my mother's cheek. "Staela. It's good to see you again. I'm sorry it took so long to get back to you."

She reached up and covered her hand with his. Tears streamed down her cheeks. "Oh, Hyrinn. I never gave up. And I never forgot."

Epilogue

Two weeks later, Rhyss and I attended the coronation of the new King Paxen and Queen Bettan of Faerie. My father sent his regrets, wanting to stay in Shonn with my mother. After so many years apart, they didn't want to miss a single moment with each other.

Thanks to Father's return, Mother recovered quickly. She was still somewhat weak, although every day she grew stronger. Father was more than happy to help her with whatever she needed. I think he felt guilty for his long absence, even though it hadn't been his fault.

After the ceremony, Rhyss and I wandered around the castle courtyard.

"Lord Rhyss! Lady Farrah!" Fionn raised a hand in greeting.

"Well met, Fionn," I said. "How have things been, since we left?"

"We have a new king and queen, as you can see," the elf said, smiling. "And while High Chancellor Lord Chela is already their advisor, Lilliana was preparing to be a secondary advisor, representing the Fairwood. Although, I don't think she'll be in that position long."

He nodded at Lilliana, who was in deep conversation with King Paxen. They stood a little close for advisor and king, and Rhyss, Fionn and I shared a knowing look.

"If she leaves—or should I say, *when* she leaves—then I will take her place." Fionn looked wistful. "I think—I think I'm looking forward to doing that."

"You'll make an excellent advisor," I assured him. "The Fairwood, and the new King and Queen, will be lucky to have you."

"Thank you, Lady Farrah."

"Oh—I meant to ask you about something. What did your mother mean, about King Balor? Watch out for—his eye?"

Fionn shrugged. "Honestly, I don't know. Just ramblings as she fell unconscious, I think."

"Yes, I suppose you're right." But privately, I wasn't so sure.

Fionn cleared his throat. "How go the wedding plans?"

Rhyss laughed. "Surprisingly, putting a coronation together is a lot easier and faster than putting together a wedding."

I swatted Rhyss lightly on the arm. "Well, maybe if our wedding didn't have so many special considerations, it would be easier. But it's now completely out of our hands."

"Completely out of your hands?" Fionn echoed. "How so?"

Rhyss chuckled. "Well, King Beyan and Queen Jennica of Calia are standing in our wedding. They're two of our best friends, and I'm godfather to their son. So we needed to worry about their security. And we thought, if they're in the wedding, we should probably invite Calia's allies, King Addan and Queen Inari of Bomora, among others. And then we invited several Fae, including your new royals. So now there are magical concerns to consider as well. It just got to be too much for us to figure out."

"Steward Henry and Taryn, the Royal Advisor in Calia, are coordinating the wedding together," I said. "I'm glad I don't have to deal with it."

Fionn chuckled. "Well, now I am definitely looking forward to it. I have never seen a human wedding before, and this sounds like it will be an interesting merging of the Fae and mortal worlds."

I beamed. "It kind of is, isn't it? I just hope nothing goes wrong on the day, after all that planning."

Rhyss said, "Hey, it's us. What could happen?"

I raised an eyebrow at him. Together, we burst out laughing.

— • —

Dear Reader: THANK YOU

What could happen? That's what I asked myself when I hit "publish" on the first book of this series years ago. And now, here we are! It's such an honor to be able to share my stories with you!

Thank you so much for reading *Heir of Secrets and Spectres*. If this is your first time in the Gifted Lands and the world of the Kingdom Legacy series, welcome! And if you're a returning reader, I'm so honored you're on this journey with me! I hope you enjoyed this fifth book in the Kingdom Legacy series as much as I enjoyed writing it.

If you have a moment, a short review on Goodreads or wherever you like to buy books and learn about new titles would be awesome.

Want to be the first to know about new adventures? Let's be friends!

□□Sign up for the Newsletter: http://www.rachanee.net/newsletter

Join the Patreon and get sneak peeks and other special stuff: https://www.patreon.com/rachanee

□□Instagram: http://www.instagram.com/rachaneelumayno

□□TikTok: https://www.tiktok.com/@rachaneelumayno

□□YouTube: https://www.youtube.com/@rachaneelumayno

□□Twitter: http://www.twitter.com/rachaneelumayno

□□Join the community on Discord: <u>Kingdom Legacy</u> (https://discord.com/invite/BRXcJJ3c6f)

— · —

JOURNEY BACK TO THE GIFTED
LANDS IN THE NEXT BOOK IN
THE KINGDOM LEGACY SERIES

PROLOGUE

THE PEDDLER WATCHED, ONE eyebrow raised, as the young man approached him on the road. Despite the young man's fine clothing and clean-cut appearance, he had a look of desperation about him. Ah, well. The young were always passionate about something, and it was following those passions that got them into trouble. The peddler pulled his mule to the side of the road to allow the young man's horse to pass him by.

But instead, the young man halted his horse. Dismounted. Practically grabbed the peddler by the collar, he was so frantic. "You're a traveling peddler, are you not?"

No, I'm the King of Calia, the peddler wanted to say sarcastically. But sarcasm never won him patronage.

"Indeed I am, sir," the peddler said instead, touching the brim of his threadbare cap respectfully. "Are you looking to sell something?"

The young man perked up. "I am. Is there anything you're looking to buy?"

The peddler eyed the young man's horse. "You've a fine mount, sir. Would you be willing to part with him?"

The young man frowned. "I—I would prefer not to. I've a long way to go, and it will only be longer if I have to travel on foot."

"Hmm. What about your clothes, then? I'd be happy to sell you something if you don't have a second outfit on you, and you'd still have money to spare."

The young man looked down at his clothing, as if just remembering what he was wearing. "I don't have a change of clothing. I ... kind of left in a hurry. And I—no, I don't want to sell this, either."

"You don't want to sell your horse, you don't want to sell your clothes," the peddler mocked. "What do you want to sell, then? Or be on your way, if all you want to do is waste my time."

"No, I—" The young man stopped and waved his hand in the air. "What about this?"

A shiny gold ring glinted in the sunlight.

"Perhaps," the peddler said. "Let me take a look at it."

The young man tugged the ring off his finger. He held it a minute, reluctant to let it go. Sweat started to bead on his forehead.

"Well?" The peddler held his hand out. "Do you want me to look at it, or not?"

"I—" The young man seemed to be having trouble forming words.

The peddler reached out, his dirty, gnarled fingers closing over the gold band the young man held between his fingers. A jolt passed through the young man, and he startled, but the peddler didn't seem to notice. He took the ring from the young man and held it up to the light, turning it this way and that.

The young man panted slightly, getting his breath back.

The peddler bit the ring, then inspected it again. Satisfied, he said, "It's genuine, all right. I'll take it."

The young man blew out a breath, and then the two men engaged in a round of haggling. They settled the price and the peddler paid the young man, commenting, "This little ring will be worth something once I melt it down, I'm sure."

"Melt it down? But—can't you see ..." The young man trailed off.

"See what?" the peddler asked.

"Ah, it's not important. It's not mine anymore, anyway. Do with it what you want."

"I will." The peddler touched the brim of his cap again. "Thank you, sir."

"Thank you. Good day."

The young man mounted his horse and rode off. The peddler watched him go, then turned back to look at his new acquisition. When he had touched the ring, he had felt the spark signaling the presence of magic. But now that he looked at the ring again, he realized its magic was for something extremely specific, and something he had no use for.

"Worthless piece of junk," he muttered, shoving the ring in his pocket.

He withdrew his hand. Instead of the gnarled, dirty fingers the young man had seen, the hand that emerged was pale and perfect, with long black fingernails. The peddler's form changed as well, growing taller, younger, leaner. Long golden hair flowed down his back, with two black strands highlighting his pale face.

King Balor, King of the Unseelie Court, sneered at the waning sunlight overhead. Fortunately it was nearly sunset, although being out in the daylight at any point was taxing on the Unseelie Fae. As the King, he had a higher tolerance than his subjects, but not by much.

The useless magic ring felt like a boulder in his pocket. He sighed. Collecting magical items was proving to be a worthless endeavor. He was searching for something ancient and specific, an item that had most likely been lost or buried by now. There had to be another way to unseal the gods' prison. Since this wasn't working ... he had another idea that might accomplish his goal. And if that didn't work ... well, as a Fae King, he had all the time in the world to come up with a plan.

All the time, in all the worlds.

CHAPTER ONE

THE PALE GREEN JEWEL winked in the sunlight that streamed through our large front windows.

"I think this will be a better fit for you, Endri," my father, Pazho, said. He shook his long, white-blond hair out of his eyes. "Tourmaline is a stone of stabilization, of protection. And," he winked, "it matches your eyes."

I smiled sadly as I reached for the green, slightly translucent pendant. It was a lovely stone, and would probably make a good soulstone for me. But—

"We've tried two others, and neither of them worked," I sighed. "Perhaps we should just accept that I'll never be able to transform."

Pazho closed my fingers around the gem. The thin leather cord it hung from trailed from my closed fist. "Oh, Endri. Don't say never. You'll get it soon, I'm sure."

I gazed out the window. Our next door neighbor was outside, beating her rugs on the stone path. Dust clouded up, and she stopped to sneeze.

I sighed again and met my father's concerned eyes. "I'll try, Father. But it's hard not to be discouraged."

"I understand." He patted my hand. "I'll go get everything."

Pazho stood up and disappeared into the kitchen. I opened my hand and studied the tourmaline, and the faint scar on my palm next to it. Yet another cut was coming. Great.

The people here in Annlyn were able to shift forms, learning at a young age which animal would be their second form. By adolescence the shapeshifters had mastered their ability, usually with the help of a soulstone. The more you used your soulstone, the more your magic became tied to it. So, picking a gem to become your soulstone was quite important. Fully connecting yourself to your soulstone required a small ceremony that involved a bit of bloodletting.

I had merged with two other soulstones before this, and both times it had failed.

With the first soulstone, I had been unable to transform, even after years of trying. Pazho., after much observation, had decided that perhaps I hadn't merged with the soulstone like we had thought, and we got rid of the jewel.

The second soulstone cracked right after I joined with it.

The failed soulstone issue wouldn't have been so worrying, except for one other fact: I was past the age of my majority. Everyone else had mastered shifting by age thirteen or fourteen. When my birth parents had brought me to Pazho, a well-respected scholar, for help, I had already been sixteen, much older than other first-time shifters.

They never came back for me. I never saw them around the capital city, where Pazho lived. Perhaps they had left the kingdom of Annlyn altogether.

I suppose they knew, deep down, that I'd never master shifting, and they decided it was a convenient way to be rid of me.

But Pazho and his mate, Denaan, never made me feel inferior, even though the cloud of my failure always hung over my head. Instead, they took me in, quietly adopting me—and proving to be truer parents than the ones who had left me behind ever were.

Pazho, his arms full, dropped several items on the table in front of me. I began organizing them, used to the routine by now. The candle went to my left. Bandages and towels, to my right. The small black pot I moved in front of me. I picked up the pitcher and poured water into the pot, while Pazho heated a knife in the fireplace.

Hmm. Something was missing. Oh—I jumped up and walked into the kitchen, scooping up some jars of dried herbs on the open pantry shelf.

"Thank you, Endri," Pazho said. "There was too much for me to carry."

"You're welcome," I said, as I added a scoop from each jar to the pot.

Pazho finished heating the knife and placed it on the table to cool. I hung the pot on a hook over the fire.

While I waited for the water to boil, I said to Pazho, "Do you think this time it will work?"

Pazho nodded. "Of course it will. This time we have the perfect jewel for you. And you're not the only one who is a late shifter. Queen Jennica of Calia was a late shifter, and now she's quite adept at transforming."

I smiled indulgently. Whenever I felt down about my lack of shapeshifting ability, Pazho often invoked Queen Jennica of Calia. I had never met her, but apparently a few years ago she had met my father, and he had given her her soulstone. She had been around my age—nineteen—when she first learned to shift into her dragon form. I refrained from commenting that the queen already had a background in magic, so she at least understood the theory even if she couldn't do it. And she didn't even *know* she could become a dragon until she met my father, so she didn't know what she was missing.

I acutely knew what I was unable to do.

Also, from the stories my father told me, Queen Jennica had shown signs of shapeshifting power when she was young. I had never manifested any powers—hence my abandonment on Pazho and Denaan's doorstep.

My silence must have spoken volumes to Pazho, for he stood up and embraced me. "We'll get it this time, Endri. We will."

Tears pricked my eyes. His encouragement gave me hope—as did the knowledge that he didn't view it as a "me" issue, but a "we" issue.

The water in the pot started bubbling. I grabbed a towel and took the pot from the flame, placing it carefully on the table.

"Shall we?" Pazho held up the now-cooled knife.

I nodded and held out my hand, palm up. Pazho made a quick cut near my old scar, and tipped my hand sideways so my blood dripped into the pot. I scrunched my nose, disgusted by the odd metallic herbal smell in the air.

When the water turned muddy, he put the necklace into the pot, pendant first. "*Junctus*. May the two become one. *Fiat*."

There was a flash, and I gagged as the sickly smell grew stronger. Then it disappeared. The pot was empty, except for my necklace.

I grabbed a strip of cloth and bandaged my hand, then reached into the pot and grabbed my new soulstone. It looked pretty good—but then again, so had the other ones.

"How does it feel?" Pazho searched my face, wide-eyed and curious.

I touched the stone with my good hand. It felt warm, and hummed with a pleasant energy. "Not bad. Time will tell, I guess."

"I guess," Pazho echoed. He sounded disappointed, as if he expected a stronger reaction. I felt a bit guilty for not being more enthusiastic, but I also didn't want to get my hopes up again.

My father sighed. "Well, let's clean up. And then we can try—"

There was a knock at the front door.

Pazho frowned. We had been so busy with the soulstone, we hadn't noticed anyone approaching the house.

He stood up and opened the front door. A middle-aged woman fell into the room, frantic. "Oh, Pazho! I'm so glad you're home! I need your help, right away!"

Acknowledgements

Wow, Book 5 already! Thank you so much to:

Tom, such a wonderful editor and friend. Thanks for reading each successive book and going along for the ride!

Jaime, my writing friend and keeper of my sanity! I couldn't make it through a project without our coffee walks.

My mother, who thought making a kitty sling was a wonderful idea so I could be hands-free for writing.

Riley, I really shouldn't thank you since you keep getting in the way and underfoot and nearly deleted several chapters, but I still love you anyway.

ABOUT THE AUTHOR

RACHANEE LUMAYNO IS AN actress, voiceover artist, screenwriter, avid gamer, and amateur dodgeball player. She grew up in Michigan, where she spent way too much of her free time reading fantasy novels. She still spends too much of her free time reading fantasy, although now she writes them as novels, narrates them as audiobooks, and creates them as improv for various roleplaying campaigns as well. *Heir of Secrets and Spectres* is her fifth novel, and the fifth book in the Kingdom Legacy series. She is also a staff writer for two web comics and an upcoming video game. You can find her online at her website, www.rachanee.net, or on Instagram, TikTok, or YouTube (@rachaneelumayno).